I0729736

HENHOUSE

This is a work of fiction. The story, all names, characters, and incidents portrayed in this production are fictitious. No identification with actual persons (living or deceased), places, buildings, and products is intended or should be inferred.

Copyright © 2025 by Emily Prescott. All rights reserved. Thank you for buying an authorized edition of this book and for complying with copyright laws by not reproducing, scanning, or distributing any part of it in any form without permission. You are supporting writers and publishers in creating books for every reader.

Library of Congress Cataloging-in-Publication-Data

Library of Congress Control Number: 2025909966
Names: Emily Prescott, author. Kaitlin Slowik, editor.
Emily Prescott, illustrator.
Title: Henhouse / Emily Prescott
Description: First edition. Campton, NH Penny Luck Studio LLC 2025.
Identifiers: LCCN # 2025909966
ISBN # 978-1-7336007-2-9 (paperback).
ISBN # 978-1-7336007-1-2 (ebook)

First Edition: September 2025

Printed in United States of America
1st Printing

Author's Note: Emily Prescott & Penny Luck Studio LLC do not consent to the use of this book (in print, digital, or audio format) to be used to train any current or future AI models.

www.emilyprescott.com

*To the women I flock with, and the men
who choose to love us fiercely.*

1

The Thatcher women were blessed with brilliant daughters, fathered by disappointing men.

At least, that was the family mantra for as long as Effie could remember. Her mother believed it of Effie's father and her sisters' father before him. Her aunt believed it, so did Effie's sisters. And so the Thatcher women, unlucky in love, lived together in the family estate of one Dorothea Thatcher, the matriarch, the polka-dot-loving, poker-playing, curse-like-a-sailor septuagenarian that Effie adored.

The one who apparently found the last good man.

Effie considered this as she took in the portrait of him that hung just to the right of the stove and below a crucifix. Grams believed him to be on par with Jesus, and Effie couldn't disagree. He had been charm and wit and sass, all things bubbly and bright. Even saying his name, Herman, gave Effie the sensation of spiced gumdrops and sunshine. Effie looked at him with his sharp beak of a nose, dark, hooded eyes, and eyebrows that would draw envy from the makeup artists at Sephora.

The monochromatic portrait was at odds with the olive-green cabinets that lined the walls and hugged an ancient, albeit beautiful, cast-iron stove. It wasn't as vibrant as the tulips in a pitcher of water that Effie's sister, Louisa, had brought home yesterday afternoon. It paled in comparison to the brightly embroidered tea towels, the copper pots and pans hanging on the rack, and the lavish wallpapers that Effie imagined some boisterous lady had ordered hung at the turn of the century.

It was the only grey thing in the house, that portrait, and Effie often wondered if it was because Grams found it easier to stomach Herman's loss when he wasn't staring back at them in lifelike color.

Effie was already to the dregs of her second cup of tea as a joyful chatter called her to the land of the living. She leaned back in her seat at the breakfast table next to the double glass doors that led out to a small veranda. The table was big enough to seat all of the Thatcher women, despite their growing numbers, and looked out over the garden beds that her oldest sister would soon seed with flowers.

Dorothea, donning her favorite sky-blue dress with white polka dots and an apron that had seen better days, planted a kiss on the soft waves of Effie's saddle-brown hair. She didn't have to bend her aging hips far as she did so. She wasn't even five feet off the ground. Effie smiled at Dorothea and snagged a piece of bacon from the plate that she carried.

Dorothea settled in her seat at the head of the table beside her sister, Beatrice, Aunt Bea. Beside them sat Effie's mom, Pamela, and her older sister Tibby. It was funny to Effie how easily you could tell they were sisters—Grams and Bea, Tibby and Pamela. It was in the eyes and the tilt of their smiles, the soft waves that used to match Effie's but were now streaked with grey or pure white. Or only evident in the growing roots, as was the case with her mother, who dyed her hair a particular shade of blonde that looked both unnatural and utterly beautiful at the same time.

Effie's eldest sister, Ellen, settled in beside her. "They did not believe it was Monday," she huffed as she gave her two little girls, kindergarten and preschool age, a sharp look. Lilah and Vivienne climbed into their seats quietly, each with a cute ponytail that reminded Effie of Pebbles from *The Flintstones*. "Is there anything else to help with?" Ellen asked.

"You ask that every morning," Effie said.

Even though Dorothea and Effie cooked breakfast most weekday mornings, Effie thought it kind that Ellen didn't take it for granted. "Oh, but I do have croissants that should be done," Effie chimed as she checked her leather-banded watch. She jumped from her seat and hurried to the stove.

"Corsanns!" came the bubbly chirp from Effie's two-year-old niece Hazel. Effie turned to her, eyes wide.

"Your favorite, right, little bird?" Effie cooed.

Louisa, hair pulled back in an effortless bun, her lips painted a pale pink that highlighted just how much she resembled a starlet of Hollywood's Golden Age, rolled her eyes as she put Hazel in the lone high chair.

"You don't have to dote on her like that," Louisa said.

Effie returned with a basket of croissants, steaming, buttery, flaky, perfect—as expected when Effie baked.

"Her cuteness demands it."

"Corsanns!" Hazel squealed, and everyone around the table lit up. Everyone but Hope, who normally had as large a soft spot for babies as the rest of them.

Effie cocked her head to the side inquiring about Hope's steelier-than-normal gaze. She may have leaned heavily into the occult, as Grams teased, but she was usually a bright spot on the astrological charts. Not this morning. The quick jerk of her head told Effie that they'd talk about it later.

Effie squeezed her cousin's hand under the table. She smiled to herself knowing that Hope would confide in her eventually. Even though Hope was twenty-five, like Louisa, Effie had always felt closer to her than her own sister. Somehow, the two years between them felt insignificant, but Louisa always treated it like an emotional chasm that couldn't be bridged.

It didn't matter though. Despite the tiffs and the slights, the borrowed and ruined blouses, the woes of a mother in Neverland, and a house full of estrogen, Effie loved her family. She loved the way they loved each other. How they could hold each other up even when they'd bickered not five minutes prior. She loved that nothing truly ever came between—

"Dad says he'll be in town come June," Louisa said and everything stilled.

Effie's mother clenched her fork like she might melt the silver with rage alone. Ellen, per usual, kept her face serene and unbothered. Or maybe she was. Effie rarely knew if her mask matched her heart. Louisa flicked her gaze to Effie, a hint of an apology there, which Effie always appreciated but never needed. It wasn't Ellen or Louisa's fault that they had a chance to see their dad every so often. Even if he was more apt to travel the world than to see his daughters, Effie was glad they had a chance at all.

"He could maybe come for dinner?" Louisa asked, her voice all hope. Effie admired Louisa's resilient belief that each visit from her father might be the one to change everything.

"I don't think—" Pamela started, her frown thwarted by the Botox that lived between her brows.

"I'm pregnant!" Hope blurted out, and Effie thought she'd never heard silence quite so loud.

The alarm on Ellen's phone pierced through the quiet. It was eight fifteen. Everyone needed to get going or they'd be late bringing the kids to school or daycare and subsequently the work that let them keep their estate on Austin Street in downtown Portsmouth, New Hampshire.

But no one got up.

Ellen silenced her alarm. Bea sipped her tea like things were about to get juicy and she was happy for a front-row seat. Effie's mother might have been surprised, but her face didn't show it. Grams held a wrinkled hand to her already full heart. Louisa's shoulders relaxed, happy for the pivot to delay the rejection of her request, and Tibby . . .

Tibby got pregnant with Hope shortly after Pamela's own positive test. The men they loved left within that same year, just a month after Hope and three months after Louisa entered the world.

Aunt Tibby was pragmatic, much like Ellen but even more so. Her long hair faded from grey to brown and she had a deeply grounding energy. She had loved Hope's father and maybe it was her trusting nature, her tendency to plan for all outcomes, or her deep intelligence that kept her blind, but she hadn't expected to raise Hope alone. Tibby wanted nothing like that for her little girl, so it came as no surprise to Effie that Tibby's jaw nearly reached the floor.

"Aunt Tibby," Effie started, but the words got stuck on the flavor of thyme. Effie's interjection nudged Tibby enough to compose herself though.

No one, other than Effie, had known Hope was seeing someone. Not even Effie had been aware of how serious they were. She opened her mouth to speak, to offer some support, but she froze.

The chasm opened between them.

Hope locked eyes with her, and she knew it too. This would change so much for them, and Hope had been afraid to tell Effie. Afraid to tell everyone, but she had done it to rip off the Band-Aid or spare Louisa another no from Effie's mother. Effie wasn't sure which was the truth. Not that it mattered.

"And I'm elated. And no, I haven't told the father yet. And no, I don't want anyone's opinion on that," Hope asserted before placing her napkin on the table and rising from her seat. "Excuse me." And then she left.

Effie stared after her. It stung that Hope hadn't told her first. The uneasy truth that Effie must have let Hope down felt even worse. She hadn't made a haven for her to share in her joy and her love—if those things were true—or else she would have told Effie. They told each other everything. *She thought.*

Ellen's alarm went off again, and this time everybody hopped to. The kitchen emptied within minutes, save for Effie, Bea, and Doro-thea. They carried plates and bowls to the dishwasher that stuck out like a sore thumb, having been retrofitted into the original cabinetry along the right-hand wall.

"How do we always get stuck with clean up?" Bea whined, eliciting a grin from Effie.

"I think it's because we're too fabulous to be constrained by the rules of society," Effie offered with a wink. "Or, you know, as much as possible."

Dorothea chuckled. "But damn if I wouldn't rather have this than dinner duty . . . suckers." Effie laughed out loud but knew firsthand the toils of dinner duty for such a large bunch. Bea and Grams were the only two *not* on the dinner rotation. Effie checked her watch.

"You're dismissed," Grams said, nudging Effie. "Go talk to her before you have to leave too."

Effie kissed Dorothea on the cheek, then Aunt Bea, before chasing Hope upstairs.

Effie hoped she'd know the right thing to say, the words that would be sincere, helpful, and honest. Words that would taste right coming from her and sweeten the truth for Hope.

Effie was not good at being anything more than a willing ear. Her advice, while well-intentioned, came from an inexperienced place. She couldn't even fathom how Hope had gotten here.

They had spent countless hours discussing that they wanted to live and travel and succeed in their own little ways before becoming mothers. Not that their family wasn't successful after motherhood, but they wanted something different.

They wanted love and devotion, partnership and great romance before they considered how life would evolve from there. That shared vision when Hope returned from college resulted in a mutual plan for celibacy. A vow to be sure they found a good man before being too vulnerable. Effie always believed they'd feared the Thatcher curse with the same gusto, but maybe that didn't mean to Hope what it meant to Effie.

To Effie, it meant keeping her twenty-three-year-old heart—and legs—closed until she found the love of her life. Effie had to be sure. She had to know it would be forever. She thought she and Hope were on the same page about that . . . Apparently not.

Effie climbed the stairs to find Tibby leaning against Hope's door. She looked defeated. Effie dropped onto the floor beside her.

"I'm showing houses to new buyers in twenty minutes." Tibby sighed. "I can't get a hold of them to reschedule, I just—I don't want her to think I'm mad or disappointed, I just. I didn't know what to say."

Effie grabbed her aunt's hand, squeezing it tight. Even if Effie didn't always know what to say either, she was excellent at the handholding. Everyone knew it. They leaned on her silent support anytime they knew words would undo them.

"I can let her know," Effie offered. Tibby patted the back of Effie's hand and stood. She wiped the tears from her eyes.

"How do I look?" Tibby asked. Effie was certain she just wanted to know if she could be seen in public and her eyes hadn't reddened too much, but Effie always admired Tibby's effortless beauty, how she embraced her laugh lines and her years.

"Stunning. As always." Effie smiled.

Tibby gave a grateful nod and hurried off to her appointment as Pamela emerged from her room down the hall in a set of NICU pink scrubs. "You never say those things to me," Pamela huffed as she pulled her shoulder-length, bottle-blonde hair into a ponytail.

"Would you believe me if I did?" Effie asked.

"Probably not," Pamela admitted. "Oh! Will you see if you got more of that baby-pink merino wool in at the store? I want to knit more hats."

"Sure."

"Thanks, love. Have a good day." Pamela paused, looking at Hope's door. "Let her know we're just giving her space. It's a good thing. An exciting thing. Another Thatcher baby!" Pamela smiled. It was such a rarity for Pamela's smiles to be real that Effie savored each one. Pamela ran off to spend her day in the NICU, where Effie imagined she must exhaust her daily allotment of compassion and selflessness.

Rolling her head against Hope's door, Effie lifted her arm and lightly rapped her knuckles against the worn walnut.

She heard the doorknob turn in time to avoid falling back as the door opened. Effie jumped up and scooted inside.

Hope plopped onto the bed made up with a violet duvet and fluffy, fringed pillows while Effie lowered herself onto the window seat bench. Both Effie and Hope had rooms on the front of the house that faced the brick-lined sidewalks of Austin Street. Estates across the paved road and on either side were built in the same New England Colonial style, but only the Thatcher's had been painted a daffodil yellow—*to stand out*, as Grams always said.

Effie pulled her gaze from the apple blossoms that were budding on the neighbor's tree to assess Hope in her cave of emotions.

"She didn't know what to say," Effie offered.

"I heard. This old house may be built like a fortress with those heavy doors, but they're not soundproof."

Effie smiled. "Do you want to talk about it?" Hope shifted in her seat. Effie tried to imagine what she must be feeling, but she never was good at future casting. Dreams and plans and imaginings about her life were unknown to Effie. She knew she wanted to find a love like Grams and Gramps, but she knew little else. Especially what it felt like for a full person to be growing inside of you.

"Louisa better bring me a large bouquet of flowers tonight," Hope said as she typed furiously on the laptop that rested on her crossed legs.

"Is that really why you blurted it out?"

"What does the name Evangeline taste like?"

Effie sighed. "Honestly? Sour grapes."

Hope grimaced. She often asked Effie what flavor a name gave. She liked knowing if the characters she wrote in her now bestselling books tasted good or not. It was always an odd question when asked out in public, but Effie didn't mind. She just couldn't explain to everyone they met that she had lexical gustatory synesthesia and therefore could taste words. Names especially gave her very strong flavors.

"Hopefully, Evangeline isn't set in stone?" Sour grapes and a mineral earthiness splashed over Effie's tongue. Her lips puckered of their own free will.

Hope huffed and closed her laptop. "Nope. Nothing is. I have the third book releasing soon, but I'm waiting on notes from my editor, so I thought I'd get started on my new series, and I . . . well, it's not working at all."

That made sense. Life-changing news had a way of wreaking havoc with routines. "Maybe you're a little distracted?" Effie suggested. She rose from her perch by the window and joined Hope on the bed.

"I wish you had told me," Effie whispered. "How far along are you?"

Hope closed her eyes as tears threatened to fall. "Almost five months."

"Five months!" Effie exclaimed, nearly falling off the bed. "How?"

"Well . . . I—I don't know. Most people don't even know until five or six weeks, and that's when they're waiting for it. I suppose I didn't realize I missed my period until I was a month late? So I was already ten weeks along when I went to the doctor. Then it seemed like it made sense to wait the whole first trimester before saying anything, in case something happened. And ever since I've been worried about telling everyone."

Effie's stomach churned. It wasn't just the family she worried over. "How did you not realize you skipped your period?"

"You know my cycle can't be trusted, plus I was locked in here careening toward drafting deadlines on book three! The release is forthcoming, and it has to be immaculate or the publisher won't want to pick up my next series . . . and then *that* pitch has to be perfect."

Effie saw her spiraling and placed a comforting hand on Hope's knee. It was as much for Hope as it was for Effie to avoid an onslaught of mashed-up flavors. *Careening,* for example, had the unfortunate association with *carrion.* Not that Effie had ever tasted dead flesh, but her brain was more than happy to try to fill in that blank.

"Okay . . ." Effie understood to an extent, but she'd never lost herself to a project or a person or anything that way. Hope tended to go all in though. Effie envied her that.

"And you haven't told him, why?"

"We've only been together for a year, but he's been busy lately, and he had this work training thing, and then he went on a trip with his moms, and I just . . . I haven't had a chance."

"You haven't created a chance," Effie corrected at the risk of getting her head bitten off. *And they'd been together a year?* Effie only first heard about him six months ago. Maybe the rift between them was already bigger than she knew.

"You're right," Hope confessed. "I'm scared. I know he's nothing like our dads or your sisters' exes, but—"

"You don't want him to prove them right."

"Exactly."

"Do you . . . Do you love him?"

Hope giggled. She actually giggled, and Effie knew before she said, "I do. So much. I feel, well . . . I am a bestselling author and have met thousands of my readers and bared my soul in my books and never have I felt as seen as when he looks at me. I don't know if he loves me as completely as I love him," Hope confessed.

It was impossible not to love Hope. Behind the witchy weirdness, she was sweet, compassionate, and so attentive. It made her an excellent observer of the human condition, even if she was rarely as aware of herself as she was of her fictional characters.

"I suppose you won't know if you don't give him a chance," Effie said.

"And you won't if you don't give *anyone* a chance," Hope deflected, though she happened to be right. But they weren't talking about Effie.

Effie hoped this man, the one that she had heard about in hushed tones late at night, whose name tasted like butter and made Hope's eyes glow as if he himself had hung the moon, was worthy of her dear cousin. Because if he wasn't, Effie would be sure that Brayden What's-His-Name regretted ever meeting her for the rest of his life.

Effie emerged from her vengeful musings when Hope handed her a photograph. No, not a photograph, a sonogram. It instantly became real. "You're going to be someone's mom," Effie said, marveling.

"I know," Hope replied, the apprehension heavy in her voice.

"I'm so happy for you." Effie wrapped Hope in a hug. She'd never tell her that happy didn't taste quite the same. The word was usually smothered in floral-noted honey. In that moment, happy honey mixed with the metallic tang of loss.

Nothing would ever be the same again.

2

Hope sank into her bed and rubbed her face with her hands. Her mind was spinning, and she didn't want to let it land anywhere but on the word count deadline that loomed before her. Somehow, sharing the news of her pregnancy had unleashed a level of distraction Hope hadn't even known was possible. On top of that, she missed Brayden. He'd been traveling and training for weeks. The phone was little substitute for his tender kisses or the feeling of his strong chest against hers.

A gentle tapping at the window had her perking up. She was a bit disheveled as she hadn't yet showered. Thankfully, she still wore an oversized T-shirt proclaiming her love for the fictional city of Velaris tucked into her flannel pajama bottoms. Anything else and her secret might hint at itself to the man crouched on the porch roof outside her window like he was little more than a lusty fifteen-year-old and not a full-grown man of almost twenty-eight.

Hope smiled in spite of herself and went to the window. She threw up the sash and settled onto the window seat. The wall became a back-rest, and she clutched a pillow to her stomach. Brayden slipped in beside her, planting one of those tender kisses on her full lips while he took her chin with his thumb and forefinger. "Hello, beautiful," he crooned as he slid back against the opposite wall, the bench barely big enough for both of them. He pulled Hope's feet onto his lap and started massaging them, to her delight.

"Hi," she whispered. "I've missed you."

"And I you," he asserted. "You know, it might be nice to use the front door every once in a while. Your family may hate men, but I don't think they've warded the entrances against me. Obviously," he said with a smirk, eyes cast at the open window.

It pleased Hope immensely when he referenced her books—the wards, the magic. "No, but they'd be waiting to grill you."

"I can take it." He spread his arms wide welcoming the challenge. Hope took the opportunity to scoot between his legs. Leaning back against him, head on his chest, she felt safer than she had a right to, lousy wretch that she was for withholding information. She kept the pillow hugged in front of her. Brayden leaned in, his breath tickling her ear from behind. The kiss he planted on the hollow of her neck sent shivers up her spine. He breathed in deeply. "Good God, you smell amazing."

"I haven't showered since yesterday," she deflected.

"Doesn't change the fact that you do." He wrapped his arms around her waist, hugging her hands, the pillow, and unbeknownst to him, their baby, close. Hope tensed at the slight pressure around her abdomen. She squirmed free, retreating to the other side of the bench, her knees now hugged to her chest. "What's wrong?" he asked, his dark brows immediately creased.

Hope hated that look on his face, the one that was all concern. Especially since she'd found out she carried his baby. She felt ill at ease receiving any worry from him. She didn't deserve it. Not with this secret between them. She started playing with the gold tassel that hung from the corner of the brocade lilac pillow she held.

Her eyes reluctantly met Brayden's. His brow had relaxed, but he held her gaze with steely intent. His dark brown eyes were depthless. His features were warm and calm like the Mediterranean beaches he imagined the sperm donor that gave him his thick black hair hailed from. Hope stared back a long moment before blinking away the sting in her crystal-blue eyes. "I win," Brayden gloated. "You blinked."

Hope's smile was weak, which had him leaning forward to brush a curl away from her face. He held his hand to her cheek. "What is it, Hope?"

Looking at him then, she knew he was everything she ever wanted to make her life complete. His was the face she wanted to wake up to every morning. He was the one she wanted to experience the world and parenthood and partnership with. The only person worthy of the heartache that would come from leaving their crazy home of Thatcher women. It was easy to fall for him. Easy to play and romance with him over weekly date nights, hours-long phone calls, and clandestine couplings in this very room. It was the most joy she'd ever felt, but they'd never taken things too seriously.

A baby was serious.

Hope should have laid her secret bare. She should have bet on Brayden to be right for the job. Her heart sang its undying support of him, but the *curse* always shadowed her. Her mother had been happy.

Louisa and Ellen too. Why did Hope think she could evade their fates?

So, instead of telling him what he really needed to know, Hope said, "I love you." And it was still a truth that needed to breathe.

That other secret had given her the gumption to utter those three words as if they were child's play compared to the baby in her belly. It felt right to say them; *she could share the rest.* But before she could, Brayden said, "I love you too." Pure joy carried in his deep voice. He kissed her with the passion of the thousands of *I love you's* they'd left unsaid these last months. Hope couldn't find a thought or a word if she tried, lost to the lifeline of Brayden's lips. Her fingers curled in the hair at the nape of his neck, and she surrendered to the moment, soaking up the taste of him.

His hands roamed across her shoulders and down to the small of her back as he swept his tongue against hers. Hope arched into his touch, her stomach brushing too close to his, and, against her will, she remembered exactly what she had to share.

Brayden pulled away with a sharp inhale, resting his forehead against hers. "I really only had time to drop in," he lamented. "But I'm glad I did," he murmured against her parted lips. He kissed her again. "I love you."

The way he said it was a pledge. A promise. Brayden stood, straightening his shirt. Hope found the words she wanted to say stuck between her teeth. They were gone altogether as she watched him move for her bedroom door. "Where are you going?"

"To use the front door?" he teased. "You love me. I am no longer a lowly townie pining for your affections from the street. My boombox can be retired, right?"

"Wrong!" Hope laughed as she pointed to the open window.

Brayden checked his watch, a bit of remorse tugging one corner of his mouth down.

"Oops. Guess I'll be a little late." He crawled over the bench hesitating long enough to peck Hope on the cheek before escaping through the window and down the porch post to the van Hope knew he parked around the corner.

Hope sighed as she breathed in the crisp April air. A pool of guilt settled in her gut. *I'm pregnant,* not *I love you* should have been the words she shared, but she let herself believe that it set them up all the better for the news when she finally revealed it. *Later that day,* she decided. Or else she'd never write another word for all the butterflies and distracting thoughts.

3

It was finally nice enough to walk to work, which Effie appreciated after the bombs that were dropped at the breakfast table. Walking helped settle the flutter in her chest. Not only was there to be another Thatcher baby—Effie wondered how many more bodies would feasibly fit in the aging mini-mansion—but Ellen and Louisa's dad would be in town soon.

Effie always struggled with his visits. Though Louisa was frequently mindful of Effie's feelings surrounding their parentage, it usually resulted in Effie feeling guilty. Which was absurd. She shouldn't feel guilty for garnering affection and concern from her big sister.

But she didn't want it.

Effie didn't want to pull from anyone else's joy—however fleeting—because her grief was so big. It didn't seem fair to them, and yet it wasn't fair in the slightest that Effie wouldn't get the chance for Pamela to reject a visit from *her* father. That was a total impossibility. Unless, of course, Hope dove full-on into the occult and was able to converse with the dead.

Effie sighed as she took another cautious step on the uneven bricks of the sidewalk. The neighbor's apple tree wasn't the only thing daring to blossom in the spring sunshine. Soft white blooms caught the rays. Tiny red buds promised verdant leaves while triumphant stems of daffodils and tulips surged from the thawing earth by front stoops and stone walkways.

Soon, Louisa and Dorothea would start planning the annual ball they hosted at their historic home every August to support funding for the arts. Vivienne and Lilah would be counting down the days until pool parties and long afternoons in the flower garden. Tibby would be readying for another riding season at the stables off Peverly Hill Road, while Pamela would be spending her evenings on the beach with romance novels as the sun set over the Atlantic. Beatrice would be working on her collection of watercolors on the back patio. Louisa would likely be auditioning for the summer musical at the community theater on Bow Street. Hope would be growing a full human in her belly and releasing another installment of her fantasy epic.

And Effie? What would Effie be doing?

It wasn't a question that usually plagued her.

She was content with her life. Cooking with Grams gave her companionship and fulfillment. Baking treats all week long delighted not just her but her entire family. She enjoyed her walks around town with Aunt Bea talking about art and science and life. Countless nights were spent with Hope at the local Book and Bar snuggled in with mulled wine or Aperol spritzes—depending on the season—and a good book. Effie found pride in her work at the craft store as a clerk and as an instructor of classes from embroidery to floral arrangement. She never wanted for more. Wanting only ever led to disappointment.

But that morning had set everything in motion. A countdown had begun for the days she had left of the life she'd been living. Sure, things changed when Hazel, Vivienne, and Lilah entered the world. Things always shifted whether Effie wanted them to or not. But this felt different. This was cataclysmic. Hope's life was filling out while Effie's remained attainably tame.

She wasn't sure that's what she wanted. In fact, she knew it wasn't. Effie wanted her life to take on the roundness of experience. She started to wonder if it could be achieved within the walls of her family home or if, to break from the thawing ground, she needed to be rooted in less crowded soils.

Effie used the rest of her walk to try to quell the rising need to be more than she already was.

⁂

"And you wouldn't want a crafty side hustle?" Basil asked as he knit a rather loud scarf that was about three inches too wide. He raised his thick, manicured brows over the rims of his thin gold glasses. Effie leaned against the counter by the register that looked out over the aisles—bolts of fabric, skeins of yarn, paintbrushes, canvases, and all manner of hobby crafts.

"No," Effie replied. "It would be too weird trying to make a buzz online or selling to faceless many." What Effie didn't say was that she battled her brain enough with comparisons to those in her immediate presence. She didn't need to include everyone online too.

"Keep it local as it were?"

"Precisely," Effie gabbed. "Why do you seem skeptical?" The bite of Sour Skittles made Effie's jaw ache. Phantom flavors still packed a punch.

"I don't know. You're always fiddling, making new recipes, dabbling. Seems like maybe you're not satisfied with just this?" He gestured to the store around them and the notes Effie made for a new recipe she wanted to try.

"I don't think that's true," Effie drawled, but felt less confident than usual.

"If you grew a backbone and opened your own damn bakery, you could find fulfillment," Basil challenged. The twinkle in his eye told Effie he was baiting her. He may have been younger than Effie, but he always seemed so much older when he made that all-knowing face.

"Not every passion needs to be monetized. Maybe you're the one lacking fulfillment," Effie argued.

"Touché," Basil said, finishing a row. Effie didn't feel like she'd truly won the argument though. It wasn't the first time she took advantage of the lull at work to devise a new raspberry tart recipe or make a shopping list for pastries for the weekend. It also wasn't the first time that someone had suggested she open a bakery. Basil himself had to be up to a dozen mentions. She'd considered it but hadn't acted on it, not yet . . . maybe not ever. She liked things the way they were. Even if they were quiet. Even if they weren't full.

They hadn't had a customer in over an hour, and they were quite prone to debates, crafting sessions, and existential musings when the store quieted. Shoulder seasons were especially bad. It wasn't nice enough for Boston tourists to flock to the seaport town, and it wasn't snowy enough for winter retreats and candlelit dinners at the noteworthy eateries around Market Square. Mondays especially were quiet with a few locals coming in to restock on yarn or pick up a gift from the kid's craft boxes. Effie never truly minded, though, because the space brimmed with creativity. It buzzed with the excitement of unrealized art, and she loved to be surrounded by it.

Basil was also a good friend and nice to be around. She loved that his name was so easily digestible. It had been a burden trying to befriend people her entire life when their names tasted anywhere on the spectrum from decadent, complex desserts to literal shit. Effie rolled her neck, stretching out the sore spots from her yoga practice that morning.

A box of chocolates entered the frame of her eyeline. "Want one?" Basil asked around a mouthful of nougat.

Effie scoured the box. "What are the flavors?" Basil scowled. "What? I don't like being surprised."

"Says the girl who is surprised with tastes all day long."

"Precisely why I like to pick my food with intention." Effie sized up the chocolates. She recognized the ones that had coarse salt ground on top as her favorite from the local chocolate shop. It coated her taste buds in its caramel, salty sweetness, and the moan that escaped Effie's lips was near indecent.

Shame had her wincing beneath Basil's scandalized gaze, but Effie played it off the best she could. "What can I say? Those chocolates are better than sex." Basil's brows flew up, ready to spew the retort that Effie knew was coming. "Don't!" Basil surrendered and went back to work on his scarf. But it was a fact. Effie had succumbed to the draw of those chocolates on more than one occasion. The same could not be said of sex.

With a shake of her head, she rattled the seeds of her insecurities back out of her awareness. It didn't do to dwell too long on what she *was not*.

Another hour passed in near silence but for the comforting clack of Basil's knitting needles and the prattle of a pair of teachers on lunch hour in need of more craft glue.

Effie looked out to the street. A blue work van parked in front of the store. A young man came around from the driver's side, stopping short with agitation, his jaw tensing as he spun around. When he emerged again, he carried the clipboard he'd apparently forgotten. He checked over the board, and Effie found herself hoping that he would come into the store.

The bell on the front door chimed.

Effie straightened, smoothing her lilac apron over the front of her light-wash jeans that had flowers she'd embroidered herself poking out from the back pocket. The subtle gesture always brought forth a giggle from Basil. Effie knew it was because she took this job more seriously than he did. He was passing through as he pursued a degree in finance at the University of New Hampshire and would eventually be led to Boston and a high-rise office in the financial district. Effie herself hadn't gone to college and bounced from job to job after high school until her crafty obsessions and knack for creative projects landed her behind the counter of Glitter & Glue three years ago.

She took the giggle in stride and made herself available for eye contact as the young man entered and meandered through the aisles. He paused briefly at the display of leather-bound journals on a turnstile beside the luxurious fountain pens. Effie made an effort to look between him and the rest of the store. Many people preferred not to be approached unless they looked like they needed something, so she did her best to stay behind the counter unless absolutely necessary.

It was hard not to admire him though. He was strikingly handsome, and her heart fluttered like it stirred to meet Hope's challenge—to put herself out there. Instead she let her eyes trace the broad lines of his shoulders and the dimple that played at his cheek while he looked over the journals. Effie couldn't tear her gaze away.

She hoped it wasn't obvious as he approached the counter. "Is there a manager I can speak with?" he asked, his voice dry and disinterested.

Effie shot Basil a look. "We're not really staffed like that. But I guess if it was anyone, it would be Henrietta." Basil nodded his agreement.

"Okay, well, can I speak to her then?" the man asked, and Effie noted the exasperation in his tone.

"She doesn't work Mondays," Effie explained. "You're stuck with me."

"Fucking perfect," the man muttered, not quite under his breath.

Effie glanced at the clipboard in his hand. "What is it that you need?" Effie asked, her tone taking on a similar edge.

"I'm here for your safety inspection. I was told that a manager would be present today to go over everything."

"Well, I wasn't informed, but I don't see why we shouldn't be able to handle it."

He gave her a tight smile that barely looked friendly below the brush of stubble that stretched across his upper lip and over his angular jaw. He held Effie's stare, and she decided that she hadn't made such intense eye contact since icebreaker games at summer camp when she was fourteen. "Let's start with the storage room, shall we?"

He pointed toward the back, the tilt of his head an inquiry. Effie nodded in agreement. The young man strode toward the storage room, and Effie followed. She quickly looked back to Basil.

His giddy eyes were wide. Biting his lower lip and fanning himself dramatically, he looked ready to swoon. Effie shot him a warning glare then hurried to catch up.

She followed the man around the stacks of boxes to the large over-head door in the back. As they walked in silence, he took notes on his clipboard. He tested an emergency light, but it didn't stay on long. The rest of the lights were dim. They sputtered and buzzed.

"Great, more dark rooms," he bemoaned.

"What?" Effie asked, not understanding why this person was being so surly. He couldn't be more than twenty-seven. He was too young and entirely too handsome to be this jaded.

"Nothing," he replied and went back to his inspection, pausing only to tame a rebellious piece of hair that dared flop into his eyes.

The thick blond waves waxed in place atop his head softened his strong brow and sharp hazel eyes. The curve of his knuckles and the ink deposited beneath his nails gave Effie the impression that he dab-bled in the arts. His broad, strong neck required him to leave the top button of his navy-blue uniform undone, revealing the prominent collarbone beneath the thin white of his undershirt.

He was a man made up of contrasts. There was a softness in his gaze where his features were all hard lines and ridges. He styled his hair and wore round black glasses that were at odds with his literal blue-collar attire. The ring on his pointer finger paired with the leath-er-banded watch made Effie want to know what he did when he wasn't performing safety checks.

And his hair. In spite of herself, she kept getting distracted by his hair and her inane desire to run her fingers through it. She hadn't been this instantly attracted to anyone since the first time she watched *Aladdin* and decided she would one day be Mrs. Street Rat. But her cartoon crush was much less prickly.

Perhaps the young man didn't always wear this edge. She let herself imagine that, in fact, he was having an off day and otherwise would have come in smiling and leaving with a new inkwell and calligraphy pen.

"You're staring," he said, strained amusement trickling off his tongue.

Her need to quell her embarrassment won out over her tendency to be shy and the words rushed out, tasting sharp. "Just waiting for you to explain all the notes you're making," she said without missing a beat as she ushered him back into the storefront. She watched him take a few measured breaths as though trying to remember to be personable.

"Well, for one thing, you're down about two fire extinguishers. You need one at each of the three exits. You want people fighting the fire on their way out, not running into an inferno to try to find an extinguisher. Also, there are a ton of boxes blocking the egress that need to be cleaned up, moved, or unpacked elsewhere. Your emergency lights only lasted about two minutes, and they need a burn time of ninety minutes to meet code, so those need to be upgraded immediately."

"Okay, so we have essentially failed your inspection?"

"Yes. And you *were* staring," he challenged. Effie couldn't tell if he was angry or flattered. *Was he flirting or did she imagine the amusement?*

The risk of humiliation was too great, so she said, "Just trying to remember your face so when I tell the sweet old woman that owns the store that we failed, she knows who to look out for."

"You gonna send her to egg my house or something?" Flattered and flirting felt a little more likely, which left Effie feeling untethered.

"No?" He chuckled, and Effie found herself considering breaking all of her old habits and programming to ask him out on a date. Surliness be damned.

"What's your name?" he asked.

"Why?" Effie said with a huff.

"You just like being obstinate, don't you?" His agitation resurfaced a bit. "I need to note who went through the inspection with me."

"Oh . . . Effie Thatcher."

"Alright, Effie. You have a lot of work to do before I come back," he mused.

"A lot, a lot?"

"Unless you'd like to pawn it off on the sweet old lady that owns the place," he replied, that bite and something like disapproval slathering his words.

"I wouldn't pawn it off," she argued. He gave Effie a once-over, looking for what, she couldn't be sure. Whatever he saw didn't convince him.

"Sure you wouldn't," he said, raising his brows with such condescension that Effie thought hard about punching him in the face. If Effie did such things. But she was tamer than that.

They rejoined Basil at the counter as he finished filling out the form. Effie leaned over, looking at the clipboard. At the top of the page was a space for the safety inspector's name. Beside it was written Theodore Tillerman. "Theodore?" Effie mused, and her face immediately scrunched.

"Wow, is my name so bad?" Theodore asked. Effie blanched,

unaware that she'd made a face.

"No, sorry."

Theodore puzzled but brushed past it. He tore off a slip from the bottom of his clipboard and handed it to Effie. "I'll have to come make sure you cleared that egress and have at least scheduled the work for the emergency lights by next Thursday. I'll go grab you a couple of fire extinguishers from my van."

Effie nodded, taking the paper. Theodore sauntered outside, and Basil pounced on her. "My God, he's gorgeous."

"I guess," Effie said before taking a sip from her water bottle that she kept tucked on the shelf beneath the register. She swished the water around before swallowing, like that would help.

"You guess? Girl, I have never seen you blush." Effie blushed plenty, prone to embarrassment and shrinking-violet syndrome as she was, but she knew what he meant. She didn't blush *like this*.

"I'm not blushing," Effie spat, and Basil took a full step back.

"My mistake." Basil lifted his hands in surrender. "But you know he's fine. And your babies would be knockouts."

Effie rolled her eyes and went back to the list of tasks they needed to accomplish to make code, her ire building over the not-at-all-cre-ative work ahead and Theodore's implication that she wouldn't be up to the job.

Theodore approached on near-silent feet, setting the extinguishers on the counter. He handed Effie an envelope. "Invoice for your boss." Effie nodded. "See you in a week and a half, Effie Thatcher."

He was irritating and dour, but she could be polite. "See you then, Theodore," Effie said with as much gusto as she could summon, but her nose scrunched all the way up as she scraped her tongue on her teeth in near disgust.

"Okay, that was a really rude face," Theodore said.

"I'm sorry, I just . . ." Effie stammered. She didn't know how to explain that she never quite managed to control how her face reacted to the names she tasted.

"You just what?" Theodore demanded, confusion, and what Effie could only guess was embarrassment, furrowing his brow. Effie stayed silent. "I'm so done with people today." He grabbed his clipboard and turned to leave.

Effie must have looked ashamed because Basil called after him, "She can taste words!" Like that somehow made her reaction any better. But it stopped Theodore from leaving in a huff.

"You're kidding," Theodore said, and the disdain and disbelief had Effie stiffening her spine.

"It has more to do with the fact that I don't know that I can accomplish your little list in the time you've given us. Especially when it likely means having to reorganize the entire stock room. You may think you're helping, but in reality, you just like lording your rules over people and being sour because you can. While I have to be the one to meet your demands." Sour, salty, sweet, spicy. Flavors crashed over each other, but Effie had the good sense to clamp down on her reaction to it all.

Theodore's face, however, flashed—a neon sign of irritation. "If you think it's so impossible, you might want to get started. I'll be back to *lord* over you all next week."

He turned on a dime and strutted out of the store. Effie leaned back on the counter, rubbing her face.

"What the hell was that about?" Basil asked.

"It's a lot," Effie whined, and the gears were already turning about how best to accomplish the tasks ahead, how to approach her boss, how to make sure everyone was happy by the end of it.

Her face must have displayed the toils of her mind because Basil said, "It's not all on you. We'll get it done. Honestly, I feel like your brain must be an exhausting place to live sometimes."

"You have no idea." Effie sighed. She noted the glint in Basil's eye. He definitely wanted to ask about the other thing. "Go ahead."

"His name can't taste that bad, can it? Not when it belongs to that face?"

Effie sighed. Theodore may have been handsome, but he was now solely responsible for her having to work late, worrying about getting in touch with her boss to make the necessary upgrades, and hating her synesthesia for the first time in forever.

"It's truly that bad," Effie said. Her disappointment and irritation with Theodore were palpable. She wouldn't even be able to curse his name while she hauled dusty boxes back and forth across the storeroom. Not without tasting the thick, filmy yuck of soggy cardboard on her tongue.

4

Hope waited until the house quieted to emerge from her room. Everyone else went off to add their bit of magic and expertise to the world. Dorothea settled in the great room with a worn copy of *Pride and Prejudice* while Aunt Bea probably painted in the hobby room.

Hope sidled into the kitchen for a fresh cup of coffee and one of Effie's croissants. It wasn't that she wanted to avoid everyone, but it had been a rather abrupt pregnancy announcement, and she felt embarrassed by it. It was an unsettling feeling. Usually, she didn't like to hide behind shame or feel sorry for how she moved through the world. She frequently took pleasure in being exactly too much for most people.

It was the circumstance of being a solitary bird, an odd duck.

Where others gathered friends, Hope gathered characters. She was prone to living in the fantasies she wove and found little interest in making friends with living, breathing people. However, the thought that nipped at her awareness while she savored the airy, buttery crois-sant was that it wouldn't matter if she wanted it. The world was not usually friendly with Hope Thatcher. People found her eccentric and existential and ethereal. All things she was proud to be, but that made barriers between her and the truly living. Except in the case of her readers. They adored her and the world she created with her *Web of Realms* series. They took her weird and celebrated it.

Brayden did that too.

Hope took a pensive sip, letting the acidity of the coffee melt the decadence of the pastry. She should have gone back upstairs and writ-ten. She should have gone to tell Brayden about the baby. Instead, she lifted another croissant from the basket and placed it on the bone china plate bedecked with paintings of wood thrushes and brambles.

The voracity with which she ate the second pastry left Hope with the realization that if she wasn't careful, she might very well eat the Thatcher women out of house and home. Hope thought Brayden would encourage it. She believed once he knew about the pregnancy, he'd dote on her in more ways than he already did. Their rare moments alone between her writing, his work and renovations, and the crazies that she lived with were filled with dinners out, foot rubs, and tender touches. She could only imagine how he'd pamper her as a moth-er-to-be.

Hope's hand drifted to her belly. It was all becoming so real. She'd read recently that she would soon feel the baby kicking. A terrifying and intriguing prospect.

It must have been the terror that appeared on her face because when Aunt Bea shuffled in, white hair piled on top of her head in a bun tied with a magenta bow, she said, "Heavens! Are you alright?"

She scurried to the table and sat beside Hope, taking both of Hope's hands in the wrinkled leather of her own.

"Yes, I'm sorry to frighten you. I was thinking about the baby starting to kick." Beatrice let out an exaggerated sigh and squeezed Hope's hands tightly.

"It hasn't happened yet?"

"No, but it should soon, and I'm afraid I'll hate it," Hope confessed.

"I wish I could tell you what to expect," Beatrice said, trailing off. Hope offered her a warm smile. She may not have birthed any babies of her own, but Aunt Bea had been just as important to Hope and all the rest as they grew up. "My only advice is to not let those next-generation Thatchers get under your skin." She winked.

Hope's smile was slow to rise. Those Thatchers were precisely the ones that she feared proving right. Louisa, Ellen, Pamela, her mother. They all had such lousy experiences in their love lives and projected them onto her and Effie. She feared they'd spoil her happiness with their worry, but it was more than that.

"I think I'm afraid of who I'll be when the baby gets here. That I'll lose what's important to me now."

Aunt Bea leaned back in her seat, and Hope could tell she was chewing over her words. "Hm," she mused. "I think the things that get lost along the way . . . the ones we put down and never remember to pick back up . . . those are probably things we outgrew anyway. The stuff that makes the heart sing demands to be picked up, even if it has to sit on the shelf a bit in wait."

"And what if I never pick it back up?" It was too depressing a thought to consider, but it had wormed its way in almost as soon as the test read positive.

"Then I can only imagine it will mean you've found something that makes you even happier than writing. But I don't think you'll stop. I can remind you to get to your laptop if you'd like . . . and to go out with Effie and read vampire novels and sing in the shower. You've got a lot of people that love you, my Hope. They'll remind you who you are, and I bet this baby will teach you a thing or two about yourself you never saw coming. Maybe this man of yours too?"

Hope leaned into Beatrice's hand as she wiped the tear Hope hadn't felt fall from her cheek. Aunt Bea was kindness untethered. "I think he will. I hope he will." Hope looked down at her lap. Doubt and anxiety brewed in her belly despite the confessions of the morning.

"I have loved one man in my eighty-three years. I loved him and stopped looking, even after he was lost to the war in Vietnam. It is enough to know that it was real."

"It's been very real," Hope whispered, the hint of a true smile on her lips.

"There's no reason it shouldn't continue as such," Bea exclaimed, her chipper tone drawing a laugh from Hope. "Just give him grace if he is a little hurt that you waited so long to tell him?"

Hope glanced at Beatrice, a bit of guilt in her gaze. "I will," she promised, but she still knew that love sometimes wasn't enough. Her family reminded her of it constantly.

Hope nervously combed her fingers through her waist-length curls. She slowed her pace. Her knee-high suede boots scuffed on the sidewalk as she pivoted back from whence she came. She halted. Summoning her nerve, she spun around once more. Her dark floral skirt fanned out around her. It was a loose smock-style dress that she wore under a lightweight wool coat. It was one of her favorites, and it had the added benefit of hiding the weight she'd gained in her lower belly. If she was being honest, she'd popped in the last week or so. Hope counted it as a miracle he hadn't noticed a difference that morning. But she needn't flaunt how long she kept his baby a secret while she shared the news.

The crisp spring air prickled her lungs. The cacophony of birds back from their winter retreats was a welcome distraction to the worst-case scenarios on loop in her head. She doubted she'd be able to write a word, let alone twelve hundred, as was her goal for the day until she unburdened herself.

The brick storefronts of Market Square gave way to old Colonial houses and mills made into apartment buildings as she turned onto Islington Street. Brayden was a few months away from finishing renovations on a beautiful home that was built in the early 1700s. It had needed a lot of love, especially since it had to be restored from its abysmal time as a funeral home. Soon, the iconic house on the corner of Islington and Bridge Street would be restored to its incomparable splendor. Hope let herself imagine them raising their baby there together, in the home he'd always dreamed of owning.

Daydreams of picnic afternoons in the backyard and walking to Market Square for dinner lifted some of her fear. Hope could clearly envision pushing a stroller to their favorite tapas bar on humid summer nights and snuggling on the couch for a movie as she came upon the rickety white picket fence that lined the front yard of the house.

Brayden should be inside.

He'd been using his lunch hour to meet with the few subcontractors he had hired to do the electrical and plumbing work. It was just about finished now, and he'd been very excited.

Hope hesitated.

In that moment, both truths existed—Brayden being overjoyed about the baby, and Brayden not wanting anything to do with fatherhood. She knew which she believed to be more likely, which she yearned for. But the reality was that one would become the truth as soon as she uttered the words, *I'm pregnant*. As minuscule a chance the latter seemed, it was enough to quicken Hope's pulse.

Until she remembered that morning.

Brayden dropping in on her and their proclamations of love were just what she needed. He always managed to do that, instinctively knowing when to show up for her, even if he never knew how much it encouraged her. They loved each other. This was good news she brought to his door. Nerves had no place here. Only joy.

Hope charged through the front gate and up the stone walkway. The barren landscape needed tending. Last spring, cosmos bloomed all around the front yard. Then, her favorite flowers seemed like a sign that she and Brayden were meant to be. She'd seen no other explanation for the traditionally annual blossoms to have welcomed her here after their first month of dating. A genuine smile made her cheeks ache as she reached the door. It vanished the instant a leggy redhead with sumptuous lips and eyes the color of milk chocolate stepped out to meet her. Hope did her best not to gawk.

"Can I help you?" the woman asked.

Hope was confused. How was this woman acting like she belonged? Hope was the one who picked the tile for the primary bathroom, the one who had imaginary picnics in the backyard. "I'm here to see

Brayden," Hope said, trying to un-ruffle as she went for the door. The redhead stepped in front of her.

"He's not here right now." There was a sharpness to her tone and her eyes burned into Hope. The air was suddenly too thick. "Why are you here?"

"I just—"

"Oh, you must be the designer he's been raving about. It's nice to finally meet you. I'm Chloe."

"Chloe?" Hope choked out as if her morning sickness flared up. Chloe's eyes narrowed. Hope didn't want to know more. She couldn't quite fill her lungs.

"Brayden's wife?" Chloe insisted, clearly pained by Hope's ignorance.

Hope recovered as best she could, but the crushing weight at her chest threatened to topple her into the dying rose bushes. Bile burned at her throat, and she thought she might vomit all over Chloe's perky chest. Everything went silent. *Had her heart stopped?* She had to get out of there. "Right, Chloe. I'm sorry. I have so many clients this spring that it's a little hard to keep everyone straight. Especially when I've only spoken with your . . . your husband."

Chloe's face brightened, while Hope's turned to ash. "No apologies necessary! I'm glad he's been using you to make decisions around here while I've been away."

"Using me. Yes," Hope echoed. She turned her wrist over, pretending to check the time. She couldn't stomach another second on this stoop. "You know what? I had our meeting time wrong. I'll—I'll have to reschedule with him."

"Anything I can help you with?" Chloe chimed, her face wholly unreadable.

"No. Sorry to bother you," Hope said and fully meant it. She hurried off the steps and out into the street, turning left toward Market Square. She needed to be surrounded by people, happy, living people who wouldn't remind her just how disappointing men could be.

5

Effie plodded into the great room past Louisa and Dorothea, her lilac apron still tied around her waist. The tufted burgundy chair that sat beside the old hearth called her name. When her head found the wooden curve of the chair back, her face turned heavenward, she closed her eyes and breathed.

Effie let the ache in her joints from moving boxes all afternoon melt off her as she listened in to Louisa and Dorothea chatting.

"I think this year we need to clear this whole room," Louisa suggested. The pause that followed told Effie that Grams didn't agree. "Just the furniture, so there can be more dancing inside and we don't have to cease the music altogether if there's inclement weather."

"I suppose you're right," Dorothea said, and Effie heard the scratch of her pen on paper. They were planning the summer ball.

It was a tradition that Dorothea and Herman had started back when they first bought the estate before they had kids. They were enamored with the history of the home. Built in the early 1800s, it had seen many celebrations hosted within its walls. When Grams had heard of the annual balls thrown in the great room that spilled through French doors onto the back patio, she was immediately struck with the desire to continue the tradition. She thought it a great way to meet her neighbors and do some good in the community. And it was romantic as hell, as Grams always said.

Effie thought the balls fun and creative but had never gotten swept up in the romance of them. They decorated the house with flowers and garlands. Dance cards were printed, champagne was poured, and decadent pastries—courtesy of Effie—filled doily-lined plates. A live orchestra played instrumental versions of modern music with a few classical pieces mixed in. The ladies donned ball gowns, and the gents wore suits with tails and cummerbunds. Normally, Dorothea left the furniture in the great room as conversation sets and now voiced her concern about not accommodating guests who wanted such a space.

"We could move the breakfast table to the veranda and arrange a seating area in the breakfast nook," Effie suggested, eyes still closed.

"That could work, but would the dining room be better?" Louisa asked.

"Let's not go rearranging the entire house for one event," Dorothea said, and Effie smiled. She imagined that Grams, at Louisa's age, would have emptied the home completely for the one event because the two of them shared a penchant for the dramatic and the wondrous. Louisa with her leading roles in the community plays year after year and Grams with the main character energy she lived by.

Effie fell into comparison again. *Was she even the leading lady of her own life?*

She let her mind wander to soggy cardboard and its mismatched face. She thought about how obnoxious Theodore had been like it was her fault he had to inspect the store at all. She also thought about his hair, which made her grit her teeth with frustration. She wasn't sure how long she lay there replaying the annoyance and intrigue of the afternoon when Louisa finally asked, "What's wrong with you?"

"God is testing my patience," Effie murmured.

"Again?" Grams asked, a twinkle in her voice.

Effie straightened in her chair and opened her eyes. The sun set through the French doors, casting an orange glow over the twice-refinished oak floors that danced across the room in a herringbone pattern. She rubbed her eyes and let her gaze float to the arrangement of porcelain vases on the mantel that Aunt Bea and Grams had collected from antique shops across New England. "I suppose it's a lesson I'm not really learning . . . to be patient."

"I would argue you're very patient," Louisa suggested, and Effie knew it was because, in comparison to the rest of the Thatcher clan, she was, in fact, quite patient. She didn't mind biding her time for the right pair of shoes, or the perfect weather for a picnic, or even the love of her life. She held no eagerness to go out and make things happen. She didn't have a passion to study or a feeling to chase. She'd always been content to let life show her how beautiful it could be instead of forcing it into submission.

Being the youngest of her generation, she was used to waiting for the bathroom, a ride, a moment, a word. She wasn't as boisterous or outgoing as Louisa. She wasn't as smart as Ellen. She wasn't as creative as Hope. And though the Thatchers insisted that Effie was splendid in her own ways, she wondered when someone outside these four walls would deign to notice. Perhaps she would have to realize it first.

"Maybe it's not my patience that's being tried," Effie mused, *patience* tasting of steamed rice, bland but savory. "Maybe instead, I am being challenged to broaden my capacity for kindness."

"Why's that?" Louisa asked as she flipped through sample swatches of napkins.

"Because we failed a safety inspection at work today and the guy that ran it was . . ." Effie trailed off, unsure how to describe Theodore. The truth of her opinion got stuck behind the same walls and locks that protected her heart and her virtue.

"Was what?" Dorothea asked.

"Infuriating," Effie decided, and her tongue burned with the cinnamon of Red Hots. "I get that he's doing his job, but I don't want to have to see him again next week."

Grams looked over at Effie, a knowing glint in her eye. Effie decided the oil painting hung above Grams's head that rendered a lavender field in impressionistic strokes was safer to look at. "His name tastes terrible, and I didn't hide my face," Effie confessed, finally meeting Dorothea's gaze.

"We've talked about your face, dear," Grams chided.

"I know, but it's hard," Effie whined. "Sometimes speaking in general is hard. I either have to choose perfect words or rush through them hoping they make a bland mush in their combination by the end of my rant." Effie scowled, the punchy tang of pineappley perfect slamming into the honeyed ham of hoping and the rancid-raspberry rant.

"And he's cute," Louisa guessed. She didn't bother to hide her teasing grin.

"He's insufferable, and his name tastes like cardboard," Effie retorted.

"That's not so bad."

"Soggy cardboard."

"Soggy from what?" Louisa asked, but she didn't actually look like she wanted to know. Effie shrugged. It didn't matter. Soggy was soggy. Cardboard was cardboard. And Theodore was Theodore.

The sun had set completely. Effie spent the last hour or so bathing and nursing a cup of tea while she read alone in her room. She was currently halfway through a pirate romance novel that would likely scandalize the entire Thatcher family if they discovered it. They'd never known Effie to have a sultry bone in her body, but that had been by design. Many of them had flaunted their desires, *and look where that got them*. Effie hadn't wanted to let her desire to see the light of day and be tempted to act on it. It felt too much like tempting fate. But just because she had vowed to keep her legs closed didn't mean her mind had to be.

She wanted to discuss the book with Hope, who had read it before her. They were in the habit of swapping criticisms, favorite characters, and passages they loved. It was often like research for Hope, but for Effie, it was just fun.

Effie checked the hobby room off the front foyer where a wall lined with bookshelves housed their beloved novels, and a credenza under the bay window stowed paints, brushes, yarns, and threads. She found Aunt Bea instead, painting another portrait of her pet conure parrot, Issa, who sat perched like a perfect model on the golden roost that stood atop the antique desk.

"Have you seen Hope?" Effie asked.

"Not since this morning. I think she was going to talk to the father today."

Effie scowled; she would have left word if she'd be out with him all night. That is, if the reaction had been positive. If, however, as Effie now feared, Brayden didn't take the news well, home would be the last place she'd find Hope.

"Must have gotten caught up café writing again," Effie lied before ducking through the double pocket doors into the foyer, through the great room, and into the kitchen, where the bustle of dinner prep was overwhelming and a bit comical.

Ellen and Pamela's night always descended into chaos. Mostly because Pamela led the charge, pulling out virtually every dish they owned while Ellen struggled to make efficient sense of the recipe in poor time to her mother's frenetic cooking style. It always ended with Ellen following Pamela with a dish rag and a compost bin, throwing away scraps and wiping up spills. Pamela's food was always fantastic, but she somehow couldn't cook without making an absolute mess. It drove Ellen crazy. The only thing that would have made her crazier would have been not tending to the hurricane chef as she passed through the kitchen.

"I don't think Hope and I will need places tonight," Effie said.

"Okay!" Pamela chirped from behind a cabinet door.

"What could you possibly need now?" Ellen reprimanded as she scrubbed an endless mountain of pots in the sink.

"The salad spinner," Pamela remarked as though it were obvious.

"I'm going to start cooking in my kitchenette for dinner."

"You'd miss me," Pamela teased.

"Plus, you only stock that kitchen enough to make instant ramen,"

Tibby added from across the room. "This is much better."

Effie turned to catch Tibby's gaze. She sat at the breakfast table with the littlest Thatchers reading a newspaper. She went from relaxed to on edge as soon as they locked eyes. Still overwhelmed, Effie guessed, with the news of her impending grandchild. Soon, though, Effie knew that Tibby would be thrilled.

Effie grabbed her coat from the closet in the foyer by the front door. It was a dusty-pink wool peacoat that belted at the waist to show off the curve of her hips. She pulled on a knit, cream-colored hat with a matching pink flower crotched into the side and gloves that made the set. It may have been spring, but the temperature dropped off significantly after the sun went down. She could drive her beat-up old Jetta that she kept parked down the street, but it was too quick. She needed the ten-minute walk in the chill of the air to soothe her nerves and steel her resolve.

Effie assumed the news was taken poorly. Effie assumed that Brayden had disappointed her. And if Effie was heartbroken that the Thatcher curse had caught up to Hope, her cousin would be too. The least Effie could do was help her nurse her wounds with a pile of pasta and a cup of cocoa for the walk home.

6

Theodore Tillerman had a terrible day. He relived it as he walked the streets of Portsmouth, warm street lamps illuminating his path past the brick buildings and glittering restaurants.

His bad day began when his sunrise alarm clock failed to do its job. The secondary alarm blared with an unholy siren that stirred fears of an air raid in his semi-conscious brain. He bolted out of bed with a spark of adrenaline that had his heart racing. It was not the ideal way to wake up. Too much in the modern world already made you feel like you were being chased by a bear, merely waking shouldn't involve a fight-or-flight response at six a.m.. But he also didn't have the luxury of relying on his natural rhythms. Those would have kept his Scorpio self up until three in the morning, waking well past eleven.

Modern society was a scam, but one he knew he had to play a part in. Which is why he had dedicated himself to being so enlightened that he knew he was not his work, not his salary, not his role in the machine of life, but rather an integral soul having a human experience. And more often than not, he could parlay his bad experiences, setbacks, irritations, and minor slights into lessons or fodder for his poetry.

But today had been a shitstorm of little things, and he was still human after all. It began with air raid–level alarms and quickly devolved from there.

His first three appointments had all added to his angst. The worst was when he collected an extinguisher from his van, only to watch some careless idiot fling his cigarette into the bushes right outside the local pharmacy. They went up like they were drenched in kerosene. He emptied the new extinguisher meant for the store to put out the flames. Instead of being thanked for quelling the inferno, the store manager yelled at him for ruining the plantings with foam.

Even worse—he had run out of extinguishers at that point and had to drive thirty minutes back to the warehouse to restock. After which, he was again berated by the pharmacy manager.

Then there was his inspection at Glitter & Glue.

He hadn't exactly been on his best behavior. He could admit that. A better version of him would have taken the lack of awareness of the inspection in stride, would have been kinder. He would have enjoyed the way Effie's gaze lingered on his eyes, his arms, his hands. She was sweet, endearing, light. Until she wasn't.

He let himself bristle at her indignation and the sour face she made when she said his name. He'd been so startled he didn't even have space to tell her to call him Theo instead. The impossibility of her condition made it hard to believe that she could taste words, taste his name. In all likelihood, she believed he enjoyed making people's work harder with his inspections and decided to put him off.

He wondered what her name would taste like. *Effie*. Eggplant was the first thing that came to mind. *That probably wasn't how that worked.*

"Are you going to brood this entire walk?" Schilling asked from beside him. They'd taken to walking off their angst together since their first week of freshman year at Keene State College when both of their roommates had locked them out with socks on the door. They'd been friends ever since.

"Just most of it," he admitted.

"Bad day too?"

There was a droop in Schilling's shoulders. "What happened to you?" Theodore inquired, happy to engage in someone else's struggles instead of dwelling on his own.

"More of the same," he said, shame marring his face. Theodore understood. Schilling had been in the midst of a bad breakup for what felt like forever. The woman who was once the light of his life had been unwilling to let him have the peace he so desired. Portsmouth was a big town, but it was small enough that skeletons rarely made it into closets. They just followed you down the street instead.

"Is there an end in sight?" Theo asked.

"I wish I knew."

"Vacation is officially over then," Theo teased. "Bet you wished you stayed on that island last week."

"Yeah, but there are things I missed here too," Schilling admitted, and the smile on his face had Theodore wondering how he could keep both things alive at once—his heartache and his hope.

7

Effie's bones ached. She'd spent every day since the inspection bringing the store back to code, and quickly realized *why* the things on Theodore's list were necessary, especially on the day that she worked in the storage room and the fire alarm went off. She couldn't make it to the exit because of all the boxes that were still waiting for new homes, and the door into the store had slipped its stop, locking her in the back. Thankfully, the alarm was a symptom of some curious two-year-old who pulled it while hoisted on his mother's hip and not an actual fire. Otherwise, Effie might have been burned to death. She could imagine the smugness on Theodore's face when he read the headline: LOCAL CRAFT CLERK TRAPPED BY KNITTING NEE-DLES BURNED ALIVE.

Effie roared a yawn and desired a catnap in the sun that filtered through the window of the hobby room. It took all of her effort to keep her head up.

"This isn't going to be a very flattering portrait if you keep doing that," Beatrice teased from behind her painting desk. A pad of cold-pressed watercolor paper lay before her as she translated the soft contours of Effie's face as lightly as she could with a mechanical pencil.

"Don't you already have four or a dozen portraits of me?"

"Yes, but I want one now. One that shows the woman that you've become."

"It's very flattering, but I don't feel as though I've changed that much since my portrait three years ago."

"Then you haven't been paying attention," Aunt Bea scolded, eyes bulging behind the bifocals she had to wear to do her paintings. Issa, who was only ten inches tall from head to tail feather, cocked her sunset yellow head to the side as though she too were chiding Effie from her perch on the desk.

She lifted off and swooped to the arm of Effie's chair. Aunt Bea had never clipped Issa's wings, and the little bird would frequently fly to her. Effie worried that it was a sign that her fate was linked to Bea's. That she'd find love just to lose it—or never find it at all.

Aunt Bea was admirable. She was creative and intelligent. She'd taught chemistry for years at the university and somehow had combined her capacity for knowledge with her capacity for wonder to become an excellent watercolor artist. In a lot of ways, Effie should want to be like Beatrice. But she often wondered if there was more to Bea's love story than she let on. If she had closed herself off and said no before she could be shown more of that blissful connection that kept the world spinning.

Effie stroked the parrot's head with her forefinger, admiring how the orange and yellow feathers of her head and breast gave way to emerald and sapphire wings. "You're very bold, little bird," Effie said, struck by the proudness of her color.

"The boldness comes from being fully what you are," Aunt Beatrice mused. "You remind me of soft pinks and dried flowers. Your essence, Effie dear, is cinnamon buns and embroidery threads and worn book pages. You are soft and sweet and timeless. *That* is who you are becoming. *That* is why I am painting you anew."

Effie smiled. If that was how Aunt Bea saw her, then she'd be happy to be painted again. Just because books and cinnamon buns, crafts, and long walks were softer and less showy than the musicals, theater, and bright makeup that Louisa loved, or the pots of paint, tropical birds, and wildflowers Aunt Bea loved didn't mean that Effie should take up less space in the world.

Beatrice began laying soft, light washes of color over her sketch, gradually building the rosy and tan tones of Effie's cheeks. She liked to work in layers, not necessarily aiming to get the right pigment in one try but rather adding bits of color on top of one another to get her portraits to sing.

"Did you find Hope the other night?" Beatrice asked as she rinsed her brush.

"I did," Effie confessed, deciding there was no harm in giving Aunt Bea the bare bones details. "She was in a state, didn't want to talk at all. We had dinner and went for cocoa after. All I learned is that she'd closed a door."

"She's not one for second chances either." Beatrice sighed, and it was the same sadness in her look that Effie had in her heart.

Hope appeared in the doorway and rapped lightly on the wall. "Am I interrupting?" she asked.

"Not at all! Come sit. Talk to us while this layer dries," Aunt Bea invited.

Hope stepped into the room, wearing a pair of black leggings that climbed almost to her rib cage with a soft, cropped, burnt-orange sweater—whose baggy sleeves pooled at her wrists—tucked into the band. Effie had seen her in it a hundred times, but today, it had the added effect of showing off Hope's baby bump. Effie almost couldn't believe she'd been so blind. Hope was clearly pregnant.

Effie must have been staring because Hope said, "I'm trying to embrace it and celebrate the changes." She sat in the chair opposite Effie and rested a hand on her belly.

"Of course. Sorry. I'm still getting used to it," Effie apologized.

"Me too."

"And this man of yours? Is he getting used to the idea?" Beatrice dared ask, and Effie was impressed with her gumption.

"I decided not to tell him," Hope admitted, but she glanced sideways at Effie while Aunt Bea checked the dryness of her paint, which meant there was more to the story. Effie had guessed things had gone sideways, but not that Hope hadn't even uttered the truth.

"I'm not sure that's fair of you," Beatrice said, giving voice to Effie's thoughts.

"I know it isn't," Hope asserted. "I'll tell him. Eventually." Effie couldn't imagine what had changed. Couldn't imagine keeping such a big thing from the father of her baby. She couldn't actually imagine being in Hope's position at all, and maybe that was even scarier.

Hope's sadness filled the air. Effie didn't say another word about it and neither did Beatrice. They knew they'd have to run interference for Hope as best they could, but the Thatcher women could only be swayed off the scent of fresh meat for so long. Eventually, Brayden would join the ranks of those devoured by their disappointment.

Effie hadn't wanted to leave Hope in such a state of distress. It was Effie's night to teach a class at the store, though, so gossip and man-hating would have to wait until later.

Effie did weekly classes in embroidery, but one Wednesday a month, she offered a special workshop where guests could bring their own wine and partake in some kind of craft. Frequently, they practiced floral arrangement, collage, or cookie decoration. Tonight, they were making faux stained glass. It was a simple enough project that wouldn't get too much in the way of the mingling and sipping her guests usually enjoyed.

Six people had registered to attend. She lamented that their system only captured emails, and she couldn't practice people's names and taste them before they arrived. She didn't need to offend anyone. Effie reached into her tote, printed with various illustrations of tea canisters, in search of her gum. Real flavors trumped word flavors, so it was easier to get through a class without too much interference from her taste buds when chewing gum. She opened the pack to find it empty. "Sugar stacks," she cursed. She couldn't very well swear like everyone else and say *shit* without tasting that too. The unfortunate circumstance of an early association being made when her mom bemoaned stepping in dog shit on a walk when she was five. She would have much preferred the word being associated with surprise or being startled; then it might taste like birthday cake or starfruit. Effie dropped her tote to the floor beside her. *She'd just have to suffer through.*

Effie laid the materials out on the large bench used for cutting fabric. She covered it with a tablecloth so it wouldn't get ruined and went to work creating stations. Each consisted of a picture frame with real glass, craft paint, Elmer's Glue, black puff paint for the leading, palettes, and junky paintbrushes that wouldn't mind the glue. She set cups of water at each station to rinse the brushes, and in the center of the long table, copies of various designs ready to be traced onto the glass.

Effie had created a design of a lady slipper orchid, her favorite flower. Another depicted a teacup atop a stack of books. The last was a simplistic rendering of a cardinal on a birch branch. Each was already divided into sections to mimic the look of stained glass so that her students could focus on tracing and color placement.

Effie picked the book and teacup design for herself and sat at the end of the bench with her supplies. She checked her watch, bouncing her knee. Her stomach always housed a swarm of butterflies before class started. The prospect that she might have to engage with someone under the age of fifty always triggered her anxiety.

The bell chimed, and a couple of greying heads bobbed down the aisle to her counter. It was Mr. and Mrs. Robecheck. They were both teachers at the local high school and very kind. They frequented Effie's classes and fondly remembered her as a quiet yet diligent student in their English Honors and culinary classes respectively.

"I'm excited for this one!" Mrs. Robecheck chimed as she took a seat and drew a bottle of cabernet from her oversized tote. Effie loved that they always brought gaudy goblets to drink from too. The ones she had tonight bore stems cast into gold talons. Effie was grateful they were the first to arrive. She settled into excitement instead of letting the butterflies win out.

The bell chimed again, and Effie recognized one of Ellen's mom friends and her husband. Not exactly Effie's peers, but it was more intimidating trying to entertain someone closer to her age. They smiled politely and took their seats as well, unpacking their picnic-style wineglasses and a bottle that Effie herself would have bought just based on the label, bedecked in dazzling floral illustrations.

"We're waiting for two more," she announced. "But if you want to choose your designs, there are few options in the center. If you're feeling extra adventurous, you can grab a blank sheet and draw your own while we wait." Everyone leaned in and picked a premade design.

"Did you draw these yourself?" Ellen's mom friend asked.

"I did," Effie proclaimed with some pride. Her little band of pupils nodded, impressed. It was a morsel compared to Hope's fame or Louisa's talent on the stage, but it was enough for Effie. At least it used to be. Rumblings of wanting to be singled out and admired rapped against her mental walls. They had worked their way forward in incremental gains since she realized life would be different all over again with the arrival of Hope's baby. She chalked it up to envy and shoved the thoughts back to their cells.

After only a couple minutes wait, the door chimed again. Effie's stomach shot up her throat as soon as she realized who walked in. Theodore Tillerman. And he wasn't alone.

8

Brayden walked the manicured path from the parking lot in the center of his condo complex carrying Thai takeout.

The buildings were nice, the green spaces well kept, but he was eager to move to his house and away from the cookie cutter he no longer fit into. Brayden noted the For Sale sign with an arrow pointing down the path toward his corner unit on the far end. He gritted his teeth, burying the anger that boiled.

He had bought the two-bedroom unit almost six years ago, right after college. His grandfather had established a trust for him when he was born, and it was bequeathed to him when he turned twenty-two. It was a substantial amount of money. Honestly, that was an understatement. He could have bought an already finished estate near Market Square with plenty to live off of for at least a decade. But Brayden's family had always been in the habit of using their wealth to make plans, make improvements, invest in their community. So he had bought a little fixer-upper condo, did the cosmetic upgrades himself, and bided his time until a property he could revitalize to raise his kids in came on the market.

He jumped at the chance to buy the Islington house, excited at its potential to hold his dreams. That was three years, endless permitting, and innumerable marital mistakes ago. He could have hired someone to do all of the work for him, but there was something satisfying about plastering walls, laying tile, and crafting his home with his own hands. He also couldn't wait for it to be finished.

That, among other things.

He pulled a key from his pocket as he reached the front door only to find the deadbolt already open. He eased inside and slipped his shoes off by the front closet in the narrow entry hall, the air stagnant and stale. *When was the last time he'd opened a window?*

He entered the small kitchen that looked over the living room with its big glass slider onto a rear deck and a woodburning stove. The stairs leading to the two bedrooms were opposite the kitchen.

He unpacked his dumplings and chicken pad Thai, but his eyes were on Chloe, who'd made herself comfortable beneath a crocheted afghan with a bottle of wine and a bowl of potato chips. "I didn't expect you for dinner," he said as he carried his meal for one to the small dining table that stood between the island and the living room.

"I imagine you expect very little of me lately," she said coolly. "I haven't seen your designer friend at the house again." She looked at Brayden, her eyes all fire.

"You're not supposed to be at the house at all. And I told you the other night, I haven't worked with her much," Brayden said, exasperated. They had been over this. He had all of two meetings with a local design firm. Best he could guess, they had sent someone to the house to check in and make sure he hadn't changed his mind about going it alone. He had no recollection of even scheduling a meeting. It was a misunderstanding of some kind, as he'd insisted already, but Chloe wouldn't let it go. It had him worried she was up to something. Or catching on to something else he didn't want her to know about.

"Fine," she said with a huff, pouring the rest of the bottle into her glass.

Brayden sat down at the table, the wooden chair feeling extra uncomfortable and stiff. The overwhelming urge to be anywhere else prickled his skin.

He really wasn't expecting her to be home. Chloe had been away a lot lately. Attending a real estate seminar in Florida for her career of the week. Traveling to Boston for a friend's bachelorette. Visiting family in Italy for two months. The last one was on his dime, but it seemed a price worth paying for the space he so desperately needed. Since she'd been back, almost two weeks, she'd been out with friends, and God knows who else most nights. He hadn't seen her in the condo in ages.

He didn't want to be baited by the For Sale sign in the yard, but he couldn't ignore it either. If the house had been ready to move into, he wouldn't have cared much. Not anymore. "I see you listed the condo," he gritted out.

"And?"

"And our last Battle Royale was over the fact that you *needed* the condo. Absolutely had to have it, had to keep it, couldn't live without it even though it was mine before we got married."

"I've decided that money in the bank is better. Safer, given your reluctance on the matter lately." Of course she had. The mere mention of money at this point set Brayden's teeth on edge.

"You're a grown woman; you shouldn't need an allowance from my trust fund."

"I beg to differ."

Brayden shoved a whole dumpling in his mouth, but it didn't taste as good as it should have. He couldn't fathom how he'd gotten here. How things had devolved and shifted to the point of wishing his *wife* wasn't home and that Hope was instead. He hadn't heard from her in over a week. Brayden knew he should count it as a blessing, especially with Chloe on a tear, but it unnerved him instead. They'd said I love you. They'd been seeing each other a whole year and finally said I love you, and this was his life. His royally fucked-up life.

He looked at Chloe again, her chocolate eyes fixated on an episode of *Love is Blind.* Not long ago, he would have been snuggled right next to her. He'd be kissing her neck at the commercials, too wise to get between his woman and her reality TV but wanting her to know how he desired her nonetheless. The thought made his stomach flip.

They'd met their senior year of college. She was a firecracker, the life of every party, and somehow she'd only had eyes for him—the smallest guy in his fraternity at five foot ten, who hadn't fully healed his acne and was better known as the class clown than a heartbreaker. She was the first person to treat him like a man. A *desirable* man. To look at him and see a future. Hope was the second.

His pad Thai turned to ash in his mouth. He'd lost his appetite. Brayden got up from the table, grabbed his wallet and keys.

"Have my food if you want. I'm going out," Brayden snapped. "And for God's sake, remember to lock the door tonight."

Chloe called after him, "I booked us another session with Dr.

Milgran!"

Brayden gripped the door handle tightly and stared at his feet. "I'm not going down that road again. Our problem is very clear: You won't give me what I want."

"And neither will you," she barked, and Brayden wondered when exactly her love turned to venom. He didn't care for it, but he didn't want to start another fight, no matter how much she begged for one. Begged for him to stay and explode with her.

He looked back over his shoulder, a mix of shame and regret in his eyes. Then he was out the door.

9

When he'd seen the flyer for the crafting class at his inspection, Theo hadn't expected Effie to be the one teaching. He thought some dowdy old lady would lead the group. Not that he had anything against dowdy old ladies. In fact, he had signed up for the class and asked Talia to join him precisely because he enjoyed trying new things and learning them from passionate people. He hadn't anticipated that Effie fit that bill.

Theo was distracted and not doing a very clean job of lining the cardinal design onto his glass with puff paint. He couldn't help but wonder if Effie was thinking about how bad his name tasted. Couldn't stop wondering what it tasted like. She would have to tell him at some point. He'd demand it. Maybe after they tussled over his follow-up inspection. *If they tussled?* They got off to another rocky start tonight. In retrospect, *oh, it's you,* probably wasn't the best greeting upon entering Effie's makeshift classroom, but then again, he was certain it's just what she'd expected of him. She'd done her best not to scowl and now went on leading the class effortlessly.

"Theodore, you might want to wipe your tip."

"Excuse me?" he said, wondering if everyone else, especially Talia, made it sound as dirty as it did in his head.

"The tip of your puff paint," Talia said, rolling her eyes. She nudged him with her elbow.

"Ah," he said and went to work clearing the glob off the end of the paint tip.

"Once you're finished with your line work, you can carry your glass to the register. I'll dry everyone's puff paint while you enjoy more wine and your dates without me hovering for a few minutes." She presented herself like an intrusion, despite being the reason they were all there in the first place. Theo caught her eye, and the subtle shade of pink that rose to her cheeks had him wondering if it was more of an effort to lead this class than she let on. What he'd assumed was a bite in their first meeting might well have been the sharper edge to shyness.

Effie led the charge by carrying her own perfectly puff-painted glass to the register at the front of the store. It was far enough away that when she started to use a blow dryer on a low setting, the hum wasn't an annoyance.

Talia poured them another glass of a smoky merlot, one of Theo's favorites. He lifted his glass. "Cheers." They clinked glasses and sipped, not breaking eye contact until they'd swallowed—*good luck and all that.*

Talia sized Effie up with a tilt of her head. "Do you think she sits at home knitting on Friday nights?" Theo shrugged. "I think she proba-bly has a cat or something. Just like a quiet little virgin with her crafts and creatures."

Theo couldn't argue that the description might be accurate as Effie tucked her feathered waves over one shoulder, her back to them. She worked the hairdryer over the puff paint; her weight shifted to the side, so one hip popped. His eyes found the little flowers that peeked out from the back pockets of the jeans that fit just right. He urged his gaze away. "Does it matter?" Theo asked, never one to like making guesses about people.

"No, it's just a fun game," Talia chirped. "But I do think you'd scare the shit out of her." She chuckled and brought her wineglass to her lips. Her eyes flicked to his crotch and back to meet his gaze. Her grin was wicked.

"You better behave yourself, or I won't invite you to craft night again," he warned.

"Heavens, no." Theo knew she'd only agreed to come in case things turned more intimate, as they were apt to do when they went out. He couldn't deny a similar train of thought had sparked the invitation.

He looked back at Effie, though, and hated himself for wondering if Talia was right. If he would intimidate her or if he could make amends for his crappy first impression. The tangible prospects before him came into crystal clear focus as Talia whispered in his ear all the ways she wanted to have him later that night.

Effie was grateful for the reprieve of drying the puff paint. She needed the five minutes to compose herself. Theodore was here with a woman who dripped sex appeal and experience and, well, everything that Effie wasn't. To top it off, Theodore persisted in being arrogant and annoying. He mentioned he'd be by in the morning for their follow-up, reminding her that passing inspection still loomed when she just wanted to make it through the class. Effie tensed remembering the sheer disappointment that *she* dared be the instructor of this class. She tried not to give it another thought.

Effie returned everyone's glass and demonstrated how to mix the paints and glue to create a transparent color, filling in the sections between the faux leading. Usually, she tried to use people's names when giving tips or little compliments, but it wasn't wise when it came to Theodore.

She'd said his name once already, and she managed to control her face, which was a feat that deserved some kind of a medal. Avoiding it for the rest of the night seemed like the right move, but she worried that he'd notice and take offense, calling back the *really rude* face she had made the first time they met. Maybe it wouldn't even come up—

"So, what does my name taste like?" Theodore asked as he brushed a mix of red paint and Elmer's Glue over the first square of his cardinal. He really was infuriating. Especially as he dared her with a look. Effie only replied so they might break their intense eye contact that had steam rising from her tiptoes to the crown of her head.

"Do you truly want to know?" Effie asked, using her project before her as an excuse to avert her gaze.

"Taste like?" Talia interjected, utterly confused. "What a weird question."

"I have lexical gustatory synesthesia, so I can taste words." She said this all while staring intently at her glass, but she felt the attention of the whole group turn on her.

"I'm dying to know," Theodore confessed.

"Fine. Theodore tastes like soggy cardboard." He didn't seem to like the answer but took it in stride. The relief she felt at admitting it startled her.

After that, everyone wanted to know what their names tasted like, so they played a little game while they painted. Effie explained that Talia tasted like seafood alfredo—something about it sounding Italian and like tilapia and rich flavor all at once. Mr. Robecheck, Arnold, had a name that tasted like asparagus. Mrs. Robecheck, Sarah, tasted like SweeTarts. Heidi adored that her name tasted like hot caramel sauce, while Colin thought that a name tasting of whipped cream was perfectly acceptable.

"So just my name then that displeases your taste buds?" Theodore asked, humor in his voice.

"It would appear so," Effie replied, apologetic. "Make sure you're adding glue to every color, Mr. Robecheck. You want it to stick to the glass." The gentleman nodded and added a dab to the blue he used.

"And what's your name taste like?" Theodore wondered. Effie wasn't sure anyone had ever asked her that.

"It's kind of hard to explain," Effie said, not interested in continuing down this line of questioning. But he waited. Effie swallowed hard, her mouth having gone a bit dry. No explanation came to save her. The silence around her felt probing, and she wished that Theodore didn't bring it up. She was back in grade school, misspelling *caricature* in front of the whole class. Her skin dampened, the room boiling over with her awkwardness. She just wanted to get back to teaching.

"I decided your name tastes like eggplant," Theodore said as he lifted his brush with a flourish. He gave her a subtle wink, and her shoulders relaxed. Disagreeable, perhaps, but not unobservant. Kind even, to have saved her from her social anxieties, even if he had triggered them.

"A flavor will frequently be related to how a name is spelled or sounds. So I guess I'll accept eggplant." She smiled faintly and settled in to work on her own stained glass. Everyone went back to their dates, allowing Effie to ponder her real answer.

Her relationship with her synesthesia was something she'd worked on in therapy for years. It took her a long time to realize that there was an emotional component to the way words tasted. Another heat wave of embarrassment tingled her spine as her name played on repeat in her mind, washing her tongue in that not-so-satisfying flavor. She shoved the regret back in its cage to examine—for the millionth time—another day and returned to her project.

Theodore finished his painting and held it proudly. "Excellent faux stained glass, Theodore," Effie said, and her nose scrunched again. It was alarming how horrible it tasted, given whatever flutter she felt when she looked at him.

"Fascinating." Theodore laughed. "It's that realistic?"

"Like licking an Amazon box that's sat out in the rain and molded," Effie joked. Theodore laughed again and she couldn't help enjoying it.

"Well then, maybe you should just call me Theo. Everyone else does."

Effie tensed. "I'll call you cardboard."

"I imagine cardboard tastes like cardboard. That can't be pleasant."

"Better than soggy cardboard," Effie rebuffed. She honestly couldn't tell if they were truly bickering or if he enjoyed the banter.

"Indulge me. I want to know if Theo is better or not."

Effie was truly hesitant. Even hearing words left her with faint flavors. Not as strong or recognizable as when she said the word, but she already knew what Theo tasted like. She didn't need him knowing that, though, because it wasn't any better. In fact, from Effie's perspective, it was much, much worse.

"I doubt it changes much," Effie warned. It struck her as funny that she hadn't considered trying to shorten his name before now. Maybe because everyone always asked if Effie was short for something, she didn't like to assume any alterations were fair play.

"Just try it," he coaxed, and it sounded flirtatious. *But that couldn't be right*, not with Talia there reminding him he promised to go to the Tipsy Moose after this and finding any excuse to brush up against him. "I'm not going to give up on this."

"Fine," Effie said. "What a lovely cardinal . . . Theo." Effie's eyes nearly rolled back in her head, and her tongue reached for the corner of her mouth where she'd certainly find—*Hope*. Honeyed ham. *Tibby*. Thyme. *Grams*. Graham crackers. She forced herself to think through different name tastes to clear her palate, but the damage was done.

"That certainly seems like an improvement," Mrs. Robecheck remarked from her stool, and Effie blushed. *She really needed to learn to control her damn face.* She quickly averted her gaze, though her skin prickled with Theo's attention.

"Definitely not cardboard," Effie offered by way of explanation.

Talia had a wicked grin on her face. "Oh, this is fun."

Theo reached for her like he was going to grab her hand to calm her. *God, how bad had her face been?* She bounced with nerves as his hand got closer, but en route he knocked his arm into his glass of wine that sat precariously near the edge. Unfortunately, it perched above Effie's open tote and cascaded all over her things.

Theo scrambled, grabbing for the roll of paper towels in the center of the table. He hurriedly unpacked her tote, dabbing at everything before Effie could even dismount her stool. "Shit. I'm sorry," he said as he continued to blot the mess. Effie could do nothing to stop the atrocious tang on her tongue. Theo noticed. "Shit—Sorry again."

"Just stop saying it," Effie blurted.

"Right. Sorry," he said, embarrassed.

Effie crouched before him as he pulled the novel she'd been reading from the bag. The one whose cover depicted a broad-chested pirate hoisting the thigh of a busty wench over his midsection as he pressed her against the wheel of his ship in the middle of a rainstorm. Rippling pectorals and stacked abs were on full display beneath his drenched shirt, now also drenched in wine. Theo's grin went crooked as he looked at the cover, then at Effie. She snatched it from him before Talia could see.

"I'll buy you a new copy. If I could just get the title," he teased, clearly enjoying the fire in Effie's cheeks. She scowled back at him.

"That's not necessary," she asserted, tucking the book onto a shelf of the cutting table. Theo held her wine-stained bag in his hands as he stood.

"You have to let me apologize somehow," he argued.

"It's not a big deal. I have other bags."

"And other books?" Effie could have melted under the heat of his gaze. He enjoyed this far too much. *Wasn't he just going to comfort her?* Now, he goaded her with flirty looks he had no right to be sharing when he was on a date.

"Yes." He kept staring. So did Talia. "Is this another thing you're not going to let go of?"

"Decidedly not," Theo asserted. "Let me apologize."

10

Effie normally wouldn't have acquiesced and joined Theo and Talia at the bar after class. It had to be a symptom of her interest in people watching. It was the only explanation for why she would willingly subject herself to a night out with near strangers as a third wheel, retribution for wine-stained romance novels aside. Or maybe she just wasn't finished studying Theo, yet.

Aunt Bea had also suggested she stay open to possibilities, so she couldn't very well say no to spontaneity even if the invite was purely apologetic. Despite Theo's innocent intentions it seemed Talia wanted to use it as an opportunity to tease Effie and stake her claim on the brooding safety inspector. It was highlighted by the fact that she kept saying Theo's name, trying to elicit some kind of reaction from her.

God was definitely testing her at this point.

Effie took her Aperol spritz and followed Theo and Talia to a high-top in the corner of the Tipsy Moose. They weren't the only ones casting judgmental looks at her fruity red drink in the dark wood bar decorated with branded beer posters, dart boards, and a large faux moose head wearing sunglasses.

"You don't go out much, do you?" Talia asked before sipping the pale ale, IPA, something-or-other that was locally brewed.

"What makes you say that?" Effie asked and followed Talia's gaze to her spritz. "I don't get weird looks at the Book and Bar," she said a bit sheepishly before taking a sip.

There was an awkward beat that ended in Talia scooting a bit closer to Theo. He didn't resist but didn't engage fully either. Effie couldn't tell what they were about, so she continued to sip her drink a bit too quickly. Theo spoke first. "You shared soggy cardboard but won't tell me what Theo tastes like?" Effie relished the tart cocktail on her tongue that kept her from experiencing *Theo* once more.

"It's irrelevant," Effie argued.

"Unlikely," Talia chimed. She held a dare in her gaze, but Effie refused to take the bait. Her face must have been very telling earlier if Talia wasn't letting it go.

"It's better than your full name, so at least we can get on without me insulting you tomorrow," Effie proclaimed. "Or better yet, I'll settle for neutral and call you Cardboard."

"Then my only recourse is to call you Eggplant," he replied.

"So be it," Effie said and went back to sipping her drink.

"Where's Schilling these days?" Talia asked.

Effie took in her surroundings. *Why had she and Hope never come here?* They liked pool and darts, people watching and a good cocktail. Maybe Effie was too settled in her ways, too sheltered.

"He's been off lately. Hasn't wanted to come out much. But what you probably want to know is a bunch of stuff I'm not at liberty to share with you," Theo said pointedly, and Talia pouted.

"You're no fun," she whined.

"I'm no gossip," Theo corrected, and Effie respected that. Even if she had meddled or gossiped more than she should, it was an admirable quality.

"But speak of the devil, isn't that him?" Talia pointed across the bar to a man with a dark, scruffy beard playing darts by himself. "Hey, Schilling!" Talia yelled. Only Effie seemed to inwardly cringe at the forthright, confident summons.

Schilling about-faced, a smile on his lips at recognizing his friends. He came over to the high-top and joined them. Theo gestured to Effie. "Schilling, this is Eggplant. Eggplant, Schilling."

"Is that—"

"It's a bit," Theo interjected. Schilling raised his brows but took a seat without inquiring further.

Effie doubted that was really his name either, but wanting to maintain some modicum of cool, she merely said, "Nice to meet you." Effie thought him to be sweetly handsome, and she wondered if Talia had called him over to watch Effie squirm even more.

"What's that?" Schilling asked, pointing to her drink.

"An Aperol spritz." His face screwed up like she had said she was drinking pure sludge. "It's good!" Theo reached over, hesitating as if to ask permission. Effie nodded her consent. He grabbed her glass and sipped. It was an intimate gesture she'd expect from Hope, not a near stranger. His face went sour with the tartness.

"I think your condition has sullied your taste buds, Eggplant," Theo teased. "Or everything you're hearing and saying is somehow making that taste better."

Effie glared. "It doesn't work like that. Whatever I'm eating or drinking overrides word tastes."

"I'm lost," Schilling said.

"Join the club," Talia ribbed, another dare in her gaze before she took Theo's palm and traced the contours of his hand, all the while fixing her predatory eyes on Effie. Talia turned to face Theo fully and held tight to his hand. "Come play pool with me, you promised."

Theo sighed. "I did. We'll be back." They took their drinks and wandered to the nearest pool table. Effie watched them a moment. They racked the balls, and Theo leaned over the table to break. Talia craned her neck and planted a kiss on his lips. Effie hated that she could tell just how much tongue was involved. Suddenly, the coaster on the table became very interesting to her.

Schilling side-eyed her. "They're not together," he offered.

"Why should I care?"

"In case you did," he said. "It's more a pairing of convenience if that makes sense."

Effie tensed but nodded. Her cheeks were on fire.

"Talia wants more than convenience," Effie asserted. "She's enjoying marking her territory."

"Then why'd you come?" Schilling asked, and he seemed genuinely curious, not judgmental or condescending at all.

"Because I'm a little tired of my life being so plain," Effie admitted. She wondered if Schilling emitted some kind of truth-telling frequency because she'd never been so transparent in her life. It could have been the kindness of his spirit or the sadness behind his eyes, but Effie felt like he was authentic. Trustworthy. "So I thought I'd see what happened if I did something I wouldn't normally do."

"And what do you normally do?" Schilling asked, and Effie was disarmed by his casual tone and willingness to chat. It put her at ease which nicely contrasted the swirling thoughts that usually accompanied the breezy exterior she forced on herself.

"Keep to myself, honestly. I bake, I craft. I taught Theo and Talia how to make faux stained glass. And when I'm not doing those things, I'm reading or trying to keep up with my loud, crazy family."

"Sounds mostly peaceful."

"Or reclusive," Effie joked, but it was the truth. It had always felt easier to live within the boundaries of what she already knew than dare to see what else was out there.

Schilling laughed. "I suppose that's another way to look at it. Maybe the recluse thing was working and now it's not?"

"Accurate. Everyone else in my life is passionate about something. It drives them. I don't have something like that. I guess I'm starting to wonder if I just haven't found it or if it doesn't exist."

"And the only way to find out is by doing things you wouldn't normally do. That makes sense."

"Does it? I feel like I sound insane." Effie hadn't been out with anyone new in so long she wasn't sure what boundaries existed in polite conversation.

"Not at all. I get it," Schilling remarked. "For me, it's okay not to have that something. I'm here to soak in what's good about life. And just because I love a thing doesn't mean I need to obsess over it or monetize it or make it my whole personality."

"Yes! Exactly!" Effie nearly screamed. She hadn't meant to be so loud, but no one had ever connected with her over this point before. She even drew a glance from Talia and Theo at the pool table.

Schilling laughed again, and it was melodic, like chickadees in the sunshine on a spring morning. Effie allowed herself a flirtatious look at him. He smiled back, and Effie thought it was a good thing that Talia tried to intimidate her by calling him over. He was cute, fun, sweet. Talia's tongue wasn't down his throat. Schilling tasted like pennies, but that wasn't terrible. Besides, his first name could be better. Even still, she couldn't help but glance over at the pool table.

She timed it perfectly to catch Talia playfully squeezing Theo's ass. Effie didn't wait to see how he responded, turning her attention back to Schilling. "You sure you don't care?"

"Definitely. I'm having fun talking to you. Must be the real reason I came out tonight," Effie mused.

"A believer in fate?" Schilling asked, and the sadness in his eyes deepened.

"Usually, but I also think that sometimes the way of the world is pure chaos."

"I feel more aligned with chaos than fate myself lately." He definitely seemed sadder now.

"Anything you want to talk about?" Effie inquired, knowing her ear might be all that was needed to turn his spirits.

"I wouldn't want to bore you with it," Schilling said before taking a long pull from his beer.

Effie considered telling him to bore her. But she knew a deflection when she saw one. It didn't matter that he was probably compelled by the same guilt she was when she didn't want her grief to sully the mood. He didn't want to talk about it, so she wouldn't force him. Instead, she asked, "So, do you come here often?"

Schilling smirked. "What a line, Eggplant!"

Effie turned ten shades of red. "I didn't mean—"

"I know," he chuckled. "But yes. This is kind of our only haunt in town. Everywhere else is trying to be some high-end mixology bar when I just want a cold beer."

"Fair enough," Effie said. She sipped her drink to bridge the silence that followed. It dragged on long enough that Effie wondered if she'd ever think of something else to say.

Instead, Schilling interrupted her rising social anxiety by asking, "How are you with candle making? Is it in your crafting repertoire?"

"Actually, yes. I've taught a couple workshops and pour my own at home. Why?"

"My mom's birthday is coming up and she is nuts for scented candles. Always burning one. Her favorite, though, is nearly burnt out, and the shop that she found it in went out of business. I was wondering if I could recreate it."

"That's thoughtful of you," Effie said with admiration.

"I like getting people thoughtful gifts, not stuff."

"Well, I think I can help with that," Effie asserted. "But we'll need the nearly dead candle to try to recreate the scent. How's Friday? We can do it at the store after closing."

"Do what at the store after closing?" Talia purred, eyebrows raised high over her sultry silver-blue eyes. She and Theo resumed their seats at the high-top, fresh drinks in hand.

Effie didn't bother to hide her glare this time, fed up with Talia's teasing. The rise in Effie only seemed to please Talia more, though, so Effie spat, "Making candles."

"Aren't you just Martha Stewart in lace?" she goaded, eyeing the modest, cream top that Effie wore. Effie wanted to rip the smirk from her face. Theo didn't even seem to notice, or if he did, he didn't care. It was Schilling who came to her rescue instead.

"And the last time you made anything but a Cup O Noodles, Talia?"

"Oh bite me, Schilling."

"Wouldn't dare," he countered. Effie smiled at him, grateful for his intervention. Maybe Schilling *was* the reason she came out tonight. It might not have been fate, but it felt like something. "Friday sounds great," he said, turning his full attention back on Effie. Something like hope bubbled in her chest, and she did her damnedest to keep the door to it open.

Theo hiked the stairs to his one-bedroom apartment in the old mill building right outside of Market Square, a fairly drunk Schilling behind him. After Effie left, claiming she needed to get up early, Talia insisted they do shots.

As Theo unlocked his front door, he was certain Talia had hoped to get him drunk enough to take her home. To her dismay, he led Schilling through the door instead.

They wandered into the modest space and sunk into the old leather sofa that sat opposite the exposed brick wall of his combination kitchen and living area. Theo leaned his head back. Under normal circumstances he would have brought Talia home, shots or not. It had been his intention all night. But when he had the choice to lay with Talia or offer his sofa to his drunk friend, he chose Schilling. He'd likely hear about that when Schilling was sober enough to call him on it. Currently, Schilling stared blankly at the wall, hugging a pillow.

"All set, buddy?" Theo asked.

"Fine. You're not though."

Theo scowled. Apparently, sobriety wasn't a prerequisite for Schilling's insights.

"You like her," Schilling said.

"Talia is fun, but we don't have the same priorities. We've been over this."

"Not her. Eggplant."

Theo choked on a laugh. That was rich. Schilling had been the one talking Effie up all night, making plans with her. Theo was just trying to make amends for ruining a tote bag. He wasn't thinking about Effie in any other way. She was merely an annoying client he had to see tomorrow, never mind that she was nicer to look at than most. And if him flirting with Talia bothered her, then she could have declined his offer. "Yeah, right," Theo rebuffed. "She's barely tolerable."

Schilling raised his hands in defense. "Seems like it bugged you when I asked for her help."

"If anything, it made me question your sanity."

"Ouch," Schilling muttered before letting out a yawn.

Theo rose, giving Schilling the rest of the couch. Poor guy couldn't hold his liquor, but people seemed to be drawn to him for it. His personality wasn't born on the bravery of booze but rather in the authenticity of his character. He patted Schilling on the shoulder as he went by, muttering, "Sleep it off."

Schilling laid down and Theo shuffled into his own room. He pulled off his shirt and pants, climbing under his comforter in just his boxers. He settled in to sleep, all the while insisting to himself that he'd take Talia home next time, and that her not warming his bed tonight had absolutely nothing to do with Effie Thatcher.

11

Hope dozed against her mountain of pillows. Her room was shrouded in hues of violet as sunlight filtered through the curtains she had drawn. She didn't want Brayden trying to come in through the window. Not again. His incessant text messages were bad enough. Apparently, he'd never been ghosted before because he didn't let up. Well, lucky him. *She prayed it hurt.*

Hope rolled onto her side to confront her open laptop. She moved the mouse, bringing the screen to life on the email she left up.

Hope!

Love the revisions; everything is coming together in this last installment of Web of Realms. *The publishers are a bit surprised by the ending, though, and so am I. You may weave some sordid tales, but you always wind up at a happy ending. We were rooting for Kiernan and Dominique. I think your readership would want it too. Try it out and send me an alt ending by next Friday.*

Talk soon,
Heather

Hope thought they'd end up together too. Maybe she could get away with telling her agent that sometimes the characters do what the characters want to do, and it's out of her hands. Pull from any number of authors who have admitted the same in interviews about different pairings or killings or seismic shifts in the plot that readers didn't see coming. It would work for Hope too, *if, in fact, it were true.* But Kiernan and Dom wanted to end up together. They needed it. It was written, well before she'd ever introduced them on the page, like they'd been drawn from her brain to find each other amidst the fictional realms that worshipped a spider goddess and were crumbling into the abyss. She just hadn't been able to write that ending. Hadn't wanted them to have what she couldn't.

Heather was being nice, as always. Not outright demanding the alternate ending but rather insisting Hope play. She knew Hope responded better to suggestions than demands, but it was clear. She'd need the happy ending to get approval from the team that made her first two books bestsellers. What was worse was she knew they were right. It had been agonizing to write the ending without bringing those two characters together. It had felt all wrong. But her wounds were too fresh when the deadline for the last three chapters had rolled around, and she couldn't bear it. She'd knocked them out in an afternoon after the whole Chloe debacle, just wanting it to be over.

Hope groaned as she drew the computer into her lap. She opened a new document, gearing up to try the romantic ending she'd been avoiding. It was an epic fantasy series after all. The romance was a subplot that she introduced in book two. It was supposed to add some levity and warmth to the otherwise dark and twisted nature of the horrors she'd fictionalized about a world falling into chaos as it disintegrated into the voids between stars. But she knew, given the outpouring of love for the characters after the second book released, that she had to find a way to save them and give them their happy ending. It was exciting when she started writing it six months ago. It felt right.

Now, it was torture.

Hope stared at the cursor blinking on the blank page. The words got stuck somewhere in the mechanism of her mind. The pressure built behind her ears. They screamed to be written to be expressed, but she'd tucked them away. Back to the cell they'd been kept locked in before she met Brayden. Where she and Effie had stuffed excitement and lust and love and waited until they could be shared safely.

A rap on the glass of her window startled her. Hope sucked in a breath, holding it tensely as though he could possibly hear her breathing within.

The window loomed before her and she couldn't move. Brayden's silhouette was cast against the thin linen of the lilac curtains, his head hung. She closed her eyes tight, tears squeaking through the dams she'd built.

"Hope, please. I don't understand. What's happened?"

Hope took a shuddering breath, her heart breaking all over again at the worry in his voice. The tenderness. He had scaled the banister to her window twice before, each time asking the same question.

She refused to answer. She'd since taped a note to the metal flashing beneath her window so it wouldn't be seen from the street and inquired over by her meddling family.

She had written three words. Three words she hoped would cut their ties and leave Brayden certain there was no future for them. They were the words he'd read in her book series. Words Kiernan had said to her first love, the one she left behind to find her true calling in the first book. The kindest breakup she could offer without diving into the depths of her own heartache.

Let me go.

"Hope, I know you're in there. I . . . I don't think I can."

She kept silent, her pain slipping into prickling rage. How dare he sound so hurt, so baffled when he was the one living a lie. He was the one who created this mess, who pursued her, made her feel seen and adored. He, who so ardently expressed his love with his words and his touch, had been nothing but a rake. A man bored with his wife and looking for other conquests. Hope nearly choked on her ironic laugh. It turned out even the light, goofy, French bulldog-loving, flower-picking sweetheart—she had once called him that—could turn out as cruel and unfeeling as the obvious womanizing pricks. Like the men she'd thought she'd loved in college. The ones that sparked her turn toward celibacy before Brayden. It pained her greatly that he joined their ranks.

Hope looked back to the window, but Brayden's silhouette was gone. She scooted off her bed and peered outside. He was nowhere in sight, but her note fluttered in the breeze, now tucked into the trim of the window. She gently lifted the sash and plucked the notecard out before the wind took it.

He had written three words of his own. The only three, she guessed, that he could think to undo whatever had been done. Like the antidote in every fairy tale, the spell to break the curse.

I love you.

Hope ripped the paper to shreds into the wastebasket that sat by the writing desk she only used when in full drafting mode. She took a steadying breath, hand resting on the marred and marked wood of the antique desk, her grief threatening to topple her.

She jolted.

Her gaze danced around the room. Hope started again, looking down at her swollen belly. She let her hand rest on the offending side and felt, for the third time now, as her baby kicked her. Hope smiled. "What? You think I should have kept it?" Another kick.

Hope moved her hands in soothing circles over her womb. She sighed deeply, returned to her pile of pillows, and drew her computer to her lap.

She took another breath and let it all go. For Kiernan and Dominque, she gave the love she had so desperately wanted for herself. For her readers too, so they might believe in love just long enough to experience it before it withered and died. Every wish and hope she had for her life with Brayden. Every glance, every touch. Everything she saw for their future. Everything she felt of their love, however brief, she poured onto the page—the only place it would ever live.

12

The stock room was spotless. Everything had been organized in tall racks securely fastened to the block walls—per Theo's instructions. The impediments to the exits had been cleared, and Effie had even managed to get someone in to work on the emergency lights within the week. They were going on minute seventy-five of burn time when Theo checked the timer on his phone.

He stretched his arms overhead, his clipboard resting on his lap. He groaned against the ache in his back. Theo commandeered a small metal chair to sit on while he waited the ninety minutes for the safety lights, and it was anything but comfortable. This was the least entertaining part of his job, waiting for the lights. Sometimes he would bring a book or his journal that housed all his poetry, but today, he'd left them in the van.

Stupidly.

Given his last visit here he thought he would have a verbal sparring match with one Miss Effie Thatcher while he performed the tests, but she was happily occupied in the store claiming she'd *leave him to it*, after smugly showcasing the hard work she had done in the back warehouse.

If she had any thoughts about how Talia flaunted her affections for Theo and how he hadn't brushed her off, Effie didn't show it. Didn't even mention last night. It was almost disappointing. He sat alone in the back room listening to the trill of her laughter roll through the door he left propped open to his right. Irritating as their first encounter had been, at least he'd had her attention.

He supposed that was something that he and Talia had in common. Their inane desire to be desired. They had bonded over the fact that neither had come into their confidence until college, at which point the fawning and flirting became like a drug.

He exhaled, his head lolling to the side. He hated that part of himself actually. The one that reveled in being looked at, admired, even if it was just for his strong jaw and curated muscle mass. It was vapid and went against everything he stood for, but he couldn't resist the allure of a sensual gaze meant only for him. He supposed he had years as the quiet emo theater kid to blame for that. He hadn't realized until he was seventeen and cast as Kilroy in *Kilroy Was Here* that he was someone who could be deemed a heartthrob. Putting on the armor of the character and wardrobe that showed off his lean muscles stirred something in him—the power of a good story.

So the one he wrote about himself became one of confidence and romance. One that would garner sultry looks at frat parties and respect on poetry slam nights. Sometimes he wondered if he was being his authentic self, or if he was only ever playing a part—the chiseled, roguish worker by day, brooding poet by night. But he realized, that in all likelihood, it didn't matter. In truth, everyone was playing a part. Best he could do was pray he'd find the fellow cast members that took his life in a more meaningful direction. Aside from Schilling and his own family who were scattered across the country, he wasn't sure he'd found them yet.

He sighed again checking the time. Ten more minutes. He gazed at the safety light that flickered once, willing it to stay lit so he wouldn't have to fail them again. It seemed to listen as time ticked on.

Effie poked her head through the open doorway. "Having fun?"

"The most," Theo crooned, eyebrows raising.

Effie wandered into the warehouse, arms crossed tight over her chest as she leaned against the wall. She looked like she was freezing or holding herself together. Theo wasn't sure which.

"Didn't know what version of you I'd get today, Cardboard. Surly safety guy or kind-of-cool craft guy, so I thought it best to steer clear."

"Kind of cool?"

Effie shrugged, but her smile spread wide, indicating that she thought he was more than *kind of cool*, and it did ridiculous things to his ego. His own smile must have shown it because she said, "Don't be so smug." She scrunched her face like she'd bitten into something sour.

"Seems like it doesn't pay to be sassy there, Effie dear," he chided.

"Don't call me that," she barked, and he couldn't help but chuckle.

"Why not?"

"My grandmother calls me that."

"Noted," Theo said as the timer on his phone went off. "Good news, Eggplant. You passed."

"Don't call me that either."

"Sign here." He pointed to the line at the bottom of the page that acknowledged they had gone over everything and that she released his company from any liability regarding accidents in the future. Just because it was his job to be thorough and make everyone as safe as possible didn't mean that things didn't occasionally go sideways and result in someone getting hurt.

He watched as Effie signed her name with a flourish, dotting the *i* with a little heart. "Do you always do that?" he found himself asking, and some insane part of him wished she did it just for him.

"Always," she said. "It was cutesy when I was twelve and I never stopped."

He took the clipboard back and lingered a beat. "What are you doing this weekend?"

"Why? You want me to watch Talia shove her tongue down your throat again?"

So she had seen, and it irked her. *Apparently.* "No? What?"

"I know you didn't really want me to come out last night. You were being nice and expected me to say no," she said a touch softer like she battled between her armor and her vulnerability.

"That's not true." Except that it was. He may have shared Talia's penchant for attention but definitely did not get off on awkward social interactions the way she did. It was like she was making up for all the bullying she'd endured by being a pot-stirring flirt in her twenties. Theo didn't know what else to say, because the look on Effie's face told him she didn't believe him anyway.

"But I'm glad you let me join," she admitted. "It was nice to do something different with new people. Even if Talia thought it was some kind of drama. Which it wasn't, by the way. You're not my type," she said flatly.

Also noted. *Wow, she knew how to draw hard lines real fast.* He didn't catch her gaze dipping to his biceps or his hair or anything. "Well, I guess we're done here."

"Guess so." Effie sighed, and Theo couldn't read the emotion behind her eyes as she forced herself to hold his gaze. Like eye contact was a challenge. It had his skin prickling, so maybe it was. He nodded once and made for the door, pausing in front of her, his face mere inches from hers.

"See you around, Effie Thatcher."

"Bye, Theo," she said through tight teeth, and he swore he heard her breath hitch behind his name.

But it didn't matter. Effie was as infuriating as the first day they met, but now for totally different reasons. He stalked through the store, giving Basil a terse wave before exiting to his van and leaving Effie—and the attention she'd stopped giving—behind. Good riddance.

13

Effie and Hope sat at their usual spot in the Book and Bar—a pair of cozy leather armchairs by the large front window. It offered the best natural light and was offset from the large farm tables so that the roar of chatter dulled to a pleasant hum in the background. Perfect for reading, sipping, and gabbing without distraction. Unless of course they turned their attentions outside and watched the flurry of people that filled the streets of Market Square, which they often did.

But today, they were both focused.

Effie, dressed casually in a pair of cropped jeans she'd embroidered with sunflowers on the cuffs and a loose white V-neck beneath her mauve cardigan, flipped through a stack of printed pages bound with a binder clip. She wielded a red pen like a teacher, the cap pinched between her teeth.

Hope's sideways glance was an impatient inquiry. "I'm almost done," Effie snipped.

"Fine," Hope groaned.

Effie smirked as her cousin took a casual sip of her club soda, but Hope's tapping foot gave away her anxiety. Effie was certain Hope hadn't actually been reading the sizable tome in her hands and likely scanned the same paragraph over and over while she waited for Effie to finish reading the rewrites of her manuscript.

Effie finished the pages and looked at Hope. "I don't know why you bother having me read these ahead of time," she confessed. Hope scowled. "It's not like I have a writing degree or any insight into how things should be written. I tell you they're great, and I feel like that's not helpful."

Hope laughed. "So they're great?"

"Yes, but I bet your writer friends would be more discerning and tell you how to make it fantastic."

"My writer friends have helped along the way, but I like your perspective. I like to know what you liked and didn't like. You're a discerning reader. Why shouldn't I want to know what you think?"

"Isn't great art supposed to be a reflection of you, not pandering to your discerning readers?" Effie quipped.

"Yes, but it's better if it can be both. Are you going to do this for the next series? It's getting tedious telling you how much I value your thoughts."

"I'll work on it."

"Good."

Effie handed Hope the pages. Hope's eyebrows shot up at the red marking the pages here and there as she flipped through. Effie looked at her feet, fiddling with her fingers while Hope scoured the chapters.

A sip from her Aperol spritz gave her the courage to say, "I mostly noted typos. And a few places where you fell into some romantic clichés when I know you had something more . . . truthful . . . vulnerable to say."

Effie dared a glance at Hope who had sighed as if she knew that criticism was coming.

"I know I don't know how it ended, or why—and I'm not asking, I know you'll tell me when you're ready—but you said it was real. While it was, anyway. Use that more. It's like ninety percent there, add the last bit you held back. Purge yourself of it so it can be remembered fondly and can inspire the rest of us to seek out a Dom and Kiernan kind of love."

"And you say you're not a writer," Hope joked, but her smile was faint.

They were quiet for a long moment. Effie thought maybe she had gone too far, said too much. She didn't like to give advice. She didn't think she'd earned that right with what little she knew of the world.

But Effie knew her own heart, how it yearned for romance and connection. How it stopped completely when she let herself imagine a life that was made beautiful and wondrous by doing it with the right person. It was how Grams had always described the love she had with Herman. It was what Effie knew was budding with Hope and Brayden. It's what had her daring to say, "Maybe you and Brayden could give things another shot."

Hope's glare could have cut glass.

"Grams always says friendship is foundational, forgiveness is freeing. Maybe—"

"You don't know what you're talking about," Hope snapped.

Effie swallowed hard. Hope didn't use that tone with her. Not since she was fifteen, Hope seventeen, and Effie had accidentally let slip that Hope had a crush on Tim Marcroft in biology class. They weren't exactly popular and he was. It made for a pretty hellish week of razzing and sideways glances.

"I'm sorry. I just think—"

"I don't care what you think!" Hope jerked up in her seat, fire in her eyes. She slammed her heavy fantasy novel on the coffee table between them. Effie flinched at the resounding thud. Hope dug her manicured nails into her hair. The assertion that she valued Effie's opinion evaporated with the steam that billowed from Hope's ears. But she wasn't the only one bubbling with anger.

Effie was fed up. They told each other everything. Always. Hope had been betraying that for over a year, apparently, and Effie couldn't take it any longer. Couldn't bear feeling like they were splitting apart at the seams. Didn't want to imagine a day where she was left standing on a ledge, Hope inaccessible across the rift between them. "Just tell me! I have done nothing to deserve you keeping me out of this. I am your friend, Hope. Just fucking let me in!" She hated cursing, it tasted like iron, blood, forbidden. She bit down on her tongue, controlling her face.

"So you can fix it for me?"

"What are you talking about?"

"What you did with Louisa and Gil?"

"Wow, that's a low blow," Effie huffed, but guilt shaded her face. Hope must have seen the shame and angst mingling and viewed it as an opportunity to push Effie over the edge.

"You know how you don't like to give advice because you're so *inexperienced*?" The word was a scathing insult. "Maybe stick to that."

Hope snatched her book from the table and began reading.

Conversation over. Like everyone in Effie's life, Hope had the final say. Effie's dad used to tell her whenever she confided that Louisa and Ellen always got what they wanted from their mother, that *the squeaky wheel gets the grease.* Effie moved through their childhood quiet as a wraith. She had never been a squeaky wheel. Never saw the point. If things were going to come her way, she wanted them to come freely, easily, with love and affection. Not because she whined for an hour straight until her mother finally gave in and let her have the nail polish, or go to the movie, or stay up past her bedtime. The trouble was it kept her from living the other bit of wisdom she'd stored in her seven-year-old memory like a time capsule—*if you don't ask, the answer is always no.*

Not wanting their relationship to devolve any further and desperately wanting to move beyond the lingering sting of Hope's condescension, Effie eased to the edge of her seat and rested her elbows on her knees. She'd ask for what she wanted without uttering a word. Effie stared at Hope, unrelenting. She waited one minute. Two minutes. Hope shifted in her seat trying to ignore Effie's stare. Three minutes. Finally, with a huff, Hope closed her book. She stared right back at Effie. It never failed to amuse Effie that despite her inexperience, her quiet floating way of living, it was the other Thatcher women who needed lessons in maturity.

"I'm sorry," Effie said, sweet sparkling strawberries on her tongue.

"Me too," Hope whispered.

"I don't want . . . I don't want things to change." Effie's glance landed on Hope's belly, though the bump was barely visible beneath her oversized sweatshirt—presumably worn because she still hadn't told Brayden.

"I don't either," she said. "I'm sorry I mentioned the Louisa thing."

"You're right, though. It—" Effie bit her quivering lip. "I regret it every day."

Hope took her hand and squeezed tight. She sucked in a deep breath before lifting her gaze again to meet Effie's. "Veritas?"

"Veritas," Effie affirmed, and she waited for the blow.

"He's married."

Effie's heart sank. "No," she breathed, not wanting it to be true.

"I stopped by his reno house to tell him about the baby and I met his wife instead."

"Hope, I'm so sorry." Effie peeled herself from her seat and strode to Hope's. The armchairs were huge, so she easily nestled in beside her cousin. She wrapped an arm around Hope, who leaned into her shoulder.

Rain pattered against the window as the sky darkened outside. Effie felt a mimicking drip of tears on her shoulder. She leaned forward and picked the novel off the table.

"Where were you?" Effie asked.

"First page." Hope sniffed.

Effie flipped open the massive book after popping a piece of gum in her mouth so she might better enjoy it. She cleared her throat loudly as though about to begin a truly dramatic reading, and Hope giggled beside her. "Valeria Winstrop had never met a man she didn't like— fantasy novel, obviously," Effie teased before continuing. Her voice soothed the anxious shivers that Hope had succumbed to in sharing the truth.

They sat like that until closing.

Effie read about royalty, magic, lust, and adventure, each word stitching together Hope's battered heart with something that felt a lot like her namesake.

Effie prayed that by the time Valeria Winstrop had tamed the dragon and claimed her birthright, Hope would be brave enough to love again. Because despite everything, despite the hate for Brayden that gnawed at the back of her mind, Effie wanted to believe in love, and she couldn't help but feel like she needed Hope to do it.

14

A chill spring rain pattered the windows as Theo entered his apartment still donning his blue-collared shirt and work boots. He was ready to swap them for soft-washed Henleys and relaxed-fit jeans. Regardless of how much he liked his job, there were still weeks he counted down the hours until the weekend. This was one of them.

Theo slipped out of his boots and hung up his messenger bag that carried all manner of release forms, code documents, and his trusty clipboard. He padded across the laminate floors to his sofa and plopped down beside Schilling, who had apparently used his spare key to let himself in.

"You look like hell," Theo remarked as he assessed Schilling from head to toe.

"I called out today," he replied.

"Yeah, I know, so why are you on my couch?"

Schilling shrugged. He didn't actually look sick. Probably just needed a day. Theo had given him the key because his friend frequently needed a change of scenery. Somewhere to sit quietly and not be bothered. Theo had once thought himself brooding and dramatic. He had nothing on Schilling's lows. The goof in daylight could turn into a real downer after dark. Especially lately.

"Sorry, I can go." Schilling moved to get up.

"Don't be stupid."

Schilling sighed, leaning back. Theo spotted the burnt-down candle sitting on his coffee table. Poured into a glass jar, its edges were stained with soot and only a trace of the wax remained at the bottom.

"It's my mom's. I'm going to meet Eggplant in a bit," Schilling explained, but his words sounded heavy, and Theo wondered what the hell had happened now to have his notoriously jovial best friend acting like Eeyore. His somber tone was made unintentionally funny by using Effie's vegetable alias. For some reason, it pleased Theo that Schilling didn't know her real name. Like it was his secret or some nonsense.

"Why don't you reschedule? I'm sure she'd prefer it to hanging out with a rain cloud."

"You're so nice," Schilling drawled. He grumbled and rubbed his hands over his face, letting out an agitated growl. "I'm sick of me too, by the way. It feels much better not being a rain cloud."

"Do you want me to go with you? I can cancel on Talia."

"What are you two doing?"

"She wants me to be on her trivia team because I'm the only one in her inner circle who knows about *literature and crap*."

Schilling filleted him with a look. It was effective enough to remind Theo that Talia was not the relationship he wanted. She wasn't his soulmate.

"It works for now," Theo snapped, not interested in being held accountable to his own ambitions at the moment. It felt like too long sometimes, that he'd spent searching for *her*, and when he was weary of the search he liked to have a warm body—to have Talia—in his bed.

"Sure." Schilling's huff was undeniably loaded, but Theo didn't take the bait. "Go to trivia. I'm cool. I'm sure we'll have fun."

"That's the spirit." Theo slapped him on the back. Schilling exhaled, and it looked like it might have been the first time he had all day.

Theo wandered to the fridge and pulled out a beer. He took a sip, then as casually as he possibly could said, "Tell her I say hi." He didn't know why he'd said it, but the grin on Schilling's face was fiendish.

"Should I not make a move then?"

"Do whatever you want," Theo responded, hoping to sound chuffed, but he could tell Schilling didn't buy his nonchalance. *He* barely bought it.

"So you'd be totally fine with me exploring things?"

"Whatever gets you out of the rain, man," Theo quipped.

Schilling loosed a laugh, and it was good to see him brighten again, even if it was at Theo's deflection. He never could hide his feelings from Schilling even if he hid them from himself. "I promise to do some recon for you, but if she kisses me first?" He raised his hands, palms up as he shrugged his shoulders. Theo smirked at him, knowing full well there would be none of that. Schilling was razzing him to try to get him to admit some kind of feeling for Effie. Trying to get him to make the right choice. Or maybe there was a chance they'd hit it off because the knot in Theo's stomach only grew as Schilling grabbed the candle and winked at him before slipping out the front door.

Theo was ninety-eight percent sure Schilling didn't want Effie. Maybe. Maybe it was eighty-twenty. It didn't matter. Except that when he slunk back to his couch and sank into the soft cushions, it felt like it absolutely did.

Effie left the lights dim in the store, leaving only a couple of lamps she'd stolen from the office lit on the fabric cutting table. She didn't want anyone to mistake the store for being open and walk in on her date with Schilling. If she could even call it that. She hadn't thought to ask, but it seemed date-like. More so than the dozen dates she'd ever been on.

Those had all been some variation of walk-and-talk meetups over coffee, ice cream, and, on one occasion, bowls of chowder to go. For some reason, she had thus far only attracted guys who preferred a get-to-know-you where they could literally turn and run at any given moment. None of them had resulted in second dates. Effie hadn't wanted them to. Either their names weren't sweet enough—because obviously her beloved's name should taste like dessert every time she spoke it—or the conversation had been so stilted it was painful. There was the one guy who wouldn't quit talking about himself, his car, or his ex-girlfriend. She did, in fact, cut and run, banking a left while he went straight through a crosswalk, and she never saw him again. Effie frequently wondered how long he kept talking before he realized she'd vanished with her cookie dough ice cream. She'd given up on dating after that.

That was two years ago.

Exactly why Hope had every right to give her grief about not getting out into the world. She was too young for spinsterhood.

But tonight felt different. There were walls, for starters. And an activity that demanded a certain amount of dedication and time commitment, and therefore couldn't be sped up like a walk and talk. She was glad for that because she liked Schilling's company the other night. He had an ease about him like dappled sunlight through spring trees.

If she was being honest with herself, which she tried hard to be, she would say she was nervous. She hadn't been kissed in far too long, and the possibility of it was enough to turn her stomach. Maybe she should take it off the table, but that thought made her sulk. Effie sighed as she sat on the stool behind the cutting bench.

Her mind was a tiresome place indeed.

It was almost six, which meant Schilling would be there any minute. Effie arranged and rearranged the bowl of beeswax flakes, essential oil bottles, and votives she had procured for their task. She checked the plugs on the two hot plates before her and promptly twiddled her thumbs as she waited. Effie tapped her fingers, bopping her head side to side, anything to edge out the nerves. Her subtle fidgeting turned into actual swaying as she hummed the tune to Taylor Swift's "Love Story."

The humming and tapping gave way to full-on singing. Unlike Hope, Effie couldn't carry a tune. But it didn't stop her from belting out her favorites or singing while she baked. Now the song lodged in her brain and demanded to be sung over and over again. Well, the chorus anyway, since she was never very good at remembering lyrics if she wasn't singing along to the actual song. This time she added some instrumental ba-doop-di-doops, closed her eyes, and wailed the chorus.

So loud that she apparently didn't hear the door chime.

"Sorry, this a party for one?"

Effie blanched, eyes popping open to find Schilling standing before her, arms loaded with charcuterie fixings. She'd never wanted to turn into a bug and crawl away more. Effie wasn't sure where to go from here. *When you sound like a dying crow with Broadway dreams there's really no use in denying it.* "I can't sing."

"I think you've demonstrated that, in truth, *you can,*" Schilling goaded, a devilish quirk to his brow.

"Let me rephrase. I'm not a good singer."

"Not everyone can be. That'd be boring. Far more so for me if I walked in here and you sounded like an angel. How dull, honestly." Schilling offered her a genuine smile that set Effie totally at ease. He began unloading his goodies onto the worktable. "So you like Taylor Swift?"

"She's okay," Effie said. "I like some of her stuff, not all."

"Yikes, don't tell Theo," Schilling warned like they'd cross paths again soon. Maybe that was a good sign. He was already thinking about taking her out again, with his friend, apparently, but it still seemed like a positive omen.

"He's a fan?"

"Taylor is his Queen," Schilling said with a chuckle. Effie couldn't help but roll her eyes. She examined the spread that Schilling brought—an aged maple cheddar, apple-baked gouda, smoked pepperoni, and a ridiculously large baguette. She noticed the bottle of red wine he uncorked. All the markings of a genuine date.

"You brought snacks," Effie said a bit redundantly, but she wanted to acknowledge the gesture while feeling out why he'd brought said snacks.

"A thank you for helping me out. I figured it could be a working dinner of sorts." He poured some wine into one of the plastic cups he brought and handed it to Effie. He filled his own and raised it in a toast. "To new friends," he cheered and clinked her glass.

Effie sipped, willing the wine to calm the drop of her stomach. *Working dinner. Friends.* Those were not good signs. Effie looked down at her glass for a long moment trying to psych herself up, but she only succeeded at looking utterly morose.

"Everything okay?" Schilling asked, reaching for the hand Effie had laid atop the table. His brown eyes were warm, ringed with hints of honey gold. Schilling's dark, near-black brows knit together like he was truly worried something bothered her. It was nice. So was the warmth of his hand on hers. That seemed like a good sign. Effie scolded herself internally to quit it with the play by plays and just try to enjoy the evening.

"Totally. Sorry. Spaced out there for a sec."

"Mulling over your setlist?" he joked. That charming, goofy smile returned to his face. All Effie could do was laugh. She rolled her eyes and playfully nudged Schilling's shoulder. "Almost forgot," he said and pulled a nearly spent candle from his backpack. "The target."

Effie took hold of the candle. Unfortunately, the label was ripped leaving only the word *winter* visible. She lifted the candle to her nose and sniffed. "I think I'm getting fir trees and . . ." She sniffed again. "Maybe frankincense and orange? What do you smell?"

Schilling took it and made a show of investigating the aroma of the candle. "Notes of honey perhaps? A touch of vanilla?"

"Really?"

"Maybe not honey. Mint?"

"I think I got that too."

"This feels very CSI: Bath & Body Works," Schilling drawled. Effie chuckled as she poured the flakes into the pans she'd set warming a few minutes prior. "So how's this work?"

"We melt the wax, mix in the oils, set the wicks, pour the wax. I thought we'd make two so you have options."

"That feels doable. Like maybe I could have googled it and saved you the effort?"

"No. I'm glad you asked. This is more fun."

He nodded in hearty agreement. "Absolutely."

Effie was having a wonderful evening. Schilling was charming and witty and good for a laugh. They bantered back and forth while the wax melted, and they gorged their way through Schilling's entire charcuterie plate. They sipped their wine and got to know each other except when they were adding oils to the wax. That apparently demanded utter silence, total concentration, and the occasional Emeril Lagasse-style *Bam!* From Schilling.

Effie learned that his favorite book was *Gulliver's Travels*, that he was an only child who had a short-lived magic career in sixth grade as Boyo the Magnificent, and that it was weird growing up not knowing his biological dad, even though he loved both his parents. Effie shared that her favorite music was by Fleetwood Mac, not Taylor Swift, that her absolute worst job required dancing in a Boo-Boo Bear costume on a hayride for a local Jellystone Campground, and that not knowing your dad or having him around in adulthood was a struggle she wouldn't wish on anyone.

The candles were set, and Effie dared lift hers to sniff the cooled wax within the short, modernly elegant glass votives she had chosen for the project. Schilling did the same with his. "I'm not sure mine's it," he confessed.

They swapped and sniffed again.

"I'm not sure either of them are." Effie pouted, turning her nostrils back to the original candle. "They're definitely in the same family, but they're not quite right."

"Agreed. But I think yours is closer."

"I think you're just being nice."

"Scout's honor, I'm telling you the truth."

"Were you a Boy Scout?" Effie asked, deadly serious.

Schilling's face went tight. "Does it matter?"

"If you weren't, then I cannot trust you at your word. You're out here masquerading as a Scout. Now if you were a Scout, I'd know you were swearing on something real."

Schilling finally realized she was pulling his leg, but still pondered for a moment. "Hadn't thought of it like that before."

Effie smiled. "I think it matters."

"Indubitably," he asserted. He leaned in close like he was about to tell Effie a secret, and whispered, "I was a Boy Scout."

The moment stilled. Butterflies flitted through her chest. He didn't pull away instantly, maybe this was her opening. She blurted, "My real name is Effie, by the way. Thought you should know that before I . . ." She leaned in closer, going for the kiss, the courage bubbling up from her toes.

But Schilling pulled back. "Effie Thatcher?"

Embarrassment and rejection hit her like the stench of burnt croissant as she deflated. "Yeah, why?"

"I was dating your cousin. I'm Brayden."

15

Effie, flour-dusted with tendrils of hair falling into her eyes from the messy bun atop her head, eased a pan of hot raspberry tarts from the oven and placed them on a waiting iron trivet. She worked in near darkness, the dimmed chandelier over the breakfast table the only light on in the whole house. It was after midnight, and the cocoon of quiet was heavy with her unspent feelings.

The pastries, perfectly puffed squares with heart-shaped centers filled with homemade raspberry compote, felt like they were taunting her. It would have been wise to use a different cookie cutter. Still, she lifted a tart from the parchment on her pan with the tenderness of a mother cradling her newborn baby and placed it on the cooling rack beside. Halfway through her task, she turned to the oven on instinct. Guided by scent alone, she knew her scones were perfectly browned. She retrieved their pan from a secondary compartment in the oven and set them on a separate trivet.

Effie pivoted again, grabbing a small bowl from the counter filled with a simple icing glaze of milk, confectioner's sugar, and vanilla. The warm scones melted the icing as it drizzled over top. It would cool like a sugary crust on the decadent lavender and honey confections. There was something peaceful in the predictability of a pastry. Unlike the torment of the evening.

When the tarts were cool enough, Effie wielded her shaker of confectioner's sugar high above them and tapped the side so that a perfect dusting, like a featherlight snow, covered the golden-brown crusts.

She dropped any lingering embarrassment to pick up her favorite plate, one painted with a smattering of red and pink roses, and placed one of each treat atop its porcelain surface. At the breakfast table, a small pot of mint tea steeped atop a pot warmer with a single tea light burning beneath. The teacup and saucer that waited for her there matched the plate. She sat before her tea party for one and poured her cup full to the brim. Effie held it daintily between two hands, blowing off the pillows of steam before taking a sip.

Her shoulders relaxed and her eyes closed as she found respite in her rituals. Much as it seemed her emotions were felt and handled with care as they arose, they had the unfortunate habit of lingering, bottling, and fermenting before bubbling over in messy waves. A lot had transpired over the last weeks, and Effie's feelings demanded the stage. That's why she had started baking, to quell the tide and ride the current in solitude.

Effie took a bite of the raspberry tart, the flaky crust depositing crumbs on the tabletop. She glanced directly at the photo of Herman. Gramps. He held her gaze as if daring her to be braver than the voice in her head. The one that said that she'd never find love. That it was hard. Difficult. A fool's hope. The voice that sounded an awful lot like her mother's.

She swallowed hard as her throat constricted and her eyes burned. The quiet started to feel an awful lot like loneliness as Effie chewed on her lip, her vision blurred behind her tears. She only let a few escape before she steeled her resolve at the sound of footsteps in the hall.

Effie composed herself the best she could as Hope rounded the corner into the kitchen rubbing sleep from her eyes. "I thought I smelled something delicious."

She padded farther into the kitchen as Effie discreetly wiped her nose on the back of her hand and smiled. Hope helped herself to a scone and some tea, taking the seat to Effie's right.

"Why are you baking in the dark?" Hope whispered, but Effie was certain her cousin knew that she was better at sharing her life as a series of activities and not so good at telling people how she felt. But her baked goods could always handle her moods.

"I had a bad night," Effie confessed, even though it was so much more than that. She had been trying to work out all night how to bring this up to Hope, how to convey all that she'd learned. Effie, however, felt rather sorry for herself and kept getting hung up on her own disappointments. On the fact that she'd literally gotten excited over the man who'd picked Hope first. It was unnerving how small it made Effie feel, knowing that she now scored zero for two in her social experiments, playing second fiddle to first Talia and now Hope. She didn't want to envy them, but she did.

Effie hoped that baking would clear her head. Give her the time to lick her wounds, shed her embarrassment at the almost not-really-even-in-the-realm-of-possibility kiss, and organize her thoughts well enough to broach the Brayden subject with Hope. She apparently landed on a quick and dirty approach, because she bit out, "I met Brayden, he's been separated from his wife for two years."

Hope nearly choked on her scone, her eyes big as moons. "What? How? Effie did you go and find him—"

"Of course not!" Effie snapped, and she let the sting reflect on her face. "I've been trying to take your advice . . . Aunt Bea's advice . . ."

Effie looked to Hope whose face was a bundle of confusion. She looked ready to puke. "Effie, could you spit it out? I'm freaking out over here."

Effie bridled her irritation and continued. "During my class last week, this guy I met doing a safety check on the store pity invited me out with him and his girlfriend after he spilled wine on my bag. While we were at the bar, his friend Schilling showed up. They only ever used that name, and there was a bit where I was being called Eggplant so he didn't know my name either . . ."

"Huh?"

Effie backtracked and filled her in on her first encounter with Theodore, how her synesthesia got in the way, and how it came back up in class. She brought her up to speed on the candle-making request, the follow-up inspection, and the ensuing incidents that brought her to revealing her real name. Hope, seemingly satisfied that this was all evidently an act of God, settled into her chair. But her gaze turned sharp as she asked, "How did he know I met his wife?"

Effie swallowed hard, bile rising in response to the anger she felt simmering off Hope's vampire-white skin.

Effie didn't tell him about the baby, didn't tell him that Hope had already decided to cut him off, didn't confess or meddle as best she could. But when he slumped onto the stool, his eyes brimming with tears, and asked how Hope could keep ignoring him when the last time they spoke they'd said *I love you*, Effie couldn't bear it.

"If you had seen him, you'd understand why I told him," Effie explained, straightening her spine. "All I said was that you'd gone to find him that afternoon at the house and met his wife. He went into a colorful string of curses, a bit of manic laughter, presumably because Chloe is insane, and then he explained everything."

"Everything?" Hope asked, and Effie thought she'd be relieved, but instead, she looked like she wanted to rip Effie's head off. "Good to know he'll confess his whole sordid backstory to *you*, and not the woman he supposedly loves."

It was Effie's turn to stare wide-eyed. She understood Hope feeling like he should have told her about Chloe, but how could she make this a bad thing? It was good. He loved her, he was dedicated to her, he was doing everything in his power to be with her, all the while trying to keep Chloe away from her. "I think he was trying to spare you from Chloe. The divorce has been dragged out because she virtually married him for his money and now she won't go quietly."

"*Spare me* your opinions, Effie. It doesn't matter. He kept it from me."

"So you're not even going to talk to him?"

"No, and neither are you," Hope said with such finality Effie wondered if there would ever come a day when she would rightfully and truly win an argument.

"Fine," Effie huffed. "But don't act like you're being any better."

"It's *my* body!"

"It's his baby!" Effie screamed.

Hope rose from the table, leaning heavily on it like she was about to breathe fire in Effie's face. "I mean it, Effie. Stay out of it. Don't see Brayden or Theo or any of them. Find other friends to experiment having a life with."

"You can't tell me who to hang out with. Schilling is a nice guy, we were starting to get along as real friends. And Theo, well—"

"Theo has a girlfriend. He obviously doesn't want you."

If Hope saw how Effie's heart bled at her words, she didn't show it. Effie wanted to yell even louder, scream in Hope's face that she was not everyone's punching bag, but instead, she did as she always does. She took a deep breath and looked at Hope deeply. She saw the bubble of hurt behind her eyes ready to pop, the anxiety in the white-knuckle grip on the table, the walls that were being built around her block by block so second-chance citizens would need a grappling hook to access her warmth and her heart. Hope's anger and fear were talking. It wasn't Hope. Effie knew that even if Hope didn't. But if she loved her, she had to help her see that she pushed away something good, maybe even fantastic.

Effie summoned her nerve, took a deep breath and whispered, "He loves you." Bright, thirst-quenching lemon water slid over Effie's tongue. "He loves you so much."

Hope barely looked at her. Didn't register the tears that were returning to Effie's eyes. "Please, just stay out of it," she barked.

Dorothea and Louisa shuffled into the room, the former in a quilted robe that brushed her ankles.

"Would you two keep it down?" Louisa scolded.

"What's going on?" Dorothea asked, settling her drowsy bones on the seat beside Effie. Hope moved to exit the kitchen.

"Effie's poking her nose where it doesn't belong . . . again." Effie's heart stopped as Hope turned to Louisa. "You might want to ask her about Gil." She stormed out of the room on a wave of fear and ignorance so big, Effie wondered if it would drown her.

Louisa's brow ruffled. "What is she talking about?"

"Louisa, I'm so sorry. I didn't . . . I only wanted you to feel loved."

"What did you do?" she demanded.

Dorothea took hold of Effie's trembling hand, worry painted on her lips. Effie was fried. She wasn't sure she could handle another argument, but she knew Louisa wouldn't let it go. "It was before Hazel was born, about a week before your shower. I went to Mario's with Hope. We sat in the bar and Gil was there with one of his friends. He didn't see us come in. We were seated right behind him at a high-top, so I heard everything . . . his friend asked about you and the baby, and he said with such conviction that the baby probably wasn't even his. That as soon as she arrived he was demanding a paternity test."

Louisa bit back a laugh like she'd expect nothing less from Gil. "And what does that have to do with you?" Her tone indicated she thought Hope had started some drama out of nothing, but Effie knew it wasn't nothing.

She wasn't sure she could get the words out. Her throat was dry, her tongue thick. "When I went out to get the balloons from my car for your shower a few days later, I saw him standing on the curb. He was dipping—which I knew he told you he'd stopped doing. I confronted him." A metallic bite tingled her taste buds. "I told him what I'd heard and said he was daft if he thought you'd try to trap him. Told him how wonderfully bright and amazing his life with you could be. He insisted he was still demanding the test. I told him if he was going to break your heart, why wait?"

Louisa was stoic and Effie's tears spilled over.

"I didn't want that beautiful little girl to come into this world surrounded by anyone who didn't already love her," Effie sobbed. "I didn't want you to break on the happiest day of your life. I'm the reason he left. I challenged him. I pushed him toward it. I'm so sorry, Lou. I'm so, so sorry."

Effie stole her hand back from Grams and buried her face in her palms. She cried for what she'd done, for Hope's harsh words, for the crushed friendship with Schilling, and for the ache in her chest that never really went away. It didn't do to let things build up this badly. She felt utterly insane and like she was overreacting to the umpteenth degree. But that knowledge didn't stop the tears. The dam had burst and now she had to ride it out.

Louisa eased off of her seat and came to kneel before her sister, grabbing Effie's wrists and pulling her hands from her face, so they rested on her lap. The only thing behind Louisa's eyes was an unwavering calm. She gripped Effie's hands with one of hers and used the other to brush the fat drops from Effie's flushed cheeks.

Grams watched them silently from the other side of the table.

"I think," Louisa whispered, pausing to clear her throat, "that if the worst thing you've done is challenge a man to reevaluate his priorities in the name of protecting me, my heart, my honor . . . then you truly are the best of us, Effie Rose." Louisa took Effie's face in both of her hands and brought her bow of a mouth to rest on Effie's forehead, planting the most tender of kisses. "You are far too hard on yourself."

Effie threw her arms around Louisa and pulled her tight. She missed her sister. Missed their late-night slumber parties beneath sheet-walled forts, the way that Louisa used to brush and braid her hair for school. How she, Hope, and Effie had once been a trio at the Book and Bar or down at the beach. The space between them had grown so big that Effie didn't know how to reclaim it. Didn't know if she could. "I thought you'd pitch into a classic Louisa screaming fit if you found out," Effie admitted into Louisa's sleep-mussed braid.

"I'm not sure any of us miss those," Grams chirped from behind them.

Both girls smiled as they separated. Louisa wiped another smear of tears from Effie's cheek. "Maybe if I found out back then," Louisa admitted. "But I'd like to think I've matured, maybe thanks to Hazel."

"I'm sorry I haven't learned much about the new you."

"Likewise," Louisa said, smiling. "Are those tarts up for grabs?"

"Absolutely."

Louisa filled a plate for her and Dorothea while Effie poured the tea. They sipped and munched until Effie's bad night ended with an unexpected lightness that only the Thatcher women knew how to bring.

16

Theo woke to Talia's giggle and the clack of her manicured daggers against the screen of her phone. He groaned and rolled onto his back, the sheets on his side of the bed a veritable nest, mussed from their passionate entanglement the night before. His navy-blue linen duvet draped over her waist, so one silken thigh was on display as she bent her knee skyward. Bare chested as she was, the sunlight through the window bathed her perfect breasts in golden warmth. If her neck weren't craned over her phone, eyes glazed in a doomscroll seeking tiny hits of dopamine, she might have made an excellent subject for one of Goya's nudes.

"Don't you even want breakfast before you mess with your brain chemistry for the day?" Theo grumbled as he picked sleep seeds from the corners of his eyes.

"Good morning to you too, pumpkin," Talia chirped. She set her phone on the nightstand and slid down into the pillows. She walked her fingers up his chest and bopped him on the nose. "My parents will be here tomorrow."

"Queen of the non sequitur."

"They're going to ask why you're not my boyfriend . . . again," Talia whined, and Theo hated the high-pitched itch of it.

"Because we want different things," Theo scolded, prying free from Talia's grasp and sitting up against the headboard. She pulled the blanket over her chest and returned to sitting, pouting.

"It didn't seem that way last night."

"*That* has never been our problem," Theo asserted. *Hadn't they had this conversation twenty times in the last year? Hadn't she assured him she wouldn't ask for more from him? Was Theo an ass for taking her at her word?* "Aren't we having fun?"

"Of course. But you claim you want something more than fun, something real. I'm saying I want that too, now. How is that not wanting the same thing?"

From across the king-sized bed, Talia looked out of place. She had teased him the first time she saw it all made up, saying he was the only bachelor in town who didn't throw a sheet-less, full-sized mattress on the floor with a comforter and call it a day. She'd actually had the nerve to scoff at his carefully selected duvet and throw pillows.

He hadn't mentioned that he bought the king-sized bed to call in his soulmate. It was a manifestation for the woman he wanted to wake to every morning, which meant making room for her in his life. So, when he moved into the apartment a little over a year ago, he bought a bigger bed. If Talia thought the duvet worthy of jest, he wasn't about to tell her all of that. So when she asked why a king-sized mattress, he had said he was a sprawling sleeper and kept the rest to himself.

For maybe the first time, Theo acknowledged that he wasn't

making room for his soulmate by letting Talia lay in her place. But it wasn't only Talia that ever laid there. In fact, it had been multiple partners in the last few months. But none of them had belonged in the unclaimed side of the bed. Not long-term. Theo never pinpointed what those engagements went without. He never landed on a trait, quality, or lack thereof that meant a woman wasn't his soulmate. Rather, he knew it like he knew the sky was blue. It was just a fact, a truth. He didn't need to know why.

It was the same with Talia. Though if he had to put it into words— Talia was far too self-important for Theo's liking. She was vain in a way that Theo had only ever dabbled in. She made it a profession—literally with her influencer Instagram and her obsession with likes and follows. He also knew that, someday, he wanted to be a dad. Talia turned her nose up at babies, and pregnant bodies made her gag while she scrolled past them. He wasn't sure which bit of truth to tell her so they could move on. He may not have wanted to spend his life with Talia or make babies with her or wake to the sunlight glowing over her breasts for the rest of his life, but he didn't want to hurt her either. They were friends, at the very least.

With all of that in mind, he answered her question as simply as he could. "I can feel my heart reaching for someone my soul knows. You want to hold flesh and bone."

"I'd think you'd prefer someone with more tangible desires," Talia grumbled. "Your hands reach for me. Your lips do. Your dick does." Talia's voice curdled against the truths she laid out. "I just assumed that someday your heart would too."

It was the most honest, bare thing she'd ever said to him, and it made his stomach ache. "I'm sorry," he whispered. He meant it too.

He didn't know she harbored such hope. It had hidden behind flirty looks, a crass mouth, and a flair for being one of the guys. He thought their sharing a bed was a result of failed romances on both sides and a need for release. He thought he was as much of a mismatch for her future happiness as she was for his.

Talia must have read the meaning behind his befuddled look because she said, "It was absolutely a friends-with-benefits situation, Theo. You don't need to be sorry. I just always wondered if it might be more."

Talia's phone chirped. She picked it up and Theo huffed a laugh when he saw the screen. A *match* on some dating app pinged her phone. She shrugged innocently. "It's not like I pinned all my relationship hope on you."

"Glad to hear it," he crooned.

Talia slipped from the covers, and the mattress breathed a sigh of relief at the absence of her weight. She wriggled into her tight-fitting jeans, and as she pulled a loose silk blouse over her head, Theo wondered if he'd ever see her naked again. Probably not. It didn't sour him as much as he thought it would.

"I know we had an . . . arrangement. We weren't dating. I don't want you thinking we weren't on the same page. But don't go seducing little Miss Effie if you're not at least moderately convinced that she's the one who the other half of this monstrous bed belongs to."

Theo tried not to let his shock show that she guessed his reasoning for buying the king-sized bed. Talia smiled, obviously proud of herself. "I know you pretty well, Tillerman," she drawled. "Don't act so surprised."

She settled onto the foot of the bed an offering in the candid use of his last name. They could be friends. It didn't have to get weird. The tension in his jaw eased. If there was one thing he lamented about the vastness of his dating experience, it was the loss of cool people in his orbit because they weren't *the one*.

"I'm not surprised, Bernardi. Just grateful."

She nodded once, then made for the bedroom door. She hesitated and looked back to where Theo cleaned a smudge from his glasses before donning them. "Tread carefully there. She's not our kind," Talia warned.

If one more person pushed him toward Effie he might scream, but instead, he merely asked, "What do you mean?"

"She's not the type to fuck around and find out, much as she tried that night. So don't fuck around."

With that, she dipped out the door and out of Theo's bed for good.

17

Brayden walked past the Thatcher house on Austin Street for the fifth time trying to summon the nerve to knock on the front door. His calls, texts, and emails had all gone unanswered. Even a message to Hope's Goodreads board went ignored. The desperation to speak with her even had him dialing the house phone, only to hang up when he heard the chipper *hello* of an elderly woman. Honestly, he would have sent a carrier pigeon if he could have gotten his hands on one. Anything to avoid doing the one thing Hope had ever asked him *not* to do.

Show up on her doorstep.

It was likely irrational on her part. Her family couldn't be that pervasively against romance and men, but she'd been pretty adamant. Scary Hope, the one that spoke in a serious whisper like she'd unleash hellhounds on your disobedient hide, had told him *never* to knock on the front door. Not until they were good and ready to face the scrutiny of the Thatcher women. Apparently *good and ready* was a determination only Hope could make.

Brayden settled on a bench at the far end of the block, the Thatcher's bricked walkway just visible beyond the bend in the road. He pulled an antacid from his pocket and popped it like a breath mint.

Of course, it was Chloe's fault that Hope cut and ran.

Realistically, it was his fault.

If he'd been honest with Hope about his never-ending divorce proceedings, then she wouldn't be holed up avoiding him. He didn't blame her. Despite the certainty that Effie conveyed the truth of his marriage, he knew Hope felt betrayed. Knew she likely felt that he didn't trust her or love her enough to be honest with her.

In truth, the shame of it all kept a gag on his confessions. Brayden wanted to tell Hope about Chloe the moment he realized *she* was his forever. That had been a month into seeing each other. The words had evaporated though when Hope told him that her family had a huge distrust of men and relationship longevity. It was a convenient excuse he snuggled right up to, not wanting to dig into the past. Not wanting Hope to see him as the divorced-before-thirty guy, the naive idiot who thought he was adored, the guy who fought tooth and nail to not have his inheritance wiped out by a scheming siren.

When he confided in Effie at Glitter & Glue he waited for the hammer to drop. For her to scream at him, to tell him he was selfish, an idiot—just like Chloe had time and again trying to break him to her will. Instead, she took his hand in hers, her eyes full of the warmth and kindness that Hope always bragged about, and told him that she understood. *She understood.* And she didn't rake him over the coals for his mistake in keeping the truth from Hope. Instead, she offered to help clear things up, to nudge Hope to reach out, even if

Effie admitted her cousin was notorious for not giving second chances, regardless of how minuscule the slight. He brightened knowing that fate had brought Effie into their little circle. If nothing else, she seemed inclined to see his relationship with Hope repaired, and having an ally in her was invaluable—in ways he was certain had yet to fully reveal themselves.

Brayden tried not to think about how Effie leaned in last night. How she slightly parted her lips and fluttered her eyes. Theo's smoldering gaze brought panties to the ground, not his. He was friendly, jovial, funny. He didn't imagine that would ever be interpreted as romantic interest and had apologized profusely if he gave Effie the wrong idea. He thought she was cool and interesting, but obviously, his heart was spoken for. She brushed him off saying it was a silly blip in judgment on her part and proceeded to prattle on about the candles and maybe trying them again if he wasn't happy with them. At the time, he wasn't sure he deserved a friend like Effie, but she'd insisted he deserved more than he'd been getting. *Odd.* But he hadn't looked too closely at it.

Brayden ran tense fingers through his hair. He checked the time. It was nearly four o'clock and he had a meeting with his lawyer—who blessedly made time over the weekend—at four thirty. If he was going to make his move it had to be now. Nerves steeled, he rose from the bench and strode for the brick walkway.

He nearly jumped out of his skin when he looked up to find a wrinkled old woman in a sun hat pruning the bushes by the sidewalk. The pointy end of a pair of shears hovered inches from his nose as she said, "You are not as stealthy as you think. Why do you keep skulking past my house?"

In that moment he looked to Hope's window. She sat at the window seat hugging a pillow to her chest. She shook her head, a subtle plea to not reveal his identity to the polka dot–clad woman before him. He choked back the ire building in his gut. It was a new feeling, being mad at Hope, but this was getting ridiculous. *She couldn't even have a conversation with him like an adult? He was supposed to lie to the old woman in front of him who shared Hope's hauntingly beautiful eyes?*

He may not have been a heartbreaker or wise enough to sniff out his gold-digging wife, but he didn't deserve this. He deserved to be heard out, spoken to, confronted, screamed at if that's what it came to. That's what you did with the people you loved. That's what he'd done after he followed Chloe to that motel three years ago . . .

"Sorry," he whispered, gaze glued on Hope. "I didn't mean to bother you."

He stormed down the street, but not before catching sight of the old woman craning her neck to scold Hope with a look. It was enough to reassure him that he was entitled to more than the ghost she'd become.

18

Theo spent most of the morning and afternoon ruminating on Talia's words. They hounded him through the night, and replayed in his head while he went to the gym the next morning, as he stood in line for a coffee and a bagel at The Works Café, and for the whole two-mile walk home he'd forced himself to take.

Even as he unlocked his front door and discarded the wrapper from his bagel, he couldn't stop thinking about it. *Had everyone been able to see something he hadn't with Effie?* It was worrisome, to say the least, given how much journaling and self-reflection he was prone to. Talia's warning also made him itch. *Was she worried Effie was actually a virgin? Did that even matter?* He supposed it did because physicality was one of the first things he explored in a new relationship. He enjoyed flinging himself into new situations and experiences seeing if he'd sink or float. But the implication that following his emotions was equivalent to *fucking around*, had him questioning his methods. He guessed that was his admission that there *were* things he felt for Effie.

Theo drained the last sips of coffee from the paper travel cup and chucked it in the trash with a sigh. He brought his diffuser that rested on the counter to life with the press of a button. The scent of frankincense filled the air around him like a bubble of calm. He took long, deep breaths as he poured himself a glass of water from the filtered jug in his refrigerator. He drank greedily, then filled it to the brim again before carrying it to the meditation cushion that sat in the far corner of the room beside the console table that housed his collection of DVDs and his television.

Theo settled onto the cushion, surprisingly flexible despite the bulk of muscles beneath his track pants. Folding his legs into a pretzel, he closed his eyes.

Theo had been meditating on and off since college, solidifying the practice in the last three years. The habit became a morning ritual that he felt the deep absence of when he missed a session, so he did his best not to. Even when it was delayed like it was that morning—a need to move and release energy superseding the practice. Now with his limbs happily exhausted, he could settle in. It was the one time of day when he could connect with that great unknown force. The one that had him believing in soulmates. That told him fate, destiny, and manifestations were real. It was the force he prayed to to make his life mean something, and the one he convinced himself daily would show him his life could be better than fiction.

Theo inhaled deeply, letting the breath circle all the way to his toes, before exhaling it back along the same path. His mind cleared as he deliberately settled into his flesh and bones and blood. He let himself be present with only his breath and the subtle hum of the diffuser across the room. The frankincense already worked magic on his senses, imbuing his energy with a tangible kind of hope and optimism.

After twenty short minutes of breathing and focus, Theo opened his eyes. He reached for an oracle deck he kept shelved beside his cushion. His sister had bought it for him for his last birthday with plants, flowers, and vegetables depicted on its seventy-two different cards. It was meant to be a joke gift after a particularly lengthy debate about signs and their meaning. Theo had argued that there was meaning and symbolism anywhere you looked for it. His sister had scoffed and said that that was impossible. When she'd gifted him the deck, she said, *I guess they can make meaning out of everything.*

He hadn't used it yet, preferring his traditional tarot deck and another built around moon phases, but intuition had him grabbing for the unopened box that morning.

Theo removed the cards and spread them out before him. He enjoyed the pattern of garden beds and hedgerows that decorated the back of the cards. Theo closed his eyes again and hovered his hands over the spread of cards, then asked aloud, "What do I need to know today?"

He waved his hands over the cards until he felt the familiar prickle that worked its way from the tip of his ring finger up to his shoulder indicating the card he needed beckoned from immediately below. He planted his finger on the card and edged it away from the rest of the deck. A tingling—like when a song hits just right—covered him in goose bumps as he turned the card over to reveal an illustration.

It was sketched in colored pencil shades like images on the front of heirloom seed packets—a perfectly ripe, seductively purple *eggplant*.

Theo puttered down Hanover Street in his black Jeep Wrangler, the sun setting behind him in tangerine hues. He itched to drive with the top off, but there'd be a few more threats of frost and rainstorms before he could shed the hard shell and bask in the summer sun.

He pulled to a stop in front of Glitter & Glue. A plump eggplant sat in the passenger seat alongside a box of chocolates. The bold move would be to go in there and offer a vegetable. It could also be construed as weird if he wasn't able to get out the greater meaning before she passed judgment. Weird might also be the deduction if she *did* hear his full explanation about how cosmically aligned his calling her eggplant now felt given the card he'd pulled and the meaning it was assigned in the realms of the mystical.

It would be a safer move to bring in the chocolates. *When had he become so pathetically indecisive?* Yes, chocolates were better.

He'd use the other offering to make eggplant parmesan for dinner instead. Maybe once they knew each other better, when he'd sussed out if the other half of his bed belonged to her, he'd tell her the intricate implications of the nightshade produce.

His eyes narrowed on the shiny purple flesh of the eggplant. The belated realization that the eggplant meant a whole lot of dirty things to the emoji generation left him queasy. *How had he not made* that *connection before now?*

Here he was calling this ethereal, quiet, sweetly seductive woman *eggplant* for weeks and she hadn't even batted an eye. Her self-restraint was admirable. If the shoe was on the other foot, he's not sure he could have left the opportunity to turn her twenty shades of red with the obvious innuendo on the table. So either she was as removed from emojis as he was or she was far kinder than he realized.

Another explanation hammered him in the head. Maybe she thought he'd been teasing her, and pride had her grinning through it. Theo raked his hands over his face. *For fuck's sake, had he ruined this before it even started?*

He refused to believe that the sharp-tongued woman he met wouldn't have said something if the nickname offended her that way. They had jested about it, but she seemed like the kind to let you know if you crossed a line with her. At least, that's what he told himself so his fingers would unbuckle his seatbelt and his feet would carry him to the door, box of chocolates in hand.

He stepped up to the cheerful craft shop, open for another ten minutes. Theo paused at the glass door where he had a clear view of Effie mopping. She'd already turned off half of the overhead lights in favor of the warm lamp on the register desk. Backlit as she was, Theo noticed the alluring dip between her chest and her full hips, and the flawless curve of her neck as she dragged the mop side to side in unhurried motions. Maybe his preconceived ideas of who he'd end up with muddied his vision. Maybe her indignation had gotten in the way of him truly seeing her at first meeting, but now, when she thought no one stood watching, she was downright beguiling.

Theo stepped through the door before he teetered into creepy territory. The chime of the bell signaled his arrival and snagged Effie's attention away from her chore.

"Hi," she chirped, her puzzled brow at odds with the airy smile that parted her plump, rosy lips. Her brunette waves were swept into a bun atop her head that left wild tendrils floating around the near angelic curve of her face. Theo hadn't let himself look at her too long before now, but something in his meditation unlocked the desire he'd kept tucked away after their first meeting.

She was radiant, beautiful. Like a dew drop on rose petals or a rustle of leaves in the wind. She stirred the very air he breathed in a way that had his heart hammering in his chest. "Hi," he finally purred.

"What brings you by?"

Theo perused the turnstile of leather-bound journals, plucking one from its resting place. "Need a new journal," he half lied. He admired them the last time he came in and thought it would be a good choice for his next collection of poems—whatever those ended up being.

He followed Effie to the register with his selection and a new fountain tip pen. He placed them on the counter as she rang him up.

"I also came to thank you," he said.

"What for?"

"Talking with Schilling. As much as he's still reeling over the fact that Chloe found a way to insert herself with your cousin, he's grateful to know why Hope was spooked."

"Happy to have helped," Effie said, and he noted the way her teeth clenched.

"But you didn't tell him everything? Why not?"

"What makes you say that?"

"Call it a hunch," Theo said, because it was the truth.

Effie gave him a once-over. He felt under a microscope beneath her gaze. Her eyes floated over his round spectacles and lingered on the stubble he wore just long enough to look roguish. Her eyes swept to his veined hands that rested on the counter and back to meet his stare. "I can't help but feel like this is some kind of a test?"

Theo laughed in spite of himself. It wasn't a test exactly, but he'd met few people who could resist the urge to meddle. He wanted to know why she'd stayed as neutral as possible in her conversation with Schilling. He didn't even want to think about what she assumed the night was. If she'd been disappointed that Schilling wasn't on the market. He swallowed that curiosity and said, "It's not. Just wondering."

"It's not any of my business. As much as I might want them to work it out, it's not my decision. And whatever I didn't tell Brayden is not mine to tell. A sentiment you seemed to mirror at the Tipsy Moose?"

"I think it's classy of you, that's all. Even if I too want them to work it out. I've never seen him so happy, even with the divorce nonsense. And Hope seems great—"

"You met?"

"Only in passing," Theo confessed, and he somehow felt like sharing that truth was not the right thing based on the hurt behind Effie's cornflower-blue eyes.

"She didn't want me to meet him," Effie uttered, her words laced with disappointment. "That's why I didn't know who he was. She never even told me his last name."

That added up. Theo wondered how the connection wasn't made that night at the bar, but if Hope kept her relationship with Schilling secret, even from Effie, it was no surprise that Effie had been blindsided. He hoped it hadn't hurt too much when she realized that their candle-making wasn't a date. *That was new, empathy before envy.* Maybe the eggplant was as prophetic as he'd read earlier that day.

Effie glanced at the box of chocolates he placed on the counter as she ran his card for his purchases. "They're for you," Theo said, feeling way off his game. He slid the box in front of her. She handed him his receipt in return.

"You're not just giving them to me as some kind of pity offering after the whole Talia, Schilling, Hope debacle?"

She definitely thought her night with Schilling was meant to be a date. *Shit.* "Believe it or not, I didn't come here to talk about any of them."

"Then why did you come? Aside from the journal of course?"

Theo's palms slicked with sweat. He hadn't been this nervous to ask someone out in ages. Probably since high school. "I came to ask you out," he said matter-of-factly.

She said nothing but fought the smile that tugged at her cheeks. Droves of buzzing bees swarmed his chest as he waited for her answer. Something about the way she carried herself, like her identity was hers to keep secret until she deemed him worthy, had him fearing her rejection. "Well?" he asked.

"You haven't actually asked me anything yet," Effie cooed, amusement dripping from her tongue.

Theo's mouth quirked. "Effie, will you go out on a date with me? Saturday night to be exact. Details redacted intentionally so I can woo you with surprises."

Her smile broke free.

But instead of answering him, she reached for the luxuriously wrapped box of chocolates he'd procured from the local sweet shop that made them in-house. She took one look at the truffles within, and her cheeks flushed a sensual shade of pink. He couldn't help but wonder how else he could elicit that heated flush as he watched Effie pluck one of the bite-sized morsels from the tray and pop it into her mouth.

Her eyes closed as she bit around the soft caramel center. A pleased moan, which she seemed unaware of, rumbled from the back of her throat. Theo's mouth went dry.

Effie worked the sticky caramel from her teeth, licking the grain of salt from the corner of her mouth that Theo had spotted seconds before. A nervous laugh tumbled from her lips and Theo thanked God he didn't opt for the eggplant. The air charged with Effie's delight, and he waited eagerly to see what she'd do next. "Do you believe in fate?"

The question nearly knocked him off his feet. *Of course, he did, but why did she want to know?* "I do. Why?"

"Because these are my favorite kind of chocolates . . ." She hesitated. Theo hung on every word. "And Theo tastes exactly like salted caramel chocolate truffles. So I guess I kind of have to say yes."

Goddamn, what was the question again? Theo calmed his racing heart enough to say, "I'll see you Saturday, Effie Thatcher."

"See you then, Theo."

Theo collected his things and sauntered out of the store. It gave him no small amount of satisfaction to know that whenever she said his name, whenever she thought it, she'd taste the sweetness that gave her such palpable pleasure.

19

Coziness enveloped the Thatcher house that evening. The air was fresh after a day of thrown-up sashes and late spring cleaning. The scent of lemon oil clung to the damp dusted surfaces of the great room, adding a zesty, uplifting energy that Hope desperately needed.

She sat on the floor, legs crossed in front of her mother. Tibby methodically pulled strands of Hope's waist-length waves into twin French braids. She'd known how to braid her own hair since she was about eleven, but it always looked better when her mother did it. It felt better too. Hope wondered aloud if there was some threshold of maturity where you were no longer allowed to get your hair braided by your mother.

"If there is, I vote we ignore it," Tibby said plainly, and it brought an ease to Hope's chest. Nights like these were usually peaceful, the entire brood gathered in a room. They sometimes played games together, but more often than not engaged in their own little hobbies while making light conversation. Hope was grateful that after the initial

Brayden-bashing, the room had fallen silent once more.

Louisa played on a floor mat with Hazel by the hearth. It still had a fire going in it to ward off the lingering chill in the air, even though summer was just around the corner. Aunt Bea dozed in her chair, Issa playing watchbird by her side. Ellen, Lilah, and Vivienne did a puzzle by the window while Pamela was enraptured in her romance novel. Hope wondered what her aunt would think if she knew Effie had the same taste in books. The thought amused her, but she'd never betray those parts of Effie that were kept hidden from the world. Especially, not after the sting of regret in revealing Effie's role in Gil's disappearance, though she'd heard it ended up being a relief for Effie. Not from Effie herself, mind you. They hadn't spoken all week. It was unkind of Hope to cast dispersions on Effie to avoid her own pain, and now Hope suffered the consequences.

Finally, Hope glanced across the room to where Dorothea sat with a new cross-stitch project. This one was a bookmark set that Grams promised to split between Effie and Hope when she finished. The old woman side-eyed Hope and shook her head in obvious disappointment. Apparently, their conversation *wasn't* finished.

"He didn't look like a delinquent to me," she barked, and Hope tensed. Everyone had already heard about the male suitor and his wife and all the gossip because it was too unbearable to let their imaginations run wilder than reality. But it still felt grating that Brayden had at least played into *some* of her cousins' fears.

"Mom, drop it. It's none of your business," Tibby scolded. "Like you can tell by his face anyway."

Guilt churned in Hope's stomach. Brayden wasn't a delinquent. He was perfect in so many ways and Hope didn't deserve him. Learning of his history with Chloe had only solidified her belief that she was the real problem in the relationship. The one with too many rules and even bigger secrets. She didn't know how to overcome it. How to fix it. She wanted Effie's help, but after how she exploded at her cousin the other night, she felt coated head to toe in shame. She could only slither into the unconditional embrace of her mother. Not even Grams could engage without making her opinions known about this one.

"He'll forgive you, you know," Grams added, her uncanny way of reading minds almost evidence that magic was real.

"I'm not sure that he will." Hope sighed. "He deserved better from me and now it feels like it's too late."

Tibby halted her braiding, and Hope could feel her mother's disbelief tangled in her hair. "I thought you told him."

"I was going to, but something happened."

"I thought Effie cleared all that up," Grams insisted.

"She told you?" Hope prickled with anger. Suddenly she wanted to be anywhere but here. Preferably between the pages of a novel that looked nothing like her life.

"Of course not. You two were not being quiet *at all* the other night. He made a mistake, but it doesn't mean you should continue making your own."

"You don't understand—"

"No. You're right. I don't. I only ever modeled a loving, respectful, joyful relationship, and yet somehow you are all so convinced that it is beneath you to need someone. Beneath you to be vulnerable even if you've been wronged. I don't know where I made the mistake, but I can assure you, your grandfather is rolling in his grave at the lot of you tarnishing his memory by refusing to let love win."

Dorothea bristled and rose from her seat. She shuffled across the room like a teakettle ready to explode. All eyes were on her. Even Ellen had the good sense to look like she'd taken the scolding to heart.

"Mom," Tibby started, but Dorothea threw her hands in the air at the mercy of her rising emotions. She nearly ran into Effie who swept into the room in a tea-length cotton dress with a corseted bodice and pearls at her ears. Dorothea's boiling grief evaporated into thin air as she grabbed Effie by the shoulders.

"And where are you off to looking so lovely?" Grams asked, but Hope was just as curious.

Effie bit her lip, a telltale sign she was nervous before she said, "On a date . . . with Theo." Effie's gaze locked on Hope, and the fear there roiled Hope's insides. Effie was clearly desperate for Hope not to be mad that she was seeing him, involving herself with Brayden's inner circle. Hope instantly regretted ever making such a demand, because Effie looked full of wonder, like she might fall into a romance novel of her own. Hope wished for nothing less for her dear cousin. Even if bitterness and envy clouded her vision, she could still see Effie for the effervescent ingenue she was.

Grams's face lit up. She grabbed Effie's with both her hands and pulled her forehead down for a proud, wet kiss. "Good for you! We want to hear all about it. No negativity, no bitterness, no doubt. Right, ladies?"

Nods from all around, though Hope wasn't sure it was a promise they all could honestly keep. Not when she noticed hers wasn't the only heart filled with envy in the room.

"Thanks," Effie whispered. "Hope, can I borrow your denim jacket?"

"Of course!" Hope replied. Tibby tied off the second of her braids and Hope clambered to her feet, her belly forcing her to adjust her center of gravity more frequently. "I think I left it in the entry closet."

Hope followed Effie into the foyer, admiring the cream, satin pumps that matched the little flowers patterning her otherwise pale pink dress. Hope rifled through the closet looking for her light-wash jacket that would dress down Effie's outfit and give her just enough warmth for the evening. She found it and extended it to Effie. Hope held tight to the garment, demanding Effie's attention for a moment. "I'm sorry."

"Me too."

"You didn't do anything wrong," Hope whispered. "I was cruel and had no right to tell you who to hang out with. For what it's worth, I'm glad you didn't listen."

"I almost called and canceled four times," Effie confessed. "No one is worth you hating me."

Hope's heart clenched. She was truly the worst. She could make excuses for herself all day long, but the fact was she let her own needs and her own fears get in the way of things. "I could never. Have so much fun." Hope kissed Effie on the cheek and squeezed her hands before turning down the hall. Her curiosity baited her to hesitate. "Where is he taking you?"

Effie's smile was a sunrise on mist-shrouded shores. "It's a surprise. Do you think I'm overdressed?" Effie pinched a pearl between her thumb and forefinger, spinning it anxiously. Hope remembered that Effie had never been on a date like this. Had never gotten to know someone outside of coffee chats and neighborhood walks or phone calls after dark.

"No. You're magnificent. So authentically Effie that you'll have him stumbling over himself all night. I'm sure of it."

Effie breezed out the door and Hope followed the urge to climb the stairs to her room. She pulled out her laptop and read through one of Brayden's emails for the umpteenth time. She clicked *reply* before she could talk herself out of it. Fingers flying over the keys she let herself reveal as much as she dared behind the safety of the email.

Dear Brayden,

I'm sorry I've been ignoring your attempts to contact me. My heart collapsed when Chloe told me she was your wife. I couldn't bear to confront you about it, because I was afraid that I would blindly forgive you and wind up shattered all over again. I needed to separate myself from you because I didn't trust myself to be discerning, not with how much you mean to me.

Effie did tell me that you are ensnared in a divorce battle that's been wearing on you for years. While it lets me breathe again, it still stings to know that you didn't tell me about her. All of this could have been avoided if you had, and I'm still angry with you for that betrayal.

But you haven't deserved the silent treatment I've been giving you since. My own stuff has been clouding my judgment and making me retreat from you further, but I want to tell you all about it . . . in person. Meet me at our spot next Sunday at three? I know I've dragged you through hell with my behavior, so I understand if you need some time.

I still love you.
Hope

Hope's cursor hovered over the send button. A rush of nausea reminded her why she thought it easier to cut ties and never look back. Happiness was too fragile. It had shattered so easily with three words from Chloe—*I'm his wife*. Greater truth aside, Hope had unwittingly rammed into her biggest fear that day. That love and joy were short-lived. If it wasn't robbed by betrayal, her happiness was at the mercy of so many other stumbling blocks. Hearts were too fragile. Bones and blood and flesh were always careening toward an inevitable end. *Was it better to love him fully and live with the fear of how long it would last?*

Hope's stomach lurched at the realization that if she felt this much anxiety over loving Brayden, she was destined to be a worrywart of a mother. The baby kicked as if to tell her to send the damn message and stop being so dramatic. Hope took Bug's—she'd taken to calling the baby Bug in the most affectionate way possible—advice and finally hit send.

After all, if everything was temporary, the least she could do was give her whole heart to her imperfect, impermanent life.

20

Effie was actually doing this. She hadn't imagined the spark between them and Theo had finally acted on it. *Theo.* Salted caramel chocolate, Theo. Realizing his nickname was her favorite confection had been unbearable. Soggy cardboard was preferable to the taunt of such bliss that couldn't be coveted. But he'd shown up, those chocolates in hand, and Effie knew that it wasn't chaos that brought him there.

She found Theo standing beside his Jeep at the end of the block as instructed. Effie may have summoned the bravado to reveal her plans to the entire Thatcher clan, but that didn't mean she needed them spying on her through the front windows while she greeted her date. The first *real* date she'd been on in over two years.

Her teeth ground together and the air suddenly felt warmer. Dating was not for the faint of heart. At least her not-date with Schilling had proven she could be social and have a good time without becoming a quivering puddle of nerves. But then she saw him.

Theo wore dark jeans and a relaxed Henley beneath his black leather jacket. Effie was absolutely overdressed. She swallowed the bile creeping up her throat, her grip like a vise around her dainty clutch. The anxious breath she sucked in sent her chest heaving. Theo's gaze lingered on her bodice for that breath before he offered a knee-wobbling smile. When she was close enough to not need to yell, she pointed at him with her clutch. "I'm going to go change—"

She pivoted on her cream-colored heels, but Theo grabbed her by the wrist. Her skirts hugged her hips as they finished their swooshing twirl. "Don't you dare." He gently tugged on her wrist and spun her back toward him. Effie landed in his arms. Even in her heels, she had to lift her chin to look him in the eye. His breath was warm on the tip of her nose and carried hints of mint. *Smart. Had she brushed her teeth since her tuna sandwich that afternoon?*

"You're beautiful," he drawled. Effie cast her eyes down as a smile crept across her lips. "Don't act like you don't know it."

Effie looked up. "Just not used to hearing it." Though she supposed she didn't let herself focus on her beauty often. It wasn't a lasting trait, as her mother demonstrated with how she fussed over her aging looks.

"Well, get used to it." Theo turned to open the passenger side door for her. "Shall we?"

Effie swallowed hard but managed a nod. She began to climb in when Theo took her hand to help her up. The door shut behind him, and Effie swore she saw him flex his hand like he was shaking off his own nerves. Somehow, imagining this stunning, sexy, experienced man was aflutter like she was made her feel much more at ease. Even if it wasn't true, it helped her pretend they were on equal footing.

The illusion only lasted until they arrived a few blocks east of

Market Square, and Theo revealed the location of their date. He led her to the back entrance of what Effie realized was her favorite tea shop, Steeped Dreams, off State Street. She puzzled as Theo rapped a coded knock on the door. The response came swiftly, followed by warm light flooding the alley from the open door. A thin woman in her fifties, hair tied in a bun, smiled broadly at them. She wrapped Theo in a warm embrace before welcoming them inside.

The dry room glowed with café lights and candles. The center table that Effie assumed was standard culinary stainless steel was draped with a lace tablecloth and filled with canisters of different herbs and tea leaves. The woman who greeted them stood poised on the other side of the table, a scale, scoops, and brown paper sachets before her. "Ready to blend some teas?" the woman asked, and Effie thought she'd never seen someone so happy to share her expertise.

Theo was so much better at this than she ever imagined. Leagues above her in dating prowess. She did her best not to let the realization summon her nerves.

Theo's hand on the small of her back ushered her forward. She finally saw the table set for two off to the side, bedecked in a similar tablecloth, candles, and a tiered tray with finger sandwiches on the bottom, a layer of mini scones in the middle, and those damn chocolate caramel truffles on top. "How did you do this?" Effie whispered as Theo draped an apron over her head then his own.

"I meet some very cool people in my line of work." He winked at the owner of the shop, but then his gaze met Effie's and she felt the double meaning of his words.

Her heart pounded in her ears. She knew next to nothing about the man in front of her, but she never wanted him to stop looking at her the way he was now—like she was a rarefied gem he'd only just discovered and couldn't wait to admire every facet of.

Theo decided it was a travesty that Effie ever wore anything but this pale pink dress that hugged her chest and waist like a second skin before flaring with the curve of her hips. It perfectly accentuated the femininity he discovered radiating from her at every encounter. And whenever she took a deep breath lifting her chest? Images of Danny Zuko falling to his knees before Sandy came to mind. He was enchanted, mesmerized, as though the minute he decided to explore this relationship the full power of her radiance beckoned to him.

Every glance his way had him wishing he could read minds. He'd never wanted to know so much about someone so quickly. Despite his constant eagerness to dive into the deep end with relationships, something here felt different. It felt like they could dive together and never reach the bottom, not in three years or ten or fifty. He didn't know what made Effie feel so special, but he knew it to be true. He'd worry about why later.

"So serious?" Effie said summoning him from his thoughts. He brushed off the weight of importance that he could feel around this first date and smiled as lightly as he could.

"Just making sure I don't overpower the delicate white tea with the dried pineapple bits. Would hate to ruin it."

"I like that blend, Theo. Should make for a zesty cuppa," Victoria praised with a hearty grin. "Try adding a bit of safflower to balance it out."

Theo nodded, happy for the tip. Of all of the safety inspections he'd done in the past few months, hers had been the breeziest, and most rewarding. Victoria had invited him to try some new teas and left a standing invitation to practice in the blending room whenever he wished. She must have sensed his innate desire to dabble his way through life, and he was grateful for it.

Especially now.

Effie lit up when she saw the space and revealed that she came in at least once a week to purchase a new tea. He could so clearly envision it as she described her morning ritual brewing a cup with her electric kettle in her room alone as the sun rose, savoring the quiet moments before joining the bustle of her sprawling family. It sounded like a sanctuary, and he wondered who she allowed across the threshold. Hope, certainly, but her room sounded off-limits to most others. He couldn't help feel like it was true of her heart as well.

"What kind are you making now?" he asked Effie.

"A Darjeeling."

"Ah, the Queen of Teas," Victoria chimed in.

Theo smirked at Effie. "How fitting."

To his surprise, she snorted. "I am no queen."

Instead of pushing, insisting that she must not have a very good mirror, he joked, "Tell that to your impeccable posture and the dainty way you're tying your sachets."

"Well, if it's strictly a matter of poise, maybe I'll concede. Queen Effie at your service." She curtsied, pulling out the sides of her gorgeous dress. It was cute as hell and Theo let his admiration flood his face. That phenomenal shade of pink rose to her cheeks again before she perfectly tied another sachet of her tea together.

Victoria gave them each a little box for the tea bags they'd blended before she cleaned up the canisters and replaced the scale on the back counter. "Have a seat, I'll bring you each a pot of hot water."

Theo escorted Effie to the small side table. He was grateful that Victoria let him decorate the back room with warm lighting so they could relax and enjoy their tea without the sting of the fluorescents overhead.

In the amber glow, Effie looked like a dream. Not just beautiful, but warm and magnetic in a way that drew him toward her body and soul.

She settled into the seat he held out for her then folded the cloth napkin into her lap. He sat across from her and actually felt comfortable in their quiet. Victoria arrived with their hot water and excused herself, reminding Theo to lock up when they left.

Then there was nothing but Effie and the clink of porcelain as she lifted the lid on her pot. The hush of paper against cardboard as she pulled a Darjeeling sachet from the box. A subtle plunk of the water as she dunked it. Sienna stains swirled from the tea as it seeped into the water, but his eyes were consumed with the curve of Effie's nose, the way she tucked her hair behind her ear, her utter and complete focus on the ritual before her. Many of his other first dates buzzed with impatience and noise, while Effie brought an unhurried curiosity that felt lost in time.

"You're staring," she whispered without meeting his gaze.

"Sorry," he said and went to work brewing his own pot. He picked the white tea with pineapple.

"Don't be. Now we're even."

Theo looked up and her grin was just shy of devilish. "Did I do alright? How's this date ranking for you so far?"

"Top of the list," Effie asserted, and he believed her. "I'm curious how you came up with the idea."

"Between the electric kettle you had hidden behind the register, the teacup drawing at stained glass night, and the tote I ruined, I kind of guessed you liked tea. I figured you might enjoy blending your own."

"How observant of you."

"I do my best." Theo winked, which had her rolling her eyes. He was happy to see she'd relaxed a bit since she climbed into the Jeep. Thankfully, he had too. First date nerves were par for the course, but this easeful banter was better. It took every ounce of his restraint not to pepper her with questions, peel back the layers, uncover what caused the palpable ache that echoed behind her. "You don't say much," he observed.

Effie wrinkled her nose as though embarrassed. "Sorry," she sighed. "If I don't know what to say I try not to babble."

Theo hoped that wasn't for fear of judgment. "You can babble at me all you like," he assured her. He took her hand from across the table and drew lazy circles on the back of her palm with his thumb. It was a habit of his. Though many found it too intimate a touch for a first date, Theo never had. Effie didn't seem to mind either, since she didn't pull away.

"It's not that . . . it's just. Babbling is dangerous for my palate. Following an errant train of thought usually results in some pretty sour, salty words."

As if in evidence of that very notion she scraped her tongue on her teeth. Presumably to get rid of the sour and salt.

"That must be challenging." Theo sighed. He wasn't sure he'd be able to handle it. Having to monitor his mind and his mouth so he didn't encounter too much unpleasantness. "You could just say my name on repeat. That'd be okay by me."

The laugh that tumbled from her was a bubbly glass of champagne.

"Theo, Theo, Theo," she drawled. The singular thought of hearing her say it as she came consumed him. "What do I have to do to make you forget I ever confessed how sweet your name tastes?"

"I will never forget."

"Oh fine," she said, the hint of a pout on her lips before she took a bite of a cucumber and cream cheese sandwich. "That's delicious."

"Made them myself," Theo boasted. He noticed the buzz of the refrigerator in back and the silence around them. "Let me put on some music."

Effie nearly leaped from her chair. "No, don't!"

Theo cocked his head to the side, utterly confused.

"This is why I've only ever been on first dates," she growled and rubbed her hands over her face, the poise cracking ever so slightly.

But Theo waited for the explanation he knew was coming.

Effie now hated her synesthesia for the second time in a month. She loved music, adored it. When it was perfectly curated, prescreened, and full of palate-friendly tunes that wouldn't spoil the mood or her taste buds. It grated on her nerves that she'd had to point to her *condition* twice now on this date as a reason that she was so awkward.

She hoped he'd realize on his own that she often spoke with morsels of her meal tucked into her cheek to stave off word tastes when gum wouldn't do.

"Your synesthesia?" Theo interjected. "I'm sorry. You shouldn't have to keep explaining what a challenge it is. It's just not something

I have to think about every day."

Effie's heart swelled at the acknowledgment. "If you want something on in the background, maybe something instrumental? Or um, Fleetwood Mac's *Rumors* album is a safe one. Beyond that, I kind of have to take it song by song. I'm sorry."

Theo squeezed the hand that he hadn't let go of for a solid five minutes. "Stop saying sorry. That makes total sense. No music it is. I just wanted the mood to be right."

"The mood is perfect, Theo."

She was totally serious. The café lights, the tea, the delicious sandwiches he'd made himself. Everything was so perfectly wonderful that she contemplated how he had gotten so good at dating. She wondered how many women he'd slept with. Effie flushed so badly she wanted to strip the denim jacket from her clammy flesh. She pulled her hand away and cradled it in her lap. "Whatever happened with Talia?"

"Ah," Theo sighed as though he hoped it wouldn't come up. "We aren't benefiting anymore. If that's what you mean."

"Since when?" Effie couldn't help but wonder what had driven him to Glitter & Glue to ask her out when he had someone like Talia warming his bed.

"About eight days ago."

"I see." She didn't know what else to say. She wanted to ask what had happened, why they broke up, or whatever it was called when you stopped *benefiting*. She kept a vise on her curiosities and sipped her tea instead. It was delicious. So rich and full-bodied. Delectable.

"That's not what I'm looking for from you," Theo said tentatively. *Well, that was a gut punch.* Maybe he'd traded in his sexy sidepiece for someone who might impress his mother, pearls and all. It must have shown on her face because he quickly corrected. "Fuck, that's not . . . I *do*. I mean eventually. I want to take this slow, and I'm not trying to seduce you or fuck around or whatever. I want to date you. Get to know you."

"Why? You seemed to have fun with Talia."

"Because, the sky is blue."

Was that supposed to make sense, because it absolutely didn't. Effie thought he might be having a stroke as she furrowed her brow. "If you don't want that from me, and you don't want Talia, what do you want?"

"What do you want, Effie?"

"I asked you first."

Theo leaned back in his seat, pouring more tea into the bone china cup painted with deep-green leaves. As he blew the steam from its surface, Effie admired the softness of his parted lips. He was heart-achingly beautiful, and she felt wholly unprepared for how much she wanted him to touch her again, even if it was just to hold her hand. Out of her depth was an understatement, but it was only because she'd never put her romantic imaginings into practice. She might have gotten up and locked him in the tea shop forever, so she could stay in this bubble pretending that they were made for each other. Where they didn't know enough about one another to decide it wasn't a fit, but they knew enough to want to try anyway.

He set the cup back on its saucer and spun the silver band around his forefinger. Effie realized for the first time that it was actually white gold, tarnished from years of wear. "You really want to know what I want?"

"Yes." Effie gulped, anticipation and anxiety burning her throat.

"I want to be here, having tea and talking with you."

Effie pushed back against every instinct to ask why he would think *she* of all people was so special, so worth a shift in priorities. Instead, she took Hope's advice. She shoved back her insecurities and told them to shut the hell up. "What's the story with your ring?"

"What makes you think there is one? Maybe I'm just fashionable." Effie raised her brows and Theo laughed. "It was my dad's wedding band."

Effie's heart sank. *Was.* She instinctively reached for his hand and he didn't pull away. "I'm sorry," she whispered.

Theo's expression was unreadable, but he blurted, "He's still alive. Sorry, I'm hearing how that sounded." Effie tried to take her hand back, something like embarrassment setting her ears on fire, but he held tight and started tracing those hypnotic circles again. She hated the disappointment that rolled across her spine that they didn't share that loss. She wouldn't wish it on anyone.

"My parents got divorced when I was sixteen," Theo explained. "As much as they had loved each other, it still didn't work out. Or they didn't evolve to let it work out?"

"What do you mean?"

"My mom wanted to travel more. My dad was a homebody. My dad wanted to make plans and budgets, while my mom wanted to be more free-flowing. By the time they filed for divorce, they claimed they'd grown apart. Don't get me wrong, theirs has to be the most amicable divorce in history, but the assertion that they didn't want the same things anymore never sat right with me. I've seen their wedding video. I know their vows by heart. They wanted the same things. What they didn't want to do was change when it became necessary to hold on to what they cherished—each other, our family. So, I wear it to remind myself that when I find my soulmate, I won't be too proud or too stubborn or too stuck in my ways."

"And what about the times when someone is just meant to make an appearance? Spend a season with you and then disappear forever?" Effie wanted to believe in soulmates but had learned instead that not everyone gets a recurring role.

"Then they aren't soulmates," Theo said matter-of-factly. "Or they shied away from doing the work."

"Isn't love supposed to be easy?" It's what Effie had always hoped, that somehow her family had failed to keep it by thinking it was hard.

"Love is easy, I think. Choosing to do life with someone can be hard, but I think it's worth the effort. I wish my parents had seen it that way."

"Me too," Effie confessed.

"Your parents split up too?"

"Yeah, but I was much younger." Effie didn't feel like washing the evening in her grief, so she didn't mention that her father was dead. Instead, she smothered a scone in crème fraiche and took a bite. They were good, but hers were better. "Did you make these too?"

"No. I'm no baker. They came from that little spot by the chapel."

"Oh, they have amazing apple turnovers."

"But not scones?" Theo asked, amused and watching as she placed the scone on her plate instead of finishing it in one bite like she had with the finger sandwiches.

"No! They're good."

"But?"

"Mine are better," Effie said as though it were a question through gritted teeth, shoulders reaching her ears.

"You can say that with more confidence, you know?"

"I'll work on that."

The night passed in easy conversation and even easier silence. It was something Theo didn't know was a priority of his, but not needing to fill the air with chatter felt right.

It felt even more right to have Effie's fingers entwined with his as they walked along Prescott Park beneath the stars on their way back to his car. They had taken the long way, at Effie's request, and he was glad she didn't want the night to end after the tea and chocolates were gone. He didn't either.

A chill breeze blew her hair from her face and he caught himself staring again. After tonight, he felt like he knew her better. He learned about her favorite music and how she got into baking by helping her grandma in the kitchen. She told him about her sisters and nieces. They went over her astrology—an Aquarius sun, which he could now point to for why she seemed in her head so frequently. He was even able to goad her into telling him about her romance novels and what drew her to them. Apparently using fiction to imagine a life beyond your wildest dreams wasn't just a pastime of his.

He fully planned to make *those kinds* of dreams a reality whenever she was ready, but he wouldn't push her. Not when he was content to hold her hand and learn about how she saw the world. And especially not when she'd seemed anxious about his reaction when she'd subtly revealed that she was a virgin. Theo had many anxieties about being her first—if he got to be—because it was so important to her. But it's the last that mattered to Theo. Sex had always been a great way to explore joy and connection and love, but he didn't believe it was the only way. He could use Effie's playbook instead of his own this time. He'd be happy to, if only because he knew the way his arm tingled at her touch meant something truly special sprouted between them.

Theo was sad when they reached his Jeep parked in the lot at Memorial Bridge.

Effie leaned against the passenger door, playing with his fingers. "Thanks for demonstrating that first dates can be great."

"It's a shame no one had shown you that before."

"Or not," she said bringing their hands down by her side. "Makes it more special with you."

Theo stepped in closer, using his free hand to tuck the waves of her hair behind her ear. He brushed his thumb along the soft line of her jaw, as she pulled on their intertwined hands, nudging him closer. A quiet plea.

Theo looked down, letting himself marinate in the bright blue of her eyes before she tilted her head back, inviting him to kiss her.

He touched his lips to hers, softly at first. The warmth of her breath on his mouth sent his spine tingling. Theo moved his hand to the nape of her neck, his fingers wrapped in the silk of her hair as he deepened the kiss.

When she wrapped her arms around his neck and held him closer, her chest pressed against his, he thought he might lose against his resolve to take things slow and fall to his knees right then and there.

Effie's tongue glided over his and he tensed with eager anticipation. *Damn, she was a good kisser.*

He lost all sense of time and place as their lips moved with a tender passion. His hand found the small of her back, a divine warmth radiating from her skin. He wanted to be wrapped up in it, but he was reminded with her hand on his chest as she slowly, *so slowly*, pulled away from their kiss that he was not here to do what he'd always done.

They stilled, his forehead against hers, their breathing a bit ragged. He leaned in once more, softly nibbling her bottom lip before unlatching the door behind her, so she could climb in. Her gaze was unreadable, but the flush of her cheeks and swell of her lips was enough to have him asking, "When can I see you again?"

21

I knew it. You *never* get so flustered! Not even when I tell you every sordid detail about my last hookup," Basil gloated. Effie regretted telling him about her date with Theo. He was far too proud of himself for *calling it*. "So when are you seeing him again?"

"We're meeting for lunch today," Effie said and damn it if she didn't blush.

"Perfect," Basil squealed before his face took on a serious tightness. "I'm proud of you. You deserve good things."

"So do you."

"Yeah, well that's a given," Basil huffed, and Effie admired the confidence with which he knew what he deserved. Effie frequently felt like she navigated her life with an outdated map. She tried not to give it another thought and just accept that she did deserve good things as she took a box cutter to the parcel in front of her. Opening the lid revealed skeins of the baby-pink merino wool her mother had been looking for, finally delivered after weeks on back order.

Effie pulled a couple to the side and stashed them under the register to ring up for herself at the end of the day. "Who are those for?" Basil asked, knowing Effie preferred an embroidery to a knitting needle.

"My mom. She wants to knit more hats for the NICU."

"What's her deal? You don't talk about her much."

Effie shrugged. Pamela Thatcher's *deal* was difficult to put into words. She had the distinct memory of watching *Peter Pan* for the first time and thinking that her mother would love Neverland. As she grew older, she frequently found herself feeling like Wendy to her mother's Tinker Bell. An unspoken web of jealousy between them over Effie's youth and prospects and Pamela's lack thereof. But for all of her faults, she was still Effie's mother. "I don't know. She's always been great at showing me exactly who I want to be."

"That's nice," Basil chimed, but he'd become distracted by a dropped stitch on the start of a very loud hat to match the very loud scarf he had finished.

It would have been nice, if it weren't for the fact that all Effie wanted for her life directly contrasted the choices that Pamela had made for hers. Effie learned much about who she wanted to be by deciding that she *did not* want to be her mother. Maybe she'd feel differently if she got to see her in action at work. It sounded like a grueling job, one that required selflessness and heart and grit. But those things were stripped away after her shift. The woman without the scrubs was attention seeking in so many ways. Effie chided herself for being cruel. Even if it was only in her thoughts. She didn't know what a broken heart felt like, but she imagined it looked an awful lot like suppressed laugh lines and bottle-blonde hair.

Basil pulled her from her thoughts. "How's the ball coming

together?"

"Pretty well. The guest list is already almost full since Lou listed the tickets for sale so early this year."

"I hope I can find a date for my second ticket."

"Should have plenty of time for that given your track record."

"No, no. We don't bring *those* dates to this function. The ball is for romance, Effie. Or have you missed that memo for the last twenty years of your life?"

"It's usually just a day that I have to sequester myself in my room until Louisa deems the house worthy of outside eyes."

Basil rolled his own before that glimmer of his lit them up. "I cannot wait to see that man of yours in a tux and cummerbund. Mmm!"

"He's not *my man*. I don't even know if he'll want to go."

Or if he'll still be around by then.

Effie ignored her pessimistic inner gremlin and continued unboxing yarn.

Hope was decidedly late, but it wasn't her fault. She was distracted. *Again.* This time, by counting down the days until she saw Brayden. He hadn't answered her email, but a mystery bouquet of flowers arrived on the doorstep the next day. She took that as a good sign.

It hadn't occurred to her that they might not have been for her.

She hurried around the kitchen, a bagel smeared with cream cheese between her teeth, and a to-go mug of herbal tea in hand.

"You need more than carbs for lunch," her mother scolded from the breakfast table.

"I'll get something nutritious for dinner," Hope garbled out from around the bagel. She took a bite and chewed. "I promise."

Tibby gave Hope a stern look, one that, in the past, had ensured Hope went to bed on time, brushed her teeth, and always had her partners wear a condom. That last one seemed to do little good recently, but it was sound advice nonetheless. Her mother was full of sound advice. Hope yearned to emulate that in the coming years too.

"I wish I could go with you, but I have a closing."

"No worries. I'll bring you new pictures." Hope wedged the rest of the bagel between her teeth to grab her purse off the counter. She rushed to the foyer and out the door before she was *really* late. One more ultrasound, two meetings with her editor, and five more days until she could see Brayden and properly tell him about all she'd been afraid of, and better yet, all she looked forward to.

"Mmm. Yours are better," Theo moaned. Effie and Theo sat on a bench in the park sharing scones she had baked the night before. Theo brought salads to their lunchtime rendezvous and Effie provided the treats and tea.

"I'm glad you agree." Effie laughed. He took another bite, and the rumble from his throat was almost certainly meant to mimic a different kind of satisfaction. "They aren't *that* good."

"Try telling my taste buds." He paused a long moment, challenging Effie's nerves with his gaze before he said, "Thank you. No one's ever baked for me before."

"No?" *Were there other ways people showed affection?* Because Effie baked to make you feel better, to spread good cheer, to tell you she cared.

"It's a rarity for someone to have your skill sets and be age-appropriate for me to date," he teased, his voice smooth as butter.

"You have an uncanny habit of making me wonder if I should be offended."

"I never mean any offense, sunshine." He grinned and side-eyed Effie like he waited to see if she'd object to the pet name.

"Vast improvement from eggplant."

"I do aim to please." He turned pensive. "What does sunshine taste like?"

"Orange mango juice." Theo scrunched his face, apparently not a fan of such a combination. "I like it!" And she did. It tasted like a vacation on the beach and the rich hues of sunset and the passion that tropical paradises promised. *Maybe the latter had more to do with who called her sunshine.*

"Well, that's all that matters then."

Theo balled their trash and tucked it into the to-go bag from their lunch. In one swift, expert move he put his arm around Effie and pulled her in close. She instinctively tensed, her stomach thrown into her throat. She was not well-versed in all the little ways you might touch or hold or shower affection on someone. It had her tingling at every touch and wondering if he could tell her heart was off to the Kentucky Derby.

Theo leaned over, lifting her opposite hand to reach his that draped over her shoulder and intertwined their fingers. *Were her hands sweaty? God, why was this so nerve-wracking?*

But Theo met her gaze, raised his brows in warning or jest, and kissed the top of her head, and her stomach settled.

Effie couldn't help but notice that when she looked into his eyes, she wasn't nervous at all. It was the not knowing where his hands might roam, or his lips, or where he wanted them to go that had her insides roiling. *What was it he'd said about her sign as an Aquarius? That it could manifest in thinking too much about everything?* Maybe it was that, but the ease with which they started seeing each other had her wary too.

In all of her imaginings, she'd have to become someone outgoing and bold with the constitution of a woman who made dating a sport in order to find a relationship. Instead, it nearly fell into her lap. She couldn't have been more grateful for how normal it felt to sit beside Theo on a park bench, the sun beating down on them on a breezy day in May. Butterfly-riddled belly aside. But it didn't change the fact that it somehow felt *too* smooth a transition.

Effie let her head relax onto Theo's shoulder, which was easy given how much taller he was than her. She rolled her head to the side so she could look him in the eye once more.

He had a face that yearned to be photographed. Not in a stylized model kind of way, but in candid moments that captured the dreamy stare she'd noticed him give the leaves on the trees and the sun as it broke through fluffy clouds. Or that caught him flashing a genuine smile that rendered him most handsome. Maybe it was his shampoo or cologne or even his laundry detergent, but some amazing scent drew her in. The taut waffle weave of his shirt over his broad shoulders had her fluttering for totally different reasons. Effie held those hazel eyes in hers and thought maybe she was already falling for him. "I kind of like you," she offered. The thump of her heart suggested instead that she just confessed she was enamored, buying a wedding dress, and planning to have lots of sex and babies with him.

"I kind of like you too, sunshine," he whispered, a broad smile on his lips. He planted them on hers and the air rushed from Effie's lungs. She didn't think it would ever stop being a shock to her system when their breath mingled and his lips claimed hers. It was exciting and intoxicating, and she could pretend she did it with confidence until it became true.

Effie never used to understand PDA. She thought people had short leashes on their libido and might do well to take a cold shower if they couldn't go a few hours in public without shoving their tongues down each other's throats.

But here, now, with Theo at the tip of her tongue, she wasn't sure why anyone did anything but kiss on park benches, in the light of day, for all the world to see.

I still love you.

The words were a relief, even if Brayden harbored his own ill feelings about Hope's behavior as of late. He knew something besides Chloe had been bothering her to have altered their dynamic so drastically.

A phone call before Sunday might have been nice.

A quick update over text.

But Hope wanted to wait until they were in person to share everything. Maybe she feared he wouldn't hear her out if they weren't face to face. She should know him better than that. It saddened him to think that she could ever conceive of a world where he was a cheater, where he wouldn't give her space to say her piece, where he would dismiss her so coolly as she had him.

The email came at the exact right time. He'd been toiling all week, fighting for ground in his divorce battle, but with each meeting, each mediation, all he saw was the life he imagined slipping through his fingers. It was excruciating to be at Chloe's mercy. Even more so was the truth that he had been so wrapped up in her, so in love that he never even noticed he wasn't what she wanted. He wasn't the prize. The week of mediation had done a lot to quell his anger with Hope, if only because he would have stayed the hell away if he could have too.

I still love you. Well, so did he. That's why he'd made up his mind almost instantly upon reading Hope's email that he would meet her on Sunday afternoon. He didn't feel her note required a response. She wanted to set a time and place? Then he'd tease out the rom-com nature of the encounter and let her wait and see if he showed, if only for the flirtation of it. He could be coy when he wanted to. Maybe it wouldn't kill him to play a little hard to get either.

That thought had him rolling his eyes at himself as he hefted another fire extinguisher onto the cart beside his van. He preferred to roll a stock of them through facilities like this, so he didn't have to make twenty trips out to the van or make detailed notes of what rooms had out-of-date equipment along the way. He generally had to replace at least three extinguishers in a place this size, so he packed six.

He loaded his forms and iPad onto the top shelf of the cart and wheeled the whole thing up the handicap ramp to the gleaming glass doors. The automatic slider opened to let him inside. He stopped at the front desk to talk with the receptionist.

"I have to check the entire building for safety code violations and make sure all of your equipment is up to date. Is the first floor clear, or are any of the rooms occupied?"

The receptionist made a few keystrokes on the laptop before her, seeming to check the schedule for the day. "They should be clear, and the staff has been warned you'd be in today. Just knock first. They'll let you know if you can come in."

"Sounds good. Thank you."

And with that, Brayden strode down the beige linoleum hall, innumerable doors flanking him all the way. He sighed. It was going to be a long afternoon.

Brayden pushed his cart down the eastern hallway on the first floor. So far, he'd only had to replace one extinguisher and encountered two occupied rooms. His sweeps didn't take long, so no one gave him grief, but he preferred not to interrupt. He still had thirty exam rooms, suites, and staff lounges to inspect before he could call it a day.

He pulled up to the next door and knocked lightly. The *come in* from the other side was barely audible, but he eased the door open nonetheless.

"Sorry to bother you I'll—"

Brayden took in the sterile exam room—the tray of tools beside the bench, the model of the female reproductive system by the window.

And Hope.

22

Hope lay back on the exam bench, her Velaris T-shirt tucked under her chest exposing her smooth, round *pregnant* belly to the chill air of the room.

Brayden staggered back. He couldn't remember how to breathe. Hope sat upright, eyes searching for his, but he had to look at his feet. Had to make sure that the ground was still solid beneath him because, for all intents and purposes, it felt like he stood atop an undulating hill of quicksand.

"Brayden—"

He held up his hand. He needed a minute. Ten. Maybe the rest of his fucking life to understand what the hell was happening in this room.

Brayden leaned against the wall, mind swirling. For times when he was overwhelmed at school, or the noise of a crowd was too much, or he needed to orient himself in the world to not feel like an insignificant speck, his moms had taught him to be observant. To find details and latch on. So he did.

The walls were beige. There was a grey rubber chair rail halfway up. There was a poster on the back wall with a fetus in the womb. The floor was the same sad linoleum. A constant *drip, drip, drip* emanated from the faucet set into the particle board cabinets painted a cheerful blue. The purse he had gotten Hope for her birthday, the purple designer one she'd been pining after every time they passed it in the shop window, sat on a bulky chair beside him.

And there. In the middle of the room, sat the woman he loved. Her long brown waves pulled away from her face with bobby pins on each side. She had navy leggings on, the band of which cupped the underside of her growing belly.

He finally looked at her face. She was ashen. Probably as pale and shocked as he looked. She obviously wasn't expecting *him* to be the one knocking. Hadn't even thought to mention the appointment, or you know, his baby.

But she would have? That's why she wanted to see him. It's not like she would have been able to keep hiding it. But that was logical. That made too much sense. He wasn't in any mood to be the good guy right now. He wanted to yell, to scream, to burst out of the room and not look back, not because he didn't want it, not because he wanted to abandon his unborn baby—

Fuck. Was it even his baby? Is that why she hadn't told him?

It would make sense. He didn't remember ever having the conversation about whether or not they were exclusive. That last morning they were together, when they'd said I love you, it felt like she had wanted to share so much more. Maybe it was all she could think to say, knowing another man had fathered her child. That she loved him and it wasn't enough. It would explain so much about what happened after everything that transpired with Chloe and Effie.

He needed to speak, to say something, to get his burning questions answered, but his voice got lost somewhere. Held hostage by the shock of it all. Brayden had a vague awareness that someone approached from down the hall.

"Brayden . . ." Hope whispered, and it ripped him open. He fully expected to see his guts on the floor, his heart a beating mess in her hand. It killed him to know she had so much power over him, just in the way she said his name. No wonder he filed for his first divorce at twenty-six.

He was a fool in love.

"Ah, so this is the infamous Brayden," a chipper voice said from behind him. Brayden made space for the woman who entered the exam room donning a white lab coat. She reached out a hand in greeting. "Nice to meet you, Dad."

Brayden shook hands but his knees wobbled. His throat contracted as he looked to Hope, the question in his eyes. *Was he dad?* She nodded, ever so subtly. One of the stones on his chest lifted. The doctor, whether a mind reader or just used to new, terrified parents, led him to the stool beside Hope, only releasing his hand when he settled in the seat. "Actually, I have to . . ." He pointed to his cart outside. His voice sounded weird. Like it wasn't his. *God, why was this so hard to digest?*

"Stay," Hope pleaded, taking his hand in hers. He managed a nod but couldn't meet her gaze. He might just lose it in front of this unsuspecting doctor and that wouldn't do. Not when she was here to make sure *his baby* was healthy. No, the fight would come. It had to. But not now. Not when the sound of his baby's heartbeat filled his eardrums and his whole life shifted.

⚜

Effie dragged herself through the door at Glitter & Glue, locking it behind her.

The store had been a madhouse when she got back from lunch with Theo. Apparently, there was some kind of knitting circle at the Strawberry Banke house—an oversight on Effie and Henrietta's part to not be more prepared. It seemed more like a horde when thirty chattering ladies came in search of as many sets of size two needles for a doll pattern they all wanted to try. Thankfully, the stock room was neat, organized, and safe since Theo's inspection, and she was able to get them what they needed without much drama. That did nothing to calm the riotous shuffling through the skeins of yarn to find the right colors, weight, and texture for said pattern. All Effie could do for that was *ooh* and *aah* over the ones they got excited about and usher them like lost ducklings to the register when closing approached.

The tension in Effie's shoulders should have eased when she spotted Theo casually leaned against a lamppost waiting for her, but the sight of him—*him*—standing there *for her* felt too good to be true. She had the unnerving feeling of being the dorky female lead in need of a glow-up to snag the hot, sophisticated dreamboat that everyone else wanted to claim as their own. Effie didn't want him to know how her anxiety exploded every time she saw him, so she inhaled sharply and strode toward him in her best imitation of Louisa, who she'd seen turn men into puddles in drive-in parking lots with just a look.

"This is a surprise," she crooned.

"A good one, I hope?" He held two steaming to-go cups stamped with the Steeped Dreams logo. She approached on aching feet, sore from standing all day and having to restock after the hurricane of knitters tore through.

"Very good," Effie said, sighing.

Theo spread his arms to welcome her close. She brought her chest to his and hugged him. *God, she could stand there all day.* She wondered if he was as affected by a mere embrace or if she was the only one giddy over it. Cautiously, she tilted her head back, opening the way for Theo to plant a kiss on her lips. Effie luxuriated in the warmth of his as they took hers for a brief hello. She wrapped her arms around his waist and slumped against his broad chest. It wasn't improbable that she would fall asleep right there.

Theo's lips found the top of her head as he mumbled, "Long day?"

She managed a nod before she pulled back, the absence of his warmth noticeable. *How could his presence bring such peace and so many nerves at once?* Theo lifted the to-go cups in sequence. "Lemon verbena and peppermint, or chamomile lavender?"

Effie reached for the lemon verbena and mint. "I fear if I drink the other I will fall asleep mid-walk home." Effie looked around but didn't see any sign of Theo's van or his Jeep. "Did you come meet me just to walk me home?"

"Maybe," he said before taking the hefty tote from her hand and slinging it over his shoulder.

"You're nice to me," Effie asserted, but Theo laughed, apparently bemused by her redundant observations.

"Isn't that kind of the point?"

"I wouldn't know." Effie sighed and immediately regretted it. She assumed Theo knew she had little experience with romantic relationships, given her confession regarding her virginity, but she didn't want it confirmed for him. It was embarrassing. She was twenty-three and hadn't ever had a real boyfriend.

Effie looked to Theo expecting the inquisition. "If you're waiting for me to grill you about your dating history, it's not gonna happen. That's your business."

"Is that because you don't want me asking about all of your past relationships?"

Theo snorted a laugh. "Maybe a little. But honestly, I think you need to get out of your head about us. Tell me what you want to tell me and forget the rest."

Effie pondered for a long moment. For whatever reason, Effie decided it would feel better to let him know the truth about her history. Maybe confirming his suspicions would free her of worrying over it. "I was good friends with this guy, Connor, in like sixth grade. We stayed pretty close through high school. Especially after Hope graduated and I had two more years of torture to endure while she was off at college. He and I talked every night, went to all the school dances together, and didn't have bigger cliques to do stuff with. We used to make out in his pickup but we were never officially in a relationship."

"Talking every night and making out means he was your boyfriend, even if he was too much of an idiot to call himself that," Theo grumbled, something like disgust dripping from his words.

"It wasn't, *romantic*, or anything," Effie confessed and began to wonder if she should be telling him all of this. "It was more an unspoken pact to learn from each other. We'd give feedback after every . . . encounter."

"Feedback? Like postgame?"

"Yep." Effie tensed. This was an utterly ridiculous thing to share with the man she *wanted* to be her boyfriend. But it felt good to unburden herself. If he didn't think her totally weird and hook a left at the next crosswalk, then she'd know he was being honest about wanting to get to know each other.

"Well, it paid off."

"It did?"

"You're a fantastic kisser. I'll be sure to thank Connor if we ever meet."

Effie nudged him with her elbow, and he took the opportunity to sling his strong arm over her shoulder as they continued down the street. She still wore a mask of confidence as they walked along, but her nerves battled in her gut.

Theo would never actually meet Connor, but the thought of it made her warm with satisfaction. She hadn't talked to or thought about Connor in a long time. They used to text each other whenever one of them waited at an airport or a bus station, since it was usually the only time Effie had her phone, and traveling felt like a reason to check in back home. She'd texted him last summer before boarding a flight to Florida with her family to take the littles to Disney World. He never texted back.

If she was being honest, he had played a huge role in her romantic insecurities. She'd always assumed if she was desirable he would have asked her to be his. But Effie learned more and more how much her dad's advice rang true. *If you don't ask, the answer is no.* It never occurred to Effie that it could be safe to let her desires be known. It never felt true.

She looked at Theo, but he didn't notice. She admired the line of his jaw, the strong column of his neck. The thought of him shirtless and performing any number of the scenes from her romance novels flashed through her mind, unwittingly dumping a fresh basket of nerves down her spine.

Theo quirked a brow. "You okay?"

Effie's throat went dry; she was ill-equipped to play it cool. She was not Louisa or Hope. She was . . . well, her. But it didn't stop her from holding on to her last shred of feigned confidence. "Yeah, why?"

"You just shivered." He brought his hand to the nape of her neck and dragged his thumb from below her ear to her collarbone, in what she could only guess was a comforting gesture, even though it unlocked a rush of desire instead. Everything inside her twitched— with what she didn't know. *Anticipation? Pleasure? Anxiety?*

Effie jerked away from his touch. "I'm not good at this."

"Walking?"

Effie huffed. She wanted this to be easy. She wanted to have what Grams and Gramps had. He would put his arm around her on the sofa and sneak kisses when he walked by emptying the trash. When they danced he'd nuzzle into her neck and seemingly forget anyone else was in the room. They were affectionate and easy. She wanted that, but her insecurities seemed to have other plans. "No," Effie sighed. She felt on the verge of a panic attack. She could really use a paper bag right now.

"Hey, hey, hey," Theo whispered noticing her rising worry and taking up the space between them. He cupped her cheek. "Just breathe. Talk to me."

Effie looked him in the eye. "Veritas?"

"Uh, truth? Yes. I want the truth."

"You make me incredibly nervous. I don't know how to . . . like the hand-holding and you kiss my forehead and . . . I haven't done the affectionate couple thing and you're so good at it and I feel like I'm one wrong step away from you realizing that I'm too weird or behind for you . . . I missed my first kiss." Well, that was a mess of sweet, sour, tangy, metallic nonsense.

"You . . . what?"

"I missed. I was fourteen. It was at camp. This really cute boy walked me back to my cabin after a mixer thing, and standing at the door . . . he made like he was going to kiss me but didn't come the whole way, I closed my eyes too early and kissed his chin. I missed. He walked out, probably thinking I was an idiot."

Theo laughed.

"It's not funny! I was mortified!"

"As anyone who missed their first kiss would be." Theo chuckled but brushed his thumb down Effie's cheek. "You seemed so confident this afternoon."

"I was pretending." He didn't like that if his scowl was any indication. Effie knew logically her inexperience wasn't a dealbreaker, that she was not the virgin sent to save the rake, but she couldn't help but feel like she dragged him backward to a level of life he'd already mastered.

"Alright, new rules. You don't pretend to be anything you're not feeling, and I will be cool with it because as previously mentioned . . ." He leaned in close and whispered, "I kind of like you."

"You might do well to see a therapist about that," Effie quipped, noting Theo's displeasure at her self-deprecation.

"Not unless she'd help me know you better." Theo looked her up and down and she wondered what mischievous thought had him grinning like a fox. "Truth or dare?"

Effie felt like she'd revealed far too many truths in one day, so she said, "Dare."

"Without thinking or stewing or mulling anything over, do something you *feel* like doing right now. A cartwheel, the Carlton dance. Whatever you feel first. Just do it."

"Okay, Nike." She grimaced at him. "This is a weird dare."

Theo shrugged.

Effie took a deep breath, clearing her mind. There was only one thing she wanted to do when she opened her eyes and saw Theo watching her, his face drenched in admiration. She didn't think and tugged him in close. Her arms wrapped around his neck and she rose onto her tiptoes, planting a deep, claiming kind of kiss on his lips. They pulled apart, both a bit breathless, Effie floating on the high of getting exactly what she wanted in that moment.

"I would have guessed cartwheel," Theo whispered.

Effie smiled at him before striding forward and sipping her tea. Much to Effie's satisfaction, it took Theo a beat to seemingly remember how to move his legs, but he caught up in a hurry, slipping his hand into hers.

Brayden shuffled to the elevator at the end of the hall, finally finished with his inspection for the day. Not only was it torture sitting through the ultrasound with Hope while the doctor made subtle commentary that indicated to him she had no idea he'd just learned about the baby, but having to step into exam room after exam room—each one identical to the one that changed his life in an instant—made for a very long, very tiring, very unpleasant day.

The bright spot, if he chose to find one, was hearing that heartbeat. It had rocked his world. Whatever surrealist dream he'd been living in when he opened the door on Hope and her pregnant belly shattered when the ultrasound started. It immediately grounded him. Hope had chosen not to learn the baby's gender, and he was glad for that. There were so few surprises in the world. But he supposed he'd already had enough of those for the day. *For a lifetime, it felt like.*

He was quiet the whole appointment, and when the doctor left to give them a moment with the profile of a little face on the machine, he had squeezed Hope's hand, kissed her on the forehead, and strode into the hallway before he said something he couldn't take back.

That had been three hours ago.

The elevator doors opened on the first floor. He wheeled his cart half full of expired extinguishers past the receptionist and out to his van.

Hope perched against the bumper waiting for him.

She jerked to standing when she saw him. He wheeled around her to the double doors in the back, opening them to unload while she watched him in silence. "I don't want to yell at you," he finally said through gritted teeth.

"So don't? This isn't how I wanted you to find out . . ."

He'd held it tight to get through the day, but now the leash on his pain snapped. He slammed the doors to the van shut and turned to face Hope fully. "Are you kidding me right now? What the actual fuck, Hope? Six months. Six months! Half the time we've been together you've been pregnant and lying to me!"

"Not quite half . . ."

"You kept this huge thing from me and had the gall to call *me* a liar!" Hope cowered and he tried to steady his voice, but his blood boiled. He'd never been so angry in his life. Not even when Chloe had all but confessed she had married him for his money and would go quietly if he met her demands. That was a blip compared to this.

"You did lie!"

"That was my past! I omitted something I want to be free of. Something I am never going back to. Chloe doesn't change who I am or what I want with you or anything that matters to our future! You omitted our baby, Hope. Our baby . . . Damn it, I would have been at every appointment! I would have done so many things and you took that from me." He barely held himself together. This sucked. He wanted to go home and drink himself stupid.

Truthfully, what he wanted to do was go home and pin the sonogram in his pocket to the refrigerator before settling in on the couch with Hope to watch a movie while he rubbed her feet.

"I was on my way to tell you when I met *her*!"

"And believed I was a cheating loser. Glad you thought so highly of me."

"She said she was your wife!"

"You should have come to me, asked me, given me a fucking chance!" This was not how Brayden imagined *I still love you* would turn out. Everything was going to shit.

"Oh, like you did here today?"

"I had to get back to work . . ."

"It could have waited and you know it."

"All I know, Hope, is that if I didn't walk by your house the other day, if your grandmother hadn't caught me, you never would have reached out. I still wouldn't know about my baby . . . I would still think you hated me for no goddamn reason."

"That's not true—"

"Isn't it? Effie telling you the truth about Chloe wasn't enough to get you to talk to me. Why should I believe you ever had any intention of telling me about the baby?"

"Brayden, stop it." He knew he was right. Hell, Effie all but confirmed it when she said Hope didn't give second chances. Well, maybe he wouldn't either.

"No. God, Hope. You must have known what this would feel like. To be treated like your fucking sperm donor." There it was. The root of the rage that had been building since he saw her on that exam bench. If he was a different man, a less persistent one, then she would have kept his baby from him. He would be no different to his kid than his dad, sperm-donor-number-whatever, was to him. That was something he wasn't sure he could ever forgive her for. Regardless of her change of heart, regardless of her email. That kernel of truth planted in the back of his mind like a cancer cell waiting to multiply. He'd never be able to be one hundred percent certain that Hope wanted him to be a true father to their baby. She'd said she loved him, but how could that be true? This wasn't how you treated someone you loved. It just wasn't.

"I'm sorry I kept my past from you, but you had no right to keep this from me."

"I know," Hope whispered, tears in her eyes. "I'm so sorry that I hurt you."

Brayden wanted to believe her, but just as she'd once written that she couldn't trust herself not to blindly accept apologies in light of his transgressions, he felt the same. He took a deep breath, scouring the parking lot.

"Where's your car?"

"I walked."

"That's like five miles round trip."

"So?" Brayden gestured to the swell of Hope's stomach that looked much smaller beneath her baggy T-shirt. "I'm pregnant, not an invalid."

Something about hearing her say it, confess it, put words to it—*I'm pregnant*—stirred a primal ache in his chest. His heart yearned to wrap her in his arms, put his hands on her belly, and feel his baby kick and squirm. It made him want to veto each other's baby names and paint one of the extra bedrooms a gender-neutral green with woodland creatures. It made him want to be a dad, to be whole and happy. But listening to his heart brought him more pain than joy in the past.

He looked at the darkening sky. She wouldn't make it home before sunset. "Get in," he commanded before moving around to the driver's side. Hope looked at him over the hood.

"Hope Lilac Thatcher get in the damn car, please." She didn't budge. Shame or guilt or pain wobbled her lip, but he couldn't hold her hurt right now. He only had space for his own at the moment. "Just let me drive my baby home."

Thankfully, Hope climbed into the passenger seat. She noted the manila folder that rested on the center console and looked at Brayden, eyes full of questions.

"My divorce was finalized yesterday."

"How?" Hope's voice was the softest he'd ever heard it.

"I gave her what she wanted, so I could finally be with you."

Not that it mattered now.

23

Theo was keen to experience life without planning it out first, happy to see where he ended up. Normally that would look like experimenting with dates and food and conversations, exploring a new partner's body, seeing what brought her pleasure, and more or less throwing himself into something until he was engrossed in it.

But not with Effie.

The sheer will of her mind kept him not quite at arm's length, but definitely scouring the perimeter to her inner workings. She wasn't as shy about being close to him anymore, in fact, if she surprised him with any more of those breathtaking, gut-churning kisses, he'd have a very hard time not creating a PowerPoint presentation to appeal to her logical sensibilities about why they should just consummate their relationship already. He wanted to worship her in that way. But even he could acknowledge that doing things his way hadn't created that soulmate bond he searched for. If nothing else, every new step with Effie felt important, and it wasn't just from her side.

And if they'd learned anything from Hope and Schilling, it was that slow was okay, boundaries were necessary, and honesty, however difficult, was crucial. Theo almost felt bad that his best friend and Effie's closest relative had given them such a good example of what *not* to do lately. Even if the love they both saw there was real enough to strangle.

Effie leaned against him on his sofa while they watched a movie. He couldn't have summarized the plot if he tried. He'd barely taken his eyes off her long enough to see who starred in it. From his angle, he could only see the tip of her nose and the fan of her lashes that extended past her brow. Theo found himself constantly wondering what she was thinking—ironic given his advice for her to get out of her own head.

He pressed a kiss to her temple. "What time is it?" she mumbled like she had been on the verge of sleep. She leaned across Theo to the side table where her watch lay, having taken it off while they made cookies earlier that afternoon. Theo's were acceptable; Effie's were melt-in-your-mouth delicious.

Theo couldn't help but notice the enticing curve of her backside while she draped across him to retrieve her timepiece.

"Why? Got another hot date?" he joked, scooping Effie into his lap. To his surprise, she didn't resist or retreat. He'd taken to sweetly, cautiously testing the boundaries of intimacy in the last week. Though she took a steadying breath, she sat there happily and draped her arms around his neck. She eyed his hair like she wanted to run her fingers through it. She resisted. Only when she seemed content to stay put did he wrap an arm around her waist to settle a hand on her hip. She sparked at his touch and it was utterly endearing.

"Is that your not-so-subtle way of asking if I'm seeing other people?" Effie let her fingers wander to his temples, but she pulled them back at the last second.

"Dare," he whispered in her ear. She did her best not to smile, which endeared him even more. She locked eyes with him as she let her fingers brush through his hair. It felt better than it should have, and he felt akin to a cat as he leaned into her touch.

Theo shrugged, trying his best to ignore his building desire. "I'm not seeing anyone else."

"Neither am I," Effie said, and Theo waited for whatever she held back. It thoroughly confused him why she wouldn't just tell him what she wanted. She kissed him instead, her fingers still tangled in his hair. She was getting good at the daring.

"That's nice to know," Theo said, teasing out the moment, playing relationship chicken at this point. He wasn't sure why it mattered, but he wanted her to say it first. "So?"

"So," Effie breathed. Theo waited. "I want to be your girlfriend."

"I want that too." He captured her lips with his and damn if nothing else mattered, not even Schilling poised to throw a pillow at them from the other end of the couch. A smile tugged at Theo's cheeks, interrupting their kiss.

"That should be sweet, but I feel nauseous," Schilling asserted while he tried to focus strictly on the movie and not on the fact that Theo was fighting an erection with his incredibly beautiful girlfriend in his lap.

Effie stifled a giggle and slid into the space beside him. "Sorry, Schilling."

"It's fine, but maybe canoodle in your bedroom?" Schilling offered, head jerking to Theo's open room. Theo wondered if Schilling saw

Effie tense—if he realized why it would be a big step to take her to his bed.

Theo rose and slapped Schilling on the shoulder as he passed into the kitchen. He was sorry too. His friend needed to crash until he got his certificate of occupancy at the house. Being out of the condo within twenty-four hours of finalizing his divorce was one of the stipulations Chloe had weaseled her way into. Just for spite.

Theo started the kettle but watched as Effie slid closer to Schilling. Without saying a word, she wriggled both her hands around his and held tight. They sat there for a long moment, and Theo noticed how Schilling's shoulders dropped, and how the tension in his jaw released. It was like watching a hypnotist, but it was just Effie, ebbing the tide of the man's unwieldy emotions.

"You're good at that," Schilling said, and he placed his hand on top of Effie's.

"So I've been told," Effie cooed, and Theo admired her all over again. Something about her ease and calm, regardless of whatever spun in her mind, had people around her steadying on their feet. She brought the ground to meet them. "I'm sorry I couldn't tell you about everything sooner."

Schilling shook his head. "I get it. We're good. I promise."

Effie threw her arms around Theo's friend and whispered something unintelligible in his ear. Whatever it was had him belly laughing and squeezing her back all the tighter before they released the embrace and Schilling tousled Effie's messy bun.

Theo tried to act like he wasn't interrupting when he brought her back a cup of tea. He settled in beside her as she scooped it up greedily.

"Ah, my little tea goblin," Theo joked as she inhaled the steam, eyes nearly rolling back in her head. He liked the way *my* sounded.

"I think I need a shirt or something that says that now," Effie replied. "But I do have to go after this one. It's my night to cook dinner with Hope."

They both cast quick glances at Schilling, who only slightly bristled at the mention of his baby's mother. "She's still going to go tomorrow, isn't she?"

"I have been given permission to confirm. She will be there at three o'clock." Effie waited a long moment before asking, "Will you go?"

"Honestly, I don't know. You have permission to tell her as much."

Effie nodded, but Theo noted the way she clenched her teeth. She clearly didn't like being their go-between. Theo wondered how often she did that—stuffed down what she felt or thought to make things easier for other people. He hoped he'd catch it if she ever did it for him because he wouldn't want it.

No, Theo wanted transparency. To feel emotions as they came up in a healthy way and to fight when it was warranted. He wanted to be in the moment and never overpower her experience. He wanted . . .

. . . A lot of things. Big things. Little things. Pain, pleasure, and everything in between. He wanted passion and friendship. Love and partnership. And he was finding, maybe too quickly, maybe too brazenly, and definitely too dangerously if you asked her, that he wanted all of those things with Effie. He just knew it.

The sky was blue.

24

Hope sat on a picnic blanket spread out by a quiet pond. It was her favorite patch of green space between the Proprietor's Burying Ground and the larger expanse of gravestones in the South Cemetery. In truth, there was no South Cemetery, it was just the name given to the collection of five public and private graveyards that abutted one another in this part of town. Her fascination with such places led to many assumptions that she dabbled in the occult. She'd been all too eager to prove to Brayden that they weren't eerie or sad. In fact, she often felt like they were brimming with life. Brayden hadn't been fond of that opinion when she shared it, but he'd come to see it her way.

The memory warmed Hope almost as much as the sunlight that crested the church steeple in the distance. It seemed like a lifetime ago, even though it was only this time last year that she invited Brayden to her favorite spot in town for a walk amongst the dead.

They first met at an author event at the largest indie bookstore in the area. She'd been asked to do a reading from her first book.

Apparently, Brayden had been in the store at the time looking for a new novel to dig into. He bought a copy of her book and made sure to introduce himself after her fans dispersed. She remembered playing a little hard to get but reveling in the notes he tucked into the free library box near her house. They were pen pals that way, swapping notes and books, for a few weeks before she finally agreed to meet him in person for a date.

The rest was an easy breeze into love. For her, it was simple to break the plans for celibacy she and Effie had laid out. It felt too good to be in love with the sweet, sensitive man who took her to minigolf courses, playgrounds, bowling alleys, and graveyards for dates that were *fun*. The reason it had taken so long, she thought, for her to tell him she loved him was because nothing felt too serious with Brayden. It felt joyful and goofy and right. It's not that the love wasn't there, but there was no need to label it or think through all it meant.

That kind of levity felt foreign to Hope. She aimed for seriousness in her work, aimed for deep unrelenting truths. But Brayden warmed her, soothed her, showed her you could have the big, beautiful, serious things in life and not take them so seriously that you forgot to enjoy them.

Or at least, he had.

Hope squirmed in her seat. The grand declaration of her email emptied like an echo behind her. The optimism it had carried deflated when she saw how much she'd hurt Brayden. She worried she could never undo the pain she caused, the feeling she'd left him with—as if he was ever just a sperm donor and not the most important person in her life. Hope wished so many things had gone differently, but now she could only try to move forward, one clunky step at a time. Starting today.

Effie told her that Brayden *might* show, but Hope wasn't expecting anything. She wasn't surprised he needed space, but she was determined to keep showing up.

Hope leaned back on her hands and stretched out her neck. Tibby warned her that in the next few weeks she would *really* pop. Hope didn't believe she could pop any more than she had, her belly already giving the subtle impression that she'd shoved a basketball under her shirt, but apparently, there was more room to grow. Sixteen weeks to be exact. So much time and not enough. Not if she wanted things back to where they'd left off with Brayden before they got messy. She desperately wanted to get there before the baby came.

Hope loosed a sigh that turned into a bit of a growl at herself and Chloe, who had to have known what she did by calling herself Brayden's wife. Hope grabbed her sweater from the ground beside her, pressed her face into it, and screamed muffled bloody murder.

"You Thatchers have a lot in common." Hope turned to see Brayden, hands shoved deep in his pockets, standing beside her. "Walked in on Effie screeching Taylor Swift to calm her nerves one time."

Hope offered him a faint smile. "She must have been mortified."

"To say the least." He gestured to the sweater. "You okay?"

"Just hating myself a little today. Chloe too, but mostly me."

Brayden didn't respond but instead settled on the blanket, just out of reach. Hope's breath hitched at the love she could still so clearly see in his eyes. *How could she ever have thought he'd betray her?* The question plagued her at night when she couldn't fall asleep.

The sight of him had her feeling twisted up in knots. If she had handled things differently, he wouldn't be untouchable with more space than she cared to acknowledge between them.

Hope's cheeks flushed and she couldn't stop the tears that escaped. "I'm sorry." She sucked in a breath. "I don't know what to say . . . I don't." Her sinuses blocked up and her eyes burned as they flooded. "I can't help it!" she whined, throwing her hands up in the air absolutely exasperated before gesturing to her swollen belly. "Everything is so screwed up, and it's my fault, and I want to go back in time and confront you about the Chloe thing and stop it all from going to hell."

Brayden crouched before her. "Unfortunately we don't have a TimeWeb."

Hope wept even harder, her words coming out strangled. "Stop quoting my book lore, it's too—too much."

Brayden moved behind her, making himself into a backrest for her to lean against, his strong legs on either side of her hips. He pulled her back into his chest. Hope took a few deep, shuddering breaths as he brushed the hair from her dampened cheeks. "You're not supposed to be making me feel better right now. I'm the one—"A new wave of sobs threatened to break through, and Hope could have cursed out her body for betraying her right now. Pregnancy hormones were not to be trifled with.

"It's okay," he whispered, but she heard the lump that had worked its way into his throat. The last time they'd sat like this was the moment she should have told him about the baby. The moment she chose to say I love you instead.

Brayden's pectorals tightened along with the air in her lungs as he reached a tentative hand over Hope's side like he was deciding if it was safe to rest his hand on her stomach, to hug her like he always did when they sat this way. She didn't dare breathe or move his hand for him. She'd already left him out of so many decisions, she wasn't literally going to force his hand on this too.

Slowly, too slowly to suggest anything but fear, Brayden laid his arm around Hope's middle, his hand landing softly on the stretched cotton of the Keene State T-shirt she wore. She had wanted to be stylish in her pregnancy but alas, tees and leggings were much simpler.

Brayden's fingers curled over her belly, stroking it with a reverence that had her wanting to spin in his arms and steal a kiss beneath the maple trees. She let herself rest on him, let herself believe that it would all be okay. Hope tried desperately not to acknowledge the voice in her head that told her that every afternoon could have felt like this if she hadn't been so goddamn scared. Instead, she let the buzz of bugs in the tall grass and the errant chirps of songbirds remind her to be here now.

"You're wearing my shirt," Brayden observed.

"I'm sorry, it's the only one I have that fits besides my Velaris one."

"Don't be sorry. I, uh . . . it's good." He cleared his throat, and Hope tried not to latch on to the need she felt behind his words.

"Brayden . . ." He tensed as a swift kick met his hand. Hope flinched a little herself. It was a big one. "Bug, settle down please." She smoothed her hand over her stomach in comforting circles. The kicking subsided, but Brayden had already jerked his hand away and shot to his feet. Hope would have fallen over backward if he didn't have the presence of mind to place a hand between her shoulder blades to steady her before he started shaking in what Hope feared was a fit of rage.

Hope spun around to face him. She hated herself even more for the warring emotions painted on his face. "Bug?"

"It's what I've been calling the baby . . ."

"I gathered that," Brayden said through clenched teeth, but he sounded more sad than angry.

Hope got to her feet and met Brayden where he stood. She placed her hands on his chest and took a deep breath with him. "I'm so, so sorry." She took his hand and guided it back to her belly where Bug did somersaults or maybe a full vault performance; it was difficult to discern, but it was definitely some kind of amniotic gymnastics. Hope melted at the smile that it brought to Brayden's face.

"Does that feel weird?"

"Very, but I think in a good way."

Brayden swallowed hard, nodding his agreement. He kept his hand still, gaze fixed on the baby he wouldn't truly see for a few more months. "Bug," he said. "It's weird but I like it."

Hope laughed. He lifted his eyes to meet hers. Hope reached for the nape of his neck and pulled him close. She softly brushed her lips against his. He broke free from the restraint he'd been showing and cupped her face in his hands. He kissed her like he needed it, needed her. Like he could live off her kisses alone.

For a few too-short moments it felt like everything was fixed.

Brayden broke from the kiss first. He ran tense fingers through his hair, while Hope waited for the shoe to drop. "I'm sorry. I shouldn't have done that, not when—"

"Not when you didn't come here to get back together."

Brayden looked at his feet, not wanting to confirm her suspicions like it somehow made it hurt less.

"We could just choose to be happy instead," Hope offered, and the idea seemed so simple that it might be the right one. "Start from here and choose each other. Choose our family." Hope's voice cracked, and she hated how much it made her sound like she was begging.

"I need you to tell me why you stayed away after Effie told you about Chloe. I need to understand."

Fair. Hope owed him that much. She had planned to give him every sordid detail of the fears that drove her to madness when she first suggested they meet here.

She could do it.

She could ignore the fault line forming in her heart and tell him what he needed to know. She could do that for him, especially if she had any hope of ever winning him back.

25

L ouisa, if you tell me one more time he's had croissants in Paris, so these need to be perfect, I'm going to kick you out of my kitchen. Respectfully," Effie scolded as she laminated butter into her pastry dough to get the perfect level of flakiness.

Louisa had the good sense to retreat to the breakfast table where a rack of finished plain croissants let off steam. The ones Effie worked on now would be chocolate.

"I'm sorry," Louisa huffed from her seat at the table. "I just want things to go well."

"I know." Not that a pastry would suddenly make their vagabonding sire put down roots and prioritize his family, but Effie supposed it couldn't hurt.

Louisa brought her forehead to the table and rapped it lightly against the worn wood. "This is the first time he's meeting Hazel," she mumbled.

Ellen took it upon herself to field that one as she entered the kitchen, laptop in hand. She sat beside Louisa and patted her on the back. "Don't worry, she won't remember being disappointed."

"Ellen!" Louisa squealed, shooting upright, her face aghast. "It could be different."

"Right, of course," Ellen said before Louisa replaced her head on the table. Ellen shared a look with Effie that said *what a fairy tale she lives in.* Effie stifled a laugh.

It wasn't funny, of course, to know that someone was going to be utterly below the bar, but it always amused Effie to witness how her two sisters had such different reactions to their father rolling through town.

Louisa always got her hopes up. She peppered him with her updates like they were worthy of being pinned to the refrigerator, and when he didn't share the right amount of enthusiasm for her role as Gypsy Rose in the local musical or her raise or her new car, she would go straight to being dour. Ellen, on the other hand, expected nothing. She always took their father to the back patio for a scotch and a chat that no one was privy to and came back looking resolute in her maintenance of a strained relationship. He would bring expensive gifts for the girls that were not age appropriate in the slightest and would suffer through grating conversations with Pamela.

That is if Pamela allowed him to come at all.

The last time he visited, Louisa was four months pregnant, and he had the audacity to speak ill of Gil who, at the time, was the picture of commitment and affection. It didn't end well for Louisa's dad.

Yet, Louisa still wanted him here, and Effie wondered if it came from a keen awareness that she at least had a chance to improve their relationship, where Effie would always have to guess if her dad would have abandoned them too.

Effie never believed it. It had been a point of contention with her and Pamela for years. Effie couldn't imagine that her father would have ever proven a disappointment. He was too good, too full of curiosity and wonder and ease to let them down like that. Her parents may have been in an *off-again* moment in their relationship when he died, but he never stopped coming around. In fact, he had shared custody. She didn't remember much before the age of five, but for three years, whether her parents were together or not, Effie spent Thursday to Sunday with her father. And then he took his motorcycle to Cape Cod for a few days and came home in a casket.

Sometimes, when she sat alone in her room, the electric kettle warming and a candle that she scented with tobacco, mint, and cloves burning, she felt like she was back in his studio apartment by the railroad tracks, sipping on the chai rooibos tea he loved. She always told her mother how wonderful her time with him was, but she only ever replied *don't get used to it*. How right she'd been.

"You okay?" Ellen asked as she clicked away on her keyboard. She paused only to look Effie in the eye and convey she *was* paying attention.

"Fine, just thinking."

Effie finished forming the chocolate croissants and set the batch that had already risen into the oven. She set a timer and joined her sisters at the table. They rarely breathed the same air for longer than a meal, everyone busy with their own main character arcs. Sometimes Effie worried they took their ties for granted, not mending or strengthening their familial bonds enough with deep conversation and attention. Other times she wished to be an only child or a recluse in the woods to have some peace and quiet. But regardless they were threaded together, through grief, triumph, and family, each taking their turn to play mother hen to the other. Apparently, it was Louisa's turn.

"Thinking about your dad?" Louisa asked, that big sister concern hugging around Effie's shoulders.

"Yeah . . . honestly I wish we could talk about him more." Effie scanned the room making sure Pamela wasn't within earshot. "I know they weren't an item when he died, but sometimes she acts like he didn't exist, or it's too painful to talk about him."

"That's probably because it is," Ellen admitted. "We lived with him for like a year or two before you were born."

"I don't remember that," Louisa said.

"You wouldn't, but I remember bringing Effie home from the hospital. It was the only time I felt like we had a family like everyone else." Ellen looked to Effie. "He was a good guy. I liked him. A lot. He used to tuck me in at night while you were wailing for your next bottle, and he'd tell me stories. Not like he'd pull a book from the shelf, but he'd come up with them on the spot. These super intricate, wildly imaginative tales about dragons and warrior princesses and magic. I wished I remembered them after he passed. I would have told them to you every night."

"Why have you never mentioned those before?" Effie asked, totally taken aback by the realization that her dad had acted like a father to her sisters too. It had her picking at the lace edge of her apron.

"Because I don't like to add to your grief. He wasn't really mine to lose."

"Of course he was." It came out softer than she intended. "Biology isn't the only thing that makes a family."

Ellen shrugged. "You say that now, but I don't know, I think you might have felt differently if I shared it sooner. I don't know. Our pathetic excuse for a father will be here any minute and I—this time I didn't want you believing for one second that you got the raw end of the deal. I would take your dad every day, even if I only got to have him for a short while, over mine who will never change."

Louisa stormed out at that, evidently having had enough dad-bashing for the evening. Effie moved to follow her, but Ellen held a hand to hers. "She'll be fine. She's always had a harder time accepting things that are painfully true."

Effie squeezed Ellen's hand. "Thank you."

"If you ever want to talk about him, come find me. I don't remember a lot, but I remember the good stuff. I didn't realize his loss still weighed on you so much."

"I'm not sure it's a thing that will ever go away."

Ellen nodded thoughtfully, though Effie knew their experiences with grief were vastly different. "So, are you out there breaking Thatcher curses? Or will this Theo character need a stern talking to when he finally dares to show his face?"

Effie stifled a laugh. "I'm cautiously optimistic. About him and Brayden."

"Glad to hear it."

Ellen turned her attention back to her laptop, typing wildly. "What are you working on?" Effie asked, never having given much thought to what Ellen did with her time. Six years difference felt like eons between sisters, so they didn't gab much. Ellen had always acted more like another caregiver in Effie's life. Maybe that could change too.

"I'm coding a new medical chart system for the hospital, so it's easier to cross-reference private care appointments with hospital data and stay current on patient notes, medications, and follow-ups."

"Sounds challenging and impressive."

Ellen laughed. "Challenging, maybe. I miss coding for Netflix's algorithm honestly. That was way more fun."

"Your brain is absolutely gigantic, isn't it?"

"Probably about as big as your heart, Effie." Ellen side-eyed her in a knowing way as Effie left the kitchen, egg timer in hand.

She found Dorothea and Beatrice in the hobby room. Aunt Bea put the finishing touches on a portrait of Grams. She swept her brush in delicate, deliberate strokes as she often did when she wanted to amplify the painting without taking it too far. Effie sank into the arm-chair that Issa perched on and stroked the bird's head. "You two know he'll have to walk right past here when he arrives?"

"So long as we're not in that foyer, we'll be safe for a bit."

"Cowards," Effie teased, the sensation of cottage cheese on her tongue screwing up her face.

"Doesn't pay to be snarky, does it?" Grams chided, brow bunched.

"Stop frowning, I'm doing your eyebrows."

Dorothea smoothed her brow. The smile she donned next was Effie's favorite. The one that brought the ripe apples of her cheeks flush with the folds of her laugh lines and hid the edges of her acorn-hued irises in squinty joy.

"We could just close the door. It's an old house. We could feasibly be stuck inside with a broken lock," Effie mused, the intentions of wielding her heart against the impending doom of the night replaced by a deep desire to do anything else.

It was Beatrice's turn to reprimand Effie with a glare.

The doorbell rang and Louisa skidded by the open hobby room door within seconds. She gushed a welcome and the crinkle of packages met Effie's ears. *More gifts.* If any one of the Thatcher women had a love language of receiving gifts, Ed Norton might have a very different reputation. Unfortunately for him, they weren't so easily bought.

Effie stiffened as Louisa hovered by the door, her arm looped through Ed's. Effie thought he looked shorter than she remembered, only standing an inch or two above Louisa, his thick grey hair coiffed like he stepped out of a cologne ad. His blue eyes were captivating, and the cut of his sleek, olive-green dress shirt hugged his broad shoulders and trim midsection. He had the sleeves rolled to reveal his strong, veined forearms.

"Edward, good to see you," Grams said. "We'll be with you in a moment, just finishing up a piece." She gestured to Bea who grinned in greeting before returning to her work.

Louisa raised her brows at Effie. "Hi." Louisa huffed, appalled Effie couldn't muster more.

"Ladies, lovely to see you again," Ed said, his Irish lilt making it ever more clear why Pamela had been putty in his hands.

Louisa and Ed slipped away, and Effie thought she'd recognize his back anywhere.

The table strained under piles of food. The spread gave the impression that Thanksgiving Day had arrived. A roasted turkey sat front and center flanked with rosemary sprigs and lemon slices. Quick breads Effie had in the freezer were sliced and steaming on their platters.

Green beans, boiled baby onions, mashed potatoes, honeyed ham, and two different salads took up the scant space left after Louisa had set the table with their finest plates and polished silver like they were having Christine McVie, Dolly Parton, and the Pope for dinner and not Ed.

Everyone was already seated when Pamela strode in beneath the twinkle of the thirty-light crystal chandelier. Her hair curled into soft waves that she pinned back on one side like a starlet from the nineteen forties. Dark denim stretched over her gym-perfected curves like a second skin, while the severe scoop of a worn Fleetwood Mac T-shirt left one shoulder bare. Effie admired her mother's perfectly painted face and pitied it all the same.

Ed let out an impressed whistle. "Pam, you haven't aged a day."

"Just trying to keep up with you," Pamela quipped, but there was a bite to her tone. If Ed noticed, he didn't let on. She took her seat beside Ellen, the image of unrelenting.

Ellen leaned in, her voice an exasperated whisper that Effie hoped didn't travel past her own ears. "Are you not wearing a bra?"

Pamela shrugged before smiling sweetly at Ed and Louisa. "So, what are we talking about?"

Pamela began filling her plate so the rest followed suit. When Ed was in town Pamela ran the show, even if it meant stealing the spotlight from the one person who actually wanted it. Louisa's shoulders rounded with anxiety, but she said, "I was showing him pictures from Hazel's last birthday."

"Yeah? Did you show him the one where she drooled—literally—on the gold bracelet she outgrew in a month?"

"It was meant to be a keepsake," Ed explained. "You understood, right, sweetie?"

"Of course, it's in her hope chest," Louisa chimed, though Effie distinctly remembered Louisa scowling at the useless and expensive gift, wondering if she should hock it and go get diapers.

"Children need affection, security, reliability, Ed. Not keepsakes."

"Here we go." Ellen huffed before pouring her wineglass full to the brim. Effie nudged her glass toward her sister and Ellen obliged with a hefty pour.

"Keepsakes are important," Tibby offered. "They give us something to connect to when we're apart." Ed cast her a grateful nod. Effie thought it a valiant effort, but Pamela was an argumentative demon, one that needed a formal exorcism to back down.

"I suppose when all you are is apart, a keepsake is all you get."

"I'm not built like you, Pam. I don't grow roots, or bleach them."

Shots fired. Effie looked to Hope who had the right idea in keeping her eyes on her plate. She had an uncanny ability to blend into the shadows when she didn't want to participate. Effie envied her that.

She also envied Grams's and Aunt Bea's stoicism on nights like this. They played it so close to the chest, that you never knew what they thought of Ed's visits. Effie, on the other hand, took every word, every jab, every flinch from her sister to heart. She felt it all, packed it in a bag, and flung it over her shoulder to carry herself even though she had no business claiming it. Not when she'd never been able to do anything to fix it.

"And I suppose your latest child bride keeps it au naturel?"

"Samantha was twenty-six," Ed growled. Effie's nose scrunched until Grams told her to check her face with a look.

"And what's this one? Older or younger than your two daughters?"

"Mom, stop. It doesn't matter," Ellen asserted, fed up with the immaturity on both sides. Effie never asked what Ellen thought of Ed's second wife. She didn't last long enough to bring around, but her social media pages, when Louisa showed them to her, were as good as reality television.

"Doesn't it? You two have always wanted a better relationship with him. Well, here's your chance. Ask your dear old dad why he has to be such a perv. Childhood trauma? Identity crisis? If I remember right it's most likely small di—"

"Enough!" Effie was as alarmed as everyone else that the outburst had come from Ed. He was known to hurl a few insults, insert himself in matters he had no business judging, but he never raised his voice. "I am tired, Pamela. You want to know how old my wife is? She's forty-eight. Not that I owe any of you an explanation about how I live my life or why."

Effie watched Louisa sink into her seat, and suddenly it felt like there were too many bodies around the table, all playing at being a family but not very convincingly. The words bubbled up her throat, every impulse telling her to defend her sisters, take her turn at being mother hen.

Dare.

"I don't think that's true," Effie whispered. Ellen cast her a glance, a subtle shake of her head telling her to *drop it*. But Effie thought it was enough of this too. "I think you owe Ellen and Louisa an explanation for why you chose the world over them."

Something in Ed softened like Effie had unwittingly found the trapdoor to his well-kept secrets. It was brief, almost too quick to notice, but Ed's eyes shifted to Ellen. Another quick shake of her head.

Don't go there. Effie wondered if Louisa saw before Ed simply said, "I showed up the only way I knew how."

"With a checkbook," Pamela scoffed.

Ed's jaw ticked in irritation. "You weren't complaining when it put them through college, were you?" Ed turned to face Louisa who flushed in an effort to keep from crying. "I meant what I said. I don't put down roots, but I am truly sorry that it has caused you such disappointment. That good enough for you there, Effie?"

Effie resisted the urge to cower. They'd heard different iterations of the same thing all their lives. A bird that couldn't be caged. If only he realized it made it sound like he viewed their personhood, their affection, as a prison and not something to come home to when his wings were tired.

26

Is it me, or does it feel like there's more to the whole Ed story than we thought?" Hope mused from her perch on Effie's bed. Her head hung over the edge, feet propped on the wall as she stared at the swirls of plaster that spanned the ceiling. Her gaze dropped to Effie, sprawled like a starfish on her faux sheepskin rug.

"What do you mean?" Effie asked, her voice quiet. Hope knew her dear cousin was still reeling. No one hated confrontation more than Effie. After her call for an explanation, dinner was tense. It culminated in a fantastic explosion of rage and pent-up resentment from Pamela that scared Issa into frantically flying about and nearly colliding with Ed's nest of perfect hair. Effie and Hope retreated shortly thereafter, vowing they'd scrape caked-on food for hours and endure dish duty later rather than stay another minute in the powder keg.

Maybe everything that happened with Brayden had Hope seeing the other side of things for the first time, but she had the distinct awareness that there were two sides to a broken heart. "In a perfect world Ed would have wanted to stay home, provide in ways that didn't require him to travel the world, but what if . . . I don't know. It's stupid."

Hope wasn't sure she could make such a leap. Not when it questioned the integrity of the stories Pamela had been telling about Ed their whole lives. She didn't want to burst Effie's bubble if she hadn't dared consider a different reality herself. But Effie sighed. "What if my mother pushed him away?"

Hope spun her feet down off the wall and came to sit cross-legged on the bed. Effie's question meant that they could travel down this road and look at their supposed curse from a new angle. "Maybe he never really wanted kids and your mom thought she could change him. Or maybe she gave him an ultimatum or wasn't willing to include him in planning their life together?"

The latter felt painfully true for Hope. She was disturbingly close to causing her unborn child the same kind of heartache she and Louisa and Ellen had endured because she never asked Brayden what he wanted. Never included him in the reality when it showed up in two pink lines. She had almost ruined her chances of a real family. Not that she and Brayden were back together. *Not yet.*

She hadn't wanted to know Brayden's side of things or how he wanted their relationship to move forward. She didn't want him to weigh-in on the being growing in her belly. She was selfish, short-sighted. It was everything she'd confessed to him at the park about why she didn't give him a chance. Why she kept the baby a secret. It was the most shame she'd ever felt, and it still formed a greasy pool in her chest.

Effie rolled onto her stomach and propped herself on her elbows.

"My mother does like to be the center of attention," Effie mused. "I wouldn't be surprised if she wanted all of him or none of him."

"But is that fair? If there are kids involved?"

"I don't think so. But Ellen wasn't exactly planned. And whatever mom thought families should look like didn't jive with Ed's vision, I'd guess. And when he didn't bend to her vision, they probably spiraled and totally collapsed under the weight of Louisa's arrival." Effie huffed and buried her face. It was more words in a row than Hope had heard Effie utter in a while. She didn't envy whatever cocktail of flavors poured over Effie's tongue as she said them.

"I suppose I know what that kind of stubbornness feels like," Hope said, hands soothing the squirming beast beneath her naval. Bug seemed an inadequate nickname as of late, given the unrelenting martial arts and acrobatics that began whenever Hope dared be still.

The pity in Effie's gaze stung like a paper cut. Hope knew she'd brought this on herself in more ways than one. "Maybe we're the problem. That's the Thatcher curse—not knowing when—"

"There is no goddamn curse," Dorothea huffed from the open doorway, a tray of tea and croissants in hand. Effie hurried to take the tray and set it on the rug with her while Grams lowered into the rocking chair Effie had saved from the front porch after everyone thought it was ready for the dumpster. Hope shimmied from the bed joining Effie on the floor, her back resting against its edge.

"Tell that to Mom, Aunt Tibby, Louisa, and Ellen," Effie quipped. "Though Ellen seems cautiously optimistic about Brayden and Theo."

"You should always be optimistic when it comes to love," Grams said. She closed her eyes and leaned back into the chair, gently swaying back and forth, her slippered feet barely reaching the ground.

"They still arguing down there?" Hope dared to ask.

"Ed and Ellen are having their scotch," Grams answered. "And I am communing with my two favorite granddaughters."

"You're not supposed to say that," Effie scolded despite her amusement.

Grams shrugged, eyes still closed. Hope had the sense she was the sage and they were the disciples ready to be passed the torch. But only silence followed.

Hope poured the tea, filling the two cups Grams brought for her and Effie. They nibbled on the chocolate croissants casting inquisitive looks at each other, waiting to see what Grams would say next.

Dorothea took a deep breath, her chest rising beneath her crimson dress with its white polka dots. She folded her leathery hands in her lap and finally opened her eyes. They squinted first at Effie then at Hope. "How's the book coming?"

"It's going to the printer this week. Ready to release next month," Hope said proudly. Sometimes it still amazed her that she lived this dream. She admonished herself for taking it for granted when everything else seemed to be going awry. She wondered if that was Grams's point.

"And did you do that by yourself?"

Hope stumbled over her words. The short answer was *no*, but it felt more complicated than that. "I wrote all the words, developed the characters, created the world. So the writing I did alone, but my editor helped polish it, Effie bounced ideas around with me. A bunch of beta readers gave me feedback. My agent got the deal for the trilogy, so I was able to be paid to write the second and third books."

"Could you have done all those things yourself?" Grams continued, and Hope wondered where she was going with all this. Effie's twisted brow told Hope she wondered too.

"I suppose. Self-publishing is big right now. I would have probably hired a cover artist, but beyond that, the actual formatting, printing, marketing, and sales would have been up to me. I could have done it, but it would have taken far more confidence than I have to see it through on my own." Hope shuddered at the thought of having to blaze her own trail online and convince the world she had a right to be published without the backing of her team. It was a daunting, terrifying prospect, one she felt relieved and grateful that she'd avoided.

"But, in the way you chose to move forward—waiting for the right agent and publisher—you get to live in the space you thrive in. The writing. And they handle the stuff that's too heavy for your hands? They make it easier for you to be great?"

"Absolutely," Hope replied.

"And you trust them to take care of you?"

Hope's shoulders softened, a smile tugging at her lips. "Yes."

"And you surrender full control when you've done your part, so the vision you have can come to life in the best and easiest way possible?"

"Yes," Hope said again, this time her smile on full display. Effie seemed to snag the thread of the conversation too, based on the twinkle in her eye as she smirked at Dorothea.

"Right then." Dorothea sighed, planting her hands firmly on the armrests. "We're not solitary creatures. We hens may flock together, but sometimes we need a protector, a confidante, someone we trust implicitly to hold our interests as sacred as their own. But it goes both ways." Dorothea stood on aching knees. "And sometimes we just need a good strong *cock*."

"Grams!" Effie blushed, her high-pitched squeal so obviously the reaction Dorothea aimed for.

"You're too easy, Effie, dear," Grams teased before shuffling toward the door. "I'll let you know when the coast is clear."

Hope bit back her laughter as Effie rolled her eyes and chomped into her croissant. Through her flakey mouthful she said, "I guess we were onto something."

"Seems like it."

"So what are you going to do about it?"

Hope gave a dramatic sigh. *What was she going to do?* Brayden had heard her out. He didn't mock her fears or blame her for having them. He didn't even seem to judge her for acting on them. He only seemed sad that she hadn't trusted him with them.

If she took Grams seriously, she would have to admit that the life she wanted, the vision she held of backyard picnics and a family with Brayden, was only possible if she was vulnerable and persistent. She'd been rejected ninety-seven times before she landed her agent. She could weather Brayden's rejections if it meant showing him how much he meant to her. Hope would choose him again and again until she demonstrated that he wasn't auditioning for a role in her life, but that he already had it—as co-parents, partners, lovers. Whatever the case, they would hold each other's dreams and bring them to fruition together. Even if it meant Hope wouldn't end her nights in his arms.

Rejection had rarely scared her. But not trying for what she wanted certainly did.

Brayden popped the caps off a couple of beers with the Leatherman multi-tool that had become a permanent fixture in his front pocket since he started renovating the house. He handed one to Theo who lounged against the wall, splattered in a pale green paint. Brayden sat beside him with a sigh, looking around the room. He was grateful Effie was busy and he could steal his friend for the night. It felt like weeks since they'd done anything just the two of them—even if house projects weren't their standard Friday night fare.

The maple floors had been restored, a few dark stains still mingled with the lighter tones of the raw wood, but Brayden thought the blemishes added character. The slight sheen of the wax over top preserved the restoration and showcased the beauty of the house's scars. Tall white baseboards lined the floor, and Brayden was grateful for Theo's steady hand. He'd cut in around the trim and intricate crown molding that Brayden had already hung. They were pristinely painted in an antique white, and not a drop of the green from Theo's brush tarnished those trim boards. It was impressive.

Brayden had to take his wins where he could get them.

A couple of months ago, he thought it would be him and Hope sharing a drink at the end of a long painting day. Instead, Theo helped him pick a shade of green that was warm and inviting and could be combined with whatever blues or pinks or yellows made their way into the room after the baby arrived.

Empty paint cans littered the drop cloth piled in the corner. Theo had shoved them aside when they finished the last coat, insisting they got in the way of Brayden seeing the full picture of the finished room—a room always destined to be a nursery. He'd thought it the first time he saw the house after he bought it at auction, sight unseen.

But this wasn't how he imagined decorating it.

It wasn't how he imagined moving in.

The certificate of occupancy had arrived at Theo's apartment the day before. Brayden should have been thrilled, but instead, he was barraged with the pang of heartache and loss of the life he'd always imagined. It didn't help that he had very few belongings—most left behind to Chloe and the condo—and needed to furnish the nearly four-thousand-square-foot house within a matter of a couple months to be a home worthy of his baby.

"I'm sorry it's not someone else here beside you," Theo said, and Brayden felt the sincerity in his voice. *Someone else.* Once it had been Chloe, when this whole project started. Then it was Hope. Now it would be Brayden's baby, however frequent that was. He'd need another lawyer soon probably . . .

"I'm not," Brayden remarked and it was only half a lie. Theo was his best friend, and it was infinitely better to have him wielding a paint-brush beside him than to be there alone. He couldn't bear the pity in his moms' eyes to allow them to come help, though they'd been fairly insistent. "I never have to wonder how you feel about me. That's uh . . . that's huge for me."

Theo took a pensive sip, nodding his understanding. Something about the fleeting nature of friendships and relationships left Brayden uneasy. Like everyone teetered on the precipice of becoming people he used to know—except Theo.

Brayden scrubbed his face.

Fall in love, get married, start a family, be happy. It seemed easy enough way back when. What he hadn't realized was that the road to bliss was littered with emotional minefields. Only Theo paralleled Brayden's journey—always en route together. He knew, regardless of their romantic relationships or families, that would never change. He was the brother Brayden never had.

"I love you," Brayden said thinking it might sound weird or out of the blue as they sat there drinking local IPAs on the floor of his baby's room in the mini mansion he'd live in alone for the foreseeable future.

But instead, Theo wrapped his arm around Brayden's shoulder and tugged him tight against his side. "I love you too, bud." And that's why Theo was his best friend. "Will I get to be Uncle Theo?"

"Seems like you'll be Bug's only uncle. Hope you're up to the task."

"Don't I look ready?" Theo asked opening his arms wide to highlight his commitment to Bug, already evident in his paint-covered clothes and light-hearted smile.

"Touché." Brayden laughed. He looked around the room, the reality of needing furniture making him uneasy. "Do you think it would be weird to ask Hope for help getting furniture? I mean, she's probably going to be here a lot and I want this place to feel like a home. Not like a bachelor's house."

Theo gave him a loaded look before innocently asking, "Do you think it would be weird?"

Brayden shrugged. *Probably.* There was still so much that needed to be said, so much he needed to understand about how they got here. He wasn't sure what the future looked like, but it needed to include more than the futon and IKEA dresser that occupied his storage unit.

If Brayden had learned anything over the last four years it was that he had to stop making plans. They always unraveled. No, Hope, his baby, his home, they had to be taken day by day. They had to be played by ear, if only to keep him from falling apart all over again.

27

Effie wandered around Glitter & Glue with a cart of her own during a lull. Louisa needed a number of items for the ball and was desperate to find them locally, so whenever people asked about the decor or the food or the dance cards she could point to an artisan or business from Portsmouth instead of directing friends and family to an Amazon link.

The rows of ribbons were a rainbow of colors and patterns, but the white lace Effie wanted for Pamela's tablecloth project evaded her. It should have been restocked a few weeks ago, but she struggled to find it. "Basil, could you check the inventory for the brocade lace ribbon?"

"Can't you check it with your eyes?"

"I need to know if we sold it all, I'm not finding it!"

"Oh fine," Basil said, sighing, and Effie heard the clink of knitting needles against the laminate countertop.

"Thank you!" Effie crooned as she rounded the corner to a different aisle, grabbing packages of paper doilies and parchments for her treats, and adding them to her cart. It already brimmed with bolts of cotton, heavy cardstock with an iridescent shimmer, floral foam, and wire, along with mountains of gold paint. She grabbed a couple of specialty icing tips from the rack before her, intent on trying a few new designs with her shortbread frosting and her cupcakes.

"Computer says there should be six fifty-yard rolls!"

Effie scowled but turned her cart back toward the ribbon. "Then where—" Effie spotted them at the bottom row. The spool was weighty as she turned it over in her hand pondering before adding it and four more to her cart. She rolled her haul to the register and Basil's reproachful stare.

"Sometimes I just need to be certain they're there before I can see them," Effie explained. She began ringing herself up, applying her employee discount to her purchases. "Also, that is a very pretty, very expensive ribbon. We should be putting it at eye level, not buried at the bottom. All the high-end materials should be at eye level."

Basil shrugged. "Then make it happen."

Effie wasn't sure she wanted to do that. It didn't feel like hers to decide, but her boss had always appreciated her initiative. Maybe she could improve the store in little ways. Be confident in that. Effie let the thought wither and turned to Basil. "Did you find a date yet?" Basil's sigh could have extinguished a campfire.

"Romance is apparently dead," he said brusquely.

"Oh, don't say that. That's not you." Effie tutted. "It's not dead, it's . . . it takes a keen eye maybe. An openness that's hard for people, but it's still there."

"So, you're to blame," Basil said with a laugh. "My romantic side has waned to allow yours to flourish. Balance and all that."

"Don't be ridiculous." But Effie wondered if there was some cosmic scale that kept track. She thought probably not. Theo insisted the universe was a flow of well-being, you either joined it or resisted it. Effie thought it a wonderfully elegant and simplistic belief. It was one she adopted almost immediately and it felt wonderful doing so. Basil might be in a period of resisting. "It will pass," Effie said sweetly.

"What will?"

"Your doubts. You'll be swooning again soon. Unless you're not Basil anymore. In which case I demand the pod person that's invaded your body to evacuate immediately."

Effie grinned at Basil who shook his head in amused frustration. "You're so weird," he teased. "But you're also probably right."

Effie finished piling her goodies into a bag with a prideful smile. Maybe she was becoming more of a romantic. At least a less closeted one. She didn't want to see Basil's eagerness to find love extinguished, especially since she had no doubts that he had helped her get excited about finding Theo. *That* she would always be grateful for.

"Louisa, where is all the furniture?" Ellen barked, laptop in one hand, a steaming cup of coffee in the other.

"I needed to clear it out for dancing. We've been over this." Louisa returned her attention to her clipboard and Hope stifled a giggle at the rage she saw in Ellen's gaze.

"Louisa," Ellen huffed through gritted teeth. "The ball is still like six weeks away."

"What's your point?" Louisa asked and Hope was tickled that she truly didn't see it as an issue, though Hope had to admit she was nearly as irate as Ellen when she came downstairs to read in the great room after a particularly grueling outlining session for her next series. But Louisa put her to work instead.

Hope held the smart end of a tape measurer across the room. "Thirty-five feet," she read off, and Louisa noted it on her clipboard. Ellen growled her frustration.

"Just go work in your private wing of the house," Louisa suggested with a dismissive wave of her hand. "Or at the breakfast table."

"I can't, you've littered it with swatches and sheet music and font samples."

"Well, dump it all in the box I left there."

"Louisa, you're being even more obtuse than usual about this."

Hope tensed at the accusation. Things had been a bit off-kilter between the sisters since their father had visited. "I'm not trying to be obtuse; I'm trying to make this great."

"It's great every year," Hope encouraged. This was Louisa's fantasy, and she wanted to best it year after year. Hope couldn't fault her for that, even if she wasn't entirely certain how emptying the space weeks ahead of time would help. Louisa always needed visual aids, so maybe it had more to do with requiring a blank canvas than anything else.

Hope understood the urge to keep getting better. It's how she felt each time she sat down to write. She never wanted to slip backward, to write less than how she had in a previous work.

Growth was life.

Louisa turned her attention to Hope, walking the end of the tape back into its reel. She held the clipboard out so Hope could see.

"Should we put the musicians in that corner blocking the doors on the right side of the fireplace, or should we go full *Bridgerton* and set them up in a circle in the center of the room?"

"Do you think the space is big enough for that?"

"Wait," Ellen said from the breakfast table where she'd shoved aside the mess. "You're going to have them play inside? They're usually on the back patio."

"Really, Ellen. Keep up. This room is going to be full ballroom this year."

"But there's more space outside. It will be too loud."

"It will be more authentic!" Louisa chirped.

"Authentic to what?" Ellen's gaze shot to Hope who shrugged her shoulders. It was the first she'd heard of it.

"Imagine it. You're in here dancing and flirting and twirling, but you need a breath of fresh air, so you go outside to the garden and patio for a quiet moment alone when you're followed by the brooding gent who's been sipping his whiskey on the outskirts of the dance floor all night. You look into each other's eyes and kiss beneath the starlight." Her eyes were aglow beneath her chocolate-brown fringe of bangs.

"You can't promise starlight. Could be overcast," Ellen mused unhelpfully.

"I can promise twinkle lights! Strung over the whole patio," Louisa snapped.

Hope wasn't sure how much more bickering she could take. Bug agreed with a swift kick. She handed the tape measure back to Louisa who was lost to her battle with Ellen. "Lou, you don't even have a date."

"Where in that scenario did I say it was a date that followed you out?"

"You're getting worked up."

"You're being difficult for no reason."

"You've overturned the entire house!"

Hope slipped out of the great room toward the foyer. She hesitated at the hobby room doors, peering inside. The space was vacant and her favorite plush chair by the window bathed in sunlight. She ducked into the room, pulling the glass doors shut behind her, dulling the sounds of Louisa and Ellen's debate. Hope snuggled into the chair, cracked open her book, and sighed.

She was only three pages in before her thoughts distracted her. Wonderings of Brayden's whereabouts, what he was thinking about the baby, whether he would ever take her back circled her like vultures. She had to see him, had to get more answers. She had to know if she'd lost him forever.

"That morning before we met, I inspected a facility that is home to a lot of confidential dealings. I had to have a special background check before I even went in. When I got there, two guys dressed in all black with guns holstered on their hips escorted me to all of my stops. In some wings, they'd make me look at my feet, lead me into a pitch-black room, and guide me to the extinguishers and AED machines. They'd turn the light on but stand right behind me to make sure I only looked at what I was inspecting. When I finished, they'd turn the light off, instruct me to look at my feet, and guide me back out. I swear they had to have night vision contacts or something because I couldn't see my own nose in there."

Effie laughed from where she lay on Theo's bed and his heart warmed. "No wonder you were so surly that day. Who knew a career in safety could be so covert?"

"Not me." Theo breathed a contented sigh. It felt comfortable laying in bed together. It felt even better that it was at her suggestion when she'd learned he kept all his old yearbooks in his room. She'd thoroughly enjoyed finding photos of him on stage for theater productions and comparing his braced baby face to the man before her. Under normal circumstances, he would have hidden away his awkward phase, but he enjoyed letting Effie see his whole evolution. "Did you really like the song or were you pacifying me?"

Effie huffed. "Trust me, I wouldn't be able to hide my hatred. 'Invisible String' is a great song and only improves my opinion of your queen."

"It makes me think of you now," he said. It was true. Something cosmic was at work bringing him and Effie closer.

"That makes it even better."

He played with her fingers that were intertwined with his. She rested beside him, her head at the foot of the bed while Theo leaned against the pillows at his headboard. Her knees were tucked, so her bare feet could shelter beneath his thigh to keep warm. With their arms stretched, their fingers barely touched. "You're too far away," he said, trying his best not to whine, despite the need for her to be nearer.

Effie rolled her eyes before crawling onto her knees beside him, then scooting into his waiting arm and leaning into his shoulder.

"So," Theo said, not sure how to test the waters without diving full in. He'd had a question on his mind ever since that first craft night. "What does Effie taste like to you?"

Effie sucked in a breath, before letting it loose. "Farro," she whispered. Theo couldn't understand the disappointment that clung to the word. He rested his chin on her head. "Care to explain why that's so frustrating?"

Effie squirmed a little before she continued. "Most of my deepest associations with words were formed when I was little with a very limited palate. And as I got older I realized that a person's name is usually a base note, but once I get to know them better it gets more layered. Brayden, for example tastes like butter. But as I've gotten to know him more there's hints of citrus and dill—bright flavors."

"Okay?" Theo wondered how salted chocolate caramels would evolve as they grew closer, but he didn't ask.

"My mom has made farro my whole life—early association. But it was bland."

"I think farro is a superior grain—nutty, elevated."

"Sure, but bland on its own."

Theo traced circles on her back where his hand rested. She nuzzled farther into his shoulder. He waited for her to say more, but her lips were zippered. "You're not bland, Effie."

"You sound like my therapist," she huffed.

"What else does your therapist say about it?" Curiosity baited him, but he treaded carefully. He hadn't realized that asking about her name was such a minefield, and he didn't want to send her running.

"That feeling like the flavor of my name is missing something—toppings or dressings, a zest or a salt or a spice—probably means I'm not seeing myself fully."

"I'd agree to that," Theo suggested.

"You thought my name sounded like eggplant. Who likes

eggplants?"

"I do!"

"Yeah, breaded with cheese and marinara. Toppings. Even you agree I'm a bland base note." She tried to wriggle free of his grasp, but he held tight.

His lips found the soft waves of her hair again as he mumbled, "You're not. Maybe you're just not a finished recipe yet. You haven't found the special sauce . . . or *maybe*, being a *bland base note* means you get to move through life trying on new identities and always ending up with something mouth-watering."

Theo felt her muscles relax as she sank back into his shoulder. "That's better than my perception."

"And what's your perception?"

"That I'm not interesting enough for a more delicious name."

"That couldn't be further from the truth." He hoped the sincerity translated in the huskiness of his voice.

"You don't know me well enough to know that." A rebuttal rushed to his lips, but he clamped it down. *No use arguing if that's what she believed.*

The crickets sang to them from the green space of the apartment building, a steady calm as Theo curled his fingers into the flesh of Effie's hip and tried to redirect the ship of their conversation. "Tell me something I don't know about you," Theo asked, his desire to uncover all her facets as present as ever.

She was quiet for a long moment before saying, "Sometimes I'm afraid I will die young . . . like my dad . . . I also think pistachio ice cream has to be the most disgusting flavor ever invented."

While both things seemed true, Theo wondered why she felt the need to counter the heavy with the light. Why she didn't let herself live in that first moment. But maybe that was how she kept her balance.

"Your turn," she whispered.

"I worry I won't like myself when I'm older, that I'll always miss being twenty-seven." It was a symptom of enjoying the way Effie looked at him, with admiration and desire. He wondered how long it would last if his jaw gave way to jowls and his hair thinned. Not that he was manifesting any of *that*.

"I don't think that will happen. You're far too self-aware to not keep embracing who you are." Theo snuggled her a little harder. "Something you hate that everyone thinks you should love?" she asked.

"Fireworks. They're loud. They're barely impressive, and they smell terrible. Something you love that you're supposed to hate?"

"Doing my taxes." Theo pulled away and gave her a quizzical look. "It's like a puzzle! Okay, mine are pretty straightforward, but Hope's? I love finding her deductions."

"That's got to be the only left-brained thing about you."

"Probably."

He looked to Effie, every possibility of their future dancing over her impossibly beautiful face. Theo didn't want her believing that eggplant or farro or her personhood lacked flavor and meaning, so he said, "Did I ever tell you about the eggplant?"

"No?" Effie sat a little straighter, crossing her legs in front of her to face Theo. "I assume there's some cosmic message there?"

"You assume correctly."

"Ah, my handsome spiritualist." She said it with such affection, and a hint of self-consciousness like she was taste-testing *my*, as she cupped his cheek then ran her fingers through his hair without a beat of hesitation. He leaned into the touch and almost forgot what he'd wanted to tell her.

"The day I asked you out, I pulled an eggplant card. Fate was telling me to find you."

"Naturally," Effie teased, but he knew she believed in fate as much as he did. He didn't call her on it.

"I looked into it and in European folklore, it is associated with love and romance. They believed placing an eggplant under the pillow of an unmarried woman would make her dream of her future husband." Theo suddenly felt self-conscious about sharing this. Insinuating that he saw himself as fit for that role in her life. If she thought it presumptuous, she didn't let on. She gave Theo one of her wistful smiles and reclaimed her spot against his shoulder.

"I better not find an eggplant under my pillow."

"Never. Wouldn't want to run the risk of you dreaming of anyone but me."

"It's not a very big risk," she mumbled, almost like she wasn't sure she wanted him to hear. "But thanks for making eggplant mean something."

"It wasn't me, it was fate," Theo countered and Effie laughed.

They settled into a comfortable quiet and Theo found himself wanting to freeze time. Effie gauged the darkness at his window. "It's late," she said.

Damn. "I hoped you wouldn't notice." It had recently felt like any amount of time with Effie wasn't enough. She'd been there since long before he'd made them dinner, but he still wanted more. More conversation. More flirting. More of *her*.

Effie traced her finger over Theo's chest and the sparks that radiated from her touch had him hugging her closer. He dropped his lips to hers. "You could stay," he suggested.

Schilling no longer occupied his couch, despite Theo's insistence that he didn't have to trade his place in Theo's apartment for an air mattress in a room that likely still smelled of paint fumes. But Schilling's spirits had lifted after making some big decisions and he wanted to move forward.

But it meant that Theo's home was his again, and he and Effie could canoodle carefree. Not that he had any *specific* intentions for the rest of the night, but he did desperately want her to stay. He already imagined her waking up beside him and it did wondrous things to his heart.

"I could," Effie murmured like perhaps the thought hadn't actually occurred to her. "Do you really want me to?"

Theo pulled back and let the shock of her inquiry color his features. "Do I want you to?" He scoffed then sighed dramatically before tumbling her over onto her back, nuzzling into her neck with a flurry of playful kisses as she squealed with laughter. Theo pressed himself onto his forearms that rested on either side of Effie's head. The weight of his chest pressed into hers and he could feel her every breath. Theo brushed his thumb across her cheek. "I really want you to stay," he said, his voice serious, if not trembling with his desire.

Effie gripped him at the nape of his neck. The electricity that her closeness ignited would never grow tiresome. "Okay, I'll stay." She pulled him into one of her taunting, deep kisses. He could drown in them and die happy. She pulled away, pushing her hand to his chest. "Give me a minute?"

Apprehension was a blow to the gut. *Why did she need a minute? Did he push too far? Was the eggplant too much?* He rolled over so he no longer smothered Effie. She gave him a quick peck on the cheek and hurried toward the door. She eyed his phone that sat charging on the dresser across the room. "Can I borrow that?"

"I'm still amazed you don't have a cell phone."

"I have one, I just don't see the point in using it unless I'm traveling."

Effie shrugged like it was totally sound logic. He gave her the okay and she scooped the phone up, puzzling when it didn't open for her face.

"114477," Theo offered. Her face was a mix of surprise and joy, like he'd given her the code to a treasure trove. She rested her hand on the brass knob but hesitated. Spun around by what looked like nerves, she added, "Stay here." And then she slipped out the door, shutting it behind her.

Theo didn't know what to expect when she returned, but he already missed her warmth beside him. He looked to the other side of the bed. *Her side.* And it was his own nerves that he had to corral or else he'd do something stupid like suggest she just go home after all.

Effie scurried to the entry where she'd hung her bag upon arriving that afternoon. Theo hadn't commented on it—she quite frequently carried a tote with a book, a craft project, and the necessities like her wallet and keys. For the past couple of weeks, she'd packed a few *other things*. Just in case.

She carried the bag to the bathroom on the other side of the apartment, beyond the dark wood cabinets of the kitchen. The penny tiles, not original but an homage to the age of the building, were a balm on her nerves, cooling her from her feet up. She hadn't realized she was on fire. She lifted an arm and sniffed, hoping her anxiety hadn't turned to malodorous sweats. For now, she was safe, but she was keenly aware that their closeness in his bed, the intimate conversation, and the unmentioned possibilities of the evening had triggered her anxiety in a big way. With Theo's phone unlocked, she set to dialing one of six numbers she knew by heart.

The screen lit up and Effie laughed at the contact name already associated with the number. *Schilling's Baby Mama.*

"Hello?" *Right, the number wasn't one Hope knew.*

"It's me," Effie whispered and immediately felt silly for doing so. "I'm at Theo's."

"Is everything okay?"

"I'm staying over . . . I think. I wanted someone to know I wouldn't be home. And, well . . . Hope, I'm nervous."

"Are you planning on having sex with him?"

"No!"

"Then don't be nervous."

"Gee, that's helpful," Effie deadpanned. Her hand reached for a phantom cord. Effie missed the coiled cord of their house phone. Every flirty call had the added benefit of a fidget fixation. *What did you do with your hands when you weren't anxiously twirling a phone cord?* An abysmal circumstance of being Gen Z.

"Effie? Where'd you go?"

"I hate cell phones."

"Okay . . ."

"They're full of the intangible and they make things distant or fake or surface. What if that's all there is anymore? What if nothing is solid and it's all ether and Wi-Fi and 5G coming to gorge our insides and turn us into the robots we're all afraid of?"

"How'd that taste?"

"Fucking terrible." Effie rubbed her hands over her face while iron coated her tongue after a potluck of artificial-sour-apple fake, corn-syrupy surface, and bile-laden gorge. She laid the phone on the white granite countertop and put it on speaker. The walls, painted a deep blue, inched ever closer. Effie leaned over the sink and took a deep breath, before braiding her hair to one side, the too-short strands framing her face in delicate waves.

"It's not just surface. Theo is very real and he cares about you."

"You don't know that," Effie mumbled. She hadn't realized how much she resisted his interest in her. How deep the insecurity ran that he would tire of her or realize she wasn't as fascinating as he initially thought. She'd all but handed him a reason to find her lacking what with her diatribe about being bland—

"What are you doing now?" Hope asked, seemingly trying to divert Effie's attentions from the maelstrom of doubts laying siege to her joy.

"I brought pajamas. I was going to brush my teeth and change and go back to his room, but maybe I should just come home. Maybe this is too much."

"Do you want to come home?" Hope's voice was soft, gentle, perfect for coaxing a jumper back from the ledge.

"No. But, Hope, I know he *wants to*." Effie's confidence waned. She didn't want to disappoint Theo, but she truly couldn't disappoint herself and this was a matter she wasn't willing to budge on. Not yet. Imagining it was any other night getting ready for bed, she brushed her teeth. Her plans to stay continued on autopilot even though her mind raged against her.

"Of course he does," Hope said matter-of-factly. "Have you *seen* you? If he cares for you like I think he does, he'll wait."

Effie glanced in the mirror and took a deep breath before disrobing and pulling on her matching set of pink satin pajamas. The shorts were . . . *short* with a slit like two petals coming together on the sides allowing her thighs a bit of rarely won freedom. The top was a camisole with lace along the neckline. She'd worn them for ages but for the first time, they looked . . . *intimate*, and her nerves rallied in her gut against her once more. "How can you be so sure that he cares that much?"

"Call it a hunch," Hope retorted. As if in confirmation, a knock sounded at the bathroom door.

Theo's voice carried through, deep, caring, if not a little hesitant. "I know you said to stay, but then I had visions of you slipping on the tile and cracking your head open on the vanity and I had to make sure you were okay."

Effie took Hope off speaker right before her bellowing laugh crescendoed at being proven right. "I'm fine," Effie replied, a flush returning to her cheeks. She cupped her hand over her mouth and whispered, "That proves nothing."

"Yeah, okay" was Hope's snarky reply. "Try to relax. Enjoy your night. There are plenty of ways to be intimate, Effie. It's not all or nothing."

Effie hung up the phone and took a steadying breath. Her gaze went heavenward. "Please, let this be easy." It was half prayer, half affirmation as she reached for the doorknob. She cracked the door open expecting to find Theo, but he'd disappeared.

Effie ducked her head into the hall, looking left and right. Still no sign of him. She steeled her resolve and padded softly down the hall-way all the while trying to hold her head high.

She found him in the kitchen. He sat on one of the stools facing the living room, elbows resting on the counter behind him. Effie noticed with no small amount of interest that his biceps stretched the already taut sleeves of his T-shirt. He'd changed too, and the cotton hugged every muscled inch of his chest before loosening around his trim waist.

He bit the corner of his mouth. Whether he was trying not to smile or say something he'd regret, Effie couldn't tell. That inner fire returned as his gaze raked over her body lingering at the whisper of fabric over her thighs and the swell of her breasts beneath the lace top. She'd opted to leave her bra on, not wanting to encourage too much by flaunting her own rising desire beneath the sheer fabric.

Hours passed before his eyes met hers. Her tongue felt thick. The silence was oppressive or maybe it was seductive. Distinguishing between the two was impossible, but the flutter in her chest was most definitely for him. He was intoxicating. A real-life love interest better than all the imagined men in her favorite books. The look in his eyes had Effie believing he thought the same of her. She couldn't bear the silence any longer and blurted, "I brought pajamas." *Her ability to remark on the obvious was unmatched.*

Theo chuckled and slid off the stool. He stood before her, and Effie had to tilt her head to find his hazel eyes. Theo's finger slipped under the thin strap of her camisole, lifting it in investigation. "*These* are pajamas?" he grumbled.

"Believe it or not," Effie breathed, "my entire pajama drawer is filled with different versions of this. So, yes. Pajamas."

"I will most definitely need to see the contents of this drawer.

Preferably one at a time." His hands slid down her arms in a tender sweep before clasping them around her own. "And preferably with you strutting down my hall wearing them like you just did."

"I did not strut," Effie said indignantly but her amusement couldn't be contained.

Theo's breath was warm against her ear as he whispered, "You certainly did and it was hot as hell." He pulled back and before Effie realized what was happening, he scooped her into the air. Her legs acted of their own accord and wrapped around his waist. His lips crashed against hers and her mind went blank. Time stopped. Her anxiety receded like the tide under a full moon, replaced with a tsunami of desire that had her wanting to keep him this close all night long.

He carried her to his bed. Effie clasped her arms around his neck, their mouths still moving in claiming kisses as he cradled her with one arm and put his weight on the other, so he could gently lay her back. With the arm around her waist, he tugged her firmly up the bed so her head rested on the downy pillows. A sharp gasp escaped her lips, exhilaration at being handled so passionately. Theo's lips found the hollow of her neck. He kept himself propped up, hovering over her. *That wouldn't do.* She pulled him closer until he pressed into her chest and between her legs, and she no longer wondered *how much* he craved her. The evidence of it had her hips lurching forward to grind against him. He let out a soft moan before Effie silenced it with a kiss.

Why she had ever been nervous to explore with him, be close to him, play with him, was a mystery now. Effie luxuriated in his touch, in the warmth of his mouth on hers. Even the crushing weight of him on top of her steadied her soul and had her feeling like he couldn't be close enough.

But his hands stayed in her hair or caressing her face. They ventured to her hip and just below the curve of her breast. But that was all. Effie's throat tightened with emotion as she realized he maintained the boundaries she'd only ever hinted at. She felt so seen. So understood. So safe.

Effie dared reach for the hem of his shirt and slid it over his rigid abdomen. He pushed to kneeling and pulled his shirt over his head. "Is this what you wanted?"

Effie, breathless, merely nodded. Her hands reached for the layered muscles of his torso. Theo let her explore each one, and she swore she felt him shiver at her touch before he gently lowered himself down beside her. He edged his hand under her satin camisole and the warmth against her rib cage anchored her to him. "Is this okay?"

"Yes," Effie said, and she found she wanted him closer again, but she resisted the urge to tackle him, something about the softness in his gaze encouraging her to slow down, savor, be present.

"Tell me when to stop," he whispered, his voice a deep vibrato that rumbled through Effie's core. He kissed her again, this time treasuring each supple touch of their lips as his hand ventured higher and higher until his palm claimed her breast. Effie sucked in a breath.

It had been so long since she'd let someone explore her body like this, and it hadn't felt the same. It was only ever hapless teenage groping. But *this. This* was new territory.

Theo's hands roamed over her body like he'd mapped every inch and knew which peaks and valleys would have her arching into him. When he trailed his fingertips down her back before cupping her backside and drawing her in with a sharp tug, Effie lost all control. She pinned him to his back, straddling him. The warmth of his skin, as she trailed kisses from his navel to his chin, was a seduction all its own.

Effie wasn't sure how long they explored each other before she had her own map of his little pleasures, but she delighted in their efficacy. The way he tensed with anticipation when she nibbled his earlobe. Or the subtle shake of his arms as she trailed a finger along the band of his shorts. Her favorite might have been the way he rippled as she dragged her nails down his back while pressing her hips against his.

Though she had thought seriously about crossing her line a time or two, she never actually had to tell Theo to stop. He seemed well aware of what was and wasn't on the table and happily slowed their passionate exchange until Effie rested on his shoulder fighting the drowsiness that pulled her eyes closed. If she had doubts before the start of their first overnight, they were washed away with the sound of Theo's slumbering breath. Nothing had ever felt so right. Effie smiled to herself as she nuzzled closer against the planes of his chest before she let sleep claim her too.

28

Who was that?" Brayden asked as Hope circled back to the bench by the cemetery where they'd been speaking. It was late, but the weight of darkness around them steadied Hope's breath. Hard conversations felt less damning beneath the moon.

"Effie," Hope replied, taking her seat beside Brayden. She had been happy for the interruption; so far it didn't seem like this conversation would go the way she wanted it to. "Sorry. I didn't recognize it and there are a few people at my publisher's office that have New Hampshire numbers."

"No worries. Are you nervous?"

"For the launch? No, not about that."

Brayden's brow furrowed, but he didn't reach for her hand, invisible shackles keeping him from doing what he'd normally do. Hope's heart ached at the realization. "What are you nervous about then?"

"You . . . us. The baby. I don't want to do this without you," Hope admitted, and she hated how much sorrow seeped into the words. She didn't want him coming back out of pity, but from the moment they'd arrived at their spot, she'd felt his guard up. It took every ounce of compassion and understanding not to throw herself at him or yell or beg. She wouldn't be reduced to such antics, not if they'd be in vain.

"You're not doing it without me, Hope," he clipped.

"But I'm not doing it *with* you, am I?" She couldn't help it, and she choked on the tears that snuck free. Hope silently cursed the streetlights that illuminated her broken heart. She wiped at her eyes, doing her best not to break any further. Brayden's silence was answer enough. "Is there anything I can do to change your mind? Name it and I'll do it. I *love* you. So much it scares me. Please, this can't . . . this can't be all we are to each other."

She gestured to her stomach. She had once thought that intimacy peaked when you brought life into the world with someone—that it formed an unbreakable bond. But she was learning that it existed all on its own. The love, the partnership, the passion all had to live and breathe separately. While a baby might be a happy circumstance of those things if they were already thriving, it wasn't a guarantee that they'd continue to exist at all. Everything felt far too familiar, far too like the sad loss of love her mother and aunt and cousins had experienced before her. Hope squeezed her eyes shut, willing her tears to dry.

"This isn't easy for me either," Brayden whispered, and Hope desperately wanted to believe him, but the strong facade had her feeling otherwise. He seemed resolved, strict. A cinderblock wall where he'd always been a sheer curtain dancing in the breeze.

"This isn't you," Hope whispered, yearning for the truth of her words to break through whatever spell Brayden had succumbed to.

"Yeah, well being me keeps bringing me heartache." He scratched at the nape of his neck, his history dragging his shoulders down with its burden.

"I'm not Chloe," Hope blurted before she could think better of it. She wanted nothing from Brayden but his heart. She didn't think she had truly done anything to join Chloe's ranks.

"No, but it doesn't change the fact that I can't trust you."

"Brayden . . ."

"No. I need you to hear this. I can't trust that you won't take an argument between us or a misunderstanding and use it as a reason to doubt my love for you. A reason to take my kid from me. I can't have a Chloe situation be the reason that you turn on a dime and walk out of my life. Keep me from my baby. Not again."

"Where is this coming from? You just admitted you still love me—"

"That's not the point."

"Isn't it? What other Chloe situation would possibly come up?"

"I don't know. But I can't risk it, not when being a good dad is so important to me. And I can't do that if I'm always afraid of what might send you running."

"Don't you think I've learned my lesson?" Hope pleaded. Her grasp on her desperation was slackening. She wasn't sure she was above groveling at this point. Everything out of Brayden's mouth sounded rehearsed, stilted.

It wasn't him.

This wasn't them.

"And you're willing to throw what we have away for someone you haven't even met yet?"

"Bug is as real as we are," Brayden said between gritted teeth, and if she wasn't clawing for the salvation of their relationship she might have swooned at the protective edge that sharpened his voice.

"Yes, but Bug's not here yet. We have time to fix this before that happens. Let me fix this." Hope thought she might have received a full pardon after everything they'd already discussed. Perhaps it had been naive to think that his understanding of her actions and the fears that led to them meant that he would also forgive them. But she thought he just needed space to clear his head. She didn't realize he'd taken that time to build a fortress to keep her out. The irony that she had done the same mere weeks ago was not lost on her. She let loose a dark laugh before burying her face in her hands.

"You once asked me if we could choose to be happy," Brayden started tentatively. "I wanted to say yes, but it's not that simple."

"Yes, it is," Hope argued but she knew she lost this battle. She might as well be bleeding out with a sword through her heart.

"I can't just choose happy. I can't keep being blindsided. I need security right now, Hope. It's the only way I know how to start off on the right foot with Bug. Please, let me do that. Let me focus on you and the baby as a dad. Not as Brayden. Not as us. Please."

"Is that forever?"

His hesitation was healing magic for her battered soul. It was a tattered shred, but it was still hope. "It's just what I need."

He hung his head, a crack in the wall showing his weariness and words he wouldn't dare say tonight. Hope pushed aside the goading inner voice that wanted to unravel his stoic facade, and merely said, "Okay."

The next morning, Effie snuck into the house well before anyone would be awake. There was no shame in her return, but she valued her sanity and her privacy, so she didn't dare walk in on a group of bright-eyed and bushy-tailed meddlers. Instead, she crept up the stairs past the many school portraits and family photos that lined the wall and let herself into Hope's room.

Effie's heart dropped as she read the room.

Used tissues littered the floor and the comforter. Hope still had one in the viselike grip of her hand as she slept, mouth agape, her red-rimmed nose probably stuffed beyond breathing. Whatever joy Effie had come to share stalled out before it left her lips, and she charged for Hope's side instead. Her eyes were puffy as they fluttered open. Hope leaned into Effie's embrace as the tears threatened an encore. "It's too late. I lost him."

"Then he's an absolute idiot," Effie asserted, her high opinion of Brayden be damned. If he couldn't come to welcome Hope's love, he didn't deserve it.

"He's not though." Hope sniffled. She pulled back and rubbed her weary eyes. "He made a lot of sense. It just wasn't what I wanted."

"But you two love each other," Effie said incredulously. How it wasn't enough to draw them back together was puzzling, upsetting, fear-inducing.

"Bug is more important. That's what he wants to focus on. Whatever he felt for me pales in comparison to his sense of responsibility."

Effie nearly popped a blood vessel trying to refrain from rolling her eyes. "How romantic," she scoffed, but she had to admit that it was admirable to put the baby first, even if it left Hope weeping all night.

"Don't hate him, Effie," Hope pleaded and Effie startled. "He doesn't deserve it and it isn't worth your energy to be mad at him. We're moving forward with what's important."

Effie nodded, but it was no small change for Hope to be so open. Love had done that. *Brayden* had done that. Where Hope had clung to her rage or her hurt in the past to prove a point or to protect herself, she was now surrendering it for something greater. If only she and Brayden could see how much they'd done for each other because Effie clearly remembered the man who laid his heart bare to her over candle wax and charcuterie. And this didn't sound like him.

Effie kept all that to herself, not presuming to know how babies and parenthood changed things, but she decided to carry the torch of faith for the both of them that they'd be reunited. She owed it to them as her own newfound happiness had sparked with their hearts daring to love in the first place.

Later that afternoon, Effie wandered to the hobby room. Aunt Bea sat behind her drawing desk studying her extensive portfolio of watercolors. Effie dipped into the chair opposite the desk and peered over at the pile of perfect paintings.

"Whatcha doin'?" Effie asked, her voice singsongy with the joy she'd suppressed in Hope's presence.

"Trying to decide if I'm finished."

"Finished?" Effie was startled. She didn't think Beatrice had an end goal in mind, not when she'd had Effie and everyone else sit for multiple portraits over the years.

"Yes. I want to share them, I think."

"At a gallery? Or would you make a book or something?" There were all kinds of options for the portraits from a live show to a coffee table book of faces to postcards of Issa the parrot.

"I think a gallery might be fun, but I'd have to rent it out myself of course. They wouldn't be accepted into an existing show."

"Pish posh." Effie huffed. "They'd be accepted."

Aunt Bea waved her off. She pulled her bifocals from her nose and rubbed the bridge like she was warding off a headache. Her face turned pensive as she scoured the pile once more. "I was too afraid to be seen for so long. I missed out I think."

"What do you mean?"

"With my work, with friends. You know Neil's family—that man I told you about—lives near here. I used to be quite close with his sister, but over the years . . . it became too taxing to hold myself authentically in a world that disdains otherness."

"I know what you mean," Effie muttered, and did she ever. It was a challenge to brave the world in the vivid truth of your identity. But Effie always thought Aunt Bea had emulated that to perfection, never daring to be anyone but who she was. "Though I don't think you give yourself enough credit. As you've told me before."

"That is the risk we old ladies run in doling out advice. Sometimes it comes back to bite us."

Effie shrugged innocently but it was true. She wouldn't let Aunt Beatrice off the hook, because if the roles were reversed she would do anything to help Effie get out of her own way. "It's not too late. To showcase your artwork or reach out to old friends. You'd tell me to get my butt out there, so you should too. I'll help if you'd like."

"Yes, you're right. Maybe you could start by helping me find a place?"

"I'd be happy to!"

"But let's wait until after the ball to say anything. Wouldn't want Louisa thinking I'm trying to steal focus from her event."

Effie had to laugh at that. Louisa was all kinds of wound up over this year's ball. So much so that she'd accused Hope of planning her book launch exactly two weeks before the ball just to torture Louisa.

"Why do you think she's so nutty about it this year?"

"I think she's hoping for a little magic and forcing it into existence," Aunt Bea proclaimed.

Issa flitted to Effie's extended arm, perching lightly on her wrist. Effie nuzzled her before looking back to Aunt Bea. "You could reach out to Neil's family in the meantime," Effie suggested. "It's nice to find new friends that make you leave these four walls."

"You would know," Aunt Bea teased. "Maybe."

"Good," Effie encouraged with a decisive nod. She turned her gaze back to Issa who tilted her head with an appraising look before lifting off Effie's arm and swooping to her perch by the window.

Effie always wondered if Issa yearned to feel freedom beyond the Thatcher walls too, or if she was content in the place that nurtured her.

29

The room was smaller than he remembered. Not that he'd spent a lot of time within its walls, and the nights he had he certainly wasn't noticing the square footage. Thoughts of hushed but passionate nights beneath the fluffy purple duvet painted a vivid picture as he looked at it now. One such night was responsible for his current task—assembling a crib.

Hope watched from her perch on the bed. "I can help, you know."

"I'm good. You rest." He had insisted that he could handle this for her. After all, he wanted things to be easy when she brought the baby home, and that meant having a space that felt safe and inviting. He was the father, he could assemble a damn crib. He wanted to do and be so much more than this. He'd done his best to demonstrate his excitement and dedication that week despite the awkward tension that lingered after their conversation and the pressure of Hope's book launch in a couple of days.

He drove her to her appointment yesterday and paid the co-pay at the office. He held her hand through the ultrasound and made sure she had a well-balanced lunch before he brought her home. He'd also taken both their cars in turn with two separate car seats to the fire station to have them inspected for proper installation. He knew they were still eight weeks out, but he was nothing if not prepared. He liked to think it eased something between them that he'd been so adamant about getting the safety measures in place and the cribs ready in case Bug decided to make an early appearance.

It had saddened him though to remove Hope's well-loved desk from the corner of the room to make space for the crib. She'd also insisted on downsizing from her queen-sized bed to a twin, so there was more room for the changing table he would assemble next. It had quickly gone from the moody cave of a witchy-minded author to a mash-up nursery bunk room.

Her bed hid behind the door, the headboard parallel to the hallway wall that was no more than six feet wide. Her nightstand piled with her current reads on the low shelf stood beside it with a reading lamp on top. On the other side of the door stood the armoire that Brayden muscled across the room from where it used to reside in the center of the long wall leading to the window seat. The corner that shared a wall with the window seat was cordoned off for the crib, and the changing table would take the place of the armoire. It was tight, but it worked.

"Are you sure you want to stay here?" Brayden asked as he finished assembling one of the side rails of the wooden crib that Hope had picked out, its warm walnut finish matching the twin-sized bed she'd swapped her cousin's daughter for. "You wouldn't rather get your own place?"

Brayden cringed at how Hope deflated. Like she thought he'd been asking something else.

He'd be lying if he said he hadn't thought of having them live together, even if they weren't *together*, but that seemed like a bad idea. Still, he should be more careful with how he worded things.

"It will be nice to have support here," Hope said in a measured tone. Still, the space made him sad. He had four thousand square feet, a separate nursery, guest rooms, and a primary suite with tile, stain, and wallpaper that Hope had picked out, and here she was in a single bedroom making it work, because he didn't know how to.

He wanted to take that pained look from her face, but he couldn't and uphold the plan he'd set forth. This was how things needed to be. This was how he could be certain he'd do right by Bug and not get left behind. Brayden gritted his teeth but nodded in acknowledgment. He got to work attaching the four sides of the crib.

"You picked some nice things," he complimented. Baby products seemed a safe topic of conversation.

"Your email with links to the highest rated in every category was helpful. As were the safety scores and notes about hidden toxins." Hope leveled him with a teasing glare.

"Too much?"

"Nooo," she drawled. "It's comforting knowing all the ways my baby can suffocate overnight if I buy the wrong mattress."

Brayden palmed his face in shame. "I'm sorry. I wasn't thinking."

"I'm messing with you . . . kind of. It is scary but it was helpful. Thank you."

"Of course. I plan on getting this crib and mattress for the nursery too." They'd tentatively agreed to joint custody, which would look mostly like Brayden spending his days off with Bug until Hope was done breastfeeding. Then he could have overnights too, but cribs were still needed for nap time, and besides, a nursery made it real.

"The nursery? At your place. You have a whole nursery." Brayden heard the embarrassment in her voice, which was entirely unwarranted. It's not like she couldn't get a place with a separate room for the baby. She *chose* to stay here for the support of it all. Brayden didn't want to think about what else she might need support on. That if he'd taken her back . . .

He interrupted his own train of thought. "Do you want to go get some clothes and diapers and things this weekend?"

"Uh, no that's okay. Effie offered to go with me."

"Okay." Brayden tried not to let his disappointment show. *What right did he have to hope she'd say yes to that?* They still had weeks to get everything.

Hope didn't want a shower, insisting that she abhorred attending the events, so why would she make other people suffer through hers? She was also adamant that she could afford what she needed without getting gifts from everyone.

They never talked about Hope's money. It was always extra in Brayden's mind. He'd be able to carry the bulk of their finances with or without the cushion of his trust fund, which was significantly smaller in size since his divorce. He and his lawyer had managed to convince Chloe to take a lump sum that was big enough to have her eyes rolling back in her head and forgetting about the allowance into perpetuity she had originally angled for. He was glad to see it go if it meant he needn't have any more contact with her. But he was still so far in the green that it hadn't occurred to him to ask Hope about how else they might split the cost of things. He assumed he'd handle it, *but if they weren't together would Hope want that?*

He'd had enough heavy conversations lately and was very much enjoying doing something nice for the woman carrying his baby, so he silenced the string of questions and pivoted to something more lighthearted.

"Have you thought of any names yet?"

"A few, but I wanted to talk to you about them."

His heart clenched. "I get a say?"

"Brayden, come on. Of course you do." He shouldn't have been surprised by her offense, but he still wasn't sure how to navigate whatever lingered between them. He had to stay practical, smart, level-headed.

"I kind of like Elliot for a boy," Brayden said.

Hope's laugh chipped away at his wall. "You think it's going to be a boy? A Thatcher boy?"

"It's supposed to be a fifty-fifty kind of thing," he teased, but it wasn't lost on him that she thought the baby's last name would be Thatcher, not Schilling. A whole new wave of heartache waited at the end of that road, so he pivoted again. "But yeah, if it's a boy, I want Elliot on the table."

"Okay," Hope said, her depthless eyes pouring such love and affection all over him, he marveled at his ability to hold her gaze.

If he stayed much longer he might just forget that she'd kept this pregnancy a secret. Might forget she believed him capable of an affair. Might forget that she didn't care enough to confront him when things looked bad. He might just forget he wasn't supposed to be giving her his soul, so he tore his eyes from her angelic face and went to work on making the room his baby's home. A home he wasn't going to be a part of.

30

The air was damp and heavy with the threat of thunderstorms. If they landed they'd be fleeting, but they had a real talent for catching drivers with their roofs down and umbrella-less pedestrians off guard. The dark clouds on the horizon were far enough away to look like they could be swayed, brushed aside with a thought or a light breeze. Effie hoped they would, if only to ensure the crowd on its way to the Book and Bar that night wouldn't get caught in the rain.

Effie wandered from the window in her silk robe, feeling the buzz of a pent-up storm beneath her skin. She'd been tamping down her anxieties in favor of good feelings with Theo and ignoring every other little hurt as of late. A snide comment from her mother, a clipped dismissal from Louisa, a wave of grief so sharp and sudden it felt like a sniper shot. They prickled to be released as she readied for the night. A night celebrating Hope. Only within these walls, in the privacy of her room would she let her envy be acknowledged. Thought of, not felt. *That would be far too slippery a slope.*

Effie stepped into a pair of dark-wash jeans that snuggled around her hips and cinched at her waist with a set of three gold buttons. They flared at the leg around her peep-toe leather heels. The peony-printed smocked top she pulled over her head boasted a sweetheart neckline that, after a few adjustments, hugged her chest most flatteringly. She pulled her curled hair into an easy ponytail that showed off the elegant curve of her neck and allowed her gold hoops to pop against her suntanned skin. Grabbing her go-to clutch, she gave herself a quick once-over in the floor length mirror hung on the backside of her door before stepping into the hallway.

She met her mother by the stairwell. "Are you going to the release?"

"I would, but I took over a weekend shift tomorrow so Anna could go away with her family for her birthday."

"Oh, okay."

Pamela checked her watch. "Isn't it a little early for a midnight release?"

"Theo's taking me to dinner first," Effie said fighting the heat that tickled her spine.

"Someone is smitten," her mother chirped before kissing Effie on the cheek. "Be careful there. You know how men are." Pamela smoothed a curl back from Effie's face, the picture of motherly affection, but Effie only felt the condescension. Condescension mixed with envy, and she was sick of it. Her anger battled its way up her throat, but Effie swallowed it down.

"I do want you to meet him," Effie said instead. It was at least partially true.

"I will if he sticks around long enough, love. Don't worry." She patted Effie on the cheek. "Have fun tonight." She slipped away and behind her bedroom door before Effie could summon the nerve to retort. Effie bottled her feelings about how her mother assumed Theo was like her own romantic disappointments and hurried down the steps. Tibby would be at the release. Louisa and Ellen said they'd make an appearance as well, so at least four Thatcher women might get the chance to meet Theo that night. The thought of it had been exciting before her mother's little display. Effie bottled that too and stepped onto the sunset-streaked street where Theo waited.

With his motorcycle.

He held a helmet out to Effie. "I thought we could take a ride down the coast before a late dinner."

Effie didn't take the helmet. She assessed the bike instead. It was a 2022 Heritage Classic 114 Harley Davidson, at least that's what he'd told Effie when he revealed he rode a motorcycle last week. She hadn't heard much else he said about the bike, her pulse hammering in her head at the mere mention of it, but she distinctly remembered saying she wouldn't ride it. She gawked at the sleek navy body and chrome detailing. He took good care of it, even if it was practically new. *Not that that mattered.*

"Effie?"

The stopper on her emotions wanted to pop, but she shoved this down as far as she could too. "We can take my car down the coast."

She shuffled through her clutch for her keys, but Theo stopped her with a hand over hers. "It'll be fun, come on."

Effie stiffened. She wasn't interested, but he looked so excited. "I thought I said I would sooner jump out of a plane than ride on this thing."

Theo cocked his head in confusion. "You were being serious?"

"Yes."

Theo looked at her again, piercing through her in an unsettling way. "Hey, what aren't you saying?" he asked.

"Nothing. It's nothing. Let's just take my car." Effie spun on her heels and made for her Jetta parked around the corner. Theo jogged after until he could edge in front and stop her in her tracks.

"Effie, tell me what's wrong?"

She didn't want to share too much. She was too close to bursting to let any bit slip. "I don't want to ride the motorcycle, okay?"

"That's fine. I'm sorry I misunderstood, but . . . you seem mad?"

"I'm not mad."

"Don't do that."

"Do what?"

"That thing you do with other people. With Hope and Brayden and probably everyone else, where you don't say what you're really feeling and you shove it aside, so no one else is uncomfortable but you. Don't do that with me."

Effie openly gaped at him. No one had ever seen through her like that. It was unnerving, to say the least. Utterly endearing, if she was being honest. But she hadn't been honest, not with her mom upstairs, not with him about the bike, and it bubbled up the bottleneck along with every other little hurt since they'd met. "I don't want to get mad."

"Why not? Do you ever experience your emotions as they come up or are they all living in bottles on a shelf somewhere?"

"You need to get out of my head," Effie huffed, trying and failing to make it sound playful. She wasn't mad at Theo, not really. She didn't feel right unloading everything on him for such a minuscule lapse in judgment.

"Let it out. Feel it. Right now. Be angry, with me, with whatever else is going on. You're allowed to take up space, Effie."

"I don't want to ruin the night."

"I promise you, you won't. Maybe I already did. I was the asshole that didn't hear you about the bike. Despite it being so super safe I'd bring Lilah for a ride—"

"It's not safe," Effie said flatly.

"Well sure, some idiots think they can push the bike until it's riding them and not the other way around."

"You don't have to be an idiot to crash it!" Effie screamed. "I hate motorcycles. I don't want to talk about them, I don't want to see them, and I sure as hell don't want to ride them, so drop it!" Effie scrambled for a piece of gum in her purse. Everything tasted too raw.

To Theo's credit, he didn't balk or try to convince her otherwise. He ran his hands from her shoulders to her elbows in comforting strokes. "Okay, good. What else?"

Effie broke from Theo's grip. "Effie, come on. Talk to me."

"This is stupid," she ground out.

"What's got you so on edge tonight? It's not just the bike."

"It's nothing, leave it alone."

The rest of Effie's feelings demanded the stage as her blood vibrated in her ears, years of stuffing down her anger surfacing with the rage of a long-dormant volcano. She stalked down the street again, but Theo caught up to her and grabbed her wrist to slow her down. "Effie . . ."

She looked him in the eye, his worry and affection so evident she nearly melted. But her anger burned hotter, roiling in her gut at how wrong her mother was. Effie tensed, ready to spill. Theo encouraged her with a nod. She huffed a little growl and dug the pads of her fingers around the base of her neck. It didn't matter that Pamela wasn't there to hear it, Effie yelled, "Not all men are disappointing, Mother! Not all of them let you down! Some of them are fantastic and never had a fucking chance to prove you wrong because they dumped their motorcycles and became roadkill!" Effie shook now, her rage and grief reaching a boiling point she'd never dared allow as she speared Theo with a glare. The venom in her eyes did nothing to quell the tears.

His arms were around her in an instant. She collapsed into him, burying her face in his chest. He gripped the back of her head and held her like he could keep the pieces of her soul from cracking apart. "I'm so sorry. I had no idea . . . you never. You never told me how he died." She cried even harder. Theo held her beneath the streetlights, taking in each crashing wave of her emotions.

"I wish you could have known him," Effie whispered. "Maybe then we'd be halfway down the coast right now." She clutched him closer, as silent tears pushed the receding tide of her grief back into calmer waters.

Theo kissed the top of her head. "What else?"

Effie caught her breath and pulled back, but Theo only slackened his grip, refusing to let her go entirely. Her tears were brushed away with a thumb. Theo took a deep breath. Together they exhaled and Effie felt lighter. "Well," she said, sniffling, "Hope is so sad that she and Brayden aren't together that I can't tell her how stupidly happy you make me."

"The evidence for that is thin tonight," Theo teased as he swept another fat tear from her cheek.

Effie huffed a laugh. "Under normal circumstances. When you're not daring me to feel my feelings."

"So feeling your feelings, not for you?"

Effie considered. Though she needed to touch up her mascara and was in desperate need of a tissue, hoping she didn't leave a snot trail on Theo's shirt, she had to admit it felt better to uncork. "It could be good if I didn't wait so long to let it out . . . this was, pent up, I think." Effie looked at him, bashful behind her damp lashes. She didn't need to voice everything that had gone into her rant. Though it was obviously more than what transpired in the last half hour.

"Does the night feel ruined?" Theo asked in earnest.

"No," Effie admitted. If anything she was falling even harder for Theo. He cupped his hand around her cheek and looked straight into her heart.

"Do you want to talk about it?"

Effie shook her head, no. She leaned forward and sank into a kiss. He wrapped his strong arms around her, and Effie knew it was safe to feel everything with Theo. "Thank you," she mumbled.

He tucked a stray curl behind her ear. "Anything for you, sunshine."

The Book and Bar was bedecked with faux candles, midnight-blue streamers, and a plethora of poster-size versions of the cover of *Magic Ensnared*, the final installment of Hope's *Web of Realms* series. The family-style tables were covered in hors d'oeuvres and postcards with Hope's author portraits. The QR code on the back gave access to special bonus chapters as an incentive to come to the live events. This one was the closest and the one Hope always planned on attending, but a few others were happening in Boston, Portland, and Burlington as her most recent novel was anticipated enough for a midnight release and parties to match across New England.

Hope hadn't ever let the success of her debut series go to her head. She knew that one series did not a career make, and she intended to keep proving herself to her readers. She kept it humble as she grabbed a cookie from the platter before her. It was shaped like Kiernan's sword, while others depicted the Goddess Arachnia and Dominique's family sigil. Effie had uncharacteristically allowed the bookstore to pay her for themed baked goods, and she'd truly outdone herself. She told her as much as Effie sidled up to her, glass of champagne in hand and Theo on her arm.

"Well, remind Grams of that when she discovers all the food coloring I couldn't get out of her favorite tea towel."

"Is she going to be here tonight?" Theo asked hopefully. Hope didn't bother to comment on how she'd watched Effie strategically avoid the Thatchers present since they'd arrived, and would likely manage it the rest of the night.

"Sadly, midnight releases are too late for dear old Grams. But she did send this." Effie paused to wrap Hope in a hug. "And this." A peck on the cheek had Hope smiling wide. Effie looked at Theo like she realized a grave error. "Sorry. Hope, Theo. Theo, Hope."

Hope laughed. "Yeah, we've met."

"Briefly before she whisked Schilling away for his birthday dinner," Theo added before reaching out a hand to shake Hope's. His gaze never strayed from hers as he offered his sincerest congratulations. "On the launch and the baby."

"Thank you," Hope said. She couldn't help the flood of curiosity that hit her. *What did he know about Brayden? Would he be coming?*

Did Theo think she was awful?

Hope wasn't certain what her face revealed, but Theo leaned in while Effie was distracted with Basil and said, "He told me he was coming. He's excited to be a dad, Hope. I'm glad he's doing this with you."

Hope's shoulders eased. She gave him a terse nod but didn't dare show any more emotion. She didn't want Brayden to think she rallied his friends to their cause to try to win him back. Across the room, Heather waved Hope over. "Excuse me." Theo cleared from her path. She looked back to catch him placing his hand affectionately on the small of Effie's back. The jealousy that rang through her was unwelcome, but she felt it nonetheless.

"Hope! I just got off the phone with the rest of the midnight release venues. We're going to stream your reading so they can all have that book launch experience with you."

"Sounds great," Hope said, a little surprised at the redundant information. They'd decided weeks ago that it was only fair since she couldn't make an appearance at every event. But Hope knew Heather. She was easing her into something.

"We want you to read chapter fifty-four."

Hope's stomach lurched. "We agreed on chapter one. Wasn't the whole point not to give it all away?"

"Yes, you and I did, but the team decided that we'll make more sales tonight if you read fifty-four. I sent you an email about it."

Hope chastised herself for letting her personal drama distract her. She recovered quickly enough. "Must have missed it."

"Right. You'll stop at the POV shift and leave them wanting more."

Hope grimaced wanting to read anything, *anything* but chapter fifty-four, especially if Brayden was coming, but she kept her mouth shut.

"Between the six venues tonight you have well over twelve hundred readers waiting to see what happens between Kiernan and Dom. Give them something to yearn for, Hope. Plus the sound bites will be useful for your socials."

Hope rolled her eyes, gut churning at having to read this particular chapter, the one that she had split open her heart and bled onto the page for in front of her audience. In front of Effie. In front of *him*. "You truly think this is the right move?"

"Don't you trust me?" Hope and Effie's conversation with Grams echoed in her mind. She wasn't the PR team, she wasn't the marketing team. She wasn't even the publisher. She was the writer, and the people who had taken her career this far—who had made it so she *could* have moved into her own home months ago without needing to take out a loan—were the ones that got her there. She wasn't ready to throw the train off the tracks, not when raising a baby was so expensive, not when her readers were so devoted, and not when it wasn't only her livelihood that rested on the book's success or failure. Hope took a deep breath. "Okay, let's do it."

When Brayden finally arrived at the Book and Bar, everyone had gathered around the small stage in the corner that was used for open mic nights and poetry slams that Theo had once been a frequent participant in. He crept toward the stage on stealthy feet until he found himself standing beside Theo and Effie. "What's going on?" he whispered.

"It's time for her reading," Effie whispered back. Brayden took in the room. Everyone in the crowd eagerly waited for a brand-new copy of *Magic Ensnared* and gazed at the stage where Hope stood, with a mix of awe, delight, and utter anticipation. The adoration for her work, *for her*, was unmistakable and it made him proud to know her. He had read the first few chapters of the book as she drafted it, but she wasn't as keen to share pages that weren't polished, so he hadn't read more. He had lost all track of her deadlines and the release with everything else that had gone on in the last few months.

Hope approached the microphone with her book open. Her navy dress stretched snugly across her chest before draping in slightly ruffled tiers over her pregnant belly. It reached the tops of her sandaled feet and gave the impression of a medieval peasant skirt. The waterfall of loose brown curls she always wore unbound cascaded over one bare shoulder nearly reaching her hip. Brayden recognized the white-gold drop earrings with tiny sapphire flowers she wore as the ones he'd gifted her for their six-month anniversary.

She was radiant.

If she weren't launching the final book in a national best-selling series he wouldn't have been surprised if all eyes *still* fell on her. Despite the distraction of seeing her up there aglow in the café lights and candles that warmed the space, he managed to clock the terse look Hope gave Effie. She seemed to make a show of how far into the book she went as she pulled out her bookmark.

Brayden's gaze shot to Effie whose eyes were round with alarm. She let out a quick breath through puckered lips before nodding firmly at Hope. Whatever was going on here, Effie was worried about Hope and doing her damnedest to give her some confidence. "Everything okay?"

Effie considered, her face crinkling between a frown and genuine curiosity. "Could be. Might be. Probably fine." Her face lightened. "Might be fantastic, actually."

Brayden was lost. Effie shrugged refusing to give him anything else before turning her attention fully on Hope. Brayden nudged Theo in the arm, *surely he knew more*. "Don't ask me. I think they might be telepathic."

Effie shushed them both as Hope cleared her throat.

"First, I want to thank you all for being here, it means so much to me," she began, and Brayden caught the tremble buried beneath the speaking voice she'd aimed to perfect for such occasions. "And I know you all are *dying* to know what happens with Kiernan and Dominique . . ." A well-timed pause allowed shrieks, giggles, and gasps to ring out amongst the hundred-person crowd. "So I thought we ought to get right to it and start with my favorite chapter in the whole book."

More shrieks and applause. *Was Hope a rock star?* He had assumed so, but to see it in the flesh, even more so than that first reading they'd met at, had him glued to the floor. He couldn't wait to see what she'd do next.

Hope's hazel eyes flicked to him for a too-brief moment. He couldn't tell if it was an apology or something else that flashed there before she took a sip from her water bottle and started to read.

"Kiernan couldn't be certain what mistake had brought her here—to the gilded steps of the Forgotten Temple. There were too many to count. All she knew was that if she didn't go inside, Dom would be lost forever. Her heart thundered in its cage, and the irony wasn't lost on her that if she had given it to him before the Crumbling began, married in secret as they had planned, it would be safely kept in the Hall of

Betrothals beating alongside his from now until eternity.

If eternity still existed.

There was so much they didn't know about why the realms had Crumbled and why others were saved. It was a miracle, a testament to the Goddess Arachnia herself, that Kiernan still had two feet to stand on, two arms to fight with, and a heart left to waste beneath her chest.

Kiernan steeled herself to enter the once pious ground, but her hand trembled as she reached for the heavy wooden door. If Dom was still inside, would he even recognize her? Would he still want her? Would he ever forgive her for fleeing when the ground had fallen from beneath them and his homeland had joined the Void? It was all she could do to stay upright. The image of his haunted face as he'd been hauled away from the Edge by the acolytes of the Forgotten Faith seared into her memory. He had feared for her safety then, made her promise to do whatever she could to stay on solid ground, but the betrayal in his eyes as she ran hurt more than any blade. He truly believed she wouldn't come back for him, and it had broken Kiernan's heart.

The Forgotten Faith needed a new Conduit, and who better than her prince—a man for whom reading emotions came easy, who lived life with fervor and joy, who spoke to the cosmos with ease and elegance?

But he was not theirs to covet, and if any of them fought her in freeing him, they would come to know her bloody wrath.

Kiernan unsheathed her blade and willed herself into the candlelit sanctuary. The stone was damp and moss-covered, evidence of the centuries of disuse. Pews crumbled before the stone dais that housed a single bench.

A bench where a hunched figure, unclothed from the waist up, bent over his knees, his dark curls hanging limply in his eyes. Shackles around each wrist bound him to the floor, the chains barely long enough to allow him to stand.

Which he did as Kiernan approached.

Her stomach ached as she took in the sight of him. Gashes like tally marks peppered his torso—the bloodletting of the Conduit to allow the acolytes to speak with the Crossed Over. Her eyes burned. Her words caught in her throat.

'Kiernan?' he rasped, his voice hoarse and coated with emotion.

Kiernan's knees wobbled as she closed the space between them. She reached a hand toward his cheek, but he jerked from her touch. 'Let me explain,' she pled. But Dom's eyes took on a hardness she wasn't sure she could break."

Hope's minuscule pause was the only indication Brayden had that reading this had become a challenge for her. That she bared some part of her he hadn't seen before. He could barely fill his lungs.

Hope continued.

"'They'll be back shortly. You should go,' Dom barked before resuming his seat on the bench. Despite the weeks, months maybe, that he'd been kept here, he was still as strong and imposing as ever. His muscled shoulders rippled with tension as he avoided her gaze.

'Not without you,' Kiernan asserted. She crouched before him to examine the shackles. Pure iron with an intricate lock that she couldn't easily pick. She tried anyway, slipping the tip of her sword into the keyhole but to no avail. Panic flooded her system; she hadn't thought this far into her plan.

'There are fates worse than this. Go.'

'No!' she bellowed, and she hoped it didn't summon their enemies sooner. She dropped her voice so only Dom could hear. 'No. I left you once. Never again.'

Kiernan kneeled before him, his legs spread wide enough in his seat that she could shuffle between them, bringing her face to meet his. She reached out a tentative hand, and this time he allowed her to cup his cheek, to comb her fingers through the tangles of his hair.

'Your realm should not have fallen. I was blindsided in the chaos and I was . . . I was so scared. Scared to die. Scared to lose you should you choose the Void like so many others before you. I didn't know if I could take it, so I let you go into the Crumbling alone. When I realized that we might stand a chance at stopping it together, I got to the Edge as fast as I could, but they already had you. It was a trap and I was a coward.' She cast her eyes downward and clutched her hands to her chest as the tears fell. 'But I didn't run because I didn't love you. I thought it was the only way for me to survive long enough to get back to you. If I had been caught . . . if they knew what you meant to me they would have used you against me, and I cannot bear the thought of you hurting. But that day I vowed that whoever brought a blade to your flesh or a wound to your soul, I would return to dust, because yours is the purest heart I know, Dominique Revengaard. It is kind and joyful and far superior to mine. I only wish that you could forgive me my cowardice, forgive me the mistakes I have made when all I ever meant to do was give my heart to you fully. When I surrender to the Void as stardust and darkness, when all that is left is pitch-black nothingness, I will carry the flame of my love for you. Wherever eternity ends, you will still find my love waiting. I just hope to prove it to you from this breath until my last.'

Dom's strong hands drew her face toward him, and his rough thumb brushed away the tearstains from her cheek before his lips crashed into hers in a fiery kiss that melted away any bit of darkness that remained shrouding her iron heart. He rested his forehead on hers, his depthless brown eyes alight with the love that had never truly faded between them. 'To the end of eternity, my love.'

The groan of rusted hinges snapped them to attention, and they were no longer alone. The heaviness between them meant only one thing—eternity might very well end today."

Hope's eyes had reddened as she read, but she appeared to use the thunderous applause as an opportunity to cage her emotions once more.

Brayden stood slack-jawed in the crowd. He couldn't move, couldn't breathe, couldn't remember anything logical. Which meant he couldn't stay.

Before he could think about what he was doing, he beelined for the exit. Out of the corner of his eye, he caught a glimpse of Hope, utterly wrecked at the sight of *him* fleeing from the edge.

31

The warmth was the first thing he noticed when he arrived. From the eclectic wallpaper to the glow of the chandeliers to the hum of the old cast-iron stove while Effie cooked. Everything in the Thatcher house radiated the feeling of freshly baked bread and going home. It was inviting, a warm embrace.

That is until you actually came upon any of the Thatchers under the age of seventy-five. Then it was all ice and sharp edges. Theo tried not to notice the sting of Pamela's glare from where she sat at the breakfast table as he finished binding the trash bag that nearly overflowed. Effie and Hope still had more mess to make and the bin wasn't going to make it.

He completely ignored Pamela as he stepped around his girlfriend—who was worth this current discomfort—and wrapped his free hand around her waist from behind. His fingers curled into her hip bone, and where his nose brushed the soft waves of her hair he was rewarded with the scent of rosemary and mint. Effie leaned into him; if he wasn't careful, he'd have to hide behind the trash bag as he left. He moved back enough so that the curve of her perfect backside no longer conformed to his body. He really needed to stop wondering what she looked like naked, especially with her mother watching his every move. "Where's this go?"

Effie craned her neck away from the pan of bubbling pasta sauce she had made from scratch. "Far end of the carriage house, twenty paces to your right after you step out the front door. Try?"

She lifted the wooden spoon to his lips. Garlic, onion, and Italian spices layered perfectly with the San Marzano tomatoes and chunks of celery and carrot that were stewed alongside the ground beef. But it was an almost smoky acid that had him groaning his approval. "Soy sauce?"

"Worcestershire," she said proudly. They'd been cooking together a lot at his place and the joy it seemed to bring her was only surpassed by her baking. In Theo's experience, nothing brought people together quite like good food. He hoped that belief held true through the rest of the night.

"It's very good," he said before dropping a kiss to her collarbone. When he straightened it took every conscious thought not to reflexively shield his balls. He sensed that Pamela wanted them in a vise somewhere. He gave her a terse smile before hauling the trash toward the front door.

He admired the decor as he took his time getting to the entry. Though he knew the home was Dorothea's first, Effie's touch was everywhere—in the embroidery pieces that hung in their hoops like frames, to the artfully arranged bookshelves and mantels, to the faux stained glass that hung in the bay window of the front room to catch the morning light. It was the latter that drew him briefly from his task. He set the garbage by the door, ignoring the snipped murmurs from the kitchen, and stepped into the room that housed all manner of crafts and books and hobbies. He didn't realize it until he walked in, but he wanted a room like it someday. He inspected the fake stained glass that had made Effie a very real part of his life. The lines were perfect, the colors translucent enough to cast hued shadows onto the windowsill. She'd taken the glass from the original picture frame and used actual solder to make a gilded edge around the glass that matched the chain she fixed to the top so it could be hung just so. Intuitively he knew that this piece was important and would be prominently displayed in their home. *Their home.* He liked the sound of that.

Theo nearly jumped out of his skin at the whoosh of feathers and the sting of claws on his shoulder. Not wanting to startle the bird back, he turned his head ever so slightly and came face to face with a perky little parrot. He held out his hand, inviting it to change perches, and lifted it out before him. "Nice to meet you," he said and felt a little stupid, but the bird cocked its head like it was listening. A sharp word almost screeched from the kitchen sent the parrot gliding back to its perch in the far corner of the darkened room.

Theo sighed and returned to the hall, the quick clip of Pamela's voice a shrill murmur he didn't care to try to understand.

Hope's voice cut through the chatter loudly enough that he could hear from the foyer as he put on his shoes. "Be nice, or I'll make you eat in your room."

She would be a good mom. Theo smiled at the thought, but it wrenched away when he considered that he hadn't heard from Schilling in a couple of days. It was a fact he immediately shared with Hope upon arriving, though it seemed to do little to quell the embarrassment she felt over her vulnerability at the book launch. He struggled to understand Schilling in that moment. Theo himself had been about ready to proclaim his love for Hope by the end of her reading. He was surprised his friend was so resigned to his decision at just being co-parents that he hadn't swept her off the stage with a romantic flourish. Schilling had never taken outside opinions so seriously. But this one had burrowed in and couldn't be taken back, regardless of what Theo had to say about it now.

Any lingering guilt about not being able to right their ship evaporated as he nearly ran into Effie's oldest sister Ellen on the sidewalk. "Sorry, didn't see you there."

"Yes, you're taking your trash duties very seriously."

"Trying to help where I can."

"I'm grateful. It's usually my job. Circumstance of getting the separate apartment." She waved to the carriage house behind them and Theo nodded. It hadn't occurred to him that they might split other chores besides the cooking. He wondered now who did the property taxes, who was in charge of the scant lawn out front, who cleaned out the gutters. He knew they *could* handle such things but he wondered if they wanted to. He also wondered what things were like when Effie's grandfather was still alive. It had been awhile, from what she'd told him, but as an outsider he could still pinpoint the Herman-sized holes left behind. Mostly in the way Dorothea moved through the home.

His face must have scrunched into something like discomfort because Ellen placed a hand on his shoulder. "Take a breath. We don't all bite."

Theo's shoulders slackened and he let out a soft chuckle. It caught in his throat when Ellen's eyes turned steely. "Unless provoked."

He nodded firmly. She left him on the sidewalk utterly convinced that Effie was the golden child they'd all go to the ends of the earth to protect.

Theo had heard rumblings from Effie about the calamitous dinner that occurred with Louisa and Ellen's dad, but he had thought the tense atmosphere she described to be an exaggeration. He realized, now being the one occupying the hot seat, that she hadn't given it *enough* credence. *Perhaps he shouldn't have insisted on coming for dinner.*

The tension was thick enough to form a noose and hang by, something Theo considered with every word he uttered. In truth, it wasn't *all* of them. It emanated in its strongest waves from Pamela and Tibby. Tibby, he assumed, because he associated with the man who refused to take her daughter back—something he guessed she was privy to if only because he had heard she tried to come to Ed's aid. Not Theo's though. Not tonight. *No wonder Effie had avoided them at the book launch.*

Louisa offered her own bit of calculating assessment, but it was far lighter than her mother's and took on a shade of envy more than anything else. Then there was Ellen, who wasn't exactly grilling him along with everyone else but wasn't helping him either. Effie's pinched, unhappy expression told Theo she had expected more from her big sister. Time slogged forward as he answered one of many questions hurled at him that snuck through Effie, Hope, Dorothea, and Bea's conversational defenses.

"They divorced when I was sixteen. My dad lives in Boston with my stepmother. My mom moved into a camper van and travels. My older sister lives in San Diego, my brother lives in Boulder, and my younger sister is still in college in Texas. No brothers- or sisters-in-law, no nieces or nephews, and my one cousin is some kind of recluse who studies fungus in the world's rainforests. My grandparents on my dad's side moved back to Germany in their retirement. My mom's parents are both deceased. And my aunt and uncle—the reasons my cousin became a recluse—keep well to themselves somewhere in Gorham, New Hampshire. So, the only person I consider family that lives near enough to see regularly is Schilling—Brayden." Hope received his apologetic glance with grace before he turned his attention back on Pamela. "Detailed enough?"

"Satisfactory." Pamela grinned over the lip of her wineglass.

"Though counting a man *like that* as family surely demonstrates a poor judge of character."

"Mother," Hope seethed. Theo would stake his life on it that Hope had tried and failed to defend Schilling to her mother.

"If you mean kind, loyal, sensitive, and goofy as hell, then yes, he is *like that*. And my judge of character is impeccable. Which is how I know not to take you insulting my family to heart, Tibby, because I can tell you're better than all that."

He was playing with fire. A bomb really, but he'd be damned if was just going to sit here and take it. She softened at his earnestness, which was nothing short of a miracle in his eyes. Then again, he always had been a good judge of character.

But Theo had a feeling things were still getting started. The squeeze of Effie's hand on his thigh all but confirmed it. He was thankful she sat on his right, left-handed as he was. Theo made a show of reaching down to hold Effie's hand his fork still held in his left. A perhaps too-bold smirk on his lips as he refused to blink first in his staring contest with Pamela. She blinked first, but he still wished he could join the kids in retiring early for the night.

"You haven't said anything about my character, Theodore."

"Theo. And you're a harder read. Strong-willed though, which is likely where Effie gets it from." He said it like a compliment and meant it as one.

"You're not so hard to read, despite your attempts at playing mysterious and suave," Louisa chimed in.

Theo's hackles rose in defense of whatever Louisa thought to spit from her twisted lips next. "I have a few friends that thought you were quite intriguing." She looked to Effie, and Theo sensed that misguided sense of protection lurking in the background. "I'm sorry, Effie, but you need to know what he's like."

"Louisa, cut it out. You're projecting." The bowl of pasta and basket of fresh rolls could have baked anew under the burn of Effie's glower. She turned to Dorothea to try to strike up a different line of conversation, but Louisa interrupted.

"Do the names Daphne, Mallory, Claire, and Hannah mean anything to you?"

Theo shut his eyes and did his best to release the desire to storm out, make a scene, and let his anger talk first. Instead, he took a deep breath. His response dammed behind his teeth as Pamela added, "Or Nicole, Beth, and Lily."

Theo couldn't believe they were making the seven women they had found, somehow by degrees of separation, into something to be ashamed of. He clocked the nudge Louisa landed in Ellen's side.

"No. I'm out," she whispered, an apology somewhere in the pitying look she cast at Effie.

"Sounds to me like you have quite the trail of broken hearts behind you, Theo," Pamela mused. Tibby had the good sense to butt out of it, while Hope looked like she might be silently hexing them all. Theo only wished he'd practiced such witchcraft so he could help.

"Leave the poor man alone, look at him! Of course he's had a few dalliances," Beatrice chirped. "You all are ruining Italian night for me."

"I agree, let's get to know him for Effie's sake," Dorothea said with every ounce of authority her seventy-some-odd years had earned her.

"That's all we're doing," Louisa said blandly. "Getting to know the man who we discovered, without much effort, is a bit of a slut."

"Did you just call me a slut?" Louisa shrugged innocently. "First of all, seven women does not a slut make—"

"But they're not the only ones, are they?" Pamela snipped. Heat flooded Theo's face. *No, they weren't the only ones.* A lot of girlfriends and hookups and just-for-one-night romances crossed his threshold. But he was never flippant about it. He cherished his time with each one of them, however short-lived, and he wouldn't apologize for it. Womanizing and predatory weren't even close to fitting. More like passionate and curious. In all his relationships, he had been looking for the love of his life, and she was currently being humiliated around her own dinner table.

"They all said pretty much the same thing though, that they thought there was something there until you broke it off, out of the blue, and usually after you got what you wanted."

The buzz of a bulb in the chandelier on the verge of burning out filled Theo's ears. His pile of pasta congealed past the point of being appetizing. He laid down his fork, uncertain how to save the night. They'd decided he was using Effie before he'd even arrived. The insult to Effie was far greater than it was to him. They couldn't see how in command of herself she was, how radiant. He was at her mercy, not the other way around.

"None of them so much as blinked in surprise when it ended. Did they tell you that even if we slept together and I knew we weren't going to see each other again after I was upfront about it? That, at least in Hannah's case, I knew the name of her childhood dog, what movies made her cry, and what fictional men made her swoon all in a matter of three weeks of dating? How about you all stop trying to make me look bad or shame me or whatever the hell this is and realize that all you're accomplishing is making your sister—your daughter—uncomfortable."

Everyone looked to Effie who had indeed gone red. Something like guilt colored Louisa's expression. *Good.* Even if Pamela refused to cow, at least someone in this room deigned to look ashamed of the ambush.

Theo never talked about his past dating record, not because he didn't want to be honest, but because he wanted, with his entire heart and soul, to keep that exact look off Effie's face. He knew she already compared herself to Talia, and it was hard enough to convince her he didn't need to have sex with her to want to be with her. He didn't need her to have a list of names to stew over alongside. He turned back to the table, but he clung to Effie's hand. Half-moons branded into his skin where her nails dug into his flesh, like if she squeezed hard enough they wouldn't see her embarrassment.

Theo stood and Effie followed his lead. "Not that it's any of your business, but I've dated a lot looking for someone to spend my life with. Effie has shown me how fully you can be with someone, and I've never been fucking happier." And he fully meant it. *She was worth taking it slow because there was no rush in living their romance.* He hadn't ever had *that* before.

He led her out of the dining room, but he didn't miss the satisfied smile on Dorothea's lips as they escaped.

Effie and her dad were excellent planners. They plotted their summer adventures at the end of May, making what Effie dubbed *Summer Funtime Must-Do Lists.* They filled their ten weekends together with trips to Old Orchard Beach, minigolf dates, day trips to Polar Caves, Whale's Tale Water Park, and Storyland. They budgeted downtime, to snuggle on rainy days and read good books, as well as little treats like ice cream walks and sunset sandcastle building. They'd barely finished plotting the Summer Funtimes of 2009 when her dad had left for Cape Cod. She stopped planning after that.

Effie was reminded of that list that she'd torn to shreds while she sat in Theo's apartment. She had the sinking feeling that she'd started to make too many plans again. Effie scrubbed the thought away as anger toward her family took its place. Her muscles quivered at the rage and shame that clung to her like splattered paint. She knew they were apt to meddle, but she didn't believe they could be so cruel, however well-intentioned they thought they were being. Her warring feelings pressurized in her skull waiting to crack with thunder at any minute.

The storm subsided upon sight of an antique tray set with a

porcelain teapot and matching cup and saucer that Theo laid before her. It looked wholly out of place atop the cheap coffee table he no doubt had since college. "What's this?"

He sat beside her and smoothed her jagged nerves with the caress of his hand on her knee. "You said your favorite teas taste better in porcelain."

"So you went out and bought a porcelain tea set?"

"Well . . . yeah." He was flummoxed and Effie didn't blame him, but she wasn't used to people just *doing* things for her without her having to ask explicitly.

"And the first thing you did when we got here was go brew me a pot of tea." To soothe her even more, set her body back to neutral, make her feel—

"Technically us, there are two cups."

If Effie weren't so splintered by their dinner she would have been overjoyed by how he took care of her. He lifted the teapot and poured. Steam curled around the lip of her cup, drawing her attention to the roses painted on the delicate china. "I know Rose is your middle name, but are they your favorite flower?"

Seems like something you should know. We have been dating for nine weeks. Effie left the barb unspoken, not wanting to succumb to her lesser inclinations. It wasn't Theo's fault her family had verbally assaulted them and given her names for the faceless others who came before her. Others that a more rational, less volatile mind wouldn't think twice about. So instead she murmured, "They're not, but I do love them. Lady slipper orchids are my favorite."

"I don't mean to be rude or impolite, but aren't those kind of funny looking?"

Effie laughed. She supposed they were kind of funny looking, shaped like little pouches, moccasins, or slippers if the legends about them were any indication. But odd as they were, Effie found them beautiful. "They're also delicate and beautiful and rare."

"I know something else like that," Theo flirted, his eyes beneath heavy lids full of something Effie wasn't confident she could handle—like he was drunk on her with one look. He leaned in and kissed her. It was soft and tender, comfort after the night she'd had. When she pulled away and grabbed her teacup, he invited her to curl up against him with an open arm. She scooted beside him, knees tucked into her chest.

"I also like that you have to go looking for them. They grow in dappled sunlight in the forest, and if you aren't paying attention you could miss them entirely."

"What is it that makes them so rare?"

"I don't know exactly, but they take a while to mature, and they're fragile. Because they're considered endangered you aren't supposed to pick them . . . or uproot them."

"Even if uprooting it would give it more space to grow?"

"They don't usually survive transplanting," Effie said, twisting the hem of her bell-bottomed linen pants between her fingers. Hunting lady slippers had been on that 2009 list.

"I see," Theo murmured, pensive.

It felt so good to let him take care of her, but the feeling battled against years of comparison in one particular area of romantic life. Years of doubting that good things could last too. The room felt too small, too hot. Effie's eyes burned with unshed tears. She didn't want to feel this way, didn't want to succumb to fear or envy about Theo or about what it would mean to finally one day be in love the way she'd always dreamed. Her voice was thin, but she dared to speak the spark of desire, saying, "But I haven't ever tried it myself."

"That makes sense; it is frowned upon."

"It could be downright illegal," Effie teased, trying to will herself back to the place where it only felt easy and good and right to sit beside Theo.

"I'm willing to break a couple rules if you are," Theo said, his voice laden with unspoken feeling.

"If I'd break them with anyone, it would be you," Effie breathed, and the truth of it rattled in her chest. She set her teacup back on the tray and melted into Theo's embrace. Her lips found his again. It was like going home, and that terrified Effie more than anything.

32

Birdsong floated through the open window, harbinger of another rising sun. The cool grey of predawn was a blanket Effie didn't want to unfurl from. A new day meant dealing with the fallout from last night's dinner, confronting her family, and calling them out for their bad behavior. Standing up for herself and being the squeaky wheel. The thought alone churned her stomach.

She turned to Theo, his bare chest still rising and falling in cadence with a deep slumber. Effie wore her usual satin pajamas, but Theo was stripped down to his boxers. Apparently, he'd been wearing shorts and tees to make her more comfortable but dared express his desire for less clothing last night. Although, if Effie was being honest it made it far less appealing to remain celibate when the barriers were fewer.

It couldn't be later than five o'clock but between the chirping birds and her reeling thoughts, Effie knew she was awake for good. She envied Theo's ability to sleep through anything—well, when properly outfitted for sleep. He'd been much more restless beneath the constraints of his modest-making attire. Effie smiled to herself, the thought of that little discomfort and sacrifice on her behalf making her heart swell. It was immediately drowned out with worry about how else she might be keeping him constricted.

The sheets clung to her clammy skin as she rolled over to face the open window. Heat seared through her in waves of humiliation. The onslaught of her family had done a number on her. Theo was right, they weren't shaming him. They were essentially saying Effie couldn't handle herself, that she was naive, doe-eyed, and too inexperienced to win the heart of a man like Theo. A subtle reminder that the way she moved through the world was not enough to find love in someone as handsome, strong, confident, and sensual as Theo Tillerman. Not that being able to please a man in bed had ever kept *their* men loyal. If she thought about it too long it would become a hurt that would be hard to forgive and move past. She didn't want that, not when all was said and done the Thatcher women were her family, her home. The air felt heavy in her lungs. *Home.* It had felt like home in Theo's arms last night like wherever he existed was where she belonged too. *That* was a terrifying thought. Her whole life she'd been taught to only belong to herself.

Theo's arm landed heavily around her middle as he snuggled into her. "You're burning up. Are you feeling okay?" His voice was thick with sleep, eyes struggling to open in the dim light. He propped himself up beside her, the back of his hand coming to rest on her forehead like a ye olde thermometer. Once satisfied that she wasn't succumbing to the plague, he placed a comforting hand against her cheek. The cool rush of his skin on hers was a relief.

"Couldn't fall back asleep," she murmured. "Thinking too much."

"Worrying, you mean."

"Is there truly a difference?"

"Yes. All worrying is thinking but not all thinking is worrying," he mused.

"Tell me, are you always so profound before six a.m.?"

"Stick around and you might find out." He lowered a kiss to her lips, tentative, questioning. A different kind of heat rushed through her and she tugged him closer with a hand to the back of his neck, greedy for a deep distraction. Emotion burned her throat. She wanted this, wanted him. Chloe. Lily. Hannah. *Had they wanted him too? Did she deserve to hold him when they hadn't?* Her mouth moved against his, letting every pent-up desire wash away the worries she'd drawn in the sand. She took his bottom lip with her teeth and let her kisses show him how much she wanted him, how much lived on the other side of the line that wouldn't be crossed.

Theo settled on top of her, his hips between her thighs, and she forgot all of the others' names for a too-brief moment. Effie decided that this was why people succumbed to physicality; it was an excellent way to keep the serious stuff at bay.

She kissed him harder, and he turned to putty in her hands as her tongue found his, as she raked her nails down his back. If she could stay in this space of bliss, this moment of connection, they could stay happy. But Effie's brain was a force to be reckoned with and it always reached a tipping point where it spoke up, reminded her not to go too far, not to be too vulnerable, not to make plans. Idiots weren't the only ones to crash motorcycles.

She pulled back quickly after another deep, claiming kiss. Theo huffed a laugh, his breath uneven, arms shaking. "Well, fuck. Good morning to you too." He caressed her face and drank her in for a tortuous moment before he rolled back onto his side, head resting on a propped elbow.

Effie looked at him curiosity trumping doubt. "You're not mad I stopped?"

"Why would I be mad?"

"Because you want more."

"I want you, Effie. Whatever that looks like. I'm not in any rush, but it's getting a bit tiring trying to convince you of that."

"It's not who you are," Effie said flatly. "You don't like to wear pajamas." He'd already made little sacrifices for her happiness. She didn't want him to change for her.

Theo jerked to sitting, muscles tensing in what Effie assumed was irritation. "Okay? And who am I?"

He sounded hurt. She supposed that made sense. She should have stopped it before it turned into an actual argument, but her brain was winning despite the pleas of her heart. "You're . . . I don't know. You're Theo. You're sexy and creative and masculine. You drive a motorcycle and wear leather without looking like a hipster. You're a sexual person and use it as a way to see if a relationship is worth pursuing." *Theo.* Salted caramel chocolates. *Sexy.* Cinnamon sticks. *Relationship.* Royal icing.

"If you were being you then you'd have bedded me to see if we were a good fit."

"Bedded you?" Theo's brows reached his luscious hairline. He took a deep breath. Then another. She'd seen him meditate, sage swirling around him on his pouf in the corner of the apartment, but this felt forced. This felt like a tool to keep a lid on his temper. She didn't care for it.

But it seemed to work because his voice when it emerged wasn't angry or measured. It was earnest in a heartbreaking kind of way.

"I like how our relationship is going. I like learning new ways of being intimate. I like that I am doing things with you in a way I've never done before. It feels right because this isn't like anything I've known before. Effie, I lo—"

"Don't." The word escaped before she could leash it.

Theo deflated. Her strong, confident, charismatic man slumped at her rejection. "Why are you doing this?"

It was an excellent question, one that likely required a good deal of the shadow work Theo was fond of. But the truth was usually the simplest answer, and the one that came to the surface was "Because I'm not like you. I don't know how to be daring and brave. I like to know things with certainty, to be able to predict them. I'm not here to try things on to see if they fit. I go out with a list, of sizes, colors, and fabrics. I carve out space for what matters to me, but I don't fall hard or fast. I don't want or yearn or imagine anything intangible . . . And I don't say things unless I know I mean them for good."

How Theo had elicited such a verbose confession was beyond her. The crush of flavors on her tongue made her want to vomit.

"You don't fall, because it's not a risk you're willing to take."

Effie couldn't deny that. *Hadn't Hope said the same thing all those weeks ago?* But it hurt coming from Theo. It stung to know he saw that in her, that cowardice and shielding, even if it wasn't his fault it was plain to see.

"And for the record, I've not said it without meaning it for good either."

"You have or else you wouldn't be here with me. You'd still be with *her*. Whichever her you actually loved out of the list of many."

Theo rubbed the grief from his eyes. "That's not . . . Never mind. I can't promise that things are always going to stay the same, but it doesn't change how I feel. It doesn't mean that I won't do everything in my power to keep us together and happy. I need you to believe that you and me . . . it's different. It's new. For fuck's sake, Effie, I don't know how else to prove it to you."

"Maybe you can't," Effie mumbled. It had less to do with Theo and more to do with Effie not being able to take a leap of faith. She hoped he heard the distinction, that it wasn't his shortcomings that would mean he couldn't prove his feelings for her, but her own. This conversation was proof enough of *that*.

"Why are you here?"

The question startled her. She fumbled for a response. "Because I like being with you."

"Why?"

"Theo, come on. You know why."

"You won't take me at my word, but I'm supposed to take you at yours? Trust that you find me charming and handsome and compatible? You're not harboring some desire for me to be more than this? Taller or funnier or less spiritual?"

"What? Of course not. Taller would be too tall, you're already six two," Effie teased trying to reel this back in a bit, but Theo didn't acknowledge it.

"But you know you want to be with me, even if you don't know everything? When will you know if it's forever? When will you know that this is a carved-out part of your life and I'm not just someone you're trying on?"

"Stop, you're twisting my words." Her own felt sour on her tongue. She stood firmly on a runaway train now.

"Am I? Or is it as ridiculous as you questioning my feelings because we haven't had sex yet?"

Effie's cheeks flushed. Suddenly the room was too small, the sheets itched like wool on a hot day. She flung the covers off needing the air. Though they were exploring new territory together, she knew Theo was being patient. He would wait to be intimate, but he wouldn't wait long for her to allow him his true feelings. Effie didn't have answers, none that would get past the mountain of doubts that buried the key to her voice box. She wanted to say how she felt. She wanted him to say it too, but it was too much. She had to be certain. It was too dangerous otherwise.

"It took Hope and Brayden a year to say that to each other," she said her voice so small and thin.

"We aren't them."

"It's too soon."

"Says who? You? Or is this some Thatcher theory that doesn't hold water?"

Effie bristled at the mention of her family. "Leave them out of this."

"I'd love to . . . sorry. I'd *like* to but they seem inextricably tied to your inability to give yourself fully to this relationship."

"And you're so devoted? You've had a string of relationships supposedly looking for *the one* and all of a sudden you're a new man?"

Theo took a deep breath, before confessing, "Usually, when you find what you're looking for you stop looking." He stared longingly at her as he fixed his dark round glasses on his nose.

Effie's stomach dropped. That might have been worse than what he was going to say before. This had heft. This was the whole of it, heavy and raw and bleeding out with every beat of silence that she left his declaration unanswered.

"You can't possibly know that."

"Why not? Because you don't?"

"No, because . . . you just can't. I'm not that special. I'm not worth waiting for. I'm not enough to be the answer to your prayers."

"And why not?" She ignored the sorrow that drenched his words. Sorrow that she couldn't see it his way, that she thought so little of herself.

"You just can't know it already!" Effie stood now, clutching a pillow to her chest.

"I do!"

"You don't! It's not how this works. You can't just *know* things!"

"The sky is blue, Effie. Let it be a fact!"

"That still doesn't make any sense!" Effie yelled, her nerves shaking her bones. She moved for the door on silent feet.

"Effie, please don't go."

"I shouldn't be worried at every turn that you're going to realize I'm not what you want." With that she grabbed her clothes and crept out the door, not bothering to mention that that fear was wholly her own. She didn't give credence to the thought that she ruined this before it started, that she was running back home, fulfilling the predictions of her lovelorn family, and hiding from what might be because she was too afraid it wouldn't last.

33

The sidewalk sizzled with the late July heat, despite the evening hour, drawing tourists and locals alike to the outdoor tables at all of Hope's favorite eateries. As she walked, she passed more than one pudgy hand coated in dribbles of ice cream that melted down too-full cones. Thankfully, the fabric of the sundress she wore was light enough that she remained dewy instead of cascading with sweat. Like Effie, she enjoyed walking when she could, and Brayden's house was near enough that she could manage it, even on a hot day.

The fence had been righted and the beds lining the foundation and walkway were filled with loam dark as coffee grounds. A deep navy, reminiscent of a moonlit midnight sky coated the front door and shutters. The bronzed, scaled face of a dragon held the door knocker between its teeth and looked down at Hope with a mystical curiosity. She had found it at a salvage shop months ago. Hope's mouth kicked up in the corners.

The door knocker, the unplanted gardens, they were all for her.

Brayden promised she could pick and plant the flowers herself when the time came, it seemed he made good on that and many other things. It felt odd to be happy when so much between them was tumultuous at best, but she chose to view it as an olive branch.

Hope lingered on the granite slabs that made up the front steps. She didn't come to pick a fight or demand to know what he thought after her reading, but she wasn't willing to wait for him to come out of hiding when they had so much to get ready before the baby came. Plus, Effie had made them each a gift for their respective nurseries giving her the perfect excuse to make a house call. Or so Effie had insisted.

Hope lifted her hand to try out the knocker, and a nauseating lurch in her stomach reminded her of the last time she tried to call on Brayden at this house. When Chloe had upended her sense of security and all but jumpstarted the end of her relationship with the only man who had ever made her want to leave the safety of her family home. Hope steadied herself with a deep breath. *It was all in the past.*

She knocked.

What felt like a small eternity later, the door eased open.

Brayden.

Hope wasn't sure it would ever stop making her muscles go slack to look upon that scruffy dark beard and those warm chocolate eyes. His lean frame, tight in all the right places, was on phenomenal display beneath a lightweight cream T-shirt. He tucked his hands into the pockets of his plum-colored shorts like he wasn't certain what to do with them.

When Hope fully met his gaze she expected to find all the warmth and longing she felt reflected back to her. But his face hardened, mouth drawn into a line. "What are you doing here?"

Hope wanted to keel over into the last remaining rose bush, but Bug deserved two living parents so she lifted the bag in her hand. "A gift from Effie. Plus, I want to see where our baby is spending half its life if that's okay with you."

Hope schooled her face into ease and contentment. She wasn't here to do anything or be anything he didn't want. Clearly, her reading fell on deaf ears and had solidified the walls between them even more. She could play happy co-parent until it became the truth.

"Of course. Sorry. You surprised me is all."

"Were you expecting someone else?" Hope looked over her shoulder like a non-pregnant, non-swollen, non-gassy trollop might be on her way to ravage her baby's father. The expression wasn't entirely wiped from her face when she turned back to him.

Brayden sighed. "No, Hope. I wasn't." He stepped aside, gesturing for her to come in.

The house looked fantastic, pristine, and far too empty.

"You need furniture," Hope offered.

"Noted."

"I could help," Hope said, trying not to sound too excited. "If you want."

"Also noted. Can I get you something to drink?"

"Water would be nice. It's a scorcher out there." Brayden barely smiled before leading her into the kitchen. Her dream kitchen, complete with Secret Garden–green cabinets, gold handles, and open shelves. The oversized stove so she could cook and bake like Effie stood beneath a gorgeous wooden vent hood that had Hope daydreaming of a visit to the Italian countryside.

She sipped the water Brayden got for her by the eat-in island that stretched impressively across the expansive kitchen. "Are you sorry you let me make so many design choices?" she asked.

"No. It looks great."

"But?"

"But nothing."

Hope nodded. Brayden was never this quiet. It was like he had a word count limit when speaking to her, and it made her dizzy. As did his drumming fingers on the countertop. He only did that when he tried to keep his mouth shut.

"Do you want me to go?"

"You'll be here a lot, best we get used to it."

"Right." The tightness of his countenance was difficult to read.

"Nursery?"

Brayden nodded once, then led her toward the empty great room. She ignored the dreadful ache in her stomach as she hiked up the refinished staircase, the treads and banister oiled an impeccable whiskey brown. By the top step, Hope was near panting. It was becoming difficult to person with the protrusion of her unborn offspring making every single thing a feat of physicality.

"You okay?"

"You try gaining thirty pounds and see if you don't get winded going upstairs," she said sarcastically, desperate for some kind of normalcy in their exchange.

"No thank you," Brayden laughed. "You wouldn't . . ." He trailed off and Hope didn't pry. She would though. Still want him, still desire him, if that's where his train of thought went. Thirty pounds, fifty, three hundred, she'd love him at any size. A fact that was bound to get her into deeper trouble if she didn't learn how to let it go.

He pushed open the door to a soft green room that instantly made the pain in her stomach more acute. The crib, like her own, stood on the far wall. A glider that looked previously loved perched in the corner by the window. A changing table that matched the crib already had a changing pad and boxes of diapers stacked beside it. Hope glided through the room, and she could imagine the tiny clothes hanging from the rail in the open closet. The window sat high enough that she could put a bookshelf and toy bin beneath it and a rug in the middle of the room to play on. She would insist Effie make a triplicate of embroidered greenery for over the crib—

Hope interrupted her daydream. *Stop it, this isn't yours to do.*

"I love it," Hope exclaimed. Her hand floated to her belly as she walked to the window. She leaned against the wall, the warmth of the sun a balm on her nerves. She could see all the way to the river from here. The bridge to Maine glinted in the low hanging light of the evening, and she was reminded that despite the ache of loss she felt over the home and the man who made it, life would go on. "It's perfect."

Brayden stayed quiet for so long that Hope wondered if he had left the room. She turned from the view she enjoyed to find him leaning against the wall staring at her. "What?"

He still said nothing. Blinking became a foreign concept to him. Hope fidgeted under the weight of his scrutiny, wondering if she'd spilled food on her dress, or if he finally noticed those thirty pounds she mentioned that took up residence in places the baby bump was not. She didn't love that she no longer looked entirely like herself. Maybe he saw it too. "I'm having a hard time getting used to how I look too. I didn't realize that everything about my face would take a slightly different shape." She reflexively brought a hand to her cheek and smoothed it toward her ear.

"Stop. You're beautiful," he snipped like it had to be said instead of it being something he wanted to tell her. He didn't continue, so Hope took a tentative step toward the door; it seemed like her cue to leave. "Please, don't move."

"Excuse me?"

"Stay there," his tone was serious, setting up for something more. "I need a minute."

"Why?"

Brayden scrubbed his face with his hands. Hope's stomach knotted as she waited for him to say something.

This was it. This was the moment she'd been worrying over. He had to have gotten a lawyer or maybe he wanted full custody now. Maybe co-parenting wasn't going to work for him. Whatever it was pained him like he didn't want to say it.

Or maybe he did and the pain came from trying to hold it back.

Hope did her best to wait, but he kept his back glued to the wall across the room, his hands firmly in his pockets, for all the world looking like he was trying to decipher the Da Vinci Code. She couldn't take it anymore. "Spit it out. I can handle it. Whatever it is, just tell me."

The simmering heat in his eyes was her only warning.

He closed the distance between them in three easy strides. His hands combed into her curls on either side of her face as he pulled her into a passionate kiss, her rounded stomach only slowing down the fire in his need by a fraction.

Hope nearly gasped as her lips parted for him. She threw her arms around his neck, tugging at his nape, drawing him as close as she could. Her heart floated with relief. *Was this happening?*

He kissed her like he never wanted to stop. Like he still loved her.

Only when the warmth of her tears dampened his nose, did Brayden pull back. He kept his hands on her face, inspecting, wiping at her cheek with his thumb. "I'm sorry," he whispered.

"What for?" Hope sniffled, a new wave of nausea rolling through her. *It was the cemetery all over again.*

"Making you cry."

Hope chuckled as she stepped away. "I'm afraid I'll only continue if that was . . . if you don't . . ."

He took her hand and pulled her back toward him. Her belly rested against his, and his hands found the small of her back. "I don't want this life without you fully in it. It was stupid to act otherwise."

Joy seeped in through her pores, but she feared it might all go away.

"You ran away the other night . . ."

"Only to keep from running to you. I truly thought it was better to keep this platonic for Bug. I was desperate to hold on to that, but it's not better for any of us." Brayden brought his forehead to meet Hope's. "You belong in that window."

"I belong with you." In this house with a wedding ring and a family that would grow by leaps and bounds until they were as weathered and grey and full of joy as Grams with the breadth of their crazy, adventurous, storybook life.

"Don't I know it," Brayden teased. Hope playfully hit him in the chest before he wrapped her in a hug, his cheek to hers.

Hope sunk into the relief, the joy, and—honestly—the pride that swelled in her heart at knowing her words had been enough. They had brought him back to her. She'd have to send Heather a thank you note.

Brayden kissed her again, and this time it was with the patience of knowing they had their whole lives to do it.

34

You did something stupid."

"And you did something slutty."

Hope glowered at her cousin. The blush of satisfaction was apparently obvious enough to Effie now that she chose to see it. "It wasn't slutty, it was a reconciliation."

Effie lit up. "Veritas?"

"Do you think I'd have sex with him if we weren't getting back together?"

"I think you've been stealing my romance novels for the past three weeks and would have deemed an orgasm a public service at this point whether it made things complicated between you two or not."

"Effie Rose, two and a half months with that man and you're as debased as the rest of us."

Effie rolled her eyes, but Hope noted the shame that clouded around her. "Do you want to talk about the stupid thing you did?"

"Why are you so certain that I did something stupid?"

Hope raised her brows at Effie who lay sprawled like a starfish on a beach towel on the back patio. The sun danced over her already tanned skin and the breeze fluttered the ruffles of her tank top. Effie was effervescent, a sparkling champagne on a hot summer day, effusive in her femininity, elegant, and all things frilly. She was a magnet and had no idea how the easy, wistful way she graced the world drew people to her. Effie was smart and kind and so beautiful that Hope had always harbored a bit of envy toward her younger cousin.

Effie was also prone to overthinking to the point of trapping herself. She, unlike Hope or Louisa or Pamela, thought her way through life instead of feeling it. But it was a different kind of thoughtfulness, not the organized logical brain of Ellen and Tibby, but the frenetic imaginings of a woman that was still looking for a safe place to land.

"You've been out here for twenty minutes. If you were sad you'd be baking. If you were happy you'd be baking. Especially given the ball next weekend, but instead, you are starfishing in the sun. That's symptomatic of an embarrassed Effie. You don't get embarrassed unless you've done something truly stupid."

"Your baby is never going to be able to lie to you."

"Good. Now, we were talking about your idiocy, not my family." She loved how the word *family* sounded. That it was official. Hope bit her bottom lip replaying her morning with Brayden. An excited shiver ran up her spine.

"That good? Even with—?" Effie scooped her hands over her stomach indicating Hope's baby bump—though bump seemed inadequate at his stage.

"It was an adjustment but then . . . Effie, I know you've always believed in God, but I think I met her today."

Effie nearly cackled. "Ew, too much information."

"Hey, you started it."

"And Brayden finished it apparently," Effie joked.

"Badumbah. Since when do you make dirty jokes?"

"It's your sex life we're discussing, so I can joke all I want. You have a more physical relationship with your physical relationships. I think I need . . . *more*."

"What do you mean?"

The birds hushed as if listening to the confessions of their ethereal princess. The breeze rustled the grass and mimicked Effie's sigh. "I think it's a mental game."

"So you need to get out of your head and into your body?"

"No. That's what I mean. The way you talk about it, or Louisa, or even my novels, it's all body forward. It's physicality and touch and that's all there, but it's not enough to fully turn me on, I don't think. I need the right headspace, I need to connect intellectually, I need words and romance, and I need it to be about intimacy, not just about getting off."

"Isn't that what Theo's been telling you? That intimacy is all-encompassing?"

"Yeah. It doesn't matter though."

"Why not?"

"It just . . . doesn't."

Hope tried to unravel the hidden meaning there. She didn't think Effie had broken up with Theo or she'd be more upset. But maybe Hope was projecting. This was the first real relationship Effie had ever had, unlike Hope who had four or five serious boyfriends in college. Maybe this was Effie post–break up. Hope didn't want to pry but couldn't quell her curiosity. "Does Theo have his tux rented for the ball?"

"I never invited him," Effie confessed. Hope wobbled to the patio stones from her perch in the shade. She sat down beside Effie and let the ground support her aching joints and swollen body. "Are you going to move in with Brayden?"

"Yeah," Hope said and it felt like a confession. It was almost too much to imagine life without Effie on the other side of her bedroom wall. They'd grown up in this house together. Hope had once viewed it as a failure to have returned to her room here after college, but now she wouldn't trade those three years together with the people she loved most for anything. She reached out a hand and laced it with Effie's. "I'm going to miss you."

"I'm going to miss you more." Effie breathed around the lump Hope heard forming in her throat. "What does it look like?"

"What?"

"Your life from now on?"

Hope sighed. She had been on such a roller coaster since learning about the baby that the answer to that question seemed to change daily. It had been dangerous to wish for a future she wasn't sure was hers to claim until that morning. "I think it looks like standing Book and Bar dates with you, and an office library where I write my next twenty books. It looks like a bigger guest list at Christmas dinner and learning what kind of mom I want to be. I think it has the same roots, Effie. I really do, but it's heartier and fuller and better than I could have ever imagined. What about you?"

"I think Book and Bar dates will be the highlight of my week."

"Don't say that." Hope couldn't keep the worry from furrowing her brow. She wanted to ask about Effie's dreams and vision for her life, but she wasn't built like that. Hope had always known what she wanted to do and be. A writer, a mother. But Effie didn't dream up possible futures, almost as if she didn't think it was safe to do so.

"It won't feel like home without you."

"I've spent time living away before."

"Never for good."

"Maybe you'll need to renegotiate what feeling at home means," Hope offered, a bit of guilt tugging at her insides about abandoning Effie amidst her turmoil when the Thatchers had been in rare form as of late.

"Yeah, maybe," Effie whispered, and Hope knew there was more she wasn't saying, but she let it lie.

Instead, she bathed in the sun, Effie's hand in hers, knowing with conviction that they would always flock together, whether they shared a wall or not.

Effie kept to herself most of the rest of the week, not wanting to engage in any actual confrontations with her sister or mother. Only Ellen had sought her out to apologize for their behavior. The other two were either afraid to approach Effie or didn't feel bad enough to say anything.

She'd managed to dodge them all weekend, keeping to her room with her nose in a romance novel or out for walks or lingering late at work.

Craft night at Glitter & Glue began with a box of chocolates left on the counter and a note from Theo. Apparently, he did his best to believe her strange departure wasn't an actual breakup, though it had felt like one to her. She didn't correct him, because her head and her heart disagreed.

Yes, she'd done well hiding, but it was Monday which meant it was her turn to cook breakfast and she could avoid no longer.

"You've been keeping well to yourself," Dorothea mused from her place in front of the cast-iron skillet warming homemade sausages they had prepped and frozen last week. The sage and thyme in the patties balanced the sweet aroma of the waffles Effie piled onto a platter.

"I'm sorry," Effie said. Grams tried to catch her eye, but Effie kept her head down. Everything felt wrong since that night, and despite all that occurred around the dinner table, Effie only had herself to blame for her current angst.

Louisa was the first one downstairs, Hazel on her hip. She set the toddler in her high chair with a sippy cup of milk and a myriad of toys. She slipped between Effie and Dorothea en route to the coffee pot that finished brewing an aromatic roast that Effie loved the smell of but hated the taste of. "Good morning," Louisa chirped.

"Morning, sweetie."

The gurgle of coffee into the ceramic mug drowned out the other sounds of the kitchen, Effie hyperaware of Louisa's location and movements. Pins pricked the back of her neck. For all her talk of confronting everyone, she was never very good at it. "Morning," Effie muttered.

Louisa huffed, resting against the counter next to the waffle iron Effie tended. "Look, I'm sorry we ambushed you. For what it's worth, I assumed you didn't know how *extensive* his history was and wanted to warn you."

"You could have done that privately," Effie said through gritted teeth, though she knew it wouldn't have felt any better without Theo there to intervene.

"I promise it came from a good place."

"I wish that mattered," Effie spat as she plopped two more fluffy waffles onto the pile. She carried the platter to the breakfast table.

"Effie, come on."

Effie spun around. "No, you come on! All you and Mom accomplished was getting in my head, unnerving *me*. You didn't embarrass him or call him out or even tell me anything I didn't already know! You just ruined things."

"If he was so easily pushed away then we were right to say something."

"He wasn't! You ruined *my* confidence, *my* faith."

Hazel fussed in her seat, not liking Effie's rising sharpness. Effie stood beside her and smoothed back her featherlight wisps of hair. "I'm sorry, little bird." She turned to Louisa. "You should have let it go."

"We didn't want you making the same mistakes we did."

"They're mine to make," Effie scolded, though something in her gut prodded her not to think of Theo as a mistake.

Louisa crossed the kitchen past Grams who quietly hummed to herself as she continued her prep, doing her best to butt out. Louisa took Effie by the shoulders and looked her in the eye. "You're right. Truly. I'm sorry."

Effie believed her, would forgive her, but hated how easy it was when it didn't change the fact that the seeds of insecurity that always lived in her head were now germinated with their meddling.

"I'll talk to Mom for you."

"It was her idea to ask around, wasn't it?" Louisa clamped her teeth around a confirmation. "We can stand up to her you know? It won't kill us."

Louisa huffed a laugh. "I've never done it. It might." Effie thought she had a point. "Regardless, I promise to apologize to him at the ball."

"He's not coming to the ball," Effie muttered. "I never invited him. I guess I was worried he'd be gone . . ."

Louisa looked a bit guilty as she took her seat, the rest of the clan meandering to the table. "Well, no one ever said we weren't excellent at self-sabotage. But he's definitely coming. He bought a ticket."

Effie nearly sloshed the tea she poured all over the table. "What? No."

"Is that a problem? Did something happen?"

"Is what a problem?" Hope asked, easing into her chair, her sleep-mussed bun flopped to one side of her head.

"Theo coming to the ball," Louisa said.

Effie clocked her mother's smug look as she settled in reaching for the coffee pot Louisa had deposited on a trivet in the center of the table. All of a sudden Effie was five with storybooks about princes interrupted with bitter truths, thirteen learning that men only want one thing, twenty-one and told love was a losing game. Effie's inner thermometer had risen past boiling before her mother even spoke. "Effie, love, what happened?"

Effie, the quiet one, the one used to waiting her turn, the least squeaky wheel of all finally snapped. "You happened!"

Pamela blanched, as shocked by Effie's tone as everyone else in the kitchen. The subtle clatter of Hazel's toy on her tray was the only indication that Effie still stood in her family home and not in the eye of a storm buzzing with pent-up electricity.

"You are petty and jealous and never look in a fucking mirror except to keep tabs on the wrinkles you insist on Botoxing away. Did it ever occur to you that you were the problem? For years I have wanted to avoid ending up like you, bitter about men and alone. But apparently, I'm an overachiever because I swung too far the other way. I can't begin to fathom why anyone would want to be *with me* when the world is full of more intelligent, more beautiful, more desirable women. In this room alone I am not the most *anything*. So what happened after your supposedly benevolent little stunt? I blew up the fucking ship!"

Effie's fingers fumbled around her apron strings, shaking with rage and shame. She couldn't get it untied. "Effie," her mother sighed, her own shame mingling with affection. The rest of the room went silent as if Effie unearthing her most private inner thoughts had finally left them speechless.

Effie released the knot on her apron and threw it on the ground before storming out. She slid on her Birkenstocks and made for the door. She wasn't due at work for a couple of hours but she wasn't about to stay here. These feelings couldn't be corked, and she didn't want to say anything else she couldn't take back.

She opened the door, strode down the front steps, and collided with a wall of muscle behind a blue-collared shirt. Theo took her by the shoulders gaze dipping to meet hers. "Hey, are you alright?"

"No." She struggled free of his grip and stomped down the sidewalk. He hustled to catch up. Effie noticed the to-go cup in his hand for the first time and was grateful he had managed to keep from scalding her with its contents.

He tried to hand it to her. "Darjeeling?"

Effie stopped on a dime, spinning to face him. Her head was swimming. Her anger, grief, and poor self-image threatened to drown her where she stood. Warning lights flashed, motorcycles crashed, good things broke and splintered making her see red. "Why are you here?"

"I wanted to see you," he said so innocently that Effie's heart broke a little more. Every feeling compelled her to sink into him, take the tea, walk together, and forget she ever freaked out. But her thoughts were screaming at her to stay safe, to walk away, to see logic and know that she was not enough of a woman for the man before her. "Why? We broke up," she snipped.

It was definitely news to him.

"That was a breakup?"

"Yes."

"I don't think it counts if only half of us knew it was a breakup," Theo teased, in a desperate attempt to hold on to her beneath a cool and collected exterior. It was also an offering, to forget the whole thing, take it back.

Effie's heart begged her to take it. But her head had always been louder. "Then I'll say it plainly now. I'm breaking up with you."

She turned before he could stop her, before she could see how her words had landed. For her, it was an icy crack of peppermint coated in acrid smoke. She knew where the smoke came from.

It was how it tasted to burn everything you'd ever wanted to the ground.

⚜

Theo hadn't had a day this horrible in a long time, and it wasn't even noon yet. He left Effie's house with a storm cloud over his head, his feet acting of their own will to vacate the Thatcher home before anyone else came rushing out to stomp on his heart that surely landed amidst the violets lining the walkway when Effie ripped it out.

He had thought Effie's outburst odd after dinner with her family, but he assumed she was merely riled, not ready to give up on them. *Maybe he shouldn't have given her so much space to calm down?*

As he drove between appointments he replayed their night, the next morning, and the brief encounter that ended in an official breakup. He tumbled each word, each look around inspecting them for any sign that she truly didn't want to be with him. He kept coming up empty-handed, but it didn't change the outcome. *I'm breaking up with you.*

Theo admired the clarity, the succinctness of it. He'd broken up with many women and always tried to convey the underlying feeling or lack thereof responsible for the ending. Questions and curiosities made it hard to move on, and right now he had so many questions. Chief among them, *how could he fix it?*

35

Effie sat at the small vanity in the corner of her room where the most natural light came in. Curlers wound atop her head, and she donned a floor-length silk robe. Chatter from downstairs worked its way under her closed door, the clink of glassware being unloaded and the hum of strings being tuned a reminder that the ball was fast approaching.

The trouble was, Effie didn't feel much like dancing. Or socializing. The only thing about the evening she looked forward to at this point was the gown Dorothea had helped her make months ago when Louisa had first decided on *enchanted garden* as the theme for this year's ball. It suited Effie wonderfully, unlike last year's masquerade or the starry night theme of the year before. This year was florals and frills and pastels, something that they'd easily reflected in the soft ballgown.

It had a corseted bodice, the boning visible beneath the sheer fabric that laid over the blush-pink satin underneath. The appliquéd organza gathered into a sweetheart neckline with two puffed, off-the-shoulder sleeves that drooped elegantly down her arms. From the fitted waist, layers of cream and blush organza created an opaque full skirt that swished when Effie walked. She favored the top layer of off-white fabric, the one with intricate appliqués of mauve and pink peonies, a mix of green and white leaves giving the folds of the dress texture and depth. She'd startled Basil with a squeal when she unpacked the fabric from a new order at the store months ago.

The dress hung, steamed and ready to wear, on the outside of her closet door. She'd never pinned any hopes on that dress, never imagined this night to be anything more than another marker of time passing. But somehow looking at it now, Effie was keenly aware that this night *could* have been something, but she'd failed again to take the advice her father whispered to her all those years ago. *If you don't ask the question, the answer is always no.*

Brayden had never worn a cummerbund in his life, but he didn't hate it. Especially not when Hope lit up at seeing him in it. She had spent the night with him, and waking with her beside him was pure bliss. They still had some of the house to furnish, the living room they were currently standing in, Hope adjusting the cornflower-blue bow tie around his neck, was barren but for a giant mirror leaned against the wall leftover from some previous owner. Somehow though, with her here in a breezy blue dress that matched him, tiny yellow flowers stitched all over, the drape perfect over her pregnant belly, the house had never felt more full.

Brayden looked forward to the night of levity and fun ahead of them since the last few days had been a whirlwind. They'd set a date for Hope to move in, hired movers, and shopped for hours for furniture and trimmings for the house that were still weeks out from delivery. They'd also told everyone about their plans, and to his surprise it had gone alright. Though he would admit that the conversation with his mothers about his reconciliation with Hope was less than ideal. They had been the ones to convince him that he needed to tread lightly moving forward for the sake of being a good dad. Their opinion of Hope had declined rapidly as light was shone on her secrets and willingness to believe the worst about him.

But after a couple of hours, too many of Ma's oatmeal chocolate chip cookies to count, and a promise to institute consistent visits with their grandbaby, things had smoothed over. Hope braved the scene toward the end of their talk, bringing with her every ultrasound photo and the exact right words to let his parents know that he meant the world to her. The latter could have been a result of the way she dropped the curtain to reveal the depth of her feelings for him. Whatever the case, they all left the exchange with a contentment where anxiety used to live.

Hope finished with his tie and laid her hands on his chest. "You are one handsome fella."

Brayden took her hands in his and kissed the tops of her knuckles. "And what are you hoping for tonight, love? Dancing? Chocolate fountain? Stolen kisses on the patio until the sun comes up?"

"Truthfully I'd like to go, have a dance, a raspberry tart, then come home and watch a movie in bed with you."

"I like that this is home now," Brayden said, and it didn't convey the breadth of the satisfaction he felt. His life had come together just as he'd imagined it that first day meeting Hope at the bookstore, after all.

"It's still weird to say, but I'm working on it. No thoughts on my plans to bail early?"

Brayden squinted at the golden light beaming through the window as the sun sank toward the horizon. "Just that we won't have internet until Tuesday, and you might be inclined to stay longer once we get there."

"Unless something truly dramatic happens, I doubt it. But I'm willing to be proven wrong."

Brayden clutched a hand to his chest in faux shock. "What? You? Wrong? Could it be, folks, that Hope Thatcher is loosening the reins? Surrendering control?"

Hope glared at him with pursed lips resisting a smile. "Let's not go that far." And as if to prove the point she adjusted his tie one more time and patted him on the cheek before leading him to the door.

It was so damn good to have her back.

Louisa had truly outdone herself. Hope was nearly convinced they'd walked into the wrong house when they arrived.

The door to the hobby room had been transformed into a coat check counter complete with a tweed-suited attendant who ran the ticketing system for leaving coats, hats, or purses. On the other side of the foyer, the dining room was already loud with the boisterous banter of a card game. The men bellied up to the large table she recognized as the high school principal, the police chief, and other notable business owners who would rather hide in a card game than twirl their wives around the dance floor. Hope didn't blame them, Louisa always insisted the dances were more intricate than your average waltz. The velvet rope across the stairs to prevent curious attendees from wandering caught Hope's attention as Brayden removed her shawl and checked it. A soft laugh left her lips at the sight of it. "What's funny?" Brayden asked.

"The rope. It's Louisa's biggest grievance that the stairs come down to the front door and not into the great room. No grand entrances like at your—our—house."

"Maybe we'll host next year so Louisa can sweep in."

"I think she might kill you if you suggest it."

"Noted." Brayden offered Hope his arm. Her hand clasped over his elbow as they eased into the great room.

It was magnificent.

The band occupied the corner of the room, blocking one set of doors to the patio, but leaving plenty of room for dancing in the center. Floral garlands hung from the mantel and the floors were buffed and waxed to a shining finish. Tall golden planters lined the walls, overflowing with peonies, baby's breath, and drooping wisteria. The latter was mirrored in the arbor Hope spotted through the French doors on the patio, the picture of enchantment with lush purple blooms and draping greenery.

It was like stepping back in time or into an elaborate scene from a movie. In another life, Louisa might have made a fabulous set designer. If the decor wasn't proof enough that it was a night of splendor, then the ethereal gowns, pastel silks, and crystal glasses of champagne served by waiters with silver trays were. Every detail invited guests to step into the decadent daydream. The commitment to the theme in dress and diligence with which the couples already on the dance floor followed along with the pair of professional dancers before them told Hope just how much people wanted a fantasy. Pride swelled in her chest, and for the first time in all the years Louisa had been hosting this event, Hope felt something like a kinship with her cousin. They both created a space for people to imagine, play, and try on an alternate reality. One with books, one with a night everyone in this room looked forward to all year.

Giving voice to her inner thoughts, Brayden said, "This is amazing. You get to do this every year?"

"And now you do too," she cooed. In earnest, she gazed at the love of her life. "Thank you for keeping your tuxedo rental through it all." She had invited him as soon as Louisa put the tickets on preorder and the next day they'd rented his tux. It wasn't long after that everything fell apart.

"To be honest, I forgot about it." He squeezed her hand. "But it seems my subconscious knew something I didn't."

Hope spotted Louisa in the crowd, and she hurried over to them. "Well?"

"Incredible, Louisa. I'm Brayden, I don't think we've met." He extended a hand and Louisa took it, beaming. Hope noted her approving assessment.

Louisa turned her eager gaze on Hope, needing more confirmation. "It's perfect, Lou. I can't believe how beautiful it is in here."

She clutched Hope's forearm and squealed. "Wait until you see the patio." Louisa's grip slackened as she stared across the room to the kitchen, past the cozy conversation set that replaced the breakfast table, where a waiter loaded desserts on a tray. "Excuse me, that's not the course order!" Louisa stalked toward the gangly teen server leaving Brayden and Hope to marvel at the glittering chandeliers and the spark in the air. Hope felt the promise of a wondrous evening in her bones.

And then he walked in.

Brayden wouldn't confirm if he'd actually show. All he'd been able to offer was that Theo was a wreck despite his best efforts to act as though he was a man with a plan. Apparently, part of that plan involved surprising Effie by actually coming tonight. For some reason, Hope sagged with relief that Effie was nowhere in sight as Theo strode toward them. She thought Effie might flee at the sight of him.

He was devastating in his midnight-black tuxedo that hugged his shoulders and tapered with his waist. The coat was left unbuttoned, flipped back with roguish confidence behind the hands that were tucked casually into his pockets. His white shirt fit so well it had to have been tailored, and where a tie should be Theo wore only an open collar. "You're gawking," Brayden teased.

Hope blushed. "I am not."

Brayden laughed. "I'd be offended, but you're not the only one." He was right, many eyes, mostly female, were securely fixed on Theo. "Hell, I think he's handsome too."

"Oh my God, shut up," Hope squeaked, Theo right by her side.

"What's going on?" Theo said by way of greeting, but his eyes quickly searched the room for the someone he yearned to see.

"Hope was checking you out." Hope slapped Brayden across the shoulder.

Theo's laugh was warm and rich. "It's the tux, I promise." But the twinkle in his eye told Hope he knew he was worth a second and third glance with or without the tux. She admired the self-assuredness and imagined it had little to do with his looks and everything to do with knowing himself. She only wished it had rubbed off on Effie more.

After a few polite exchanges and small talk about the decor, Theo seemed ready to crack. "Is she coming?"

Hope's developing motherly instincts compelled her to wrap him in a hug and smooth the worry from his brow. Despite his palpable anxiety and vulnerability, she kept her hands to herself. "She should be."

"Or she's sitting upstairs alone and missing out because she heard I was coming."

"No one knew for certain. Louisa just told her you bought a ticket."

"I shouldn't have come. She would have invited me if she wanted me here." Theo shot a sharp look at Brayden.

His path to the entrance was now blocked anyway by a woman in a ravishing gown fit for an enchanted queen with side-swept curls tumbling below her collarbone.

The woman Hope, Aunt Bea, Grams, and now Theo saw so much more clearly than she ever saw herself.

Effie Rose Thatcher.

The one and only.

36

Seeing her was an arrow through the heart. It was a special kind of anguish being on the precipice of forever to have it yanked away without warning. Without cause. Though Theo supposed from Effie's perspective there was plenty of cause, she just wasn't sharing what it was.

Effie smiled through a few greetings as she meandered through the gathered guests. His jaw ticked with every gaze that trailed behind her with a longing he knew intimately. It took more strength than he knew he possessed to keep from whisking her onto the dance floor for all to see, to claim her lips, and to show her off. But when she finally found him in the room, her face dropped and Theo swore his heart stopped right along with it.

She wasn't happy to see him.

He was going to kill Schilling. Theo hoped the daggers he threw at him conveyed as much. Schilling's cowed shrug said he understood, but not that he was sorry.

Theo supposed that was only fair. It would all be over soon and he could leave Effie in peace.

Effie arrived at their little group avoiding Theo and pinning her eyes on Hope. "Show-off. I should have had you and Grams do mine, though I guess it would have been wasted this year." Hope smoothed her skirt over her rounded stomach, and Theo unwittingly imagined what Effie might look like carrying their baby. *Fuck.* That was not a train of thought he should entertain.

He speared his awareness back on the present, looking at Effie's dress anew. "You made that?" She was truly an impressive creature. He fancied himself a creative person, but he was a hobbyist. Effie made creativity a lifestyle.

"With some help. Grams is determined to make a seamstress of me yet." She spoke directly to him but there was a tightness to it, a chain attached.

Her gaze lingered on Theo for a breath, too short to read what lay beneath her oceanic eyes. Hope, thankfully, intervened before he could put his foot in his mouth. "Let's go get a snack, I'm famished. Get your dancing shoes ready, gentlemen."

She led Effie toward a waiter in the corner with a tray of flakey samosas, bacon-wrapped scallops, and something that looked like seared tofu skewers.

Theo's shoulders dropped their tension with his exhale. "I'm sorry," Schilling whispered.

"It's not your fault, but don't expect me to linger," Theo said tightly.

The pity on Schilling's face was a twist of the knife. "You're not even going to try to get her back?"

"I'm not going to push her. I just want her to know I'm here, whenever she's ready to be here with me." Theo scratched a phantom itch at the back of his neck. He couldn't very well respect her wishes and lay the truth of his feelings at her feet.

"But?"

"But that's assuming I'm right. That she got spooked but still wants me. If she doesn't . . ." Schilling's hand gripped Theo's shoulder in a show of support.

Not until she'd accused him of trying their relationship on for size and declaring that he couldn't know how deep their connection ran already, did he realize how tenuous their bond was. He thought they were falling together. Apparently, he had leapt while she remained firmly on the ledge, and he'd come splattering across rock-bottom with no way of knowing if she ever intended to jump at all. His self-pitying reverie was cut short as the ladies returned, Hope offering a samosa to Schilling.

The band played the final notes of the current song, one Theo knew he recognized but couldn't parse out in its instrumental version. He expected Effie to delight in the tide of the beautiful melody—no threat of unpleasant word tastes to ruin the evening. But she was stoic. Refusing, it seemed, to let herself enjoy the evening. The quiet before the next song filled with Hope's request for a dance.

"As the lady desires," Schilling replied while sketching a bow. Hope led him to the dance floor with a flick of her brows at Effie who stood beside Theo twiddling her fingers around the dance card on her wrist.

"Do you have room on your dance card?" Theo asked, wanting to get lost in the fantasy along with everyone else.

"They're more for show, but I guess so. One dance."

Theo nodded. He'd take it.

He offered his arm, a less intimate point of contact, to lead her to the floor in time for the next song to kick up. Theo clocked the dancers at the front of the room and recognized the dance almost immediately. Perks of being in the chorus for the high school's rendition of *Anastasia* his freshman year. He'd keep Effie in his arms through most of it, but there was a moment when partners would change hands at the end. He positioned them to Schilling and Hope's left, catching the former's eye and giving him a subtle nod.

Theo let his body guide him in remembering the steps, only checking in with the pros at the front now and again. Theo lifted their hands in delicate arches. He pushed Effie away to welcome her back with a twirl, all the while keeping his eyes fixed on hers.

The music became a hum to keep time to and nothing more. The chatter was consumed by the swish of Effie's skirts, the soft hush of her breath. This should be a night to remember, romantic as hell with him whispering to her all the ways she moved him. His fingers curled into her waist against his will but if she felt the longing in the gesture, she didn't let on. Theo forced himself to focus on the steps, and not on his desire to kiss her.

"I'm usually terrible at this," Effie mused.

Theo executed another wistful twirl and welcomed her back to his embrace. "You didn't have the right partner," he said matter-of-factly. "It's easy because I know the steps, and you're trusting me to lead."

Effie didn't reply but glanced over to Hope and Schilling. They were good, but it wasn't as effortless. When she faced Theo again she looked ready to speak, but she held her tongue. Theo filled the silence instead. "I was reading up on your lady slippers. Did you know that they can take up to sixteen years to develop their first flower?"

"That's a long time."

"So how much has to go right for us to see them in the woods. The right soil pH, the presence of a symbiotic fungus to help them germinate and grow, no disturbances to their root systems, and the right amount of sunshine. If any of those things were rushed or missing, we would never get to see one. And to think that the fleeting blooms we do find could have been working to that exact moment for so long, with no one noticing is kind of heartbreaking."

Effie's brow furrowed. "Why?"

"Because too few people are awed by the patience and process of the things they admire coming into existence. I don't want to be one of them. Some things are worth the wait."

Effie's grip warmed his shoulder, and he could tell her anxiety bubbled up causing clammy hands. She tried to ask it with a bit of playfulness, but it came out blunt instead. "So you want to be my fungus?" He bit back his smile at her scrunched nose. Fungus probably didn't taste great.

Theo checked on Schilling beside him, he didn't have much time, and he wouldn't dare say what he burned to, what she'd prevented him from telling her that morning, so instead he said. "No, Effie, I want to be your forest."

Before she could answer Theo passed her to the gentleman on their left, receiving Hope mid-spin. Theo seamlessly led her in a slow circle, their palms touching right above their foreheads, so they lost sight of Schilling for a beat as the music ended.

For a brief moment the room went dark, the overhead chandelier and lighting all switched off. He held Hope steady and spun her toward the center of the dance floor as the lights came back up.

Schilling stood on one knee with an engagement ring in a velvet box in one hand, and a bouquet of cosmos in the other. "Hope Thatcher, will you marry me?"

Hope brought her hands to her face, smothering the squeal or sob that wanted to break through. "Yes. Yes, yes, yes." She hurried forward and Schilling slipped the ring on her finger. He stood and kissed her, cheers and applause breaking out through the ballroom that was really Effie's living room.

Theo turned his attention to Dorothea and Beatrice who stood by the light switches clutching each other on the far end of the room. Dorothea winked at him and he nodded his thanks. Louisa and Ellen donned authentic smiles, while Tibby's tears were pure joy. Even Pamela looked excited as she squeezed her sister's hand. These were the women he knew Effie loved, the ones who knew how good it really *could* be.

Then he saw Effie, stunned. Not unhappy or even rattled, just surprised like she pieced together why Theo was here in the first place. He hoped that it didn't upset her. He hoped she knew that proposal or not he would have *wanted* to spend this evening with her, but only if she had wanted the same. Theo prayed to whatever gods were listening that at the very least, Effie could believe that Theo was hers entirely. He gave her a sad sort of smile, one that would have carried so much more if she was ready for the depth of his feelings for her, then turned and walked out the door.

Louisa hadn't oversold the patio. Lights like stars twinkled over the expanse of the bluestone that stretched from the French doors to the hedgerow that delineated their property from the neighbors'. The arbor of wisteria welcomed guests to the maze of planters that created alcoves of privacy under the summer sky. Benches and wicker chairs populated each nook so cocktails could be sipped and private moments could be shared.

Hope and Brayden sat together at one such bench, Hope's hand extended before her, her new engagement ring glimmering in the faux starlight. It was so beautiful, Hope thought she might cry. It had a platinum band with intricate filigree that gave the impression that elves had crafted it in another world. The prongs formed a pointed star shape inset with small diamonds to cradle the large oval sapphire in the center. It was the fantasy ring of her dreams and she couldn't believe it decorated her finger. "It looks like that one I loved at the Christmas market we went to."

Hope beamed at Brayden who looked on cloud nine, eyebrows raised. "It *is* the one from the Christmas market. I went back the next day and bought it."

Hope gaped at him. They'd only been dating a few months at that point. He had still technically been married. She was almost, if not already, pregnant with Bug. It was almost too much to fathom. "And you've held on to it since?"

"I know we've had our issues, Hope, but how much I love you was never in question."

She took his face in her hands and kissed him with no small amount of joy at realizing that not only would she get to do it forever, but she would do it as his wife with him as her husband. Hope liked the way that sounded.

"And if Effie asks," Brayden ventured, "that's why Theo was here.

He got his ticket with me when Louisa first posted them for sale. I had always planned on asking you tonight . . . before everything went sideways with us . . . and wanted my best man by my side. He wasn't trying to impose when she didn't want him around. He was helping me."

Hope thought on that for a moment. She couldn't be certain Effie *didn't* want Theo around, but she kept that to herself. "It was a simply fun way to find you down on one knee. I'm glad he came."

"Me too," Brayden said. "It's weird though. Nothing about how I feel about you has changed in the last ten minutes, but I *feel* changed. Like this is all just beginning. It all feels new."

"I know what you mean," Hope said smiling. She rested her head on Brayden's shoulder, hand on her belly, as she enjoyed the majesty of Louisa's garden ball.

Hope saw the lavender bell of her dress before she saw Louisa wander through the arbor to a patch of grass beneath the lights. She looked heavenward, unaware of Hope's attention. The deep breath that lifted her chest felt like it released a monster from her back. The wind rustled and the music carried farther through the backyard garden as a new set of footsteps shuffled across the bluestone.

Hope squeezed Brayden's hand and watched with bated breath as a gentleman caller handed Louisa a glass of champagne. Louisa's returning smile was coquettish and warm—nothing like the cynical, overprotective sister Hope experienced the other night.

"You're right," she whispered to Brayden. "Everything is new." Hope smiled, a magic settling over the Thatcher house in the wake of Brayden's proposal. A magic that felt an awful lot like breaking a curse.

37

Effie didn't waste any time after the ball searching for a gallery space for Aunt Beatrice. It was a nice distraction from her self-pity and the boxes that piled up in Hope's bedroom.

Effie's inquiries around town had led her to the doors of the Portsmouth Historical Society. They had a few rental spaces within their two buildings that would do nicely for a watercolor show complete with light appetizers, drinks, and mingling. Effie had scoped out the spaces ahead of time and invited Aunt Beatrice out to approve the one she liked best.

They walked along the second-story gallery in the federal-style building on Middle Street. A white wooden railing marked out the open center of the floor, looking down on the well-kept interior. Paneled walls made great frames for art pieces that the event coordinator assured them could be swapped out for Beatrice's paintings.

"What do you think?" Effie asked.

"It's perfect." Beatrice beamed, patting Effie's arm where she held it for support during their turn about the space.

"We have an opening two weeks from today," the coordinator exclaimed from behind her clipboard. "Since you're doing appetizers and cocktails I should be able to pull it together quickly for you."

"Perfect." Effie bubbled with excitement at making these plans for her dear great-aunt. "But we will require a signature cocktail for the lady of the hour. Something with gin and lavender."

"Oh, Effie. Don't fuss."

"Fuss I must. You're too important to let this be glossed over. We aren't just renting a space. We're celebrating your *years* of beautiful artwork." Effie turned to the event coordinator. "Do you have a weekly newsletter we could announce the show in?"

"Of course, but we do charge for advertisements."

"Whatever it is, I'll pay it," Effie said with such confidence she wondered why everything in her life wasn't so easy to decide.

"I'll go draw up your contract and make a note about the cocktail. Feel free to peruse and plan," she said gesturing to the space.

Effie led a quiet Aunt Beatrice in another turn about the room, noting which walls would be best for a display of Issa portraits and how they might lay out the evolution of the Thatcher women along the four walls that made up the expansive circle of the balcony-like room. "What's on your mind?" Effie finally asked.

A pensive beat before Beatrice replied, "You don't have to go through so much trouble. I only wanted them displayed for a night. I didn't need a *show*."

"I know you didn't need it, but it feels right, don't you think?"

"It feels like *something*, and it's been a good long while since I've had *something* to look forward to. For that, I will be forever grateful."

Effie paused before an oil painting of a bowl of fruit. She had never understood still life paintings, finding them to be more evidence of skill or practice in color theory than actual artwork. But this one, with its blue lace tablecloth and ceramic bowl filled with berries and stone fruits, had her wondering if she'd judged the style too harshly. There was a sweetness to the brush strokes, a calm in the beam of light through the blurred window in the background.

It reminded her of their kitchen, their own bowl of fruit that rested in the center of the breakfast table. It became an emblem of life lived around the objects and a sentience radiated from the blue lace, the worn wood, the fruit that would never rot or be eaten.

"Aunt Bea?"

"Yes, Effie dear?"

"Does it ever get easier to let yourself be happy?"

A sigh emanated from the sturdy, wrinkled frame of the woman beside her. "I think it's the hardest thing in the world to let yourself be happy."

"Why?"

"Because then we have to admit that we were the only thing keeping us from it all along."

Effie nodded, eyes drifting to the bowl of fruit. At first glance, it was pristine, almost too good to be true. Until Effie noticed the bruise on one of the peaches, the chip in the bowl on its lip, and the stain on the napkin that was draped beside it.

It was messy and blemished on close inspection, but when she took in the whole picture it was absolutely perfect.

Hope forgot how annoying moving was. Not that her single room at Thatcher house had enough space for too many belongings, but combing through bookshelves and cabinets in their shared spaces for her favorite novels, photo albums, and boxes of memorabilia from high school and college had been a monumental task.

Effie had been right, she had never moved away without some thought that she'd eventually wind up back within the walls of 53 Austin Street. It was bittersweet to box her yearbooks and college sweatshirts to carry on to her forever home.

As for the crib and changing table Brayden had set up in her room, they'd been disassembled and brought to the attic for storage. *In case someone else needs them soon* Grams had said. Hope was on the cusp of donating them but couldn't argue that they were in better shape than Louisa's crib that had been handed down through the generations. It would be retired as soon as Hazel was old enough for a big girl bed.

Time moved too fast.

Hazel already talked and walked and would soon be three. Hope wondered who would be next to need the crib or if it would gather dust in the attic for years to come.

Brayden interrupted her thoughts with a rap on her open window. "You ready?"

"I thought you used the front door now?"

He ducked into the room from his perch on the roof. "One last climb, for old time's sake." Brayden came up behind her and wrapped his arms around her shoulders, kissing the side of her forehead. Hope sighed, a pang of sadness at the emptiness of the room around her.

The twin bed remained, stripped of the purple duvet. The walls were bare, dark squares left behind where Hope's photos and framed book covers had hung on her wall. The small closet was empty, and the space felt enormous without her large armoire. Hope assumed someone else would take over the room eventually. Maybe Hazel, if the upstairs great room with its private bath stopped serving the little tot and her mother.

Brayden must have sensed the sadness in her heart because he whispered in her ear. "We're a few blocks away. You can come home anytime."

"Home is with you now," Hope replied but it still felt odd to strip her house here, her family, of that title.

"It's wherever you want it to be, Hope. I saw a tea towel at the market yesterday that said home is where your mom is. Other people say it's where your heart lives. I say it's where you're always welcome to be yourself, and that can be applied to more than one place."

"Or person," Hope said, spinning in Brayden's arms to face him. She leaned into him for a kiss, her lips lingering for a long moment.

He mumbled against the bow of her mouth, "The movers are going to beat us there."

"Will you go ahead?" Hope asked. "I want to walk with Effie."

Brayden kissed her forehead. "I'll see you over there." He made for the window and Hope couldn't help but smile. He saluted her before scaling down the porch banister. Hope shut the window behind him and locked it tight.

Hope found Effie in her room, an embroidery hoop in hand. "I have one type of fern finished already for the baby's room. Halfway done with this one." Effie turned the oversized hoop to face Hope, an olive-green thread danced along the linen fabric in the curves of woodland greenery. "Thank you," she said.

The quiet pause triggered Effie to ask, "Time to go?"

"For now," Hope mustered. Effie rose from her seat by the window where she preferred to work in the sunlight and walked to Hope's side.

"For good," she countered but her words weren't angry. "Yes, you'll come by often, but you're moving into your new life, and it's okay."

She looped her arm through Hope's and led her across the hall, down the stairs, and out the door into the humid summer heat. Effie wasn't telling her that she was shutting them out completely, but that she had to close the door on her chapter at 53 Austin. It was okay to let it live in the past because she needed to give herself fully to her new life with Brayden, her new house. Her whole bright future.

They walked in silence for a bit, the sun threatening to burn Hope's delicate cheeks when Effie finally said, "We'll have to institute Saturday morning breakfasts at the house or something. Easy enough since you can walk over."

"I like the sound of that," Hope uttered, the anxiety about moving out for good rounding out into the picture Effie painted. It was just as she'd told Effie on the patio, things were fuller and better. The move was growth, not an ending. It felt much better to view it that way.

They reached the white fence, and the new flowers Hope picked sat in their pots ready to be planted where she'd laid them out. She looked to Effie who took in the large house before them, the fairy tale come true. Her face turned solemn, but it wasn't the house she looked at.

It was the motorcycle parked on the street by the driveway.

"I told Brayden you were coming today," Hope said a bit angry that he'd ask Theo to help without consulting her first.

"It's fine," Effie croaked, but the tension in her jaw said otherwise.

"We are supposed to get some heavy pieces delivered today . . ." Hope mused, certain that Brayden was in search of some extra brawn since she was not in the mood or condition to heft furniture around.

"I promise, it's fine." But her tone had sharpened.

They walked through the front door and sure enough, Theo was there with Brayden muscling the new sofa into position across from the mantel. It was a large sectional that they assembled by clipping the extending L shape into the hooks of the other piece. It looked heavy if the glistening sweat on both of their brows was any indication. Theo looked up meeting their surprised looks. "Hey."

Effie turned to Hope. "Where do you want this?" she asked, lifting the reusable grocery bag she'd carried for Hope into the air.

It wasn't much, a few things she hadn't wanted boxed or in the truck. A carved jewelry box that her dad had given her mom before she was born, a ratty, old stuffed rabbit that she'd loved to near death, the first copy of her first book, and an embroidered lilac Effie had made for Hope's middle name. "It should all go upstairs, but you don't—"

"I'll figure it out."

Effie hurried up the stairs and away from Theo, who was shirtless and sweating and far too handsome to keep a rational distance from. She hadn't reached out to him since the ball, and she hadn't heard from him either. She supposed he'd said it all, laid it all bare, if only in sentiment. *I want to be your forest.* To Effie that meant he wanted to protect her, nurture her, help her grow, and be her home. He'd never let her read his poems, but his turns of phrase were loaded enough that if she ever read them, she might combust.

Hope and Brayden's bedroom was at the top of the stairs. The dark walls and brooding tones were made inviting and cozy with little touches of light wood and linen when they might otherwise have turned austere. Effie opened the bag and retrieved the jewelry box within. She placed it atop the natural-wood bureau that stood under the large window on the back wall. If she played it right, she might make unpacking this bag last long enough to avoid Theo altogether.

The embroidery hoop she placed beside the jewelry box, propped against the wall in temporary display. Effie assumed that Hope wanted the stuffed animal in the baby's room, so she ventured down the hall to the nursery.

It was sweet and inviting, just as Hope had described. Effie put the stuffed bunny on one of the floating shelves that housed empty picture frames ready to display baby's firsts. She adjusted the bunny until it sat with one leg dangling over the edge of the thin shelf looking for all the world like the main character of a children's book.

The creak of old floorboards was her only warning. "Are you going to avoid me forever?" Theo was tall enough to take up most of the doorframe, his broad shoulders reaching for the jambs on either side. It hurt to look at him, to know she wanted him yet had turned him away. Maybe it was enough to know that for a fleeting moment in time, she had been desired by someone like him. Someone strong and handsome, kind and inquisitive, intoxicating and wholly out of her league. Though if the way his eyes grazed over her was any indication, it was Theo who felt undeserving of Effie. She almost laughed at the absurdity.

"Just until you stop looking at me like that," Effie confessed. She could see it clear as day, the longing, the heartache over the distance between them. But she couldn't see a way to move forward while she didn't love herself enough to believe she deserved this. Deserved him.

"I don't think I'll ever stop . . . but I'll try. If that's what you want."

Effie's breath caught in her throat. It wasn't what she wanted, *was it?* "I'm sure you won't have to try once you find someone who can love you better than me." The word had wedged through her mental screens. They'd dodged it all this time and yet it still lingered, waiting to be let free. If he heard it as the confession it was, Effie couldn't tell. His face remained stoic, but his teeth turned to diamonds with how hard he clenched them.

"One day, Effie, I hope you see yourself the way everyone else does."

Effie deflected with a huff. "Why?"

"Because maybe then you'll realize there is no one better for me. Maybe you'd let me in. Maybe we'd just be happy." He took a tentative step toward her. "Aren't you tired of talking around this?"

Yes. "No," Effie said instead. There was too much she was uncertain of, herself, the longevity of his affection for her, the way life looked if she let herself not just be contented or at peace, but *happy.*

In all her life she had never wanted for anything. She liked to float and bake and stay unattached to the outcome of things because it was safer. The only plans she made involved recipes and sewing patterns. But almost as soon as she met Theo she *wanted.* It was a feeling that had only ever been mirrored in how much she wanted to talk to her dad again, to see his face, to get his advice now that she'd grown up. It was dangerous to want because there was no guarantee that you'd get what your heart desired.

And as if God herself was demonstrating the ephemerality of joy, Hope screamed from downstairs, "Effie! We have to go!"

38

The smell of antiseptic stung Effie's nose. Each word she caught from the doctors and nurses around them through the fog of her grief carried with it a horrid new taste.

Stroke. Too much salt. *Unconscious.* Rusted copper. *Hospice.* Hot wax.

Somehow the rest of her family was able to give the medical professionals their full attention as they discussed the palliative care ahead. But Effie could only stare at Aunt Beatrice, laying horribly still in a hospital bed, wires and tubes connected to her. Machines beeping was the only real sign that she hadn't been lost yet.

Effie settled into a stiff chair with its plasticky upholstery and took Aunt Bea's hand in hers. She traced the veins visible beneath her fragile skin with her thumb. Bits of paint clung to the underside of her fingernails, and Effie couldn't have stopped the tears that came for anything.

It didn't matter that eighty-three was a good long life. It didn't matter that she'd had a fulfilling career in the sciences and shared her wisdom with countless students. It didn't matter that Beatrice had loved her Thatcher women with her whole heart and given the rest to a man who never came home from war. All that mattered to Effie in that moment was that Aunt Bea wouldn't see her own art show. She wouldn't meet up with those old friends. She wouldn't get to do all the things she'd put off, because her time had finally run out.

At least that's what the doctors were saying around her. That this was nearly impossible to come back from. But if Effie knew anything, it was that Aunt Beatrice was as unpredictable as they come. She had turned from chemistry to watercolors. She brought home exotic birds and dished like a schoolgirl in the cafeteria. She was too vivacious to be snuffed out. Though Effie knew it was an inevitability, being faced with the reality was entirely different.

People filtered in and out of the room all afternoon, but Effie remained.

Finally, when the sky had darkened outside the open window of Beatrice's hospital room, Effie felt a firm hand on her shoulder.

She looked up to see Pamela beside her, eyes red-rimmed from crying. "We're heading home," she said. "There's no support we can give her if we don't get some rest."

"I don't want to leave her. Someone should stay."

Pamela combed her fingers through Effie's hair the way mothers do when they want to soothe away the hurts of the world. "Let me."

Effie didn't know what else was baked into the offer. An olive branch. Maybe a show of solidarity or a desire to shield Effie from some bit of pain.

"That's okay," Effie said. "I want to stay. Besides, you should go be with Grams." Pamela didn't say it aloud but Effie knew she was grateful. Pamela had always preferred to grapple with the tangible problems before her, and making her own mother tea and rubbing her back until she fell asleep was something Pamela had the capacity for. Effie wasn't sure holding vigil in the quiet alone was.

Long into the night, Effie sat beside Beatrice. Her hands, usually clammy and sweating when her emotions were heightened, were steady and warm while Beatrice's grew colder.

She wondered what Beatrice was like when she was Effie's age. *Did she always wear bright pink bows in her hair? Had she been as sassy and bright when she met the only man she'd ever loved? Did she always dream of the life she'd built or was she just along for the ride? Did she regret not doing things sooner to set her heart on fire?*

Effie watched as Beatrice exhaled her last breath, any hope of getting to ask her vanishing with it.

It felt wrong for the sun to rise. For the birds to chirp and the streets to be filled with people going about their day like nothing happened as Effie walked home. It was a substantial distance, five miles or more, but Effie didn't care. She needed the air. After Aunt Beatrice finally fell into her endless slumber, Effie became paralyzed. The lone, piercing beep of a flatline was her only company for what felt like an eternity, though Effie supposed it was only a few moments before the nurses rushed in.

In all of Tibby's estate planning, she'd made sure to get directives from everyone in the house about what to do in case of such things. Beatrice wanted no extreme measures taken. When she went, she wanted to be let go. Effie thought that made sense at eighty-three if the alternative was a half-life of illness, but for herself, she wanted every extreme measure. At least until she reached a benchmark where her death would be sad instead of tragic. Her arms turned to gooseflesh. A life cut short without experiencing the breadth of existence did not sit well.

She thought of her dad.

He was only thirty-eight when he died. Effie wondered if he greeted Aunt Beatrice. If they were getting to know each other again in the afterlife. The thought eased something in Effie's chest as she plodded along, the day near sizzling as the sun rose even higher.

Effie had apologized profusely for wanting to leave once her family arrived. But nobody blamed her. In fact, they'd tried to encourage her to wait for Tibby to give her a ride home, but the walls of the hospital were closing in, a sort of helplessness piercing through her.

So she walked.

Effie's favorite thing about walking was how it cleared her mind. How it brought everything into sharper focus and had her feeling grounded. It didn't fix every hurt or help her understand life's bigger problems, but if she could focus on putting one foot in front of the other, even the hardest days felt a little lighter.

As she turned onto her street, the scent of lilac in the air, Effie wished she wasn't so familiar with grief. Fifteen years had passed since she'd lost her father, eight since Gramps, but the road looked the same. An aching heart, a hole in her mind where musings of Aunt Bea's activities used to live, a vile nausea at realizing she'd never hear her voice again. But as she rounded the corner onto the brick path that led to the house that would now feel a little more empty, she noticed something different about the journey of her grief.

And it sat on the front steps waiting for her.

Theo stood when he saw her, a tightness to his expression, none of the deep feelings she had seen before, like he tried to mask it and be here for her without any expectations. "Your mom called me," Theo said in his rich timbre.

Effie stood before him. Whether it was seeing him or the fact that her mother had thought he was what Effie needed that broke the veneer of calm, she couldn't say. But Effie melted into Theo's embrace and let the tears come.

He held her through the wave. Thoughts of the art show and sitting for Beatrice's portraits, bifocals, and the quirk of her lips when the gossip was getting deliciously good. Every bit of Beatrice branded on Effie's life flashed through her mind as she stood there in the sturdy arms of a man who wanted to love her.

At some point, he had ushered her inside. Exhaustion and heartache made everything fuzzy as she watched him move through Dorothea's kitchen like he'd lived there all his life. He found Effie's stash of tea in the cabinet by the kettle and fixed a pot for her, taking down a china cup and saucer from the open shelves to his right. He grabbed a copper pan and rummaged in the fridge for eggs and vegetables, concocting a delicious-smelling omelet that he put in front of her.

"You don't have to eat it all, just a bit before you go rest."

Effie wanted to thank him as much as she wanted to push him away. It felt too good to be taken care of and even good things had an expiration date. But she nibbled on the omelet in silence, washing it down with the queen of teas he had brewed for her. She wasn't sure what he saw in her face, but he stated more than asked, "You stayed with her all night?"

Effie nodded. "She was more than family. She was my friend." Effie hated how *was* tasted today. It didn't usually carry much flavor. It was bland like water, but today it was spiked with the tang of sulfur like the filter had failed.

"I wish I could have known her better," Theo confessed and it sounded sincere. All Effie heard was that if she wasn't such a loser when it came to relationships he would have had the chance. The walls went up and she set her fork on the table.

"Thanks for stopping by. I think I'll go try to sleep for a bit."

She didn't wait for a reply, and he showed no reaction to her terseness. Effie tramped out of the kitchen, and as she climbed the stairs heard the distinct clatter of dishes being washed. Her heart ached for a whole different reason.

Aunt Beatrice would have been so disappointed in her for pushing away the best thing the world had ever brought to her doorstep.

39

It was a beautiful day. The rain the night before had brought the late summer heat back to a pleasant warmth, the smell of damp earth a reprieve from the baking asphalt of the week before. A light breeze tickled the daylilies in bloom outside of the Portsmouth Historical Society. The air was fresh and bright in Hope's lungs as she and Brayden scaled the steps to honor her dear Aunt Beatrice.

Effie had brilliantly suggested that the show be arranged as Aunt Bea's memorial. Hope could think of no better way to celebrate the cheeky old bird than to admire her most treasured work while sharing stories of her charm and wit with people who loved her.

Hope wasn't expecting the dozens of others who milled about the mezzanine as they approached. People she'd never seen, and who she knew were no acquaintances of Aunt Beatrice, had turned out for the show. It warmed her heart that the gallery was a success. She hoped that wherever souls went to rest there was a viewing area to Earth and that Aunt Beatrice had a front-row seat to her own celebration, her own artistic success.

Hope had helped Effie with mounting each and every watercolor piece they found in Beatrice's portfolio. They now hung all about the room, an homage to the woman who painted them and the subjects she loved enough to paint in the first place. Hope spotted Effie standing with Louisa at the golden urn by the front window. Effie held a microphone in one hand and tentatively raised it to her lips, clearing her throat once before she began.

"I wanted to welcome everyone to the Beatrice Thatcher Watercolor Exhibition. This was not initially meant to be in memoriam. Aunt Beatrice should have been amongst you sipping her signature cocktail and asking you all which were your favorite pieces. But God had other plans." She raised her lavender-tinted beverage in the air. "A toast to Aunt Bea, thanks for letting us love you."

Hope noted Effie's effort to keep from crying at the last words. She turned to find Brayden poised before a portrait of Hope. It was surrounded by four or five others. In one, her three-year-old self hugged the bunny stuffed animal that now lived in the baby's room. Another she was missing her two front teeth. Another she wore heavy eyeliner and dark clothes, her emo phase in high school. The one that Brayden couldn't stop staring at had been done a couple of months prior, Hope in her burnt-orange sweater, the swell of her baby bump visible beneath her hand. "I want all of these," Brayden said, entwining his hand with Hope's.

"We might be able to arrange that."

The Aunt Bea was delicious. Lavender gin, a touch of lavender syrup, lemonade, topped with club soda. Effie thought Beatrice would have approved. Looking to the unknown crowd that pointed at paintings with admiration and the friends and churchgoers that offered Grams their condolences, Effie knew she'd have been pleased with the whole event.

Grams separated herself from the well-wishers for a moment and came to catch her breath with Effie. And with Aunt Bea who stood beside them in her golden urn, tied with a pink bow. The bow was a direct order according to Tibby.

"How are you?" Effie asked.

"It's a good day, but a sad day," Grams said and Effie agreed.

"Was Aunt Bea always so . . ."

"Gossipy? Creative? Clever?"

"Open," Effie asked. It was one of her favorite things about Aunt Beatrice. The bald-faced way she met the world, the brightness in her spirit, the sense that she welcomed whatever came her way.

"No," Grams finally said after pondering it for a bit. "The fact that she put off doing this show on her own is proof enough of that."

Grams stole Effie's glass and took a long sip of the cocktail before answering. "There's two ways people change. You're either inspired by something great or you're transformed by something painful."

"Which was it for her do you think?"

"Well, both probably. Though, Effie dear, I think she'd tell you to run like hell toward the greatness because the pain will find you no matter what."

"So it's a choice to let the good stuff mold us, where the effects of hardship are unavoidable?"

"I think so, don't you? How many people in this room do you think spend their time thinking about how all the bad stuff in their lives has made whatever difference without acknowledging the good? It's always that terrible breakup, or the loss of a house, or a loved one . . . not the epic romance, or the building of a home, or the life that was lived that we focus on. Once Bea decided to do that instead, the world became wonderful, and her right along with it."

"I don't only want my life defined by the bad things I've survived," Effie said. Though she knew her pains were fewer than many, they were deep.

"So don't," Grams dared.

Effie found herself standing before her own portraits moments later—the evolution of her spirit on full display through Aunt Beatrice's eyes. The colors she used for Effie's paintings were softer than all the others. Effie hadn't ever compared them before, but looking now she noticed that every other portrait from Ellen to Issa had defined edges, the colors of the subject's clothing and hair kept within the bounds of the sketch.

For Effie, though, Beatrice had let go of constraint. The puddles of dusty pink that rendered one of her favorite tops on the page faded into watery edges that spilled in cloud-like plumes where Effie's arms should be. Her soft brown hair, whether in the pigtails of her childhood portraits or the loose layers of her most recent sitting, faded into the blankness of the background the same way giving a ghostly, ethereal effect to the images.

Effie didn't recognize the woman who came to stand beside her. She dared a sideways glance to see the look of wonder in her eyes. The woman turned to face Effie, realizing she stood with the subject herself. "It's you." She looked between Effie and the paintings. "I love her choice to part with definition here," she said pointing to the very splotches Effie was noticing for the first time.

"What do you think it means?" Effie asked, some part of her hoping that the woman beside her was versed in fine art.

The woman tilted her head to the side as though assessing. "Maybe that the subject isn't fully formed yet. The edges and solidity are not yet defined. Or maybe it's a reflection of the soft, feminine palette, a warmth that emanates outwardly."

Effie nodded her thanks and the woman moved on to the portraits of Issa to their right. Effie thought it only fitting that she and the little bird share a wall since no one else in the house had managed to make friends with her. In fact, Aunt Beatrice had left Issa to Effie in her will along with some money to build a solarium off the back of the carriage house as she and Grams had always discussed for lemon trees and tropical plants and a space to endure the cold New England winters. A place for Issa to fly free.

Effie tried not to think about how it felt like it meant staying at 53 Austin for the foreseeable future. How she was irked by things staying so much the same moving forward, despite the massive loss she currently endured.

But she would see Aunt Beatrice's wishes through. It was the least she could do for the woman who had changed Effie's whole perspective with a painting.

Effie wasn't finished yet. She could be malleable and undefined. She could shift and expand and radiate her inner self for all the world to see. And she could change as much or as little as she wanted. Looking at the bleeding edges of her form on the page before her, Effie realized her walls were imaginary. She didn't keep people out, not in the ways that mattered. If she did, Aunt Beatrice would have given her firm edges, hard lines, and decisive colors. But Effie was soft and open-hearted when she was being herself—and it was high time she started acting like it.

Otherwise, she'd never know how good it could get. Otherwise, she'd always wonder. Otherwise, the answer would always be *no*.

40

Theo's Jeep idled at a stoplight on his way home from work. He was getting home later than usual, the sun had already sunk well below the horizon. He'd had another difficult client for his last appointment. After the inspection, the manager reprimanded him about all the work he created for *no goddamn reason*. Though Theo insisted safety and code and the staff's wellbeing were reason enough, it didn't stop the onslaught of insults he'd had to endure in order to get the guy to sign off on receiving his instructions.

In some ways, it reminded him of his first meeting with Effie. Her irritation at having to meet his standards to pass inspection. He wondered if it colored the rest of their interactions. If she thought herself being inspected for approval, like he had a list of requirements for his girlfriend the same as he did for a commercial building to meet safety codes.

He choked on a laugh as he let his foot off the brake. Safety was his career, yet he had somehow failed to make Effie feel safe with him.

Failed to show her that he was there to take care of things and that all she needed to do was be herself.

Theo ached at the thought of her sitting at home, navigating her grief. He felt for all of the Thatcher women and had been torn about whether to go to Beatrice's art show and memorial.

After doing what he could for Effie that heavy morning nearly two weeks ago, he felt like he was becoming more burden than help. Like seeing him unsettled Effie in a way that had her covered in shame and confusion. He didn't want to bring that to a day of celebration, so he stayed away.

The Jeep was quiet but for the rhythmic clink of his blinker as he waited to turn left into his parking garage. He stretched his neck side to side searching for an opening. Before long he parked and unloaded his things. His messenger bag felt heavier than usual, each step a monumental task as he moved for the stairwell.

Theo almost forgot what it felt like to be optimistic about finding his soulmate. He'd once been happy to float from relationship to relationship in search of the love he knew existed. It had excited him to know that *she* was out there somewhere. But now, knowing who she was, where she was, and that she didn't want him back felt like a sick cosmic joke.

He didn't want to keep fooling himself, that he just had to wait and she'd realize she wanted to be with him too, but he also didn't want to admit defeat. He'd told her he'd wait, so wait he would. At least until it became less painful to move on than to stew in unrequited affection.

Theo reached into his pocket for his keys, not looking forward to another night without Effie asleep beside him. It might have seemed rash to anyone else that after only a few months of knowing her, he was certain it was forever. To Theo, it felt natural. As Effie had said with such self-loathing, she was the answer to his prayers, and he supposed that if all he got was those couple months, he would be grateful nonetheless.

He rubbed his eyes like he could unsee their breakup as he stepped through the door, shutting it behind him.

Theo hung up his bag and turned to find Effie sitting on his sofa.

"Brayden gave me his key," she said lifting it as evidence she didn't manage to pick the lock and break in.

Theo nodded and walked into the kitchen, despite the live-wire buzz that vibrated through him at seeing her. He rested his elbows on the counter, his eyes trained on Effie. He kept his distance, like trying not to spook a deer in the woods, but everything in him screamed to be near her. She stood, clutching a leather-bound journal in her hands. With a few steps, she landed on the other side of the island.

Theo couldn't keep from drinking her in head to toe. The blue and white striped sundress she wore bared her shoulders and hugged her curves to her hips where it fell in a soft bell shape to the tops of her knees. She'd braided her hair to one side and the sensuous curve of her neck was on full display. He wanted to trace its contours all the way to the pearl earrings that studded her ears.

Effie placed the journal on the counter. "It's the one you bought from the store, right?"

Theo nodded. "Did you read it?" He wasn't certain if he hoped she had or hadn't. He had been out of habit in sharing his poetry with anyone and felt insecure about how good it was. After poetry slams in college, it became more of a personal form of therapy than anything to be read aloud.

"I wanted to," she confessed, and her cheeks reddened in that sweet embarrassment that had him wanting to brush away the color. "But I didn't."

Theo debated whether it was a good idea to ask why she came by and risk sending her running when Effie blurted, "I don't want to die without knowing if this is real. I don't . . . I don't want to put off the good things."

Theo ventured around the counter until he breathed Effie's air. She smelled like rosemary and mint. Her cornflower-blue eyes met his and he couldn't stop the hand that reached for her cheek, his thumb smoothing over its blushed curve.

Relief eddied around him. The sense of optimism returned. He wanted to confess everything. To say the words they'd danced around for weeks, but still not wanting to speak, lest this moment was as fragile as it felt, he pointed to the journal. "Flip to the last poem."

Effie quirked her brow but did as she was told. She pulled her bottom lip between her teeth as she flipped through page after page, presumably noting that every poem within was about her. About them. She reached the last page and looked up at him. "This is dated a week before we broke up," she said a bit breathless, and Theo couldn't help but stare.

The Sky Is Blue

Some things I know (like the sky is blue) without a thought
or feeling. (It is truth in vibration and spirit and faith.)

I yield to no doubt (for doubting is not knowing). I need
no proof (for Sunshine, the proof is in the language of our
souls when we are silent.) I trust no other to share my life
(because in knowing there is no returning
To ignorance
To before
To without.)

This is the marvel of receiving that which my soul yearned
for (the solidity of the untouchable.) This is the heartstring
plucked on its perfect note. It is the vow of a man who fol-
lows his knowing (like a compass through the jungle.)

Some things I know (like the sky is blue) and you and I are
what they meant when they spoke of destiny wrapped in
Sunshine on the dark side of the moon.

Effie's cheeks hurt from smiling as she read. Whatever fear she had about Theo knowing what they were to each other so quickly, so assuredly was washed away with every word. As she read aloud she was treated to a palate of flavors like a sumptuous seven-course meal. Theo, whether knowingly or not, had written a poem that had her mouth watering with every savory remark, every delectable, filling phrase, every sweet notion.

She laid the book back on the counter, her curiosity over what other lovely things he'd written about her pushed aside for the time being. Theo gripped her waist with his strong hands.

He looked at her like she was the whole universe wrapped in a sundress.

There was a question in the way he held her, the way he wouldn't take his eyes off hers. She was ready and she said so with a nod.

The smile that spread across his handsome face sent Effie's knees wobbling. She knew if his fingers weren't curled into the flesh at her hips she'd have fallen right over. "Effie Rose Thatcher," he said, voice heavy with importance and laced with a deep yearning. "I love you."

Effie knew it was coming but her heart fluttered all the same. "I love you too."

Effie had said I love you many times. To Grams, Hope, and all her family. She'd said it to the cat they had when she was little and to Issa on more than one occasion. Each time it had tasted the same, like crisp lemon water, refreshing and bright and full of zest. But when she said it to Theo, it was fuller, sweeter. Like freshly squeezed lemonade on a hot summer day.

"What does it taste like?" he asked, and Effie nearly swooned all over again at his awareness that her mind mulled over the way her synesthesia responded to *I love you.*

"Like the sweetest lemonade I could drink every day for the rest of my life."

His fingers were soft as they brushed her hair back from her face. "I've seen you all along, Effie. Soft." He brushed a teasing touch down her neck. "Sweet." He brought his hand to her cheek. "Magnetic. The only woman I've ever loved."

She barely had time to inhale before he hoisted her onto the counter. His lips met hers and she welcomed him closer, her thighs cinched around his waist. He placed one hand on the counter, the other bracing her back as he worked his way up the column of her neck with tender kisses.

Effie tingled all over as she arched into his touch. He took his time exploring the curve of her collarbone, his hand roaming over her back. Theo planted taunting kisses along her jaw whispering thirst-quenching, lemonade *I love you's* between breaths. He tried to bypass her lips, but that wouldn't do.

Effie clutched the back of his head, fingers tangled in the thick blond locks she'd imagined running her hands through so many weeks ago. She couldn't get him close enough. The taste of his lips and the sweetness of his breath were driving her wild. She scooted closer to the edge of the counter suffocating the last bit of space between them.

This was what she'd been waiting for. This devotion, this affection. This promise of forever and the love that went with it. It had been there all along, but she'd kept it blocked, unable to receive it before. She tried not to chastise herself for the wasted weeks when she could have been savoring this feeling. Every touch made her shiver with a desire she'd only ever brushed against. She felt it fully now. She needed him, all of him. The certainty she'd craved and received in more ways than one had her drawing back and whispering his name. "Theo." Sweet salted caramel chocolate.

His warm hazel eyes assessed her face, reading her decision. "Are you sure?"

She nodded and he kissed her again. Effie fed off the love and desire she felt with the press of his lips. He lifted her up, her legs wrapping around his waist. She laughed. "Where are you taking me?"

"I'm not making love to you against the kitchen counter," he said. "At least not yet," he grumbled with a devilish kind of grin. A thrill went through Effie. Her insides twisted with anticipation as they crossed into his bedroom and he laid her gently on the mattress.

Their passionate need softened to a romantic sensuality as his hands explored her body like a work of art. His kisses promised to make her feel adored, and as their clothes were shed Effie was aware that she had never in her life been so certain of anything.

She wanted everything with Theo, and she was pleased as punch she was finally letting herself have it.

41

Theo, for all of his experience and sexual prowess, hadn't realized it could be like that. The moment she'd said I love you, said yes, he felt something greater tethering them together. He knew it was a spiritual connection, their souls or their energy colliding along with their bodies. He'd been well aware what kind of connection Effie saved her virginity for, because it was the same one he'd wanted to find. It was soulmates. It was devotion. It was a forever kind of love, whatever came their way.

Making love to Effie was a bliss like he'd never known. And he realized that was the difference. He'd had a lot of sex, but he had never made love. Not like he knew it now.

If he'd thought he was enamored before, crossing that final line in their physical relationship had only solidified for him that Effie was his person. It was all he could do to get out of bed in the morning and go to work the next day. As though it were any other day. As though his world hadn't come into crystal clear focus, forever changed by the woman who held his heart in her hands. It could only be called blasphemous that everyone he passed on the street didn't stop to congratulate him on being so in love, so utterly and completely devoted to Effie Thatcher.

In the days that followed, Effie spent every night with him. He'd made good on his promise to take her against the kitchen island and it was better than he ever imagined. Everything about them was good, at least when she wasn't missing the family dinners or breakfasts she'd become accustomed to over the last two decades of her life. Her angst over the changes had him encouraging her to go home and be with her family for a few nights, though—honestly—the emptiness in bed made it hard for him to sleep.

⁂

Effie stood beside Hope, zesting a lemon for the lemon bars she was making for dessert while Hope slathered chicken breasts with her favorite marinade before popping the pan in the oven. Though popping probably wasn't the right word, since Hope's movements had become slow and deliberate, holding her belly like she thought it might fall off. "How ya doing there?"

Hope huffed a breath but laughed. "Oh you know, three days past my due date, so stellar, fantastic, didn't know existing could be so exhausting."

"I can finish up, go sit."

Hope dragged the stool from beside the landline phone into the kitchen instead, propping herself on it while she peeled potatoes.

The house was quiet for once. The sizzle of the stove warming water and the hum of the oven the only constants in the room. Each swipe of the vegetable peeler was a sharp slice into the silence between them. Effie put her lemon bars in another chamber of the oven and set her egg timer before taking up the cutting board beside Hope. She cut the peeled potatoes into chunks and plopped them into the boiling water.

"So what's next?" Effie asked.

"What do you mean?"

Effie fidgeted, unsure what words made her point clearest. A feeling like shedding many skins had settled over her in the last couple of weeks. Standing there beside Hope like they'd done a thousand times only highlighted the shift. "It seems like the start of something, you know? Everything feels so different and . . . raw, I guess. I don't know. It seems like something is coming. I wasn't sure if you knew what it was . . ."

Hope's eyes crinkled with her smile. "Well, besides Bug, I think it's just life now."

"Life."

"Remember how we used to play all the time? The board game? How we'd drag the box from the closet to the rug in front of the fireplace and organize all the cash and cards. We'd pick our favorite color car, set our tokens on a track, and get everything situated? Mugs of cider and doughnuts beside us, Grams's knitting needles clinking in the background, the stage set for the game?"

"I remember."

"That's what it feels like to me. The stage is set, everything is lined up. Now we get to start playing."

Effie sighed. She liked the analogy, but a niggling reminder fluttered in her chest. "You always won that game."

"Yet you kept playing with me." Hope nudged Effie with her elbow.

It was nice that Pamela worked late and Tibby had a last-minute appointment. That Louisa and Ellen had taken the girls to a dance class and Grams read in the living room. It got to be just the two of them, for however brief a moment. A moment, Effie realized, that would become all too rare when Bug arrived. That was rare enough already given that Hope had moved out. "Thanks for coming tonight. I think I needed to go back to start for a minute."

"Me too," Hope said, though Effie could tell Hope needed the touchstone less than she did. Effie placed the last chunk of potato in the water and took her utensils to the sink to wash up. Hope remained on her stool, a hand laid over her stomach as she stretched like a cat. "Are you happy, Effie?"

Effie paused her washing, warm suds dripping from her delicate fingers. Happy had been relative for so long, she wasn't sure she could trust the feeling, the big deep resounding yes that bubbled from her toes. "Yeah, I am happy." *Floral-noted honey.*

Hope smiled broadly. "I could tell. I just thought you needed to hear yourself say it."

Effie savored the last bit of quiet, the honey sweetness of her happiness, as it flooded her senses and overflowed with the creak of the front door, the patter of little feet, and the effervescent chatter of the women she loved as they came home to share a meal.

Tibby landed in the kitchen first. "Anything I can help with?"

"Just waiting at this point," Effie asserted.

"Brayden joining us?" Tibby asked. Effie encouraged her eyebrows to stay put as she waited for Hope's reply.

"Yeah, he had a performance review at work, so he's running a little late."

"Whose performance are we reviewing?" Pamela crooned as she walked into the kitchen and took up a seat at the breakfast table beside Tibby.

"Brayden's. At work," Effie said with a look that she hoped conveyed to her mother to play nice. Pamela nodded and Effie's shoulders relaxed.

"Theo coming for dinner too?" Tibby inquired, her look telling Effie's mother to behave. To Effie's surprise, Pamela didn't even flinch.

Effie plunged her salad tongs into the mix of greens and cucumbers and cherry tomatoes. She tossed the contents of the bowl a few times, coating them in her lemon vinaigrette before daring to answer. "No. I wanted a nice dinner with everyone. His being here would have made things awkward." She kept her eyes trained on the bowl, her heart hammering in her ears. She didn't like how small she felt, how much like a child waiting for permission. It was maddening, especially given how free and confident she'd felt as of late. How womanly and sensual and—

Pamela cleared her throat. Effie looked up to find all eyes on her. She was grateful it was only three pairs because the whole of the Thatcher clan would have been too much. Hope's grin was wicked. "Effie Rose Thatcher, you had sex with that man!"

"What? How did you..."

"You let me sit here talking about my swollen ankles when you're having sex!"

Effie buried her face in her hands. "Ugh, let it go."

"I will not!" Hope turned to Tibby and Pamela. "You know what this means, don't you?"

Pamela looked straight at Effie and her throat constricted. She wasn't sure she'd ever shared her plans with her mother. How she'd remained celibate to protect her heart. Maybe in passing or defense against her mother's man-hating, but she couldn't be sure. So when Pamela said, "She loves him," Effie couldn't have been more relieved.

Effie squeaked out in faux embarrassment, "I do."

Pamela did the one thing that truly cleared the air, set everything to rights, and made it all perfect. She smiled. Her genuine, full, real smile that told Effie that Pamela was as happy as she was. Happy had never tasted so good.

42

Hope woke to pain like bad period cramps in the middle of the night, and not long after the sheets were damp with the breaking of her water.

The bags for the hospital were packed and waiting by the door. Brayden ran around like everything wasn't ready to pick up and walk out with. Hope laughed at the frantic energy that bubbled around him as the clock neared one a.m.. She checked the timer she'd started on his phone, waiting for her contractions to be close enough together to warrant going to the maternity ward. She didn't want to labor long in the sterile environment that still smelled too much like a reminder of her last visit to the hospital to say goodbye to Aunt Beatrice.

But at some point, it would be unavoidable, and that point was now. "Time to go," Hope said, swinging her feet over the side of the bed. Brayden rushed to her side, holding her steady as another contraction ripped through her.

"That seemed like a bad one," Brayden said with a wince.

"Oh, we're just getting started," Hope teased, intent to stay light-hearted through the labor, especially because if she stopped too long to think, to take this seriously, she'd be wracked with worry. It was time. She would have a baby in her arms within hours, and there would be no version of her that wasn't a mom ever again.

It was thrilling and terrifying all at once.

Brayden guided her down the stairs and out to the car. He ran back inside for the bags before hopping into the driver's seat. He started the car and fumbled through neutral and reverse and drive. Hope placed a reassuring hand over his on the shift stick. "Breathe," she said.

Brayden inhaled and exhaled along with Hope. "Bug is really coming," he said as though he too had thought it was some distant possibility, not a promise. "What if he hates me?"

"*She* will love you, but only if you get me to the hospital in one piece." Hope's face scrunched in pain as she breathed through another contraction. "And soon."

Brayden's hand steadied as he put the car in drive and pulled onto the road. Hope's stomach fluttered with anticipation. She could not wait to meet the being that made the picture of her life complete. Writer. Mother. Wife. *What more could she want?*

The labor was a blur of nurses and breathing techniques and grunts of pain Brayden could do nothing to ease. He stood solid beside Hope, his arm or his hand ready to be squeezed to a pulp if that's what she needed.

She was so strong, so beautiful.

By the end of it, Brayden decided that there was nothing more impressive, more amazing, more awe-inspiring than watching the woman you love bring your baby into the world through will and grit and instinct. Because that's what Hope did. When she felt something was off, she changed positions. When she wanted to walk around the room, she did. Every breath, every movement was born of some womanly instinct that Brayden could only marvel at.

And the bundle he now held in his arms, well he was another kind of miracle. A gift from Hope. She'd taken the building blocks of them and combined them into a living, breathing little boy, with ten fingers and ten toes—he'd checked—and a personality he could already feel forming with each twist of his nose and lips. Brayden was so grateful that Hope had cooked this little man to perfection, and he could not wait to see who he would become.

Hope leaned against his shoulder, a gentle hand smoothing back the peach fuzz that coated the baby's head. "What should we name him?"

"Him!" Tibby exclaimed from the open doorway, the rest of the Thatcher women behind her. "A Thatcher boy? We've never heard of such a thing."

"Well, now maybe he isn't a Thatcher," Ellen mused setting down a gift bag on the windowsill before kissing Hope on the head and waggling a single finger in greeting to Brayden's son.

"Posh," Dorothea said as she shuffled into the room, bright-eyed and bushy-tailed as the rest of them despite the early hour. "The only reason any of you are Thatchers is because I demanded my daughters take my name."

"You did?" Brayden asked, never having heard this particular story.

"I did. Herman's last name was King, and wonderful as he was, he didn't have to carry them for nine months and push them out his hoo-ha. It's arbitrary that babies take their father's last name, so I made my case, and he agreed."

"A king indeed," Theo drawled from the doorway, arm draped around Effie's shoulder. Dorothea harrumphed her agreement before settling into one of the empty seats on the other side of the room. Louisa and Pamela wrangled the three little girls onto the couch under the window, each clutching a gift for the baby.

For the first time since meeting Hope, he was grateful for her wild, crazy family. They had become his and he couldn't be happier, especially since Uncle Theo had officially joined the fold. If it was a numbers game, there'd be more votes for Thatcher than Schilling, but he didn't care what the baby's name was. He'd learned long ago that family was made, sometimes in blood and name, but more often in action and love. "Well, what's it gonna be?" he asked of his future bride.

"Elliot Schilling Thatcher," she said with a bit of worry that he might be upset. "Grams and I agree on this one." She laughed. A chorus of *amens* from her aunts and cousins confirmed the strain of labor earned naming rights.

Brayden laughed and looked down at his son. "Welcome to the world, Elliot."

43

Theo walked up the brick walkway, the site of the only breakup that had ever threatened to undo him, to join the Thatchers for dinner.

What he found instead was a bustle of activity, the front door thrown open as the ladies shuffled in and out with furniture and belongings from the carriage house. Ellen marched behind her two little ones, each carrying pillows and blankets. "Hey, Theo," Ellen said like it was just another day.

"Hi?"

He followed behind her in search of Effie. He found her in the great room scolding her sister as she paraded through on her way to Beatrice's room. "I didn't mean you had to do it now!"

"No time like the present!" Ellen retorted before continuing down the hall. The girls had disappeared upstairs with their bedding.

Theo sidled up to Effie, dropping a kiss to the top of her head, the scent of herbal mint wrapping him in a calm embrace. "What's going on?"

"I asked Ellen if she *might* consider moving into the main house so I could try living on my own in the apartment."

Theo raised his brow; the carriage house wasn't *exactly* living on her own, but he guessed it was within Effie's comfort level to be a few steps away. He tried not to worry over what it meant for them that she still wanted her own space. That living together hadn't even crossed her mind. Maybe that was a line she wasn't willing to cross until they were married . . . *well that could be arranged.*

He shut it down. They may have said forever and meant it, but he was still a little gun-shy about suggesting such monumental changes when their reconciliation was still fresh. "And she just started hauling stuff over?"

"Yes!" Effie exclaimed.

Ellen returned from Beatrice's room, arms crossed. "Did you expect me to say no?"

"Well, kind of," Effie confessed. Ellen laughed but rolled her eyes at Theo like they were in on the same joke.

Ellen turned her attention to Effie. "Look, the alternative is that you move out completely, yes?" Her eyes flicked to Theo but he kept a lock on his words.

"Eventually . . . maybe," Effie said, a bit of that trepidation from before *forever* sneaking through. "I don't want to have to choose."

"I know this," Ellen said, and Theo thought it sweet how matter-of-fact she was about the whole thing. Logically, Ellen could take over Beatrice's room, the girls could take Effie's and Hope's rooms, and Effie could have the apartment for whatever life she was building. Ellen seemed resolved. "I don't know where we'll all be in a few years, but if it makes everyone happy to move around and make room now"—again her eyes flicked to Theo—"then that's an arrangement I can get behind. Besides, the girls are excited to have their own rooms. And if a little bit of Aunt Bea can rub off on me, I'll consider myself lucky."

Effie looked at her sister through lowered lashes. "You still didn't have to start moving tonight," she challenged.

Ellen waved her off before continuing on in the moving march. Tibby and Pamela joined the fray, and Effie and Theo helped too, a line of worker ants trudging from one building to the next. He grabbed Effie's stained glass on their last trip out, an idea brewing about Effie's new home.

When everything had been moved, they sat down to the meal that Tibby had prepared. Dinner was a vastly improved experience. Theo got to know the Thatcher women without their fears and disappointments talking. They'd swapped stories about favorite concerts and must-read novels over roasted chicken, baby potatoes, and green beans like Theo had never tasted. He saw the deep threads that wove between the women around him at the dining table and felt lucky as hell that they viewed him as *breaking the curse*. Even though Dorothea retorted rather animatedly that there was *no fucking curse*. He decided during post-dinner cocktails around the card table, playing poker with Grams and all the rest, that he was going to enjoy being a part of this family. His cast was really shaping up.

After the festivities, Theo found himself in the nearly emptied two-bedroom carriage house apartment. All that remained were the girls' beds, stripped and left behind because their new rooms were already furnished.

It was outfitted with a galley kitchen on one wall in the main living area. Plenty of room for a sofa and television where the girls play rug and toys used to live—no need for a real living room when they were always in the main house anyway. The front bedroom that had been Ellen's was smaller, a good size for an office or guest room or miniature hobby room for Effie. The back room that the girls shared was larger, with closets built into the eaves on either side.

Theo finished touring the apartment, only smaller than his in terms of the kitchen, and circled back to where Effie stood in the main room. Her clothes, vanity, rocking chair, rug, and bedding were piled unceremoniously in the center of the space. Laundry baskets filled with the books and crafts she'd kept in her room littered the floor. She seemed unsure of what to do, so Theo lifted the electric kettle she'd kept in her bedroom out of a box and set it warming on the kitchen counter. He found a couple of cups and saucers that were hers as well and went about brewing a pot of tea.

By the time it was steeped and ready to drink, Effie had settled against the wall beneath one of three windows facing the street—the one he'd hung her stained glass in. She lifted the cup but stopped before bringing it to her lips. She frowned at Theo and he wondered what she was thinking. Maybe she already regretted the spontaneous move or felt odd having him stay the night here. He didn't have to wait long to find out.

"If I don't ask the answer is no," she said.

"True . . ." Theo replied wondering where this was going.

"Would you want to live here . . . with me? I know it's kind of like moving in with my family but maybe we can see how it goes—"

He interrupted her prattling before she could get too worked up. "I want to be wherever you are."

Her smile undid him. She lifted her teacup. "You can drink now. Our first cup in our new home."

Theo loved the sound of that. But he was distracted by wisps of satin draped over the edge of a laundry basket to his right. "Are those what I think they are?" He held up a lacy camisole, his devilish grin matching his rising desire at the thought of her strutting through *their* home in her barely there pajamas. Effie snatched them from his grasp and silenced his rebuttal with a kiss.

The tea and pajamas were forgotten as they tangled on the floor, both breathy and eager for another first in their new home. It turned out to be a night of firsts, seconds, and thirds, as Theo showed Effie the upside of his years of sexual exploration. *And the sounds she'd made?* He hoped they couldn't be heard in the main house, but he almost didn't care, because they were followed by her gasping his name as she careened over the edge. That was the benefit of Effie's synesthesia, it made her say his name in a way that had never sounded so good.

Theo cradled Effie, naked in his arms beneath the sheet they'd thrown on the bed in the bigger back room. He propped himself on an elbow. "You think my bed will fit in here? I did not have enough room to work on this queen-sized bed," Theo teased.

"I think you worked just fine," Effie laughed burying her face in her hands. It was cute as hell, and Theo's heart exploded with so much fucking joy he might have been confused for a less broody sun sign. "But yes. It should fit."

Theo combed his fingers through Effie's hair, brushing it back from her flushed cheeks. "You know it's a magic bed?"

Effie rolled her eyes. "Oh yeah?"

"I bought it knowing that the other half belonged to my soulmate."

"You manifested me with a bed? Is that what you're saying?"

"Well, it sounds weird when you put it like that," Theo muttered, feigning offense. But Effie took his face in her hands, all jests aside.

"Whatever brought me to you, I'm glad that it did. Thanks for invoking magic for me."

"Anything for you, sunshine," he breathed. Then they fell asleep and Theo spent his first night in the Thatcher henhouse, right where he belonged.

44

On the other side of the glass, the world was painted in oranges, yellows, and reds. The air had chilled to a pleasant crispness that enlivened Effie's spirit and reminded her of going back to school. On her side of the glass, the solarium did its job keeping the heat and humidity in for the myriad of plants she'd brought in so far.

Theo had built the structure for her, its entrance off the back side of the carriage house. The sunlight poured through the windowed roof and had the waxy leaves of the monstera reaching for more. Effie brushed her fingers along the spiky crown of a yucca and through the unfurling buds of the lemon tree she'd potted in the corner. She looked up in time to see Issa swoop through the air from the window on the second story. Theo had managed to create a shed roof for the solarium that met up with the back window of their apartment, so Issa could fly between the two when it was left open. Effie sighed contentedly as Issa perched on her shoulder.

Theo's voice rang out from the doorway to the carriage house, "You coming?"

Effie smoothed a finger over Issa's head. "I'll see you later?" As if in response she flew to her new perch amongst the fronds of young palms with a squawk that sounded an awful lot like joy.

Effie joined Theo at the door. His arm found its home around her shoulders and she reached up to lace her fingers with his. They walked the twenty paces to the front door and continued into the chatter that emanated from the kitchen.

Though it might have made more sense to move their family breakfasts to the dining room, they opted to get a bigger table for the breakfast nook instead. Everyone was already in their seats, Hope with the baby nestled in the crook of her arm rocking the infant as though she'd been doing it her whole life. Brayden chatted with Dorothea who sat beside him telling a tale with her hands.

Hazel demanded croissants that were not on the menu given that it wasn't Effie's turn to cook while Lilah and Vivienne whispered secrets to each other next to their mother. Pamela brushed behind Effie, placing a hand on her daughter's back, and kissed her lightly on the cheek. "Morning, love." She continued on for coffee as Effie and Theo rounded the table.

He pulled out her chair for her and took his seat beside her. His eyes widened at the food before him. "Louisa's omelets?" he said excitedly.

Effie's sister beamed at the inherent compliment as she placed more on the table. "That one has turkey sausage and spinach for you," she chimed.

Theo brought his hands together like a prayer and bowed in gratitude.

Effie caught Grams's eye, a twinkle of warmth behind the wrinkles. She smiled back, wondering if Grams's heart was as full as her own.

This was the good stuff. The stuff that had made her.

Effie looked past the table and the piles of food to the cross on the wall and the two portraits hung beside it.

One of a man in greyscale by which all others were measured. The other in bright watercolors of a woman who'd loved her family more than anything.

Together, they represented the forces that made Effie's world go round, that showed her what it meant to feel safe, loved, and hopeful about her life.

The other force that made her world spin sat beside her. A man who had her heart, who kept her safe, and made her feel womanly and adored. He was hers, equal and opposite.

She knew now what Theo meant when his gut had said yes to her. It was a certainty she couldn't shake like the Thatcher women flocking together, she and Theo were meant to be. She knew it like she knew the sky was blue.

Theo's brow twisted in curiosity at Effie's stare. "What?"

"I love you, Theo," she said.

"I love you too."

With that, Effie settled into a lifetime full of love, sweet lemonade, and salted caramel truffles.

ACKNOWLEDGMENTS

Though at times it feels like I fell into novel writing after years pursuing a career as a screenwriter, I think the truth is that this book was a long time coming. Long before I knew I wanted to write movies, I knew I wanted to be a storyteller. I wrote during reading writing marathons in elementary school, and loved the weeks in second grade when we bound our own books with cardboard and cloth. All this to say, I'm so grateful for all of the people that encouraged me to tell stories, in whatever form from such a young age.

The two biggest supporters of my career—of my life—are my mom and dad. Their encouragement to keep trying, to keep going, has been the life raft I've needed in the choppy waters of becoming a published and produced writer. Though my dad is no longer earthside, and it breaks my heart that I won't be watching him read this with his magnifier glasses and cup of Sumatran blend coffee, I know he's relieved I finally listened and tried writing a book. Thank you both for loving me through the ups and downs of dedicating my life to the craft of storytelling.

When I finally finished writing the actual book, there were two people I trusted to tear it apart and tell me what wasn't working. My fellow writers, my forever beta-readers, and best friends in the writing trenches, Marguerite and Lauren. Thank you for reading draft after draft, and helping me make this sparkle. I couldn't have done it without you.

To my other early readers, my sister, Amanda, and my husband, Gabe, thank you for giving me your thoughts, for telling me what moved you, what felt too easy, and where you needed more. Your insight helped me take this project to the next level and I'm so grateful!

Though it might seem like the number of eyes on this project meant that it was polished and ready for publishing, I have one more person to thank for the magic within these pages. Kaitlin, my editor, you are a dream. Thank you for catching my multiple uses of grey and gray, for combing through for timeline errors and continuity errors and confusing sentence structure. I'm so glad I found you on the world wide web, and can't wait to keep working together.

I'd like to formally thank my husband for putting up with me. Gabe, we have navigated my career and how I haven't really been living it the way I imagined for fifteen years (only five of those married). Thank you for carrying us while I pursue my dreams. Thank you for reading everything I've ever written, good, bad, and in between. Thank you for believing my success was a *when* and not an *if*. I'm so lucky to have you as my partner and best friend.

Finally, thanks to you, dear reader, for picking up this book and for spending your hard earned dollars on a new name in the indie publishing space. You know not what it means that my work wasn't just released, but *received*. Bless you, baby-angel-readers. Until next time, and with much love and gratitude — Emily.

www.ingramcontent.com/pod-product-compliance
Lightning Source LLC
Chambersburg PA
CBHW030521190726

48283CB00006B/1720

* 9 7 8 1 7 3 3 6 0 0 7 2 9 *